THE LEARNING CURVE OF PAIN

SHAWE RUCKUS

Editing, Design, typesetting and publishing by UK Book Publishing
www.ukbookpublishing.com
ISBN: 978-1-915338-23-5

SADNESS IS A BONFIRE

CONFIDENTIAL PAGE 1/2
TRANSCRIBED AND TRANSLATED IN JULY 1985

Tell us about her.

Emma was my *duenna* [GOVERNESS]. She came from England. She always wore a dainty blue silk scarf that her uncle bought her from Liberty of London. I want to visit there one day.

Tell us about your family's doctor.

Father has always been frail and bedridden for long spells. Our doctor Francis and his daughter Vanessa live with us; so do the maid and driver. Vanessa is three months and nine days older than me. We sneak out to visit the nearby botanical garden sometimes.

Tell us what you saw that afternoon.

I got back and saw the ground-floor bedroom window half-open. And I heard someone groaning. I wanted to peek inside; then I heard my father calling from behind. I ran away in fear of his scolding. They always scolded me whenever I grazed my knees.

Tell us what happened to her.

It was a hot day when Emma died. Mother and Father had gone to town, and the maid took us to the beach. By the time we found her, she was sleeping peacefully, like a Lladró figurine. Her skin was stiff and as cold as my dead grandmother's. They said she had committed suicide, but I didn't think so. I saw Francis coming out of the room, and he told me: "Don't be afraid. Now, get me some ice."

Why did you think otherwise?

One night I sneaked downstairs to get to the kitchen. I like to have my figs chilled. As I passed her room, noises and light were coming under the door. I peeked this time and saw Mother disrobing her, touching her, and kissing her frantically. On the night of the fireworks, Mother cried so hard and said that she could not live without Miss E.

Tell us what happened that night.

When we got home, Francis was talking to my parents. At that time, ETA was capturing a lot of attention, and my father had an Astra pistol. It happened very fast [CONTINUED OVERLEAF]

CHAPTER 1

December 2015.
London.
Covent Garden, Slingsby Place.

"Don't be afraid," Melody Baldwin said as she cut a length of floral tape. "It's unlikely that you'll break the wire." She turned on her heel to Catherine Roxborough, her student who had joined the floral academy in April. "Now, get me another 22-gauge, will you?"

"Of course." Catherine grabbed a piece of dark green floral wire from her apron pocket.

"First, we fold the wire in two-thirds, take the shorter end, then twist it like this."

Catherine watched as Melody demonstrated with her gardening snips.

"When designing wedding bouquets, we need to think about the flowers, and we need to think about the person who will be holding the flowers. If the person in mind has a petite figure, a hemispherical design with the right accents could accentuate the figure very well." Her teacher picked up a cut white rose. "In wintertime, the weather often demands less. But for June brides, pay more attention to keeping the flowers moisturised. The easiest way is to layer up on the tape and secure them with twine. The golden rule is 'less is more'. You should remove anything you can from your design until it doesn't work anymore, then you add back the last item. Baby's breath always works nicely and it represents long-lasting love."

They continued to work on the bouquet, adding a few Casablanca lilies and periwinkles. Finally, Catherine used a pastel blue ribbon to conceal the wires.

"Oh, and Catherine? We'll start our pre-orders for Christmas today. We are going to be rushed off our feet for a while."

Christmas...

Catherine thought about the festive season; it would be the first Christmas that she and her darling would spend together. She thought she'd go to town with the celebrations.

Lunch break arrived.

Catherine arranged her tools and made her way into the locker room.

"Cat, c'mere. I saw your man just now," Orla, another student and part-time at the academy, informed her as soon as she entered.

"He was with a chic Latina," Orla proclaimed, her face florid. "They had a rather open display of affection in front of the Hotel Chocolat on Monmouth Street. I'll spare you the details of their PDA."

It can't be!

Catherine's heart fluttered. "Are you quite certain?"

"I've seen enough of him waiting on that bench outside. I was getting coffee from across the street and they were there..."

"He didn't see you?"

"Gwad no!" Orla shook her head fervently. "They went into the

Radisson Blu Edwardian..." She paused and she looked as though she had crossed her heart. "Look, I know you must be going clean mad. I'm only telling you for your own good, like. Don't get your knickers in a twist. You should see what's wet and what's dry. You should cop on and mind more for yourself! Catherine, immigration marriage fraud could happen to anyone! Better get away from that skittery whelp." She primmed her lips. "I watched *Before I Go to Sleep* the other day. Creepy, innit? As my ma would say, it's always the quiet ones that you fall for... and it's always the silent ones messing around. You know, I saw a post online the other day that eighty per cent of relationships end because of romps and cheaters."

It can't be...

Catherine's appetite suddenly gave way to an emotional cauldron. She tried to calm herself but to no use.

She had been on the rebound when she met Changxi Yang, a former M&A consultant, a scant seven and a half months ago. To a smaller circle of friends, he was known as Chance Yang. He'd spent a few nights at her house (on her sofa) and offered some anti-stalking consultation after someone broke her kitchen window, which turned out to be a misunderstanding over a missing pet. Initially, they got off on the wrong foot, but life brought them together in October. Then they'd spent... how long? Hardly three weeks in each other's company, in between when Catherine attended a short course on floral design at the Boerma Instituut in Holland.

They had no relationship status uncertainty. There were calls and messages and dinners and snogs...

But nothing else.

Catherine was glad to have things going slowly. She had learnt some lessons the hard way from her failed engagement. But going too slowly was a different matter. Any initiatives, any ungainly advances on his part, she would have met them with alacrity.

But none came.

She had thought he was a fine specimen!

And now...

"I saw your man just now. He was with a chic Latina..."

What did she know about him?

She knew that he had grown up in Inner Mongolia in China, spent some of his middle school years in the US, then studied Computing at Imperial and had previously worked for Mercury Investments and Securities.

She knew that he had a good grasp of Spanish and Japanese...that he liked to have his tea with salt...that he was not on any social media and he didn't like runny yolks...that his last name was not that of Yin and Yang but meant a poplar tree....

Come to think about it, she knew hardly anything about him.

She didn't even know what his first name meant. And he never offered an answer.

He hadn't even invited her to his rented flat on Kean Street.

Orla changed into her apron and gave Catherine a meaningful glance. "I better give you some peace."

After she left, Catherine called him.

It didn't connect.

It can't be. Or...can it be?

He was planning to open a jazz bar on Catherine Street with a friend. She decided to try her luck there.

The walk was short yet unsettling. She almost ran into a group of chuggers.

Truth be told, dealing with an unfaithful partner was not new for her. Her engagement had terminated on similar grounds.

Who said that jealousy doesn't show how much you love somebody, but how insecure you are?

She was demented with fear and worry.

The festive finery on the streets did not warm her heart but bothered her like a foreshadowing of a tedious argument.

Catherine quickly found her way to the newly established retro-cool venue. The bar had been recently refurnished and smelt faintly of varnish.

"Hey, Catherine, how's it been?" Turner, a fit, feisty fellow, greeted her. He was making an inventory of liquor glasses as he burnished them. His jumper had a design with three flying geese.

"Have you seen Chance?" She tried to hide the quaver in her voice.

"He said he'd come in in the afternoon. Got a previous appointment." Turner pointed to a corner of the bar counter. "I've been thinking of getting some flowers here. Some very bright ones to drum up new business. Have you got any tiger lilies? Maybe I can drop by the academy later today?"

"Sure."

"Do you want me to tell him you were looking for him?"

"Hmm...no, that won't be necessary." Catherine forced a tenuous smile. "We're having dinner with his cousin tonight."

The cousin in question, An, was doing a Master's at King's College London.

"Ah well, I better grab my lunch. I'm down for a croque monsieur or a chip butty, so..." Turner gestured, and they ventured downstairs together.

She parted with him and called Chance again.

He didn't pick up.

Catherine had remembered that a family friend, Felipe Kazama, once said that cheating spouses are like teenagers who watch porn: nine out of ten deny it, so you should commend the one who has the guts to admit it.

**

Later.

"Follow me, please." The waiter confirmed his reservation and led him further down into the restaurant.

The Sticks'n'Sushi in Covent Garden was rather crowded that night.

A few lamps protruded from the ceiling like octopus tentacles. Unknown music played in the ambient air and chopstick rests made of pebbles were everywhere.

"Would you like something to drink?" the ponytailed waiter inquired as he pulled out a chair.

"I think I will have a pot of the Coziness tea. I'm waiting for my friends. We will order later."

"Of course." The waiter nodded and left.

Chance sat down; the chair was a little too firm for his liking.

He looked up. A painting of a giant eyeball watched him from the wall opposite.

He browsed the menu and waited.

Ten or so minutes passed, tea was served, and he had suppressed several yawns.

Then he saw Catherine walking into the restaurant with such speed that her movements carried a hint of fury.

He stood up. "Sorry I missed your calls earlier. Is everything alright? Turner said you were looking for me."

Nothing is alright!

Catherine sat down and warmed her hands with the teacup. "Nothing...really."

He settled again, took up his cup and sipped as he watched her.

She flipped through the menu. "Turner placed a recurring order with us."

"Yes," he nodded. "I thought some flowers would be nice."

She gulped. "How was your day?"

"Well, not bad considering that I'm having dinner with two charming ladies."

He took note of the time. An was late.

Catherine straightened.

How should one address situations like this? The dalliance? The copine? The confidante? The lover? The fling?

She cleared her throat. "Orla told me that...she saw you today during our lunch break."

He almost choked. *NO WAY!*

He fidgeted in his chair and calmed himself by pouring more tea. He hesitated before asking, "Where...uhm...did she see me exactly?"

His attitude irked her.

She stammered, "She saw you on Monmouth Street...with someone."

His tone lightened. "Oh, she must be mistaken."

Catherine fell silent for a moment and made a last-ditch effort. "She saw you...going into a hotel...with someone."

He took a deep breath. "I was not at *any* hotel today. I was nowhere near Monmouth Street."

Catherine watched him intently as he tugged his shirt collar. She seethed at the sight and she bridled at his lies. Yet she didn't say anything.

He considered for a while and said, "You don't believe me?" His emotion was plain.

She knew it was more a statement than a question.

She glowered at him. "No! I mean...no, I...I want to, but she was quite certain that she saw you."

"My word against hers and you don't believe me." He said this simply and with a degree of incredulity.

She bristled at his evasiveness. "Tell me where you've been, then. And why didn't you answer my calls?"

His shoulders slumped. "Well, I prefer not to say, but–"

"So sorry to keep you guys waiting!" An announced as she dropped her tote bag and settled on the chair in between the two. "My group project meeting dragged on. You know what it's like when a seminar is about to end, but someone asks an Einstein-level question."

An continued talking about her thesis plan as Catherine sipped her tea and smiled feebly.

It seemed they would need to digress for now.

***

Two hours later.

The dinner ended, the bill was split, An parted, and they had to face each other again.

The rain had stopped.

Their footsteps echoed on the miry streets, making the ambience doubly cold.

The giant, ornate Christmas tree in Covent Garden glowed with silver and gold baubles. A long queue of diners lined up outside the Shake Shack. 'Hungarian Dance No. 5' played live in the background. There was a Santa Express made from Lego in real train size. Pentachromic lights sparkled as visitors waited their turn for selfies. Two police officers on horses patrolled the area. People everywhere had smiles on their faces.

London in December is the worst setting for a break-up, Catherine thought as she looked at the waning gibbous moon.

They walked in silence.

She had enjoyed the dish of fried cauliflower. She would have enjoyed her supper more had she been in a better mood. She felt a bit heavy-headed. Perhaps she had had a few more drinks than she had intended.

Heck, one must prepare for the hard truth...

Her patience was ebbing away.

They got to Kean Street shortly after; his black Audi Q5 was parked not far from a modern furniture store called Aram.

He spoke tentatively. "Catherine...do you want to come up to the flat for some tea? I've managed to tidy it up. We can talk..."

Huh. So, this is how it starts...and ends.

There was no way she'd let him hurt her in foreign territory.

"No. It's been a tiring day," she said tartly. "I have an early start tomorrow."

"Then let's go. Mr Darcy must be waiting," he said.

They drove in silence as 'Last Christmas' played on the radio.

They did not speak. Catherine was waiting for him to speak.

What was she waiting for?

An explanation or an apology?

The night traffic was lighter than she had expected. They reached her house in Holland Park in less than half an hour.

Catherine's parents had passed away in a car crash when she was twelve years old. Since then, her uncle Alexander Roxborough, a university professor in sociology, and her godfather Cecil Stone, a barrister, had taken her into their care.

And now, no one waited up for her except for her ginger cat, Mr Darcy.

They got out of the car. Then Chance said warily, "To answer your questions...it was not a topic suitable for dinner discussions, I'm afraid. But..." he paused, not knowing how to continue.

He looked up and saw Mr Darcy perching on the second-floor bedroom window. "Oh! I bought you something."

Catherine watched him as he opened the trunk and took out a large bag from Hotel Chocolat. She felt the stinging sensation of Dijon mustard climbing right up her nose.

She was livid.

"How dare you do this to me! Guess what? I notice things as well! I thought you had no *bloody* bodily desires, but no, just not for me! Don't you know you can't run around and shit where you eat? Good heavens, right under my nose! It's not even a furlong from where I work!"

Her fiery words and teary eyes nearly vanquished him.

"Please, Catherine, I'm so sorry–" His face blanched under the moonlight.

"Don't apologise! I've had enough apologies. If you have the guts to apologise, why didn't you have the wits to resist in the first place!? Don't tell me that it was a moment of weakness!" Hot tears scalded her eyes.

"But *please* listen to me..." Her tears had cut him to the quick.

She refuted indignantly, "Get stuffed! My uncle tells me to listen, Cecil tells me to listen. Don't you start too!"

"But...but I can explain. It's not what you think," he hastened to clarify.

"I'm too tired to bandy words with you! And stop badgering me! You don't care a straw for what I think! You don't care a pin! You care damn all for me!" She shoved him hard, grabbed the bag and his car keys and threw them as far away as she could. "GET OUT OF MY LIFE!"

She slammed the door in his face.

He pressed the smart doorbell once, twice.... He called her cell phone a few times and her landline some more. They didn't connect.

Then he saw Mrs Ferguson, Catherine's neighbour and a curtain twitcher, wanting to know what was happening.

To his dismay, it took him nearly ten minutes to find his car keys.

He heaved a heavy sigh and drove off into the windswept night.

***

Christmas Eve.

An got to his flat at eight pm sharp.

"Come in," he said, opening the door.

"An, you're just in time!" Catherine emerged from the kitchen with two glasses in her hands. "Here's some mulled wine to warm you up."

"Thanks a lot." An took off her down jacket and rubbed her hands. "It's freezing outside. Must be below zero."

They chatted and enjoyed the panoramic view of Covent Garden. Even the BT Tower looked a lot nicer during this festive season.

An said, "The other day I went to Sagar. It's a great vegetarian curry place. You guys should try it."

He winced. *Curry...curry and codeine...*

The oven alarm went off.

He checked the turkey as the girls chattered.

"When you cry for my guinea pigs, I mourn for your turkey."

He had heard a voice.

"How is your coursework?" Catherine asked An.

"Okay-ish. I like my lecturers...minus the complication of the assessments," An joked. "I've been living in the Maughan Library. I never know if I pronounce it the right way. We have this Round Reading Room where Jay Chou once made a music video. It can be difficult to find a seat in exam season."

"They also filmed *Johnny English* there," Catherine added.

"I quite like it. It's so much more comfortable than the LSE library... only I didn't expect to see so many rats in London. I literally jumped the first time I saw one."

Rats...rats and rivets...

"What harm can a lil Mickey Mouse do?" The voice haunted him.

He shook away these thoughts and focused on his task.

They had a lovely meal.

There was mushroom salad, garlic toast in the shape of Christmas trees garnished with chopped parsley; roasted baby potatoes and boiled Brussels sprouts. He even made some fried cauliflower with black truffle sauce. Catherine seemed to like it.

"Do you know that there's a medieval legend..." he wanted to show off a bit. "That if you put a black truffle next to a fresh egg, the egg will become as fragrant as the truffle." He continued, "And do you know that only the poor ate lobsters in the old times?"

Lobsters...

"Do you know the other name for lobsters? Cockroaches of the sea. And do you know what is so scary about cockroaches? That if you find one in your house, there are probably a hundred undiscovered ones. The same goes for merger and acquisition. Murder is a field where there is a chasm between theory and practice."

The glottal voice continued.

They finished dinner, chatted a little longer, and An left to seek solace in her reading lists.

Catherine had gone to the bathroom upstairs.

He noticed the time. She had stayed in there for too long.

He ventured upstairs and knocked on the door.

"Catherine?"

"Yes?"

"Are you alright?"

"Perfectly fine. I've bought something from Agent Provocateur that I wanted to try on tonight."

NO!

He panicked.

Not on this bed!

Not on the bed where...

Not on the bed where Joyce Peng had died...

***

He woke up from his trance, his neck as wet as a dog's nose. His sweat-soaked pyjamas clung to his back. The candle on the lampstand by the sofa had long been extinguished.

He checked his phone. No messages, no calls.

It had been two days since they parted on less than...no, *unfriendly* terms.

He wondered if there was a remedy to her silent treatment.

Or was the treatment itself a remedy?

Chance regretted having this dream, though it was not something that he had control over. It seemed rather treacherous.

He watched as a tiny spider crawled on the wall. He didn't know if he should go to the floral academy and seek out Catherine during her lunch break.

He got out of his sleeping bag and changed his clothes.

The BT Tower glowed beams of red and blue through the fog in the still early morning. A few aeroplane trails loomed in the oyster dawning sky, one of which drew a tangent with the fading moon.

The furniture store downstairs opened its gate for delivery. Many office buildings lit up in unison. The illumination theme of the Space House changed from time to time; on that day it was a shade of blue.

London awakened.

He prepared two slices of toast with Gouda cheese and ham and a glass of water with lime.

After breakfast, he opened the door to the balcony. Damp air mingled with the sounds of wind, cars, and seagulls burrowed into the room.

He looked at the rolling clouds.

Gone like clouds...

Now, he had to add curry, codeine, rats, and rivets to his list of things to avoid, together with alcohol, white bedsheets, and economy seats.

Death seemed to be on his heels.

He went inside and hoovered the downstairs areas but did not venture upstairs.

The bed where Joyce Peng last slept was still waiting for its next dreamer.

He finally decided to get rid of it.

A salmon-pink sunrise peeked out of the sky, and a red tower crane in the distance slanted its neck like a giraffe feasting on an acacia tree.

He went into the study. The dimly lit room was windowless, making it appear airtight. A ladybird-themed beanbag rested in a corner.

He opened his desktop and the Bloomberg terminal that he had installed recently. There were no emails of particular importance. He needed to meet up with Turner at the bar at nine.

His cell phone rang. It was Catherine's uncle, Alexander Roxborough.

"Hi...hello?" He was still groggy from the paracetamol he had taken earlier.

"I was surprised not to see you at supper yesterday. I don't know what happened with you two. I thought that you were getting along well?" His tone was not reprimanding.

"Hmmm...Professor. Could you ask Catherine if...if she'd...never mind. There's a little misunderstanding, I suppose."

"I ought to leave things to you two to sort out. I never listened to my parents, anyway, regarding matters of the heart. I can't say that I've never been a bounder myself." Alexander Roxborough paused, "Take some time apart. Cathy can be headstrong at times. Do you know why she decided to become a vegetarian?"

He sat down. "Yes, I think I do know."

"And what might the reason be?"

"Was it not because she didn't go to a vegetarian restaurant with her parents on the night when they passed away on their way back?"

"Did Felipe Kazama tell you this?" Alexander sounded disdainful.

"He didn't mention any specifics, but I connected the dots."

To Chance, Felipe Kazama was a dangerous man. You never knew when he was lying or when he was joking or when he was telling the truth. Or how terrifying the truth might be. A Harvard Business School graduate and a bookworm who liked to pick apart others' narratives, Felipe had some nefarious side hustles that would fail to comply with any legal system in any country.

Alexander Roxborough continued, "Do you remember you once told me that you could help me to track someone down?"

He scratched his forehead. "Yes. I do remember."

"I need to ask you a favour," Alexander Roxborough sighed. "A friend of mine wants to find someone...someone who's dead."

***

After a routine lunch at an old spot in Leadenhall Market, Lewis Milken strode back to his office.

When he reached the high-rise entrance, he did not hurry, but idled on the grey cobbled pavement and took a drag. Then he entered the building, passed the security controls, and took the lift to the eighteenth floor.

The polpettine he had eaten earlier was a bit salty, and he licked his lips as he headed to his office.

Some youngsters chewed over their holiday plans.

"Trust me, Len! If you ever get the chance to go to Cuba, you have to try this place's mojito. It was Hemingway's personal favourite!"

Another pair thrashed out their corporate revamps to sell and lease back the headquarters next year.

Lewis listened as he fixed himself up with a cup of builder's tea, dolloped some sugar, and moved on.

He had a gracious corner office with a minimalist design. Through the room's floor-to-ceiling windows, he could see the Gherkin.

He always went to where the money went.

He had dissected so many sunset industries and cherry-picked the best performers.

Now his own end was looming.

Lewis sighed as he loosened his tie.

A while ago, a junior executive at his firm had collapsed on his way back home and was fortunate enough to be saved by passers-by.

Lewis took his time with his tea and did not bother to check the Asian market.

From Wigan Pier to Canary Wharf and the City, Lewis Milken had made himself a success story.

He had a house in Belgravia, a holiday home in Deauville, several luxury sports cars, a ridiculously high-paid job, a somewhat broken family, an excellent cigar collection and a cellar that would not be frowned upon, not even by the most sophisticated London circles.

What more could he ask for?

A little bit of life, perhaps.

His hand found its way to the cigarette case in his suit pocket.

Lung cancer stage IV.

His physician had delivered him his death sentence a month ago with the same ease with which Lewis gave keynote speeches and television talks.

The markets and the bourses could wait, yet his clock was ticking.

He would not live to see another Christmas. He knew it.

It had come a bit sooner than he had expected.

Lewis smiled bitterly; at least he had time to update his will and make his funeral arrangements. He would tithe a generous legacy for his alma mater. He once wrote a eulogy for himself as part of an assignment during his course at LBS. Now it was time to dig it out and put it to use.

He took out a folder from the drawer on his left-hand side. He opened the folder but stared blankly out of the window at the swarm of clouds flying by.

Emma...I will live until I find you...

It looked like it was going to rain again.

Chapter 2

Night.

C hance got to the bar and found his business partner Dominic
Turner grimacing while holding a half-eaten Gregg's sandwich
and an ice bag.

"What happened?" he asked as he noticed the swelling on Turner's
face.

"I got onto the Tube, there was a commotion, a man was pie-eyed,
and he insulted a lady in hijab. He said some *disgusting* things. Then I
decided to try some of the Krav Maga techniques that we learnt. I guess
I was a bit rusty, but, anyway, a bloke helped me, and we got him. We
scuffled with him, and he was more challenging than I thought. He
should be charged with bodily harm..." Turner looked like a deflated
balloon. "Things are crook in Tallarook...Pish. I don't know why these
things always happen to me." He stopped. "How've you been?"

Chance sat down and stood up quickly again. "I'm alright. The
medication works." He checked his watch. "It's been a long day. You
better go home."

"I'll go now. My mother will skin me alive if she sees me like this.

She'll be doing her nut. I better find her a really decent pressie." Turner picked up his helmet, zipped up his jacket, and glanced at the door. "See you." He moved towards the door and turned. "And remember that the ablutions...loos are still not up and running."

"Got it."

He waited until Turner was gone, then pulled out his phone and sent a few messages.

A quarter to nine.

Lewis Milken emerged from Covent Garden Station.

"Free guides!" The rickshaw drivers and hawkers near the Underground entrance touted for customers in a variety of accents and sold overpriced umbrellas and raincoats.

Someone played 'Jolene' on the guitar.

Street art performers were disguised as Master Yoda, Mr Bean, buffoons, Pierrots, and even dogs and duff magicians shouted the 'last show of today' for the nth time.

He stood under the streetlight and lit up a cigarette with his silver Dupont. The neon backdrop dwarfed the sparks from the lighter.

He walked uneasily eastwards as he took a few puffs on his cigarette.

It drizzled as Lewis found his way to the new jazz bar on Catherine Street.

Tempting snacks and desserts filled the store windows, adding the danger of a calorie overload to a festive evening awash with alcohol.

He found a pub that resembled an ants' nest.

Lewis looked in between teeming heads and saw its name, 'The Prince of Wales', in golden capital letters.

He turned the corner just as a young lad came out of a door.

"Sorry, mate, excuse me!" Lewis called out. "Do you happen to know a jazz bar around these parts?"

The lad nodded and held the door open with his helmet. "Take the lift, third floor."

He thanked him, found a bin, ditched his smoke, and walked inside.

At the end of the dimly lit corridor waited an old-style lift. Lewis got in and the lift creaked upwards.

The door opened, and he found himself in a big room, as spacious as a dance hall.

The room smelt like new cars, garnished here and there with film posters. Barstools stacked on top of pub tables and unopened crates clustered around.

"Good evening," an Asian man greeted him. He was of medium build, on the lean side, and had a clean-shaven face. "Mr Milken?"

Chance took a good look at Lewis Milken. He was a corpulent man with grey flecks in his tawny hair.

"You must be Chance Yang." Lewis tipped his hat. "I've heard a lot about you from Felipe. All good things."

"Oh..." the man hesitated, "I thought you were a friend of Alexander Roxborough?"

"Alex and I go back to Trinity, but..." He took off his hat and raincoat. "Felipe's the one who helped with these matters."

"With finding your sister, I take it?"

He swallowed. "Quite right."

"I'm afraid that we have not fully stocked the bar yet. I do have some mineral water; would you like a bottle?" the man offered.

"No. That won't be necessary."

"You don't need to worry about extra ears here."

"Yes. I've heard that you are tight-lipped." He settled on a leather chair and gestured to the man to do the same.

"If it's not too much trouble, I'll stand for now."

"How should I start..." Lewis mused. "I grew up in Wigan. My dad died in a work accident when I was five, and my mother was devastated and soon followed him. We were paupers and we always lived in squalor. So poor that we had to dilute the family's bottle of ink, so it lasted longer. My notes were always a shade lighter than my peers'. My sister, Emma, she was eight years older than me. When my parents died, we were entrusted to the care of my father's brother. Uncle Benson never married and treated us as his own. Emma got a teaching qualification, then decided to work in Spain. She got a post as a governess with a family in Barcelona in 1979 with the help of a friend. During this time, she hardly ever came back, not even for Christmas. It went on like that for two or three years, I think. Then one day when I was in class—Latin, I believe—the headmaster summoned me and told me my uncle was there to see me. There was a telegram. Emma had contracted tuberculosis in Spain and had died." He pursed his lips.

"You were never able to verify it?"

"There was a death certificate, of course. The family posted it after her funeral..." Lewis paused and pondered. "Then I fell out with my uncle...let's put it like that. The last time I saw him he was very ill. The man cried and begged me to find Emma and bring her back home. That's where Felipe came in to help. I thought it would be a straightforward matter until he showed me this..."

Lewis Milken opened his suitcase and took out a folder. "Read it and tell me what you think."

Chance took the folder containing a telegram from a post office in Barcelona informing the family of the passing, and a dog-eared file page. A smudgy photo was also inside. It showed a young girl in a long buttermilk-coloured dress with a pinafore over it and a silk scarf around her neck, and a boy beside her in a starched white shirt and braces.

He took his time with the page marked 'CONFIDENTIAL'. He felt that it opened up a lot of room for imagination.

"Any other clue about your sister's employer?"

"There were some postcards from Blanes at the beginning. The girl Emma taught was named Irati and she was in poor health as well. Emma wrote to us saying that they were a well-known trading family. They even had two fridges in the kitchen. One was always locked up." Lewis shook his head, regretfully. "I only know that she was introduced to the family by a friend."

"Nothing else? No other correspondence?"

"Maybe she wrote to my uncle. I didn't find anything useful after his funeral." Lewis continued in a distraught voice, "I've asked a few friends at the Embassy. No luck there either..."

"I see." Chance finally sat down. "I've tracked down people before... living persons. You must understand, Mr Milken, that I cannot promise anything."

"But will you try?" Lewis exhorted.

He said after a while, "I'll try, but don't keep your hopes up."

"My uncle once told me that sadness is a bonfire and our thoughts are firewood. If I can find out what happened to my Emma, at least I can die with my eyes closed."

"Someone once told me that sadness burns like no end." Chance furrowed his brow. "But...life's not like debugging: knowing what went wrong won't necessarily make you happier."

Lewis smiled sadly. "It's a chance that I'm willing to take."

***

Ten-thirty.

Cecil Stone shut down his desktop, jotted down a quick memo, removed his gold-rimmed glasses, and rubbed his face.

It had been days since he had had a decent night's sleep.

He slumped in his swivel chair as he strained to breathe, then picked up his watch and checked the time.

"Ah-ye-ye."

He scratched his balding head and muttered.

He began to pack his things into his Tusting briefcase, hoping to sleep well tonight. The briefcase had been gifted to him by his late wife, who had passed away shortly before their pearl wedding anniversary.

Until death did us part...

There was half a BLT sandwich left over from lunch. He hesitated and tucked it into his coat pocket. Then he checked his phone.

There was a message from Vodafone, telling him to collect his unused Rewards, and a calendar reminder of his meeting with someone from Doughty Street next Monday.

His screensaver showed his daughter Sophie and his grandson Brendon who resided in Munich.

Life had treated him well.

Regrets, he had a few. Probably more than a few, one of them being that his goddaughter, Catherine, had chosen flower arranging as a career, much to his contempt.

He checked his wallet, picked up his bowler hat and umbrella, and made his way out.

"Have a good weekend, Mr Stone," the night security guard said kindly.

He doffed his hat and nodded before walking out of his office.

The sombre night air was not so kind outside.

He navigated his way from his Chambers at Pump Court to Fleet Street, ran a red light and turned into Chancery Lane.

The Law Society's Hall was undergoing external renovations, and he stopped to touch the sitting lion decorating the doorpost.

He was once a nobody from Derbyshire, and was now a Queen's Counsel.

A few students loitered around the Maughan Library, reminding him of his pupillage days.

Those days, like his wife Elizabeth, were only memories now.

A few cars were parked in the side spaces and raindrops battered the stone pavements with an eerie glow.

He snuffled and held his umbrella tightly as it defended his body in the winds and sleet. The Arctic cold front that he had read about in the morning paper did not belie its name. He wondered if London would have a truly White Christmas this time. Brendon would love that. He felt cold, yet he sweated like a pig as his scalp tingled.

Someone coughed not far away.

Under the faint streetlight, he saw a bedraggled, gaunt silhouette carrying a huge knapsack.

Could be a homeless person.

He knew that every Friday night some charity would provide free food in Lincoln's Inn Fields. There had been grousing from the neighbourhood about this.

In a way, Cecil thought, he was homeless.

His daughter would visit him once, twice, or thrice a year. And there were video calls and short trips, but...he wanted some longer-term company.

His house had been empty; only him and his Bowers & Wilkins.

Catherine would sometimes keep him company, but she had a life of her own.

An old school friend who headed the Royal Society of Medicine once told him that single elders lost their minds much faster than couples.

He wanted a change.

He needed a change...a change from the humdrum nature of his life.

The downpour intensified in seconds.

Cecil staggered into a makeshift passage made of scaffolding and collapsed before he made it out to the other end.

***

After Lewis Milken left, Chance took a moment with the file, then put on his jacket, locked the door, and made his way out.

He took the stairs, pressed the green 'EXIT' button on the wall and pushed open the door.

The rain had petered out.

As he passed the LSE Grosvenor House, a cat meowed.

He looked up; a tabby cat looked down from a half-opened window. It had a red bowtie.

Mr Darcy, does she still wish to keep me in her sight? Chance felt himself asking.

He wended his way down Drury Lane. The evergreens resting in the corner of the street shone. A Turkish restaurant, Sarastro, where he had once dined with Catherine, was packed. A street cleaner for the City of Westminster smoked, slouching against the decorative wooden piano outside the place.

A passer-by had decided to drop his cigarette butt into a bin, and the cleaner snapped.

"Hey!" he yelled, went forward, and caught the man. "Didn't you see the warning? Don't put it there!"

"Oh, I'm so sorry," the man said and still threw the butt into the bin.

"Hey!"

"What? Didn't I say sorry? Bother!"

"Don't I know you thick lot? You say 'sorry' as 'fuck you'!"

The man escaped quickly enough to dodge a blow. The moon had escaped from the clouds, and the streetlights stretched his shadow long.

Chance walked past a red brick wall with half a clown's face of graffiti, then took out his key card and swiped it on the card reader next to a glass door. He had no mail except for an estate agent's postcard asking about his willingness to sell the flat.

He got back to his flat on Kean Street. His neighbours, the Robinsons, had just returned from a hiking trip to Croatia. He could hear Hannah Robinson merrily asking her husband Eddy about his preferred choice of nightcap for that evening.

The last time Chance saw her in the lift, she had acquired some new home fitness products: kettlebells and a yoga mat.

A bird croaked.

He found his way into the kitchen, drank some water, and started to make dinner.

He rinsed a portion of rice for one in a measuring cup, put it inside his rice cooker, took out a Coeur de Boeuf tomato from the fridge, cut it in half and put the sections in the rice cooker as well. He set the program and took a shower as he charged his phone. By the time he had changed into his loungewear, the rice was ready. He took a pan and cooked some eggs with crushed cashew nuts.

He ate as he thought about his dream from last night.

How he wished she would allow him a chance to speak...to explain...

By the time he was ready to relax on the sofa, someone had called.

Not Catherine.

He listened to a helicopter overhead that buzzed like a plague of locusts, fought with himself and called back in the end.

Every conversation he had had with Felipe Kazama was mentally taxing. The oldest son of an indigenous mother and a Nikkei father from Peru, Felipe had always liked jokes, riddles, and hocus-pocus.

The call connected; he could hear Yamashita Tatsuro's 'Christmas Eve' playing in the background.

Felipe spoke first.

"I've been reading a book called *Hotel Shanghai* by Vicki Baum. It brings back old memories, doesn't it?"

Chance didn't want to think about those memories.

"I'm disheartened that you never gave me a tinkle on the blower. What can I say? That I'm glad you haven't blocked my number yet? Remember our tango last time? You know, it would probably hurt more if you used your watch dial. Y, how have you been? Enjoying life and its offerings of assorted chocolates? I'm well...alive and well and busy as a spider and...still at large. *Jaja*, just joking. Still batting around between Congo and the States. In this festive season, I'm just calling to express my gratitude for your constant support and patient guidance in the past year and...to say thank you...and you'll always be my favourite assistant in the global talent pool."

"If there is nothing else..." He yawned.

"*Oh là* là. So eager to get my goat? How's London? Did you get your feet under the table yet? And did you like the mezzotint that I hand-picked myself? I didn't think you had it in you to become a part-time fixer. I always felt that you shared my sense of shrewdness and not my lewdness. Do you no longer have your wits about you? Now, tell me, did you take it up because you don't want to decline another *dying* man's last wish, or was it because you can't help peeking into others' secrets? Don't you want to know what transpired between Bobby Moore and the Bogotá Bracelet? Did our last collaboration defile your good-natured character so much?"

He remained silent.

"No one can be pure after touching tar, and no one can avoid getting photokeratitis after staring at the abyss. Wouldn't we all want to deep-dive into others' innermost secrets? The chambers of the heart, that we are not allowed to mention, let alone to visit? I'll wager. We might as well be hanged for a sheep as for a lamb. Are you as bright-eyed and bushy-tailed as I am wanting to know what happened in Carfax Abbey? Privy, aren't we? The children of God can have some really off-colour hobbies. One guy I know likes to drink tigers' urine. Told me it's good for virility. He has his own tiger, of course. He tells me that a Siberian has a more tannic taste than a Bengal. And he tells me that now the dogs don't dare go near him because of the smell. Drinking it did him no good; he even bought the shit heap from Theranos. Can't say I'm happy for him. And what an interesting case, don't you think? Another suicide. Must be our word of the year. Absurd as it may sound, I knew someone who committed suicide by shooting himself in the back seven or eight times. He had legal blindness, so to speak. And such a pity that they didn't have a butler.... So, we cannot conclude that it was the butler who did it. Are we not all voyeurs when it comes to the skeletons in the closet? Peter Drucker said that you cannot keep a corpse from stinking, but I'd say that you surely can stop someone from talking. I always knew that it's not the gutter that's scummy, but the critters' doings."

"I only did what I felt was right," he said, a little lamely.

"Or maybe you are just bored. It's like having a top trader teaching kindergarten math. Talk about allocative inefficiency. I wonder if *jubilación** does indeed bring jubilation? One has to make strategic decisions. My fees are quite high and my billable hours short. And I'm not interested in projects that feature neither merger nor acquisition. You know what I mean."

Of course, he knew.

Felipe had once hinted.

"In our not-so-small world of investment banking, there's a company

with an arcane division known to a cabal of a few as 'MIS', which stands for 'Mercenaries in Suits'. Urban legend has it that they use code names for their dodgy business. For example, a 'merger' meant murder, and an 'acquisition' meant an abduction. The professionals never develop Lima Syndrome."

Perhaps Felipe had sensed his unease, yet he continued to goad him still.

"As the old saying goes, don't shoot butterflies with rifles, don't use a sledgehammer to crack a nut, and don't do away peaceful civilians with Special Forces. My days spent in Ica, on my dad's farm, taught me that farming does not pay: retailing does. I'm just a middle man on the totem and I've decided to let you keep the less chewy bones. 'Horses for courses' as an old friend would say. I'm very good at sorting the wheat from the chaff and I'm never a fair-weather friend. Ex-Mercuries always benefit from our life-long mentoring commitment. We can be good buddies and peers for life. Jos de Blok once said that they have no CFOs and hence no financial problems. They also didn't have HR, so their employees are the most satisfied. Why put up with a tin cow when you can get milk for free? If you go freelance, everyone's happy. Especially me. I'm still waiting in the wings to make the acquaintance of your stepmother....

"Ever drunk alpaca milk? My old man had his personal favourite alpaca that he worshipped. He'd sing to it and give it massages. Sara once told me that 'milk is blood'. But sometimes, we draw blood not to hurt. Milk's an everyday essential—Thatcher, Thatcher, Milk Snatcher. If you don't milk a cow, the udder could swell and lead to nasty infections. Speaking of the devil, we broke up. Sara and I. *Même pas mal!* Christmas is a superb holiday to spend unattached...saves all the hassle of gift-finding..." The acidity in Felipe's tone betrayed him.

Chance recalled that he had once told Catherine that his grandmother would let some blood out of his fingertip whenever he caught a cold. He told her that it was a niche remedy that worked.

He wondered if they would ever talk again. He had a sinking feeling in his chest.

He should have known better than shying away from her insistent questioning.

"GET OUT OF MY LIFE!"

He remembered her charged words.

How could he not?

Felipe continued languidly, "Who's to blame? I haven't opened all my Johari windows to her. And I can't deliver her a...macerated, milder disposition of me. Her moral bearings are antithetical to mine. A life that's half-truth is as destructive as a lie. I hope that whatever we had, it was not all phony. Awww... We were quite a pair à la folie, always quibbling, like a pair of Australian dollars and Japanese yen. She stepped on my toes quite often in our *pas de deux*. I am glad that I saved the juicier bits of my life from her. Like once I helped to import some Wagyu genetics involuntarily...let's call it that. We both had our moments. Didn't we? Her caprices changed like the British weather. I won't stoop so low as to call her a munter now. She really got me going. She had taken my heart hostage, and I've paid a smarting lesson. Her beauty is only skin-deep. No wonder people say that there are no more relentless flirts in the world than English girls. Always pettifogging... always lambasting. Whenever I eat meat, I'm contributing to thawing glaciers. Whenever I use *leche de tigre**, I'm partaking in animal torture. She might as well blame the extinction of dinosaurs on humankind.

It's a bane too much for my lonely hunter to heft. She really whipped me up. Do you know that blaming and shaming follow a set pattern of psychological behaviour? People are more comfortable blaming the easy target. That's the ambivalence. Instead of condemning rapists, they blame the victims who go out at night. Instead of blaming the US military for its enormous contribution to greenhouse gas emissions, they overtax honest citizens who prefer some meat in their nourishment. The tree-huggers only pluck soft persimmons..."

Chance listened as Felipe rambled on. He was always a good listener...and an active one even when he wanted an escape.

They had met Sara White in a club in Soho in April earlier that year. Felipe had made a scene when they discovered that Sara's date had spiked her drink.

He knew that Felipe was a man who lived by his own terms of justice. Perhaps there was the slightest chance that under his truculent style something tender still lingered.

"Do you know who else has been on my mind lately? Sara's ex. He wasn't as lily-livered as I thought. Someone nabbed him again. I heard he was large as life and twice as ugly. I hope he's well. I've heard that phantom pains do not limit themselves to the limbs only. I wonder if... if codeine could treat it?" Felipe laughed innocently. "Such a hapless incident. One must be careful with where one's going. Those who gamble must expect to lose. Those who transgress must expect to cry."

Curry and codeine. Rats and rivets.

"I don't want to ruin your appetite for menudo forever. But if you insist... Urban legend has that if you wish to torture someone the old way, you find a basement, tie your targets to some nice, sturdy chairs bolted to the floor

with strong rivets, then put a few rats inside. What harm could a lil Mickey Mouse do? You will know when you start pumping water into that basement. The rats, so desperate to survive, could burrow holes in certain objects and eventually pull out the guts."

Chance felt another surge of vertigo. He looked out of the window. The BT Tower had lost its appeal in the light-polluted night sky.

"Now, will you enlighten me on your proposed approach to problem-solving?" Felipe asked.

He thought for a few seconds. "I told him that I could not promise anything."

Felipe hummed. "Of course you can. Just put a tiger in your tank and be on your mettle...and be agile. And use divergent and creative and design thinking. Did you know that Spain is the largest fig producer in Western Europe? *Atonement* and the Kielce pogrom tell us that when children lie, the consequences are severe. Would you say that God is a child who doesn't have a belief system? The defence of infancy resides on dilatancy and poignancy. Children are such innocent and naive creatures. If you tell them that little puppies like to eat chocolate, they'll feed them chocolate. One kid I know always confuses 'Santa' and 'Satan'."

Chance had learnt to treat everything that Felipe Kazama said at face value.

"It might not be what we think."

"Already imagining things, I see. Care to share, debate, and develop them? In my view, imagination's the worst form of sacrilege. Not that I don't do it from time to time; I've never been a religious devotee. Imagination's the mainstay of human existence. The heart is a lonely hunter. And the mind is a fat liar."

He heard Felipe lighting a cigarette.

"As for you, *amigo mío*, you've been sitting down for too long. It's bad for your digestive system, and you must shake your legs. You must stop your lifestyle as a mouse potato and a homebody. Have you not heard that sitting down is the new smoking? As they say, variety is the spice of life." Felipe laughed like a drain. "Wonder what that spice might be: organic turmeric, perhaps. Wasabi sounds better. *Wabi-sabi* *. Sushi Samba. Oh, I do miss it there. Now, to update you on a mutual acquaintance, I made sure that she bought a one-way ticket on the Sancho Panza of Boston. Hmm...let's hope that she spends the rest of her life living in interesting times come hell or high water, come rain or shine. All voyages have their hardships, and you cannot avoid getting damaged goods sometimes because of *force majeure* or the fickle finger of fate. It's sod's law."

Chance's heart sank like a lead coffin foundering in a tourbillon.

"Have you ever met her face to face?" he could not help himself asking.

"Of course. I love to meet new people. I always prefer to meet the parties involved in a merger at least once, even though I only meet them once and for all. I have a penchant for *ichigo ichie** and *ichigo ame** and the sweets from Minamoto Kitchoan. Or where do you think I got that ipecac syrup from? She had a perfect poker face. Acting might be a better career choice. If she hadn't done such a lousy job and failed so grotesquely, I would have suspected if someone else didn't plan for anything. And as I've said before, not all writers can pull off a pastiche. It was an admirable attempt. Silly girl, she should have done her due diligence. I've heard the malady was not getting better. She got want she wanted...for want of a nail, so to speak...and she must pay. How about curry for their last dinner? A man's gotta do what a man's gotta do. Did she think that a gentleman or a gentle woman or a gentle human is someone she could take advantage of? If you churn milk, you get butter, if you punch a nose, it bleeds, and if you stir up anger, you'll get into trouble."

Felipe continued, "It was said that before Miyazawa Kenji's sister died, she asked him to fetch a bowl of snow so that he wouldn't have to see her dying and suffering—such a tender-hearted girl."

"I saw Francis coming out of the room, and he told me: "Don't be afraid. Now, get me some ice."

Chance recalled the foxed page.

"Cowards run away from death, and the cab-forwards hurried to the rocks happily as they drank the Kool-Aid from the poisoned chalice that I gifted for their housewarming. Do you know that crocodiles are close relatives of birds? When a fox invites a hen to dinner, the wise hen asks, who's on the menu? One must accept the good, the bad, and the ugly with equanimity and *sangfroid*. Mind the gap, says Captain Hook." Felipe laughed at his jokes once more. "Have you imagined what happened between the two?"

After a long pause, Chance responded. "No."

"Let me enlighten you, then. Once upon a time, there were two friends. Good friends they were. Then one day, the parents on one side discovered that they were more than friends. What did they do? They gave the little lady a big hand. Not in a figurative way. And they gave their daughter an ultimatum: leave or remain. She chose to leave. Things didn't work out when the other party went away for exchange. You know, not everyone can pull off a long-distance relationship. Money was tight, and she didn't have anyone to fall back on. Then what did she do? By and by, she decided to become a surrogate and got herself into an interesting condition. It worked, only halfway."

"She asked me if I had children. For that, I hated her."

Chance sighed deeply.

"When and where money is involved, it's always dangerous. What can I say? I guess that parents should, by and large, stand by their children more often. Such a pity that people don't need a licence to parent."

"If there was no fire..." Chance murmured to himself.

Felipe ignored his remarks, "A zero-sum game that added quite a few zeros to my balance at Julius Baer. Can you think of a better Christmas present than a cash cow and an escrow? But the brother got the lion's share." Felipe chortled, "Now, I know your Schengen visa is still valid. I've booked you a flight tomorrow to Barcelona so you can start hunting your hoard of treasure yonder. Lewis Milken holds something of interest to me. He's very cagey about it. Business is all trading favours—still more for politics. The barbarians are all socioemotionally selective animals and they still love bartering from the old days. Ah. It's quite late, and I won't delay you any further. Hope you enjoy the nice weather and...pleasant dreams in spades."

"I'll only take it on if you promise *never* to hurt Catherine again."

"Don't worry, the two of you are my most-favoured nations for now."

The call ended, and he sat there for—how long? He'd lost track of time.

Then he did two things.

First, he placed an order for a new bed from Arketipo through the website of the furniture store downstairs, and then he looked up the 'Sancho Panza of Boston'.

It was a nineteenth-century barque bound for Liverpool that was never heard from again.

CHAPTER 3

Cecil Stone saw a face.

A face that belonged to someone he did not recognise.

He opened his bleary eyes, and a middle-aged woman in a light blue uniform appeared in his field of vision.

"Mr Stone, how are you feeling? And how many fingers am I holding up?" she asked intently. He told her the answer as he collected himself.

He took in his surroundings slowly with his swimmy eyes, like an old cat waking up from a long siesta, and realised he was in a hospital ward.

The nurse introduced herself, but Cecil was still not quite himself. He had bilious urges and his tongue felt tripled in size.

"Here's your medication," she offered.

"Where..." He recovered from his stupor and harrumphed, "Where am I?"

"Rest assured," the nurse smiled thinly. "This is–"

He didn't catch the name of the hospital.

"An ambulance brought you in last night around ten forty-five."

He puffed with exertion and said waveringly, "W...what?"

The nurse helped him to get up.

"It seemed that you fell down on Chancery Lane. Your consultant will update you on your situation during the ward rounds at nine."

The nurse offered his medication again, and he found out that his right hand had a layer of gauze around the centre of his palm while his left hand had an IV infusion.

"You might have gashed your hand trying to grab on some jagged edges when you fell; we stitched it up," the nurse explained.

Cecil stared blankly at his wounded right hand. Perhaps because of the anaesthetic, he felt only a dull ache.

"Thank you…" He craned forward to look at the nurse's identity badge without his reading glasses. He narrowed his eyes, "Nurse… Bennett."

"Just call me Patsy." She had beady blue eyes.

"Thank you, Patsy…"

The nurse asked him his dietary needs, gave him a welcome booklet and some basic toiletries, detailed the mealtimes and introduced the facilities on the ward. There were radios for free and television that you needed to pay for, though calls were free.

Then Patsy briefed him on the status of his belongings.

His coat, hat, and umbrella were there; his signet ring was there. Much to his relief, his briefcase and watch were there.

She finished. Cecil thought for a moment and asked some questions to clarify.

His wallet, along with his half-eaten BLT, was gone.

***

Catherine received a call from her godfather in the early morning and hurried to the hospital during visiting hours.

She found the Acute Admissions ward. Tobias, Cecil's pupil, was there and she saw them whispering. Cecil looked quite raddled and frail.

They had a few more words about postponing a meeting with a client, and Tobias left.

"Oh! Cecil!" Catherine walked up to the bed, noticed his gnarled hand swathed in bandages, and kissed him on his ashen, gaunt cheeks. "What did the doctor say? Is it serious? Sophie's so concerned..."

"I'm fine. It was piercingly cold last night, and I probably needed some more rest. Hypertension...angina...old stories. A slight concussion..." Her godfather squeezed out a small smile. "I'll stay for another night or two."

"Where was Eamonn and what happened to your hand?" she asked. He hadn't mentioned the wound in their call earlier.

Eamonn was Cecil's driver.

"Nothing serious. A shallow cut. He had some family business last night." He grunted, "Did you manage to bring me a change of clothes and my spare reading glasses? Need it to report my lost cards on my mobile banking app. Ay, technology..."

"Yes." She handed him a paper bag with the requested items, together with the latest *Strad* magazine.

Cecil sighed, "Cathy, I'm so relieved."

"Hmm? Why is that?" she asked as she took out his backup reading glasses case.

He said plaintively, "Nothing in my wallet that can't be replaced. And my Tusting is still with me. Three students found me last night. One

44

of them had first-aid training and even put me in a recovery position because they thought I was drunk and worried that I might suffocate. Lord knows, I'm very fortunate to still be here..." he trailed off.

Catherine stayed for half an hour or so and asked if there were anything he might need when she visited again and left the ward. Before leaving the hospital, she talked with the charge nurse and informed him of Cecil's haemophobia.

Her godfather never admitted it, but she had discovered his unease once when they took Mr Darcy for a cat blood donation. The nurse gave an understanding nod and reassured Catherine that the team would take note of this information.

"I have to say that I'm rather good at noticing things."

She drove out that echo from her mind.

It was drizzling as she wandered the streets still fresh with Christmas bunting.

She still had two good hours until her afternoon shift at the flower academy. She took out her folded brolly and walked toward London Bridge Underground Station.

A group of tourists exited the Shard and shared their selfies excitedly.

Catherine suddenly had an urge to go up the tallest building in the European Union.

She had once had dinner with her uncle at the Hutong, a Chinese restaurant in the Shard. It was her uncle who once said that 'tall buildings symbolise elitism'. It was also her uncle who told her, after another broken relationship, that 'love is all about economics: you'll never know if you'll get a lemon or a peach'.

A lemon...

How she wished for another kind of lemon...

"Designed by the renowned Italian architect Renzo Piano, the Shard is currently the tallest building in Britain and the European Union...A new London landmark."

She listened as the high-speed lift ascended.

"Would you like some complimentary champagne?" someone asked as she stepped out of the lift. Catherine declined their offering numbly and heard a guide introducing the observation deck.

She hid from the crowd and stood in the corner away from the lift.

The buildings beneath the Shard were reduced to the size of Tetra Pak cartons. Her eyes traced the iconic chimney of the Tate and then the South Bank...Waterloo Bridge... then the London Eye. The sky beyond the inky horizon revealed a hint of gold.

The crowd marvelled at the London skyline.

Catherine was relieved that her godfather was still here.

She remembered how her father had brought a set of Matryoshka dolls from the then USSR as her first Christmas present. Her parents were gone...everyone around her would be gone...and she would be gone as well...

Gone...inevitable, like the weather...

Angela Carter was wrong, she thought in her despondency. Nostalgia was not only the vice of the aged but the bitter of the lonely.

She took out her phone and checked again. She had not heard from him since then.

No messages and no calls. Nothing and without so much as a by-your-leave...

They had first met on somewhat stand-offish grounds, then his presence had grown on her in time with the help of bees, ice, and fire. She believed that a complete cut-off was tantamount to the end of their relationship. He had simply left her cooling her heels.

Catherine thought she had felt 'chemistry', as cliched as it might be. But the chemistry between lovers was, as Felipe once said, bumbling fools' gold. Because lovers often dream of their ideal partners as if they live in an alternative universe.

Chemistry is only a figment of lovers' imagination.

She was ghosted and jilted, she was quite sure.

Catherine had a very sore heart.

She felt as though someone had pummelled her heart with a bludgeon; or that a sack of cotton had combusted in her chest incompletely.

Drilling holes in the heart might help with angina, but not with her case.

Paulo Coelho said that life always waits for some crisis to occur before the most brilliant moments.... She had had one crisis after another, and she was being hurt by someone who didn't even care to say he was sorry.

She had cared for him.

Her uncle was right.

Love was all about psychology and behavioural economics. And there's undoubtedly an endowment effect in romantic relationships: it takes a lot of effort to tear yourself away from the person you have cared for.

And now what?

They would become acquaintances with only a history...

No, not even a history...

She was in a wax of dangerous melancholy.

History does indeed repeat itself...

Why did she always attract philanderers and wanderers and liars and miscreants and heartbreakers and rascals and shirkers and Lotharios?

She had brooded over this puzzle many times.

Perhaps it would remain the biggest mystery of her twenty-first century.

She vowed that, if she ever believed in another person's lies, she would never find any flying saucers again...

***

By the time Catherine descended from the Shard and passed the Old Operating Theatre Museum, she saw Tobias, Cecil's pupil, heading in Borough Market's direction as if he were tailing someone.

The streets were cold and humid and full of exhaust fumes. She continued her path and followed the rich aromas wafting out from Borough Market.

There was a live kitchen show; the guest speaker in a sari explained how to make the best Masala chai at home. A lanky British Sign Language professional translated in real time.

Catherine watched for a while and learnt how to choose good nutmeg, then carried herself towards South Bank.

Herring gulls hovered while mallards and drakes roamed in the Thames.

A sand artist worked on a *Star Wars* painting with a warning on his left that said 'NO TIP NO PHOTO'. Occasionally, the tourists and pedestrians would toss out penny coins and take selfies with the sand work.

Someone busked 'Last Christmas' in an area where no busking was allowed. A group of tourists chattered about completing the Jubilee Walkway in a day and going for a pub crawl afterwards.

Catherine made her way to the Tate and took a right onto the Millennium Bridge. The wind was not so strong that day; the bridge swayed only slightly.

She wondered when J.M.W. Turner's *Snow Storm: Hannibal and his Army Crossing the Alps* would be on show again.

Someone walking her dog smiled apologetically at Catherine. She made way for the large creature then thought she had remained a blind dog all this time.

When the copper railings outside Oxford Circus Station are hot to touch, you know that summer has come to London.

Catherine recalled what her pen pal had once written to her and grabbed on to the railing.

It was cold to touch.

"My hands are a bit cold, sorry."

On that winter day, her heart was cold as any stone.

Cold as a stepmother's breath...as Orla would say.

Someone was selling hot nuts at the far end of the bridge. The smell of caramel and vanilla enticed her and reminded her of the toffees from her childhood.

She hankered to go back to her childhood, when her parents were alive and lived in her now lonely house. They had always celebrated grandly, and she looked forward to the events: the jollies, the candy cane hunts, and Stir-up Sundays were her favourite.

If only things were different.

If she had gone to that vegetarian restaurant with her parents...

If they had stalled after dinner, maybe gone to a film at the Prince Charles Cinema...

Now, Christmas was nearing, and she wasn't even interested in her advent calendar anymore.

She was still in mourning.

Catherine mused as she walked towards Blackfriars Bridge, where a couple kissed fervently on a bench by the river.

Perhaps it was the way it should be.

Sometimes, people were meant to be passers-by in life.

***

Chance got back to his hotel at just past nine.

The crummy room was quite stale and, on the bed, lay a plate of chocolates.

He took off his jacket and opened the window. Light seeped through the cranny and the sheer white curtains.

A cool ocean breeze swept in along with the notes of the Buena Vista Social Club, and the glowing beacons in the distant cove illuminated like amber fireflies in a stalactite cavern.

He leaned against the window frame and listened as waves lapped the shore.

Blanes was a tourist town famous for its coast and natural scenery.

But he was in no mood to enjoy his escapade.

He had taken the earliest flight from Heathrow and got to El Prat Airport in Barcelona before noon local time. Then he caught a taxi, had a flapjack as a light snack, and listened as the taxi driver flirted with someone over the phone and complained about the NiNis or the NEETs.

The weather was not comfortable, but it was quite a comfort to the eye.

He lowered the rear window and gazed at the shimmering Balearic Sea where the Costa Brava's idyllic sandy beaches stretched for miles and seagulls glided their way above the water and hissed like cats.

He had arrived at the hotel shortly before two in the afternoon.

It was a decent hotel with quite a few holiday-seekers.

He had lunch, selected some brochures on the Marimurtra Botanical Garden, deposited his carry-on suitcase in his room, then found his way to the Garden and had a tour.

There was a bookshop not far from his hotel where he obtained more detailed maps in English, Spanish, and Catalan on the local landscape.

Cemeteries were what he was after...

Not my favourite pastime, he thought as he nosed around the neighbourhood with the façade of an eager tourist.

Cemeteries...

One can't go into cemeteries and columbaria as if one were going to a singing taster session...

Something kept nagging at the back of his mind. He could not put his finger on what exactly. Perhaps it was something Felipe had said or hinted at.

"Another suicide."

He racked his brain for inklings.

An older man and a schnauzer walked past Chance.

"Children are such innocent and naive creatures. If you tell them that little puppies like to eat chocolate, they'll feed them chocolate. Do you think that childhood is a human invention? Rabbits don't even like to eat carrots. Nintendo's Miyamoto Shigeru said that adults are only children with more ethics and morals. My question is, are they? And do they?"

He found a café, ordered a bottle of mineral water and a portion of membrillo with Manchego cheese, took out a copy of the file that he had made and reread it, again.

"I heard someone groaning... I wanted to peek inside... I ran away in fear of his scolding... One night I saw Mother disrobing Emma and kissing her frantically... Her skin was stiff and as cold as my dead grandmother's... On the night of the fireworks, Mother cried so hard and said that she could not live without Miss E."

She could not live without Miss E...

Then he called Lewis Milken.

Lewis Milken was surprised at his speed of action. He had expected him to start his quest after the New Year.

Chance listened as the man flumped on a leather sofa, coughed for a long time, and took a gulp of something.

His own father had passed away from lung cancer. He knew it was a long torment.

"Now, tell me, did you take it up because you don't want to decline another dying man's last wish, or was it because you can't help peeking into others' secrets? Did our last collaboration defile your good-natured character so much?"

He dismissed Felipe's reedy voice and updated Lewis on his findings, or the lack of them. Then he asked him two questions.

"How did your sister meet the friend who got her the job?"

"Well, as far as I can remember, they met during some volunteering event for a charitable cause. Emma was always kind-hearted."

"And..." he paused, "what happened between you and your uncle?"

Lewis half-laughed. "He decided to take up gambling as a hobby. In fact, more than a hobby..." He continued, "Then he got into some trouble and faded out of my life."

"On Monday I'm going to check the local libraries for newspaper archives. Just to see."

After some more dry coughs, Lewis said, "Thank you for trying."

***

A call pulled him back from his reverie.

It was Felipe.

The bar downstairs was now playing a remorseful sarabande.

He turned on but muted the TV.

A programme called *La Sexta Noche* aired, and the same song by Yamashita Tatsuro played on the other end.

"No need to thank me for the suite and the sweets," Felipe said, "Did you enjoy your hotel and your mint chocolate? I've heard that you went into a hotel with a female companion for some rather heated moments. News travels fast hell for leather, and it travels at the rate of knots." Felipe lowered his voice, "Oh, Cathy is giving you the silent treatment, isn't she? As someone who has had many similar situations in the past, I feel for you."

"I've tried to explain–"

"Now, now. Don't fret. Everyone makes hideous mistakes. Courting is not as simple as 'click and collect'. Don't expect to send a few corny, mushy, and cheesy messages and see her standing on your doorsteps with arms wide open. Catherine has for sure told you that patience is a virtue. One missed-out hyphen could crash a NASA rocket, and one small mishap could endanger a blossoming relationship. Allow some time to cool off. Let her consider her Return on Capital Employed and see who is missing."

He chuckled inwardly at the not-so-layman joke.

"And I take it that you haven't heard the bad news, have you?" Felipe asked compassionately.

Bad news. How he hated bad news.

"What happened?"

"Old Cecil collapsed before one can say Jack Robinson. Don't worry, he got to his Jesus Hilton on loaded miles. But I think he'll have a hard time there. Do you know that he fears seeing blood? I only found out recently. Do you know that hospitals often use the colour green to soothe moody patients and for doctors to refresh their vision? Filmmakers use green screens for all sorts of fancy background swaps. I've heard that they even made the roof of the Shad Hall at Harvard Business School green. It's my favourite place at HBS. Green is a fab colour except when applied on hats. Even the carpet in the House of Commons is green.

"Unwitting Cecil really needs some refreshment and time for reflection and recollection. For sure, the Queen does not wish to see her staid counsel curling up with only a career. Someone needs to help him

to unstuff and untuck his shirt. Hmm, come to think about it, Cecil's
the one who often sets the balloon debate in his chamber's pupillage
interviews. He is, undoubtedly, throwing himself out of that sinking,
cockamamie hot-air balloon. He really needs to change that circumspect
attitude of his. Let me put it this way...bluntly...the odious humanity-
mongers and their compeers should really spare some miserly mercy for
themselves and call to improve their own deplorable living conditions.
Why do they always fancy CSR over CPR? Why do they always risk
their lives and limbs?"

He made a mental note to call Catherine later, then, remembering
Felipe's words, he scratched that note and fed it to a shredder.

"I do hope that Cecil was properly attired. Once I saw a leaflet on
how to know when it's the right time to buy new underwear. You need
to imagine that you are having an emergency and if at any time you'd be
embarrassed by your underwear when paramedics remove your clothes,
then you need to procure new ones. Do you know that according to the
WHO, the average life expectancy of an adult male in the UK is around
eighty years? I'm not saying that he should lech, but Cecil should do
himself a favour and stop wasting the remains of his days. The odds
are not so bad for a heterosexual single man who has both money and
status. You can't say that he's not a gregarious man. He's good at making
overtures. I can think of better ways to beguile some of that...let's
see...630,720,000 seconds," Felipe counted.

"Once I worked on a project related to hospitals. Customer
Relationship Management training with nurses to enhance the patients'
customer experiences. Funny that you can categorise the whole ball of
wax in terms of buyers and sellers. It's an interesting study, and we found

that the introduction of CRM led to higher readmission rate for people with chronic disease. They'd grown too fond of their nurses."

Chance listened as he watched the TV screen flicker.

"And do you know why in the US you're better off seeing doctors that are not too old? Especially in towns and counties. Because the old doctors are often rusty if they don't have the number of patients available to achieve the learning curve. No one would expect a decrepit senile person to detail the eight bones of the wrist eloquently. And emotionally they suffer less if a patient dies than a novice. Old doctors often have higher patient death rates than young ones. Who knows, maybe there's a learning curve for detachment and nonchalance...but Cecil's alright. He's taken care of by very caring and light-fingered medical staff. I'm sure they won't draw too much blood. And here's an in-joke among medics: the patient had refused an autopsy. Just joking; Cecil's in good hands. And I mean it in the right way."

"The brother had handpicked the deluxe option. They will be in good hands."

He remembered.

"Anyway, the bad news was that he'd lost his wallet and half a sandwich. Then, in the wee hours, his cards were used in Brazil. How wonderful..." Felipe was amused. "From the known burglar, the juvenile, the booster, the junkies... *Qué mona!* Technology does empower all. The professionals compromise the SWIFT, and the less able-bodied filch half a skimpy BLT. Do you know where everybody's most sensitive spot is? Someone from Israel tells me it's the wallet because no one wants to spend but only to earn more money."

Chance didn't reply. On the television screen, a guest was grinning broadly.

"Do you know that Wigan has the world's largest baked bean factory? Orwell never did justice with his unflattering portrait of the town. One has to live, especially the poor ones. When I was still a hick and a nobody, I once found a lost wallet," Felipe recalled. "I was so poor back then, but not as poor as poor Lewis. At least I never needed to debase my ink. But still, I needed to make buckle and tongue meet. And, guess what I did after finding the wallet?" Felipe didn't wait for his guesses. "I took all the cash, and found the owner, saying 'hey, here's your wallet, sorry it was looted already when I saw it. But you still got your cards and *unten menkyo*' and your *hokenshou*' and your 001, so that entitles me to some honorarium.' And he was very grateful, he bowed thrice, and gave me ten thousand yen. Well, the money was not his, technically, but his wife's. That's why I was the top of my negotiation class."

"Hmm..." Chance curled his legs up on the sofa, found a comfortable position and said, "Rather impressive."

"Now, don't be sarcastic," Felipe dismissed him with a flippant remark. "You were never good at it. I read an interesting study today on kissing. Researchers found only about forty-six per cent of kissing couples in one hundred and sixty-eight cultures. Do you know that Bronisław Malinowski found on the Trobriand Islands that lovers would not kiss but bite off each other's eyelashes? I keep on wondering how it would feel. I don't even have a partner to practise on now...I have no one to hold in my courting seat..."

"Someone from Mercury's Hong Kong branch tells me that a comedian once said listening to love songs after a break-up is like having an indoor gas leak and deciding to seal the windows. Even a sea bream loses its flavour when eaten alone. The songs got it all wrong. Not every average man prefers his favourite sport when the temperature is low. London is no place for golf in December, I tell you. Today, I decided to stop looping sappy songs and allow myself a respite by recharging my battery on the course. It didn't work. Guess who I ran into? Raymond at the Meadow. He complained that he hadn't seen Howard for a while. You do remember Howard, don't you?"

He could hardly forget.

"We didn't get the rub of the green when we played with him the last time. It's his turn now. What you lose on the swings you gain on the roundabouts. Those who-have-had-it-alls would soon cry over spilt milk. Poor Howard, I'm sure that his wife was not too pleased to find his name on the Ashley Madison hack list. When poverty comes in the door, love flies out of the window. Do you know that the oldest buildings in London have their windowsills facing out? And did you know that there was once a window tax in Great Britain? It might be useful for a pub quiz.

"Christmas is a terrible time to be indicted for white-collar crime. Santa Claus must think that he had been a bad boy. As a Chinese saying goes, if a son is nescient, his father is to blame. I wouldn't be surprised to find both of them on Santa's naughty list. Naughty boys indeed. Naughty and nasty. Santa must feel that some people are meant to wither and die on the vine. Sometimes when life shuts a door, it shuts another, and another until they reach their nadirs. Howard certainly makes a better door than a window. A golden key can open any door, and a hokey-pokey can close many more. What can I say? That no one can always get the rub of the green? If you dig a hole in the road, disguise it, and wait for

your enemy to walk by, you are springing a trap. If you hire someone to
approach your enemy and say, 'hey, here's a hundred bucks, I want you
to dig a hole in the ground for me', if he takes the money without even
asking what the hole is for, and picks up a shovel and dives right in...that
is called depravity on his part." Felipe cleared his throat.

"But really. When Rajoy is being punched in the face on the home
field, you know no one is safe. Safety is on relative terms. Trouble never
rains but it pours. And nothing is as safe as spending time with the dead,
which brings me to the topic at hand...and I'm very good at easing into
heavier subjects. How was your walk among the tombstones? Any leads?"

"No."

"Not yet."

"I can't say."

"Don't say 'I can't say'. You can say, 'I'm confident I will make
progress'. Cathy shares one common hobby with me. She likes to read
and watch thrillers. And recently, I've discovered a secret. I call it the 'rule
of WOWOW'. That in all books and films and TV, ninety-nine per cent
of the time the murderer is for sure in the casting. If only life worked
that way. Maybe we should try a séance. You know what you should do?"

Felipe continued nonchalantly, "You should think about dirty objects
more often. Such a pity that they scrapped Page 3. I once had a great
time at Lloret de Mar. Maybe you should take some time off. Blanes
has some amazing restaurants. My personal favourite is Bistrot de Tot.
Do you know that lobster's blood is colourless? It only turns a tint of
blue when the blood is exposed to oxygen. And *bogavante* does taste a
lot better than its American counterpart. Maybe you can go and explore
that neck of the woods...sow some wild oats and improve the local

biodiversity?" He joked.

"I was there in Spain to see the cormorants and the *basajaun*. Really, I'd be a dog if I lied. Do you know that a flock of cormorants is called a 'gulp'? And did you know that Lloret de Mar was a backward fishing village in the nineteenth century? People who were dissatisfied with their lives went to the New World and sought wealth from the mines in Peru and the coffee plantations in Costa Rica. That's why you get to see the ornate and frilly building styles."

Chance tucked this trivia away.

"You will continue your *drôles de jeux* tomorrow, will you? Speaking of games...once, I accompanied a big gun...no, he was actually a bowhunter, on a whitetail hunting session. The guy was really an expert at blood trailing. He taught me how to tell apart a lung hit, a meat hit, or a liver hit, and a paunch hit. Then one day, we were there, and he shot his bow. And he was all balled up, saying that he'd never seen such a blood trail of a whitetail. Then it dawned upon him that he had shot someone," Felipe paused, "and you know what he said to me? He wiped his sweat and said, 'Phil, one witness is no witness. You do understand what I mean, don't you?'"

Chance dreamt of straggling ducks that night.

CHAPTER 4

The alarm awoke Catherine from her fitful sleep.

She dreamt again of a glob of blue fire.

She had long finished the book that he had given her and consumed half a bottle of vodka. And her drinking last night had thrown her body out of its kilter.

A splitting hangover followed her like a shadow as she got up. Mr Darcy, her cat, meowed and urged her for breakfast. His diet regime had, undoubtedly, failed again.

There was a message on her cell phone from Mick, Catherine's best friend who had recently married.

"Hey, Cathy. We've thought that we can give him a good lesson and by that we may or may not mean a hard beating. Kean Street sounds like a doable place for an ambush. I can do some preliminary research today after work. No kidding. I won't do anything, but please take care. Give me a bell if you need a broad shoulder to cry on."

She smacked her forehead. "Good God, oh dear, what did I say?"

A quick check on her cell told Catherine that she had called Mick, her uncle, and even Sophie last night.

She could not remember the details of their conversations...not even the salient points. Heck, she could not for the life of her remember anything they had discussed.

What she did know was that she had ranted and railed.

Just great...

Several DVDs were scattered on her carpet. *Killing Me Softly*, *In the Cut*, *Before I Go to Sleep* and her favourite films...

"You don't believe me. My word against hers and you don't believe me."

She diverted her attention by applying some carpet cleaner foam on the splotchy wine stains, then rearranged her DVD collection. Her TV was on, and a telethon played, then fundraising commercials.

She'd remembered that Felipe had once said, 'the children in LEDCs do not only starve at Christmas. The TV producers, do they know it's Kwanzaa?'

Catherine changed the channel. A chat show played, and some experts debated the influx of refugees in the EU.

"The European Parliament should come up with a practical solution. Are we just sitting here and letting crime rates in our already turbulent neighbourhoods rise? We want no more immigrants and no more terrorists," a man argued indignantly.

"I'm genuinely brassed off with all this drivel! We need to tone down this whole rhetoric on crime. Is this a community of values?" The camera panned, and a commentator in a black dress suit retorted, "Even if you add up all the refugees, the number is less than one per cent of the entire EU population. Not mentioning that we have strict border control. Think of Alan Kurdi. Is the spirit of humanitarianism already dead?" Her protest went unheeded.

Catherine turned off the TV and raised her central heating by a notch.

The weather was a cold snap and so was her heart.

She considered whether to visit Cecil later in the day and decided she would go after her shift at the flower academy.

Catherine prepared muesli for herself and food for her cat, checked her calendar on the fridge, and got ready for work.

It was still a bit early.

The motion detectors in her house were up and running. Mr Darcy had lost interest with them long ago. His new play items were her Anglepoise and the pot of cat grass she got him.

Her house phone rang, and she rushed to check the caller.

An unknown number was calling; an international number.

Orla had told her about a recent scam involving missed international calls: the scammers would hang up and wait for you to call back, to charge you high rates per minute and you shouldn't call 1471 afterwards either. She let it ring the full duration and didn't pick it up. She had long erased her answering machine message and disabled the device.

Mr Darcy rubbed against her leg, asking for attention, and she played with him for a while with a ball of worsted yarn. She had remembered to make a vet's appointment for his check-up.

She left her house without faffing around, thinking about the Swiss Glockenspiel.

A boy on the Tube was playing 'Everybody Hurts' on his headphones, and Catherine could hear the lyrics clearly in the not-so-rushed morning rush. She arrived at Covent Garden Station shortly before half past seven.

The Underground advertisements promoted a sculpture exhibition on happiness at Tate Modern, and an Ibsen play, *The Master Builder*, at the Old Vic.

Cleaners scrubbed the shop windows as Catherine made her way to work. A dull yellow puddle lay under a bin, most likely the by-product of someone's happy hours.

A homeless man sat not far from the Underground station with his Rottweiler.

She had bought a copy of the *Big Issue* the other day, but she bought another from this man.

"Well, thank your mother for the rabbit, lovey, and 'ave a nice day!"

The dog stared at her with big watery, rheumy eyes.

He turned back once again, slowly, and his eyes were dreading and entreating.

"Goodbye then, Miss Roxborough."

Catherine pulled herself from her foggy haze and hurried under the overcast sky.

Her mood became, once again, as soggy as the London streets.

***

Orla was already at the shop, preparing flowers.

She wore a green apron with the flower academy's logo.

"Good morning, Melody. Morning, Orla." Catherine hurried down the steps to the basement. It smelled like a greenhouse, damp and mouldy.

"Why don't you get us some floral clay, wire, and tape?" Melody instructed as she cleaned her work station.

Catherine changed into her apron in the locker room, grabbed her herb snips, and gathered the requested items. Then she moved the small blackboard out with information on their latest promotions and gift card discounts.

She noticed that the 'PULL' label on the door was about to fall off. She went inside, retrieved some tape and secured the sticker.

It was a hectic morning with customers buying and ordering flowers and mistletoe for the festive season.

Catherine sat down on a chair after making two bouquets and a vase of orchids and took out an eye spray. Then she realised that, unknowingly, she had a cut on her right index finger.

A slight occupational hazard when you have to work with thorns, scissors, and wires...

She bandaged her finger with a plaster, in fear that the chemical solutions they used to preserve flowers could cause further harm. Then she closed her eyes and applied the spray.

He smiled ruefully. "That's okay. At least I know where the Band-Aids are."

Unwelcome memories...

She sat there, massaged her temples, and sighed.

How she wished she could shut off her memories the same way as a TV.

Orla came into the room and saved her from another bout of simmering bitterness.

Catherine opened her eyes. The room seemed a lot brighter.

There was a replica of *The Flower Makers* by Samuel Melton Turner on the wall. She stared at it languidly for a few seconds.

Orla was sending her boyfriend a voice message: 'Hey. How's the audition?' Then she yawned and stretched. "I want to steer away from mornings at New Covent Garden at all costs. How do they manage to get up at three in the morning and do business?" She combed her tresses with her fingers and waffled on querulously. "Winning bread is hard. It's a pig of a job. I've been losing a lot of hair, and I don't get to see him that often... Though we always sparred, and Melody's always having a go at me, and I have to accompany my nephew for his dialysis. He's always acting the maggot at the hospital. Bree, my sister, is still in a tug of love. I even got cyberflashed yesterday on the bus. Jaysus, why can't anyone leave me in peace?" She pouted.

George, Orla's boyfriend, was an aspiring actor who made his living with various precarious employment opportunities. He always carried a satchel with a badge that said 'LOCALS ONLY' and liked to wear stackable rings on his left hand.

Orla picked up a banana with a fair-trade label on it and a bottle of Innocent juice as an early elevenses. "I should shack up with George to save on rent. My granny once asked me how we make up when we quarrel. I told her that we haven't even quarrelled once. I guess I can't complain much. George says that so many places are using zero-hour contracts. People just don't care about social welfare. He always blamed the Poles. His friend was harassed by a gang of Polish punks in Whitechapel last month. She walked by them, and her watch was gone." She chuntered on about her life.

Catherine said nothing. Her best friend Mick was half Polish.

Orla took out some hand cream from her apron pocket, squeezed a generous amount on her hands and began to massage them.

He dipped his hand into the bowl and scooped some blue fire onto his palm. He held it carefully and rubbed it quickly on her ankle...

Catherine stopped that train of thought before it even departed.

"Melody says there's another course at the Boerma Instituut and she wonders if you would like to go? It starts early in January."

"Sure." Catherine gave a perfunctory nod.

She could ask her uncle to take care of her cat. And indeed, no one would miss her if she was gone for a few days, maybe even a few weeks.

Or a year...

She had tried it before. She was very good at running away from her problems and worries. The last time, she had run as far as India. She might even pull up her stakes and relocate again.

This time maybe she would go to Argentina...maybe Buenos Aires...

This time she would bring Mr Darcy...

The rest of the world would manage perfectly without her...

It would suit everybody.

"Here's the itinerary for the flights. You can fill out the reimbursement form now." Orla took out a sheet of paper from her apron pocket. "We'll be staying at Melody's friend's tulip farm. We'll be there in time for their National Tulip Day. Oh, and Cat, I've read that Dutch guys like high heels, so be sure to pack a pair or two." She threw her a wink.

Melody called, "Orla, dear! My laptop is frozen. Come and help me with the order list, will you?"

"You can try to press control-alt-delete on the keyboard. It usually works!" Orla shouted back.

Catherine found a biro and filled out the form. Then it was time to work at the till.

The front of the shop played a jazz tune called 'Can't Smile Without You'.

Catherine emerged from the basement. A chubby lady was standing in the shop browsing their flowers.

Catherine had recognised her—Hannah Robinson, *someone's* neighbour.

They had once chatted briefly at the Petersham Nurseries shop in Covent Garden. Hannah had moved to London from the US with her husband Eddy, who worked as a legal counsel for a Fintech and knew Cecil.

"Hi. Catherine, right?" Hannah Robinson extended her warm smile. "How are things going? I almost forgot that you work here. I saw the flowers and I thought that I would pop in to say hi. I was at the White Company getting some knick-knacks and I'm waiting to get some groceries when Marks & Spencer opens."

"Good morning and thanks for dropping by." Catherine put on her polite, commercial smile begrudgingly. "What are we looking for today?"

"The poinsettias are quite gay and so is the holly." Hannah Robinson looked around like a kid in a sweet shop, "The white roses are garden-fresh. Wow, look at these sprigs! I have a difficult decision. I always have a difficult time deciding. I'm spoilt for choice." She turned to examine the Italian ruscus and the hypericum berries.

His eyes bore into hers and smiled again. "I did notice certain...sparks. But, I dare not to assert." He paused. "If all goes well, perhaps I can get some white roses to celebrate a new beginning."

The saccharine background music wasn't helping at all.

Catherine pretended to check the till. "Well, our flowers are delivered by air freight, and we have very high standards in sourcing."

"Umm, I haven't seen you in Chance's flat. No, I don't think that I ever saw you there. You have to come someday; we could have dinner after he comes back from Spain. I'm sure you'll enjoy my relishes. I make great Hoppin' John, tater salad, gumbo, and beef Stroganoff. All of Eddy's friends love it. Oh! You're a vegetarian, aren't you? I make a great Waldorf salad. We have a fabulous rooftop where you can see the Palace of Westminster. Did I pronounce that right? I always tend to stress the 'min' part... But the panorama is better in the summer when London is as warm as toast and everything is so pretty...except that London has no jar flies. You know what? You two should join us for the New Year's Eve fireworks! We have a great view!" Hannah Robinson jabbered.

Under any other circumstances, Catherine would warm instantly to her Virginian accent and her friendly invitations, but she listened as she jarred the keys on the till hard in vexation.

She did not know that he had gone to Spain. For a second, she wondered if he had done a moonlight flit.

"I will not go without saying goodbye."

Catherine decided that she hated him.

Her customer gave her a cryptic smile. "Don't worry. He's getting rid of the old bed. He left his keys with me. Some workers will take it, and there'll be a new bed delivery and a new mattress. How exciting. I'll see to it myself."

Catherine was genuinely puzzled. "I don't quite understand."

Hannah Robinson lowered her voice and checked no one was eavesdropping. "He hadn't told you, has he? Golly! Look at my big mouth..." She clicked her tongue. "I reckoned that you knew already. It's kinda awkward for me to tell you..."

"About?" Catherine asked.

"Really, it's not for me to say, but he'd have to tell you sooner or later and maybe it's okay for me to tell you. He for sure had some reservations about inviting you up there. I would if I were him. I can only call a spade a spade..." Hannah Robinson spluttered as she explained. "Long story short, the previous tenant of that flat passed away in there. She did herself in during the Holborn fire. Eddy and I were away. Our cleaner Sarnai found her. She's got gumption. Poor darlin'. The girl died on that bed. Thank God that we didn't know her. It...it happens every day. People should really think 'bout their lives. Everyone lives in a hell of a frumpy mess. Eddy knew somebody who jumped onto the train tracks at Victoria. But...but the flat's okay. You don't need to be nervous as a long-tailed cat in a room full of rocking chairs. Sarnai made sure it's clean, and there was no blood involved. You've got nothin' to worry 'bout."

Huh.

Catherine should have felt sympathy, but she listened as a cauldron of seething anger welled up inside her again.

Bastard.

No wonder he had to go to a hotel.

Damn him to hell.

***

Cecil Stone pondered thoughtfully for a while after his pupil left.

Catherine called, asking if he wanted any flowers, but to her dismay, the ward did not allow flowers or plants.

He did not have any food that he particularly liked or wanted, not even gooseberry pie or lemon meringue pie. In the end, he had turned down his goddaughter's wish to visit again in the afternoon.

"How are you feeling today? Mr Stone?" Patsy's voice broke him from his reverie.

Cecil closed his magazine. "Much better." He raised his wounded hand and checked. He was glad that he could not see any blood. "Can I ask you a question, Patsy? If it's not too much trouble."

"Certainly," Patsy said as she arranged some items for another in-patient.

"I have very little medical knowledge, but would you give a tot of whisky to someone with hypothermia to warm them up?" He smiled faintly. "I had a friend who read Medicine, and once he raised this question as a challenge, but I never heard the answer..."

"Umm...interesting question. I believe that..." Patsy paused to remind a visitor to not sit on a patient's bed. "I do believe that you shouldn't. As alcohol is a vasodilator, meaning that it relaxes the peripheral blood vessels and allows more warm blood to flow from the core of the body to the skin and tissues, it could cause more heat loss." She sighed. "We always see people who are blotto and suffer from hypothermia during the festive seasons. The Beast from the East is quite savage."

"Isn't it just?" Cecil nodded. "Hmm. Patsy, any plans for Christmas?" he asked, trying not to appear too keen.

"The usual. I've got nowt special. The chit-chat, the niggle, the binge, the stodgy puddings...the Full Monty and the *Downton Abbey* omnibus," Patsy said meekly and smiled. The wrinkles around her eyes did not do her justice. "We have quite a goodly diddlum this year. And how about you, Mr Stone? You will be discharged soon. Wouldn't it be wonderful to spend the Yuletide with your family and enjoy the dainties and the jollity? It's awful to fall ill in the merry season."

"Yes. It is..." Cecil muttered. "Wasn't there an illness called the... 'Christmas Disease'?" He coughed slightly. "My daughter and my grandson are coming to visit from Germany." He decided to change the topic. "Do you live far away?" He paused in discomfort. "It must be terrible to commute in this beastly weather, particularly after night shifts."

"I'm one of the lucky ones. I have accommodation provided by the hospital. The waiting lists are very long. We have a nearby indoor pool and great social facilities like karaoke and pub quizzes," she said. "We have some events planned...carols and cantatas..." Patsy thought for a few seconds. "I once went inside a public gallery to see a trial at the Old Bailey. They said Dickens was a regular there to get inspiration for his books."

"Yes. Charles Dickens was a court reporter. Magwitch in *Great Expectations* was based on a convicted thief. He was caught in flagrante delicto and was deported and later returned to England." Cecil stopped to gather his breath. "Patsy, do you know that the Lady of Justice at the Old Bailey is not blindfolded?"

Patsy didn't bat an eyelid. "Umm...I haven't a Scooby. Maybe next time when I pass there, I'll stop and have a look," she said and left to check another patient's drug chart.

Cecil sat there, and his feelings silted up for a long time.

***

That day, Felipe Kazama wiled his morning away at Le Méridien Piccadilly.

He later went to Hyde Park to see the Garden of Tranquillity, a memorial in honour of the victims of Harold Shipman, a British medical doctor who had murdered his patients with morphine injections.

As an avid reader, Felipe had kept Francis Bacon's words close to his heart: 'a man that studieth revenge keeps his own wounds green'. He had learnt from a young age that medics were a dangerous species of people who could hurt and heal and who certainly knew how to make people hurt the most. Truth be told, his visit to the Garden of Tranquillity did not quell his inner turmoil.

In marketing, all products need positioning. Felipe Kazama positioned himself as a finagler, an interloper, an outsider, and an angler, just as there are crisp sets and fuzzy sets in maths and in life.

It was a rainy and misty day; the familiar, leaching scenery in London.

There were a few people in the park. Squirrels dashed around, and a young father in a transparent raincoat played with his daughter.

Felipe traipsed aimlessly through the park, hiding under his Brigg umbrella, his John Lobb shoes squelching on winter mud. Once he had met a man at the World Economic Forum who told him that it was no use wearing new shoes in Mongolia...

Two horses flashed out on the riding path to his left and swished by as they trotted through the muddy water. The riders did not look very happy.

Mallards and swans gathered at the lake.

He remembered the tale of *The Hunter and the Seven Swans* and decided to rest on the bench not far from the lake.

Rain splashed on his umbrella and he watched as the birds waddled, dabbled, and quacked and his emotions ruffled.

He collected himself and later visited the Princess Diana Memorial Fountain.

Afterwards, Felipe made his way to Covent Garden on the Piccadilly line and got coffee from the famous Monmouth Coffee Company.

Someone called as soon as he left the coffee shop.

He put on his Jabra earphones as he sipped the hot beverage. "Well, well, isn't this the will-o'-the-wisp? Hanging loose in there? You make me feel that you are the one who's on the lam."

"Aren't you the one who prided himself on his splendid plans and what has taken so *bloody* long this time? I've another perfect storm waiting," his caller questioned.

"Tut-tut. Do not gee me; I'm not your horse. And don't be so antsy. Did your mother not teach you to never answer a question with a question? And how bloody is bloody? Did you know that the Father of the Blood Bank was an African American? He resigned from the Red Cross because, during World War Two, the Red Cross prohibited blood donations from African Americans as they didn't want the blacks' blood mixed with the whites. How ironic."

"You are going off-piste again."

"Oh yes, I've been enjoying my time in London. It's good to be a butter-and-egg man once in a while. I'm just on my way to the British Museum to see the Parthenon sculptures, and later today, I'm going to the V&A to check out the watercolour *Figs* by Jacques le Moyne. To enhance my cross-cultural competency, you know." Felipe watched a group of tourists gathering at Seven Dials with their hubbub. "Haven't you heard that sadness is a bonfire? And to stoke up the flames, some gimmicks are certainly needed."

The other end laughed. "So has the tight spot in the cart been solved?"

"Rather a titillating image," Felipe mused. "Why waste UK taxpayers' money when we can handle the larceny quite nicely ourselves? Do you know that Nintendo started as a small workshop producing playing cards? It's called *hanafuda* in Japanese. Card games and mergers are all about planning; planning in advance. Hope for the worst and prepare for the best. I never borrow trouble; I only lend it. I never invite danger; I only hire it out. I have many tried and tested fancy recipes for problems."

Felipe opened the lid of his foam cup as he always had a *nekojita*. "I once went to watch a movie...a horror movie. It was good, but not that good when you had to shell out the extortionate amount of five dollars. It had the usual elements of horror: a cult, an exorcist, lots of gore. But you know what put me off? The protagonist walks into a murky hostel in the middle of nowhere. In the middle of the night, he sees a dreadful creature who resembles a clerk, and he asks if he can use a Mastercard. A single line marred the whole show. Unlike cinemas that profit from popcorn, I gain by putting up a show. Michelin restaurants don't sell food, but an experience, or the scarcity of it. Hunger marketing is all it takes."

"Marketing again, eh? You know what the shop owners say about the Hatton Garden heist? It was the best advertising campaign they ever had for their jewellery district."

"It's a pity that the Litvinenko case never brought the same fame to Itsu. Do you know that 'itsu' means 'when' in Japanese? And do you know that 'wagamama' means selfish? The more desperate one is, the more willing one is to surrender, and the easier for me to up the ante. Your fellow serviceman James Bond was wrong. Small portions are best suited to entertain curiosity."

"Measured doses may be fine for treatments, but not chicanery."

The sky cleared.

A few cirrus clouds floated like whipped egg whites.

"Precisely. And time's our ally." Felipe continued to sip his coffee as he watched Londoners splurging on their sundries in the shopping season. "I once helped a client with an international expansion of his coffee chain. He was eager to conquer the EMEA markets. All the shops were doing well, except for one place in one particular country. At first, we thought there were some venal specialities involved. And he sent me as part of the outfit. I went in as a 'mystery customer' to investigate. It turned out that those shops, in place of selling coffee, provided an altogether different service. The shops were known locally as sleazy meeting points that served as platforms for people who engaged in the world's oldest profession. I got back, and I told the CEO what was happening there. I told him that 'yes siree, it's all chaos out there... chaos, not *ciaos*... It's like *The Night Café* by Vincent van Gogh'. You know what he did? They partnered with a non-profit to provide free STD examinations and contraceptives. I asked him why, and he said, 'Phil, it's better to be loved than hated'. He always called me Phil even though he knew that I absolutely hated it. The last time we dined, we had some luscious wine. It was his last dinner. I'm not sure if he liked being on the receiving end of a harpoon. He was really pitchforked. Not in a figurative way. What was the name of that fellow...never mind. I never bothered with those who bit the dust. Yeah, I'm known for being crooked as a barrel of fish hooks. So now, tell me, do you want things to run their course or do you want to avert the downspout? I'd say it would be better if Lewis Milken did it off his own bat. Capitulation is better served voluntarily. It's like coffee production: the first three years you plant the tree, and then you wait."

"Now I do feel bad for your spaced-out protégé. He could have avoided the bootless trip and the whole wild goose chase," the other end said with a contrite tone.

"A chaperone must mind his own business first—not to mention that I have a bigger fish to trawl and to fry. I believe that the key with tutoring is for the students to deduce the answers by themselves. As Drucker says, there's nothing more dangerous than the right answer to the wrong question. Some people have a smart mouth like me. And others have attentive ears. Sam Antar said that the art of distraction is always more important than lies. Lewis Milken needs a tree hole more than a brash pair of fire tongs now. When you meet him, you will know that Chance Yang is damn good at worming information out of people. He's curiously attractive to the general public and hence a hard act to follow. And no one is hurt. He will be home and dry soon." The steam from the coffee blocked Felipe's vision. "And never say I never helped my favourite assistant. John Stuart Mill, your fellow countryman, said that love requited is love extinguished. Absence makes the heart grow fonder. I did embolden him and even told him that he should think about dirty objects more often."

"And who is titillating now?"

"*Jaja*. Does the *New* Scotland Yard sport such a prudish climate? Page 3 will always be in between page 2 and 4. Do you know that Clos Maggiore has a wine list 85 pages long? The devil is in the details, and the evil is in the entrails of the human mind. I love tits."

He paused, and the other end remained silent.

Felipe continued, "I love tits and I love blue tits and coal tits. You don't know what a 'dirty object' is, do you? Let me enlighten you. A 'dirty object' has altered content that is out of synch with the database. It's a name that we can call Lewis Milken. He knows something that we don't and we hold something that he doesn't."

"Lewis Milken is not getting any better. I hope his rot won't last."

"Arson is always better with a degree of urgency and he's not going anywhere." Felipe's eyes half-smiled as he found his pack of Marlboro. "Maybe I should quit smoking. It's a wonderful world out here." He considered. "Have I ever told you the story about how I found a lost wallet? I took all the cash and went to the owner, saying, 'hey, cheer up, you still have all your credentials and cards'. His wife gave me some money as a token of gratitude. And the man did not disappoint. He found the note that I left in his wallet, and he bought his address book back for quite a bonny sum. It had a good collection of girls' names and addresses and their interests. No one really fought against Franco, and his dictatorship only ended when he died. Tigers leave their hide when they die, and men leave their name...and maybe a black leather notebook...or some home videos, like Rurik Jutting did. Here's my piece of advice for advancement: shuffle paper and look busy."

"I need a date."

"Hasn't your mother ever told you to ask for favours nicely? You should at least say: tell me *cuando, cuando, cuando*." Felipe waited for a reply. When none came, he sucked his gums. "Epiphany is on 6th January. You don't need to kick your plan into touch. Poor Lewis will soon get the sticks in his craw...the bitterest misery is to know so much and to have control over nothing."

"Will you be there?"

"Of course, I'll be there and be square. I'm the product owner in this. And I'm fashionable yet never fashionably late. If I'm ever late, it means that I'm dead..." He stopped to lend a theatrical pause. "Or that I'm beat...or that I'm a deadbeat..."

The other end chuckled.

"See, I can make anyone laugh. I didn't have a career ambition to be an M&A consultant, and if I didn't entertain finance, I'd be a great comedian." Felipe observed a pigeon eating breadcrumbs while another cooed. "Do you know what a flock of crows is called?"

"It's called a 'murder'. After all, it's my line of duty."

Felipe said, "No. Sometimes it's called a 'congress', and a group of owls is known as a 'parliament'. Might be helpful for pub quizzes, who knows. Isn't it funny that you can't stand for MP as a Bow Street Runner, but a tried criminal can? That's why I never plan the future by the past. We can assume nothing *a priori*."

"A lot of cats and dogs get in, but politics never interested me."

"I know the MP for Wigan and I feel truly sorry for the Wigan people. Just call me a well-informed individual. All politics is local. As the Tories would tell you, if you want me for a neighbour, vote Labour.

Did you know that the London tour guidebooks were never written for non-white people? I shall find my bearings around in the tangled leafy town. Oh, you think it's fun to hang out with caviar environmentalists and champagne socialists? And all the MPs I know are deadly dull. All the party animals talk about is how to party and not about their Party. It makes you wonder if they have two operating systems: one for showing and one for living. Some of the MPs have the worst handwriting that I've ever seen. Way worse than chicken scratches; AIs won't even recognise them. If there were no receivers, there would be no thieves. If there were no humans, there would be no mergers and acquisitions. One thing I like about politics is that it always hurls forward buckets of boulders and it usually whacks some people. Now, I believe it's time that we dial 'M' for... Merry Christmas!"

The other end hung up briskly.

Felipe tucked away his Jabra, grabbed his furled umbrella and continued to rove on the London streets.

Chapter 5

H is visits to the local archives yielded no fruit.

Chance gleaned some pieces from old newspapers on obituaries. He even managed to get a copy of a list of house owners from 1980 to 1990 in Blanes. Despite his Spanish coming in handy, the list did not reveal much; no, nothing at all.

He had mooched around the marina, the dinghies, the vast swaths of beaches, and the surrounding vibrancy for a dozen times. Yet he hadn't a clue how to move things forward, with the case or with Catherine.

"Aren't you grateful that I helped to move things forward? A little catalysing...bonding... where the rubber meets the road? And she's a lot stronger than you think. You're doing her an injustice, thinking that she's a damsel in distress."

He had often contemplated these words from Felipe.

Felipe did not call; nor did Catherine.

Lewis Milken called, almost every day, to ask for progress, and he offered none every day. They talked mostly over dinner and plates of salmagundis and Moutabel dips. He made sure he had plenty of vegetables and fruits.

Lewis spoke about his sister for hours: how she got her favourite dress...what Beatles songs she liked...her favourite illustrations by Beatrix Potter...how she loved to visit the Daunt bookshop...how she wanted to go on safari...

He felt that he was getting to know Emma Milken very well...just like he had known Joyce Peng.

Felipe once told him that, 'if we are to be spongers, at least let us leave a neat trail'.

Chance felt he was like a sponge, for he had soaked up all of Lewis Milken's simmered sorrows and regrets.

Was he bearing the brunt of Lewis Milken's loss?

He could hardly bear his own.

There is more than one place called London in this world...

There is more than one European town known for its botanical garden and fireworks...

Was he looking for a cat in a coal hole?

He worried that he was after a lump of coal that was long burnt and turned into soot.

He dwelled on these thoughts often.

A week went by and Christmas came and went.

On Christmas Eve, he sent a dozen emails, made some calls, and wrote some New Year's greeting messages. Cecil replied, telling him that he had returned home and thanking him for his kind words.

Later, he video-chatted with his cousin An.

She was with some Chinese friends; they did not mind him joining their jolly long distance.

Like him and An, the group had not grown up in religious families other than occasional visits to Buddhist and Taoist temples. They were happy to get a break from their reading lists and assignments.

He listened as they shared their London experiences and episodes over hot pot and effervescent drinks.

One student recounted that his flat had a malfunctioning smoke alarm that woke the whole house one winter night. They had followed the landlord's instructions and called an emergency contact number. Then they asked the other end if they should evacuate the building, and the receiver said, 'Mister, I'm in Delhi, and you are in your apartment. Do you need me to tell you if there is a fire or not?'

Someone shared a story of how his Economic History lecturer took a hammer and an iPhone 4S to class and smashed it in front of the whole class. The lecturer then explained which country made the chip, which country made the screen, which country made the camera, and which country made the battery.

A girl mulled over her summer in Budapest when she lost a backpack and her passport. She reminded everyone else to safeguard their belongings when travelling.

He remembered his student days.

The hectic exams...the pub crawls...the mistakes...

Then the group talked about ice skating at Somerset House...the best hot pots in Chinatown...their favourite Jay Chou albums. Then bizarre happenings in London: one saw a man naked below his waist on the Underground...another was molested by someone who barked at her like a dog...how people intentionally told them the wrong directions... how surprising it was for them to find pastries with poppy seeds on sale in bakeries; to find so many homeless persons on Fleet Street; to find people commuting on scooters...foxes window-shopping at midnight on

Oxford Street...how smelly the red telephone booths are...neighbours who kept parakeets as pets...how they were asked for ID in clubs...how a Chinese man always played the tune 'Weeping Sand' on his *sheng*ˢ in Covent Garden...the sad song made them want to cry every time they passed it.

He listened as they argued whether Pret a Manger or Caffè Nero or Starbucks had the best coffee with respective price-quality ratios, and where to find the best condiments...

As the night went on, the students moved onto more sentimental topics.

One blurted out the items on her bucket list. Another cried for not being able to travel back home for the Chinese New Year; it would be his first time away from home...

Chance listened as he clipped his nails.

Then someone brought up the news of a food shop near the Strand whose mascot, a clay pig called Pepe, had been smashed by frantic vegans who had also smashed the shop's display window and left a warning note.

The shop was called Viandas de Salamanca. He had been there to buy Ibérico ham.

Catherine never interfered with his diet options, nor he with hers. She had allowed Mr Darcy to choose his favourite cat food, as he was not partial to plant-based products...

Chance listened on.

Another said that once she was at a Topshop store, and someone's mink was stomped on and peed on by another when the owner went to try on clothes. A biologist in the group mentioned that, unlike its Chinese name, 'fruits without flowers', figs do have flowers and insects known as fig wasps are digested by an enzyme inside figs during the pollination process. Therefore, there was controversy among vegans about whether to eat figs, as many did not consider the fruit vegan.

"I like to have my figs chilled..."

He hung on their every word. Suddenly, he felt that he was very close to something.

"A woman groaned...I wanted to peek...I ran away in fear of his scolding...One night I saw Mother disrobing Miss E and kissing her frantically...On the night of the fireworks, Mother cried so hard and said that she could not live without Miss E..."

He excused himself, ended the video chat and stood by the window.

An idea had flitted through his mind as he thought about his conversations with Felipe once more.

"You know what people say about the mute and the dead? That they cannot speak for themselves.... Children are such innocent and naive creatures.... Imagination's the worst form of sacrilege...."

He ran some searches on his tablet. The more he read, the more unsettled he became.

He had a thought. It was a horrifying yet feasible thought.

Just as he was about to contact Felipe, another call came in.

He connected it, and a cheering female voice said, "Happy holidays. It's been days since you called me. *¿Me has olvidado?* Have you forgotten me?"

Chance smiled wistfully.

Before he went to bed that night, he called Catherine and found her line busy again.

**

On the morning of 31st December, Felipe finally called.

Chance put away his Dopp kit, dried his hands on a towel, and connected the call.

"Hey, kid. How are you holding up? I'm sorry that you had to stay away for Christmas. How about I recompense you for spending New Year's Eve with Cathy? 2015 is almost turned pages now. I hope you can start afresh in 2016. Tomorrow's a new day! And... hmm...I have some updates with Lewis Milken's case."

He wanted to ask Felipe a question, but in the end, he asked a different one.

"What kind of updates?"

"Enough to say that he can shuffle off his mortal coil with his eyes closed. I've obtained some intel from another source. You know, I never put my traders on the same trading floor, not even in the same building. As your visa's about to expire, why don't you come back to London and take some days off for the New Year and meet me at the cocktail bar at Le Méridien Piccadilly at two pm sharp on the 6th of January? Epiphany is on the 6th. I've sent you an email with your ticket."

He checked his email and found the ticket.

Then he asked Felipe a question, the one he wanted to ask but dreaded the answer.

"As Keynes said, it's better to be roughly right than to be precisely wrong. Looks like you have the bare bones all figured out. I'll tell you the gory details when we meet again. Oh, and remember to go to the jazz bar opening tonight. I'm planning to coax Cathy to join you at the party."

And with this, Felipe hung up.

He packed his meagre belongings, checked out, took the hotel's shuttle bus to Barcelona airport, and boarded his flight on time.

It was the third time that year that he had flown to London.

The first time, he had arrived on a last-minute charter flight from Tokyo in April to help Felipe to resolve another dying man's last wish. The second time, he had flown in business class in October hoping for some new beginnings, and now...

Now.

Catherine had not called, nor replied to his messages.

He had thought about some possibilities, then he baulked at the very idea, but they still lingered like the after-taste of an irritating mouthwash.

He could only hope for the best and prepare for the worst.

Maybe it wouldn't be so bad, after all, if he returned to China and spent the New Year with An's parents. He had not seen his aunt and uncle for a while.

An old couple conversed on how they would spend Hogmanay and a family sitting in the row in front played 'I spy with my little eye'.

The flight was not a bumpy one, and he soon fell asleep thinking about chilled figs.

"Dear passengers, we have arrived at London Heathrow Terminal 5. We wish you all a happy New Year."

He opened his eyes, checked the time, put back the British Airways *High Life* magazine, and unbuckled his seatbelt only after the seatbelt light had gone off.

Unlike most passengers, who travelled with heavy luggage and bags of souvenirs, he only had a carry-on suitcase.

He grabbed his suitcase in one hand, and his landing card and Arrivals Fast Track voucher in the other as he followed the queue to UK border control. He then handed the voucher to a member of staff and lined up behind a couple from Thailand.

Chance watched as they took out a folder of printed material from their hand luggage and explained that they were visiting their daughter who lived in Stratford. He waited as they supplied their fingerprints. Finally, the border control officer called him to step forward.

He passed border control, used the washroom, found his way out as travellers rubbed their hands and waited to reunite with their families and friends and jostled against him, and headed for the parking area.

He found his car in the teeming car park and got in. Turner pinged, asking him if he would be there at the bar tonight. He confirmed with a 'yes'.

Even if Catherine would not be there, she would be there...

The radio played 'My Foolish Heart' by Rod Stewart.

He checked the fascia and drove off, once again, into the windswept winter scene.

***

Orla had had a terrible day that day.

She almost argued with an ill-tempered customer who questioned the freshness of the flowers he had ordered for a centrepiece. Melody had had to intervene to resolve the issue.

At last, the shop was near to closing time as she kicked her heels.

Orla could not wait to join her boyfriend, George. They had some crazy New Year's Eve plans. She was immersed in their previous night's romance when someone hit the call bell strongly.

"Oi!" she recalled her thoughts. "Hiya, sorry, sir to have kept you waiting. Happy holidays and how can I help you?" she greeted the customer as she eyed the clock.

A man who was dressed like a dog's dinner looked at the flowers. "Don't say sorry and don't call me 'sir'; it makes me feel old."

"Sorry. How can I help you si–sorry...mister?"

"Don't say sorry, just don't do it again." Felipe looked at the girl with a mealy complexion in front of him. "Do you know the one common problem of you British and the Japanese? You dish out apologies every day for trivial issues, but you scruple to discuss the dense matter at all costs. Countries steeped in aggression. Isn't the British Empire the epitome of commerce without conscience? Slave trade, opium, smuggling of cultural relics, to name a few topics on the agenda. Each of them would merit a tome. The British should apologise for what happened at the Boer concentration camps, for what happened at the Parthenon, and for what happened at the Summer Palace."

Blargh! Why is everyone winding me up today? Mercury's not in retrograde yet!

His unstopping words and imperious attitude rankled her. "Sheesh! Just give over, will you! Will you *please* stop giving out say-sos? And for your information, si–mister, I'm Irish."

He gave her a sardonic grin. "Ha! Even better! So, the next time you meet a Brit, you can tell them this...and maybe add a few details on the Great Famine, which is pathologically ignored, in my humble opinion."

I will, yeah, she thought.

He looked at the glass jar on the counter that was raising funds for Red Nose Day. "A penny for your thoughts."

Orla tried not to roll her eyes as she gave out to him. "Bleh. I hope to have better-quality customers next year."

"Flattery will get you anywhere. I bet that you would not meet generous customers like me that often." Felipe took out his wallet and inserted two fifty-pound notes into the jar. "Unlike *some,* I'm well aware that a penny soul never came to twopence. And I try to do one good deed every day. Girlie, if you find my words aggravating, that's understandable. One must watch where one's going and pay attention to what one condemns. It's not only the chattering classes who chatter. One may use choice words, but one need to choose words very carefully. Sometimes, words can do irrevocable damage...like Gerald Ratner. If you gift a rose to someone, a nice scent stays on your fingers, and if you badmouth someone, your tonsil stones will stink. Tidbits and tittle-tattle especially. It's an ill wind that blows nobody good. Sometimes you let the wrong cats out of the bag, and they can foul your own nest before you have the time to cry. Do you know that not seeing is a flower?"

For cripes' sakes! What a brash and conceited man!

Orla blew a raspberry as she stared at this outlandish man in his ludicrous outfit like he'd come out from a party hosted by the Great Gatsby. "Thank you for your generosity...puh-lease...Sir... Mister... I'd appreciate if you'd save your harangue for another day. Do you need *any* flowers or–"

"Yes, I'd like a bouquet of white roses."

"Aye...and would you like to include a message card?"

"Is it free?"

"Yes, it's complimentary."

"Sure, why not? I do like bells and whistles."

"What would you like to include in your message? We can write it for you in several calligraphy styles," Orla said as she took out a message card and the calligraphy set with a ruling pen.

"You can write *'Tsumaranai mono desu ga"*."

"Wait...come again? How do you spell that?" She looked genuinely puzzled.

"Ah. I do think that your shop should customise for an international clientele. 'Global Britain' should be more than nomenclature. It's a title that needs to be earned and not declared. Here, let me write it for you." He took the pen and wrote down a line on the card. "Let me sign my name as well. The name's Felipe Kazama. Kazama is a Japanese word that means the time when wind passes." He folded the card. "Not passing wind, mind you."

She tried to suppress her giggles.

"Orla? Macushla! Let's meet at Heathrow on the 5th...and remember not to be late for our flight! Woe betide anyone running late! I read in *The Telegraph* that Heathrow stress can trigger a heart attack, think of it..." Melody called from the basement. "And the 'PULL' label on the door is about to fall off again. Would you mind securing it with some tape?"

"Ahh...can't it wait? I mean...it's not like we'll have many more customers today. And surely, they would be able to tell. It's fierce windy out there!" Orla shouted back.

"But it could be dangerous. What if people bump into each other?

We must adhere to the health and safety protocols," the teacher said.

"I'll do it." Catherine moved to the front of the shop, and she saw Felipe lolling beside the counter.

"Aha! Here comes the assiduous Cathy. I'm buying a bouquet to celebrate the opening of the new jazz bar. In Japan, people would gift *hanawa* or large wreaths for new business openings, but in China they often do it at funerals, so a propitious nosegay would do. And do you know that in Russia, people send an odd number of flowers to the living and an even number to the dead? I'm always very careful with cultural nuance."

"That's very thoughtful of you." Catherine avoided the topic at hand. "Wow, don't you look dashing today?" She knew that Felipe was pedantic about preening himself. She then said to Orla, "I've got this customer handled, could you help me to secure the label on the door?"

"Fine... fine..." Orla took the tape and headed out.

Catherine asked, "How've you been?"

"Mega *bien*."

"And what brings you to London?"

"Well, I came to attend a funeral, actually. This is the fourth funeral I've attended in this quarter and still no wedding on my schedule yet. I've been busting my ass these days. M&A is a trying profession. But I do love to meet new people, even if they are just oafs."

Felipe selected some bright flowers in addition to the white roses. "And how's work been recently? I'm never fond of the legal sector, so I'm glad that you managed to escape like a rat up a drainpipe. *Ikebana** is a well-esteemed profession in Japan. As Katherine Hepburn would say, if you do what interests you, at least one person is pleased." He shot her a glance, "*y dime una cosa*, do you hear the roses scream?"

"Nice try, Felipe. I can hear them singing." Catherine helped him with the flowers.

"But do you not hear your love affair screaming like a strangled kitten?"

She pretended not to have heard his question.

"Do you know that mistletoe is a parasitic plant, Cathy? People are sick, I tell you. Kissing is only a process of exchanging microbes and food debris. And I was told that honey is like bees' half vomit." Felipe cleared his throat. "Funny for him to open a jazz bar; he doesn't even drink. But you know what's even funnier: there are so-called 'Chinese experts' in the Pentagon who have never been to China, so I say all is well. I know someone from the Department of Defence who's in charge of sanitary management. They have like 184 toilet rooms. No wonder it's the twentieth largest economy in the world. Imagine how much toilet paper they need in there. And no wonder their financial statements are unauditable. I wonder how many toilets the DOJ has."

Catherine listened as she bundled the flowers with a length of floral wire.

"Got any plans for tonight?" Felipe asked rather abruptly.

"Uh-huh: dinner with my uncle and Cecil."

"The same old tripartite, I see. No alternative entertainment planned?"

"No. I wish."

"*Gracias a mi mismo.* I got a ticket for the Vienna Philharmonic Orchestra New Year's Concert tomorrow."

"Aren't you the lucky one." She chose a wrapper from the drawer under the till.

"Yes, I'm quite proud of myself. Although I did not read a hundred books this year, I did reach my goal of attending a hundred restaurants." Felipe took a deep breath. "Well, Cathy, I'm not here to mollify anyone, and I do not wish to wax sentimental...but I can vouch for him. I'd never imagined him to be the leching sort. He's such a greenhorn when it comes to matters of the heart. I'd buy it if you told me that he was a stool pigeon for Scotland Yard rather than him being a cad and stooping so low as to pull off unseemly stunts and trifle with women's hearts. Do you know why?"

Catherine pretended not to have heard him again.

"Because that man hates hotel rooms to the extent that he would only sleep on the sofa in his sleeping bag. That's why we didn't grace the hotel chains with our presence in April. And do you know why he hates hotels?"

"And why might that be?" She worked hard to seem impervious to his words.

Felipe's tone was delighted. "Because he hates white bedsheets, but who knows. He might overcome this phobia if someone's willing to provide some redeeming... consultation...on strictly professional terms, of course."

"And how do you know that?" Catherine tried to keep her tone uninterested.

"Well. I might as well tell you," Felipe shrugged. "We worked on a project once, and an intelligencer leaked our offer to other bidders. I tipped Housekeeping so they could keep their eyes on the team for me. This person told me that he never used his bed. Ho. I thought perhaps he didn't stay in his room at all. He might have partied all night. Then I asked him, and he told me why. I checked the CCTV, and it seemed that he was telling the truth. You know, I seldom vaunt anyone. He's such a taciturn fella. But once he gave me some punches because I said some things about you. Nothing offensive, just some bog-standard observations. And he was very angry. He even used language. It was stupid of me. I had had a few drinks and I deserved it. He raised such hell that our neighbour knocked on our door and complained to our face. I've never seen him so agitated..." Felipe trailed off.

Catherine frowned. She put down the bouquet then said airily, "Really? Why? What did you say?"

He studied her. "I think it's better if you find out from him." Felipe shifted his stance. "You caught Pierre in the act, but this is different. You must be familiar with the legal jargon and the grimgribber more than I do. You know, innocent until proven guilty... *Testis Unus, Testis Nullus*... one witness is no witness...due process...the benefit of the doubt.... Why don't you bring your buddy who's out there smoking and go treat yourselves to a girls' night out? You can bring this bouquet to him. I'm not in the mood for a peart party tonight, and I don't want to be a party-pooper. I do not wish to steal away anything, not even myself. You can help me to avoid that tawdry pomp and circumstance. I understand your quandary; I really do. Of all of the *mochis*, my least favourite one is *yakimochi*. And I do think that people should play responsibly. Talk to him. If he did do it, at least slap him hard and teach him a lesson."

"I can't. I need to meet my uncle and Cecil."

"Stop abrogating with your puerile excuses. Do you need a corsage for your next date or do you need a date for your next corsage? A career is wonderful, but I can't curl up with it on a cold night. Would you instead write to your pen pal and reminisce about the sloppy what-might-have-beens? Do you know what I didn't learn in business school? Just because you can do something doesn't mean you should do it. And just because you don't want to do something doesn't mean that you shouldn't do it. Do you need me to remind you of what Bertrand Russell said about caution in love? I think not."

Felipe took out his wallet again and drew out another fifty-pound note. "I won't prattle on for any longer. I think this would cover the bouquet and it's always lovely chatting with you. The decision is yours to make and chance favours the prepared mind. No pun intended. The only reward for love is the experience of loving. I can't remember who said it. If you don't wish to go, give the flowers to Cecil so he can brighten the rooms in his bleak house."

***

Catherine clutched the bouquet tight as she scuffed along Long Acre in the winter night. She had to admit that what Felipe said earlier piqued her interest and curiosity and put her out of sorts.

He knows me too well. He knows exactly what to say.

Why did they fight over her...no, not over.... Why did they fight because of her?

She knew that Felipe could sometimes speak out of turn with his zany humour and rub people up the wrong way, but he never said anything that was utterly offensive in the most blatant ways, not to mention that Felipe had asked her some questions to which she didn't have the answers.

Catherine touched her alexandrite necklace over her jumper that had once belonged to her mother.

If they were at a dead end, at least they should say goodbye.

She found her way to the bar. A live jazz band was playing something by Sinatra, and the cheery notes mingled with the touches of laughter as the crowd guzzled.

"Ah! Coach Sidney, so good to see you!"

Catherine saw Turner slinking through the throng of merrymakers and offering fawning greetings to someone who wore at least four-inch heels.

"Ee, Turner! Hoofing! You are looking swish! Do I get the discount still? I've brought some old buddies to heat up tonight." the coach asked amusedly.

"Of course! You have my most sincere gratitude. As you said, I did a bit more research and found out that the venture was not as appealing as it seemed. Chance has a mate who wants to lease out this place. So, we decided to strike out on our own. Have lots of fun, and I'll catch up with you later," Turner said fulsomely.

"Sure. I think I could do with some rum and coke."

Catherine reached up to Turner before he moved away.

"Hey." She eyed her surroundings and handed him the bouquet. "Hope you and your business have a wonderful New Year."

"Thank you so much, Cat." Turner took the flowers and looked around. "Chance is about, probably spending a penny or so. Why don't you enjoy the bar? We have some great sopes and ouzo. Or how would you like some Michelada? I'll tell him you're here."

"That's fine. I'll go now. I have a dinner with my uncle and my godfather. Happy New Year." She retreated and almost stepped on someone.

The band began to play Norah Jones' 'Don't Know Why'; an abysmal choice for a New Year's Eve function, she thought.

Then a figure lazing by the bar caught her eye.

"The last time I was in Spain, my taxi driver, knowing that I'm from Mexico, told me that he was ashamed of my country. I told him 'likewise'. Another said that it was great that I only had a little accent. I tell these episodes as jokes now." A woman in a red backless dress sitting on a high-back bar stool bantered with the bartender.

"Tell me about it! I was once asked on the Tube if I speak English! Typical!" the bartender said.

The woman continued. "And someone at my hotel asked me whether I was a beneficiary of the DREAM Act. What the fudge nuts!? I told her that I would take it as a backhanded compliment. I guess I don't look like my age and, you know, age is only a number. But I did have a nice watsu massage and some wonderful Roman punches. I was asked for my ID yesterday when buying vodka."

"How would you like some V.A.T? Wait...lemme get you some Sipsmith to try." The bartender poured a shot for her.

"*Qué Padre!* We must ask Chance to stock some Jose Cuervo. I'll make sure to drop by from time to time."

"I favour Alipus," the bartender said.

"I saw your man just now. He was with a chic Latina..."

Catherine glared at the woman pointedly. She did not look her age indeed.

"Catherine!" someone called out behind her.

Not someone: *him.*

She turned and wanted to snub him, but he sidled up to her.

"Happy New Year..." He had jitters before speaking up. "Do you have a minute? Maybe we can talk?" he said with agonising politeness.

She was annoyed with his poor efforts and his half-hearted conciliatory approach. "Don't you dare 'Happy New Year' me! Do you think you can just *waltz* into my life whenever you want!? To hell with your flipping ghosting! Do you think that I'll be putty in your hands again!? Well, Mr Yang, I'm not at your beck and call!"

He gave her a tremulous smile. "Umm...one possibility that I can think of is that...you might have blocked my number."

The woman saw them and approached. She stood proudly like a blossoming Checkmate rose. "Well, well. I do believe that we have not been *properly* introduced. Lynette Sun." She reached out her hand.

Catherine did not want to make this woman an agreeable acquaintance, or an acquaintance of any kind.

Why did he have to hang her out to dry in the open?

Why did she come here only to be mangled and scalded?

She bit her lip and glared at him, and they locked eyes. Then he smiled sadly and gestured. "This is Miss Catherine Roxborough. My... umm...a friend. And Catherine, this is my stepmother, Lynette."

Chapter 6

Cecil Stone typed a quick reply on his phone one-handedly, put it down, and picked up his chopsticks.

The Hakkasan Hanway Place in Fitzrovia was a favourite of his long-term friend, Alexander Roxborough. It had excellent food but somewhat uneven lighting and a noisier ambience than he liked.

He glanced at his dinner companion. "Cathy said that she wouldn't join us tonight. She's very sorry, but she's spending some time at the jazz bar. There seemed to be some misunderstanding that's been resolved."

Alexander nodded. "I would rather that they reconcile than have her spend New Year's Eve with the two of us...and her cat. I hope she'll be in august company."

"I'll check on the cat on my way back."

"I've never liked its name," Alexander Roxborough said.

They ate in silence for a while.

"Thinking about Isabel?" Cecil asked after finishing his pork rib.

"Sometimes, yes." Alexander Roxborough swallowed. "And Catherine's parents." He picked up a cashew nut from the sizzling fried prawns with chilli and dropped it on his plate. "I'm ill at ease...I never have...I don't feel comfortable letting that sod Felipe Kazama near her. Cecil, you must promise me, if I go before you, you will keep your vigilance."

Cecil smiled bitterly. "I might go before you do." He took a sip from his soft drink with a copper decoration denoting the Year of the Monkey.

They sat in silence again, then Alexander said, "And Chance Yang...I do not know if he knew the real Felipe Kazama...and his true intentions."

"I hope they can navigate safely through the perils." Cecil rearranged his napkin and said after a pregnant pause, "Alex...there's something else...or should I say someone... that's been troubling me."

They talked until their food went cold.

***

They strolled down Drury Lane and turned onto Kean Street without speaking.

She trailed him through the glass gate and into the lift. It was a small lift with mirrored walls accommodating a maximum of nine persons.

They came out of the lift on the ninth floor and moved through a short wooden passage that gave onto a petite, open atrium with rows of large terracotta flowerpots.

Peals of laughter and music drifted in the air; the Robinsons were having a shindig.

Catherine hesitated before speaking. "Mrs Robinson told me of the... unfortunate happening in your flat."

She observed him, and he did not look surprised. "I would have preferred to tell you myself, but I understand if you don't want to..." He cast his eyes down.

"No...I'm fine."

He took out his keys and unlocked the door.

Hannah Robinson did not exaggerate: it was a lovely penthouse with a balcony, and a panorama of Covent Garden. Catherine could see the BT Tower from afar.

They took off their coats and shoes and walked like a pair of cats on the heated flooring. Catherine wore a jumper from Brora. She tugged its hem nervously and looked around as he turned on the accent lighting.

The living room was spacious with a mahogany kitchen island. A suitcase, the one she had seen in April, stood not far from the beige sofa. There was an engraving on the wall. It had whorls and squares. Beside it was a pier glass. A white spiral staircase led to the upper floor.

The bedroom is probably upstairs...

She wondered what the previous tenant was like and if she had enjoyed her view.

Catherine looked around without appearing overly inquisitive.

A small, half-opened green scrappy fabrics pouch lay on the kitchen counter; it had a sewn avatar of a tiger and contained various receipts and used boarding passes.

"Mrs Robinson told me that you went to Spain."

"Yes." He retrieved the pouch and put it away. "I went for some...side hustle."

He hated to use that term, yet he continued. "I did message you."

Ay.

Catherine decided to change course. "The receipts, why do you collect them?"

"I always shred them for personal information safety purposes." He walked to a cabinet and took out a stamp-like thing and a sheet of paper. "When I don't have a shredder at hand, I use this stamp to smear the texts, so they are unreadable by malicious individuals." He demonstrated on the paper. "You can refill it with printer ink cartridges."

She felt she was watching a cack-handed teleshopping programme.

"He's such a greenhorn when it comes to the matters of the heart."

Maybe Felipe was right after all...

She smiled inwardly before a thought tugged her mind.

"Oh, that time..." she reflected. "When we met under the Swiss Glockenspiel. You weren't asking me out discreetly, but you needed the cartridges for the stamp." She sounded like a private investigator deducing a lead.

He put down the stamp and smiled sheepishly. "Umm...that time... we had a shredder in that flat in Oval."

"Hah!" Catherine let out an incredulous huff and tilted her chin upwards. "It's only your word..." Then she trailed off.

"My word against hers and you don't believe me."

She looked at him in awkward silence.

"Maybe next time you see Felipe, you can ask him." He smiled again, took out a candle lighter from another drawer, and lit a candle in a votive.

It didn't take long before a redolent citrus scent roamed the room.

"Do you light a candle to remember the deceased?" she asked.

He shook his head slightly. "I'm afraid I don't do it for altruistic reasons..." He looked at her, and Catherine avoided his gaze. "Tomb robbers would light a candle or a torch before they broke in so they would know if there was enough oxygen or not." He sighed. "I don't think the deceased would do me any harm. Besides, I do like its scent."

She felt they had become terrible at small talk.

"Do you like..." She reined herself in. "What else do you like?"

"Well, I like sweets but not liquorice. Chocolate, of course. Sometimes I play badminton, and I collect mechanical pencils."

"Do you like me?" she blurted out her most pressing question.

His eyes bored into hers as if saying, 'do you have to ask?'. Then he said, "Catherine, I like you very much."

She steeled herself mentally and countered sullenly, "Please...I can't...I cannot take any more lip service."

"Oh, Catherine." His head dropped as he announced dejectedly, "If something is bothering you, you need to tell me."

"You still...you still haven't told me where you'd gone that afternoon," she told her socks then looked up.

He deadpanned. "Are you sure you want to know?"

"Yes."

He stepped closer. "A hundred per cent sure?"

"Do tell."

He gave her a roguish smile. "And you promise that you will not think less of me?"

"No...I mean, yes, I promise. Scout's honour."

He walked over to a cabinet and took out an A4-sized, recycled-paper folder. He opened it, found a page, and handed it to her. "I was...I was at a colorectal clinic." He sounded all cringey.

She took the folder and thoroughly examined the appointment printout before bursting out laughing. Never in a million scenarios had she imagined this combination of events.

"Does my alibi pass inspection?" he asked sincerely. "Would you like a detailed account of my consultation with the specialist regarding... regarding my piles? Or his email address and number?" He showed her an innocent, hurting smile.

"I'm sorry," she murmured gingerly. "And...I'm sorry for kicking off at you at the bar just now. Sorry for the set-to. I was hot-headed–"

He stopped her mid-sentence. "Catherine, I am sorry if I made you feel insecure about this relationship in any way."

His disarming smile assuaged all her gnawing doubts.

"We could have celebrated our first Christmas," she bemoaned.

"We can still celebrate our first New Year's Eve...our first Chinese New Year...and our first Valentine," he said as he invited her to sit on the sofa.

"Will you make me happy on Valentine's Day?" she asked, trying not to sound cheeky.

He considered. "I hope to make you happy every day. If you will let me."

"Promises, promises."

"Guess I'll have to remedy that." They snuggled together, and he gave her a quick peck. "Will you take a chance?" he smiled. "No pun intended."

"Now you sound like Felipe," she said as they nuzzled closer. "You know what your problem is, Mr Yang? You should be more persistent."

"Should I?"

"Uh-huh. You should have at least called me with a different number."

"I did. I called you from my hotel in Blanes. But I couldn't leave a message."

"Oh." Catherine remembered the international number that called her quite annoyingly every day before she added it to her blacklist.

He considered. "Will you tell me what Orla said about me...no...the person she mistook for me?"

So, she did, and after her account, she asked, "Are you still angry?"

"No, no. I hold you very high in my estimation." He thought for a while. "But now I understand why you *were* angry. Give me a moment." He stood up and disappeared upstairs. A minute or so passed and he re-emerged with a large bag from Hotel Chocolat.

"An told me that you liked it...and I saw it the other day after my appointment at the clinic. I didn't ask for another bag because I had this one to hand."

She eyed him suspiciously, then he took out a shoebox from the bag.

It was a pair of Charlotte Olympia kitty style flats.

Catherine would find it too much if he bent down and helped her with the shoes, but he didn't, and she tried them on.

"Did I get the size right?"

"As right as a trivet. It's a topping pair of shoes."

A gleam danced in his eyes. "Happy?"

"Yeah. You do catch on quickly, Mr Yang." She put the shoebox away, and they nestled up again.

She wanted to ask him about his fight with Felipe but decided to save it for later.

He mused, "Umm, Catherine, you are quite a firecracker when you are angry."

She buried her face in his arms. "I'll take it as a backhanded compliment. Having second thoughts?"

"No. I like to see a different side of you." He took hold of her fingers; they were quite cold.

"Well. I'm glad that I can surprise you, Mr Yang."

"Tomorrow's a new beginning for us?"

"Yes."

Just as they were about to share a proper kiss, a static spark shocked them both on their lips.

They collapsed into gales of laughter.

"Let's try that again," she said, still laughing.

They had finally reached closure and were engaged in an unalloyed, passionate clinch when someone knocked. They parted arms reluctantly, and Chance stood up to answer the door.

"Hi! I saw your lights on!" Hannah Robinson invited herself in. "Come and join us for the fireworks! We got Aplets'n'Cotlets, hot toddies, and many more goodies that will stick to your ribs! C'mon, let's kick up our heels!" She invited them in the most effusive manner.

He asked Catherine if she would like to see the fireworks and she said yes.

Chance extinguished the candle with a snuffer, they put on their coats, and before they headed out, he lingered in the washroom for a minute as she changed her shoes.

The Robinsons' place had the same layout, except they had a view of the river. Some colleagues of Eddy Robinson were gathered there and clacked as 'It's Too Darn Hot' played on the stereo.

The fireworks had just started strobing when they got onto the balcony.

The night air had descended a few degrees, but Catherine felt giddy and warm-hearted.

Giddy...in a good way...

Last year today, she had celebrated the New Year with her students. Who would have thought she would end up here?

The party oohed and aahed at the fireworks, and she felt him squeezing her hand gently. He gave her a hand warmer and held her other hand in his overcoat pocket.

She thanked Felipe a thousand times.

All was not lost after all.

***

The fireworks were sublime and the party was a success.

They talked with some people, had a few bites, and finally stole themselves away when the powwow started on if and how Donald Trump could beat Ted Cruz in the upcoming Republican primary race.

"Donald may have a babbling mouth, or sometimes act as a blowhard, but who didn't say one or two funny things when they were young over a couple of drinks?" said the lady of the house.

Catherine had found it difficult to believe that Hannah Robinson was a zealous Trump supporter. She also noticed that Eddy Robinson had refrained from joining the discussions and chose to smoke on the balcony instead.

The BT Tower glowed a merry hue when they got back. Then he offered, "I better drive you back..."

"This sofa is not so crowded for two." Catherine sat down and bounced up again. "I don't want to go home. I'm enjoying some congenial company."

"Better not to get cricks?" he offered tentatively.

"But I want to talk. We hardly had any time to talk."

And whose fault was that? Who's the one who assumed? Don't you know what happens when you assume?

She quelled her upsetting inner voice. "We can banter all night!"

"If you say so." He relit the candle then asked her if she would like to charge her phone before settling beside her on the sofa. She made sure to unblock his number before recharging it. Catherine had also borrowed a spare toothbrush, remembering what Felipe had said about kissing.

They were relaxed and replete.

They talked about how they had spent Christmas. She told him how Mr Darcy had mauled off the cover of the *Big Issue* featuring Bob the Street Cat... but her cat didn't know that she had another copy in the safe. And they remembered the time when her cat had peed on his shirt and how they made use of a memorial half bottle of vodka.

She thought for a moment then asked, "Why did you fall from a tree? Once you told me you fell out of a tree..."

He recalled, "We were out playing in the field, An and I. I was about seven or eight. We saw a fledgeling had fallen out of its nest, a sparrow. I wanted to return it, so I climbed up the tree and I was attacked by wasps."

She nodded with concern. "It must have hurt quite badly." She played with her fingers before asking, "Do you know...umm...how to spoof a MAC address?"

He scratched his brow. "A rather random question, I have to say, and the answer is yes."

"Felipe said that everyone should learn how to spoof MAC addresses with the same dedication that they pose for selfies." She leaned back into the sofa arm and turned her body so she could read his face. "He told me that you dislike hotels and white bedsheets. Will you tell me why?"

"Well..." He wrung his hands. "My dad was a heavy smoker and developed lung cancer. One morning I went to visit him in hospital, but he was not there. The first thing I saw in the room was the sheets on his bed. Then I knew that...he was gone." He bit his lip. "Since then, I haven't been able to sleep on white sheets."

Some small talk.

Catherine had expected a case of mysophobia. She scolded herself for her poor choice of question as she drew a parallel with her life.

She feared driving at night and...then she remembered the question that she longed to ask.

"Felipe also told me that you once fought with him because he had said some things about me. Is that true?"

The way he looked at her was like Mr Darcy when he did some misdeed.

"Yes. It was on that day when you...sprained your ankle in front of the stairs at the National Gallery. Felipe...he did...he said some things about you that I didn't like. I did not like them at all." Then he laughed a little. "You know what he told me? He told me not to wrinkle his bespoke suit." He said this with brooding eyes.

"He told me that it's funny that someone who doesn't drink would open a jazz bar." She waited patiently, as cops would do during an interrogation.

He did not disappoint. "I want it to be a place where even those who don't drink can have a relaxed time. As for why I don't drink...I failed myself on a night when I got pie-eyed." He then sighed. "Before I started at Imperial, there were some welcoming events for freshers. One night I went to a pub, hoping to meet some course mates. I was a bit of an anorak back then. This guy ordered some Jägerbomb shots and asked if I would like some. I didn't want to back down, so I said, why not?" He smiled a bit. "I didn't know what they were, or how strong they were."

"Oh..." She felt sorry, yet she felt that she was getting to know a different side of him.

"That's how I missed my very first lecture. Another lesson learnt, I guess," he said, then looked away.

Not a lie.

The omission of subsequent events cannot be called a lie.

Or so he had convinced himself.

They each took a minute or two to collect themselves, then Catherine told him of her plan to attend another short course at the Boerma Instituut.

He supported her decision as always, and he looked at her with mischievous eyes.

"Now, do I get to ask questions?"

"Of course." She paused. "You tell me things about you, and I'll tell you things about me."

"I see. Like computer handshaking," he decided.

It was in times like this she remembered his tech-enthusiastic nature.

"Do you...do you not remember..." He considered for a while.

"During our time...umm... apart...did you think about me?"

"Yes," she said, borrowing a line from her favourite book protagonist, "I've been out of temper for some days. I think about you like...a bad habit."

He gave a small laugh. "Oh, I was hoping more...in terms of... entranced."

She decided that she liked to see him laughing.

"Did you obsess over me, Mr Yang?" she countered playfully. Then she added, "Don't lie or I'll know."

"Well...you made me headier than a Jägerbomb..." His eyes dodged her scrutiny, "and..." Then he had the audacity to stop.

"And?" she prompted him like a bad cop. "Mr Yang, I have yet to find out where you are most ticklish; don't make me force it out."

The corners of his lips curled up once again. "When you gave me the silent treatment, I had a somewhat...suggestive dream."

"Do tell."

"You bought some lingerie from Agent Provocateur, and you said you'd try it on. I guess it was because I saw their store the other day when I bought the shoes."

"Hmmm...naughty day's residues. Someone said that dreams are an involuntary art of poetry. And I can think of another *agent provocateur*..." She gave him a matching, wry smile, then tapped her finger lightly on the tip of his nose. "I always wear flannel nighties, but..." She moved very close to him and crooned by his ear, "I suppose sometimes a change is good?" Then she pulled away quickly again. "When will your new bed arrive?"

"Another week for the mattress and another two weeks for the bed.

They got delayed with the holidays."

"Better be a good one," she declared.

"I did buy a Dux mattress."

Then perhaps to distract themselves, they moved on to less heated territories as she asked more questions: what his first name meant in Chinese...why had he decided to live in this flat...how he felt when he massaged her ankle...

She also offered advice to alleviate his ailment: a daily half stalk of fresh celery. Her uncle did it, and she heard it worked.

They discussed how they might spend the next Christmas. They spoke about Lynette, his stepmother, a jewellery designer, who was on a visit to Hatton Garden preparing for her next showcase. Catherine told him that she saw Mr Spencer and his re-found cat Silos during Mr Darcy's vet visit. Mr Spencer had a ginger striped cat that did indeed look very much like hers. He worked as a barista in Richmond and they had met him over a misunderstanding about a missing pet in April. Though Silos was a lot fitter than Mr Darcy, Mr Spencer said that Silos sometimes used his washing machine drum as a treadmill.

They talked into the wee hours and fell asleep on the sofa.

When they woke up, they found out that they did get cricks and the candle had burnt all night.

The New Year came and went, so did Catherine's holiday.

They spent some time in the flat in *dolce far niente*, and she found, in his study, a computer screen stand that looked like the Two-Headed Monster with a funny-looking keyboard. Catherine also found a ladybird-themed beanbag in the study. He told her that it belonged to the former tenant, and they decided to keep it.

They also had lunches with her uncle, Cecil, and Lynette, played with Mr Darcy, and then the day arrived for her to depart again.

He drove her to the airport. Needless to say, Orla was astounded to see them together.

Catherine did not explain; she felt no obligation to do so. She did feel that she walked a little taller.

He saw them to security screening. Before parting, he gave her a set of spare keys for the flat and said, "Miss Roxborough, do you know what I'm thinking? If my Schengen visa has not expired, I would stick around..."

Catherine was very pleased and told him, quoting Dickens, that the pain of parting was nothing to the joy of meeting again.

Later, she had the most wonderful in-flight nap she had ever had.

She knew that she would no longer be alone.

Chapter 7

6th January.
Epiphany.

After breakfast, he got ready to go.

His spouse had gone to work already. He opened the door, and cold wind lashed his face.

He left the Georgian building where they rented their apartment and walked unhurriedly along the Albert Embankment towards Lambeth Palace. As he passed Vauxhall Bridge, he looked at the MI6 Building from afar, thinking that it resembled the Ministry of Love. A patrol boat glided by quickly on the Thames, stirring up the river.

He continued his morning walk. He could see the Palace of Westminster now.

He thought about Catherine and her previous calls.

What Pierre did had rocked him on his heels, and now he sincerely hoped that she had found happiness.

A small dog hung back on the pavement, yapping at its owner's heels as she put away her pooper-scooper. Tourists held selfie sticks on the bridge and raised their thumbs.

He had remembered what Felipe Kazama said to him after the wedding was called off.

*"Micky, I think we need to ask him to return the ring. Do you think that we should return it off the finger or **on** the finger?"*

He shuddered in the wind.

He had a brief walk in Hyde Park, went back, packed his dancing shoes, grabbed his briefcase, and headed out again for work.

***

Someone called in the morning.

An unknown number.

Chance hesitated before picking it up. It was Mick, Catherine's best friend he had yet to meet.

They decided to meet up during Mick's lunch break as he was giving ballroom dancing lessons at the Pineapple Dance Studios in Covent Garden.

It didn't take much time to locate the Studios' neon signs in an alley near the M&S Simply Foods on Long Acre.

He pulled open the glass door and followed a parent and child inside. Then a young lad at the front desk pressed a security switch and let them in.

There was a small café on the ground floor.

He climbed the narrow stairs. One class on the first floor played a blasting techno version of 'Outside' featuring Ellie Goulding. He peered through the doorway, at a group immersed in callisthenics.

Chance could also hear the theme song from *Mamma Mia* faintly upstairs; Catherine had told him that the musical's cast would rehearse on the third floor from time to time.

He found his way to classroom Ten; the white wooden door was ajar. A man in a blue silk shirt and black Noschese dance trousers sat on a piano bench in the corner, drinking coffee from a thermos. There was also a full wall of mirror and wood ballet barres.

Mick noticed his presence; he stood up and gestured him to come into the room.

Mick was quite tall, standing over six feet. He had short, parted brown hair and distinct features.

He also looked familiar.

Chance wondered if they had passed by each other on the streets of London before.

He waited as Mick rolled up his shirt sleeves. Then Mick said sternly: "I've known Cathy since I was five. We entered so many competitions that I've lost count of the number. I love her. We are literally family. So, if you make Catherine cry, I'll make you cry. Is that clear?"

He knew Mick was only bluffing, and he nodded softly. "Yes."

Mick approached him, his well-defined features in agony. "Don't behave rashly. I'm warning you of the consequences. Do you know what happened to the ex?"

"No."

"I hope not. I hope that you never have the *chance* to find out."

He might have been startled by Mick's words if he hadn't worked with Felipe.

"Marek Grant." Mick stepped forward and extended his hand.

"Hope you do justice to her affection."

"Changxi Yang. Thank you for caring for her."

They shook hands. He noticed Mick had a ring on his ring finger, then he remembered.

"Well..." he said, "Congratulations on your wedding. I once attended a singing taster session with Sam. Please send my regards."

They talked a bit more, decided on a date for dinner after Catherine returned from Holland, then he left.

It was a quarter to one when he exited the dance studios.

He passed the Swiss Glockenspiel in M&M-scented air and arrived at Le Méridien Piccadilly half an hour later. Outside the hotel, a saloon changing lanes had jammed a bus carrying an ad for *The Revenant*. He entered the lobby as he caught a glimpse of the bus driver giving the finger.

The cocktail lounge had a few customers chatting and indulging. He sat on a sofa not far from the bar. There was a vast white glass panel displaying a pair of khaki overalls on the wall.

Soft music played; he was not sure if it was Art Tatum or Thelonious Monk.

A waiter brought him the drinks list. He ordered a non-alcoholic cocktail named Oriental Passion. His drink soon arrived. It had fresh raspberries and passion fruit and even tasted like fig.

"I like to have my figs chilled... I heard someone groaning... I wanted to peek... I ran away in fear of his scolding... One night I saw Mother disrobing Emma and kissing her frantically... Her skin was stiff and as cold as my dead grandmother's... I saw Francis coming out of the room, and he told me: 'Don't be afraid. Now, get me some ice.' On the night of the fireworks, Mother cried so

hard and said that she could not live without Miss E..."

He sipped his drink and was bothered by a feeling he had recognised as remorse. No, not remorse, powerlessness.

Felipe showed up at a minute to two, followed by Lewis Milken.

Felipe held something in his arms that resembled a cremation urn. He was dressed to the nines including a pair of John Lobb shoes.

"Happy New Year!" Felipe said with a cunning light in his eyes. "Hope you had a great time in Blanes. Lewis and I greatly appreciate your hard work and effort."

He felt somewhat uneasy as he stood up, and the three of them shook hands.

"Well, Lewis, without further ado, you know the rules of barter." Felipe set the urn on the table. "Got the item requested? Chance will serve as our witness."

He watched as Lewis took out a small USB from his suit's breast pocket and handed it to Felipe.

"I like to have deals done. A done deal merits a good meal." Felipe handed Lewis the urn and took out a key card. *"Mi casa es tu casa."* He then retrieved his hand quickly. "Be very sure that you want to know what went wrong. As resourceful as I am, there's no remedy for regrets."

Lewis Milken looked as though he were on tenterhooks. He held the urn as if he would hold a baby, took the card, and left without a word.

Chance continued with his Oriental Passion as Felipe placed an order for whisky.

"Umm..." Felipe checked the USB as he nursed his drink, "A pity that I don't have a USB condom at hand. Do you have one?"

"Back at the flat."

"Never mind. I'll check it once he finishes his business in my dingy room."

"Who's he meeting?"

"The doctor's daughter."

"Oh."

"Now, enlighten me." Felipe pocketed the USB and said, "How did you connect the dots?"

"I knew that you would never tell me the whole story, but you would give me some hints," Chance sighed. "On Christmas Eve I called my cousin. She was with some friends, and I listened as they talked. There was one girl, she got a little tipsy and shared some items from her bucket list. One of them was that she would become a blood donor once she went back to China. Another told her that she couldn't if she had lived in the UK or anywhere in Europe for more than six months after 1980. It was a very specific prerequisite, so I looked up why."

"Blame it on Mad Cow Disease. It has a long incubation period: up to fifty years."

"Then, I thought, if people keep tigers for their urine, and if they raise cattle for their milk, if Emma Milken had a rare blood type, they could..." He paused to collect himself, "I searched what diseases require patients to receive regular blood transfusions. Then I knew. It was not a kiss; it was CPR."

***

"Let me walk you through my thinking. When I took over this project..." Felipe responded, "it didn't take long to find out who the family was...

if you know where to go and whom to contact...if you know where to
send the bush telegraph, so to speak. A connection from the Mafia got
me the file, whom the UK had imported involuntarily on a van. A man
on a van...hehe. The Mafia is not a sunset industry, mind you. They are
learning a great deal from their Japanese counterpart about diversifying.
They no longer busy themselves with oranges and lemons. Anyways...
But the pages obscured my line of vision. I scoured it every day, word by
word, and I did imagine things. Told you that imagination is the worst
form of sacrilege. I thought the file an excellent story for an R-rated
movie. There was violence, taboo, suspense. What bothered me the most
was the phrase 'get me some ice'. You know, the illustrations on the big
screens would always feature a scene like this. So why didn't the doctor
shout 'get me the phone' or 'get me the first-aid kit' or 'get me the police'?
Even 'get me some tobacco' or 'get me some booze' or 'get me *Playboy*'?
Why did it have to be ice?" Felipe had a gulp of his drink. "Did you bring
the file?"

He took out the page and laid it on the table.

"One day I was watching a documentary on how a missed hyphen
crashed a NASA rocket. Then I had a bath, and I had a 'Eureka!'
moment. I thought, what if I do this?" Felipe took out a fountain pen,
marked twice, and underlined once, then the text became:

On the night of the fireworks, Mother cried so hard and said that
"she could not live without Miss E".

"I told you that I had learnt a lot from my days spent at the farm;
ergo I connected the dots right away. If you milk a cow too hard, it'll
kick you. If you enslave people, they'll die. Then I did some groundwork.
Emma Milken had met the so-called friend at a charitable cause

advocating blood donation. People should be more careful about what they show to others and not make any trashy friends. The friend knew the family's doctor, a quack who knew nothing about Thalassemia. If you add a lot of fertilisers to a plot of land, the plants will wither, and their roots rot. With too frequent transfusions, people become dependent on them. They get worse; it's a vicious cycle. His daughter told me that Emma Milken died like Snow White. I tell you, never believe in quacks. The uncle had a share in this venture as well."

Felipe took a swig of his drink. "I do believe in karma, manufactured or not: he died of leukaemia."

"She did not die in Blanes," Chance said after a minute.

"No."

"What happened, then?"

"The driver shot the parents and the doctor. He's a good man, at least he had some conscience. A wise fellow I knew once said that not all wrongful homicides are wrong because they are homicides." Felipe folded the pages and roughly stored them in his wallet. "I had long covered the grunt work, but I was not satisfied. The terms of my negotiations with Lewis were an unequal treaty. He said he would pay me handsomely. He's such a barnacle. Why would I need his ducats when I'm a lot richer than he is? So, I thought, I might hold this banana until it matures or I could throw its skin on the ground and see who slips." Felipe grinned. "I'm no master of compromise. Those who got promoted in the corporate rat race are often not the most productive, but those who could show others that they have busied themselves with business affairs and those who pretend to have clients' interests at heart. It's all for show."

He looked into Felipe's glassy eyes.

"Then, the chance presented itself when he was diagnosed with terminal cancer. I got the news before he did. He's desperate now. He's racing against time." Felipe cleared his throat before asking for another whisky on the rocks. "Do you know why people call him 'Relentless Lewis'? He's relentless at blackmailing, at marauding, at reaving, and at embezzling. Rumour has it that our trumpet-playing alligator has a figurative black leather notebook containing the innermost secrets and desires of the London circles. He force-fed many families full cups of hemlock and shot them with flintlocks. What can I say? I guess doing some good deeds, and some other not-so-good ones, doesn't make him, on average, a good person, no matter how many indulgences he buys. The same goes for me. He came to me again begging me to bear a hand. As wily as I am, I told him that I know someone who is very good at tracking down people only if he's willing to grant me a memento."

Chance looked up. "The urn..."

"The urn is triple A, and what's inside that urn is also triple A. Humans can fake death certificates and DNA reports, but believe it or not, I do have a conscience, however small a morsel of it. And I'll not waste them on grifting. Make no boo-boos. I can lie to you, but I cannot lie to my conscience. Life could not be gainsaid. Once, I was told to kill a calf, and I made a mess. I fired the bolt stunner in between its eyes. I thought that I was giving it a *coup de grâce*, but I was wrong. The shot had missed the brain completely. I watched it suffer...for a long time."

They sat there for a while and watched as the ice melted in Felipe's glass.

Lewis Milken came down after half an hour.

"I wish I *hadn't* known," he said glumly. "Life is indeed not like debugging."

Felipe saw Chance to the hotel entrance. "I saw the Chinese New Year decorations in Chinatown, and I thought about our time in Yokohama. Gee, time gallops. Got any plans later?"

"No."

"Let's part here then. My job is like winemaking: to do it well, I stay away from the light. Hell, I didn't even put any sunblock on. I'll go and get some fish and chips with tartar sauce and maybe enjoy a double Irish coffee with a Dutch sandwich. Better keep an eye on everything; even an errand as simple as ordering delivery can lead to a camel's nose under the tent. It's all chaos out there. Chaos not *ciaos*. Do you know that the word 'ciao' actually comes from a Venetian dialect word that means 'slave'?" Felipe continued sullenly, "There's more than one Crossbones Garden, and there's more than one Tuam. We should not cry over spilt milk; we should mourn for the slaughtered calf or the ones sitting down in the corral. Why am I basking in negativity today? Maybe I need a hair of the dog. Cheer up, buddy. I'll be gone, and you'll be gone."

He walked back as he weighed upon Felipe's words. By the time he reached the Swiss Glockenspiel, he had received a message from Turner:

'This message card came with Catherine's flowers; do you know what it means?'

He clicked open the photo and recognised Felipe's handwriting in Japanese. It was a proverb that said: 'If you speak of tomorrow, the rats in the ceiling will laugh'.

He carried himself back to Covent Garden on Shaftesbury Avenue like a brougham with bad wear and tear. A yacht chandler, Arthur Beale, caught his eye.

Chance looked at the nautical and surveying instruments in the shop's display window and had a feeling that the Sancho Panza of Boston would sail soon and never be heard from again.

Then he remembered something Felipe had said: he took a right and continued along Monmouth Street.

It didn't take him long to find the hair salon he was looking for; he went in and made an appointment.

⁂

A quarter to four.

She finished her shift, rubbed her temples in the changing room, changed, put on her NHS-blue winter coat, and felt heavy-headed as she walked towards Borough Market.

She waited for a green light and was about to dart across the pavement when a Bentley stopped beside her. The front door opened, and she recognised the spindly passenger instantly.

The assistant...no...the...the pupil...

"Nurse Bennett, Mr Stone would like to have a word with you." He held the rear door open for her.

She was not baffled. She crouched a bit and saw the man sitting at the back of the car.

"Hi, Patsy." He gave her a hesitant, warm smile.

She got into the car somewhat unwillingly.

They sat in there without conversing as the driver crossed the river. Finally, they stopped at a spot where they could see the Lady of Justice at the Old Bailey.

She observed the statue. Indeed, it was not blindfolded.

The driver got out and went into a street café.

"I wish this conversation to take place in discretion," Cecil Stone said. "A colleague of mine writes books on electronic disclosure and he tells me that you cannot hide anything anywhere nowadays."

"Mr Stone, I..."

"Once, I took my daughter and my goddaughter on vacation to Thailand..."

"Mr Stone..."

"Please..." Cecil Stone refuted softly. "Please let me finish. We were on holiday but my daughter, Sophie, had some school assignments. Then something terrible happened: she had lost her luggage and her laptop was in there as well. It had some very important files. Fortunately, we managed to get it back. Since then...a friend has suggested to me that to prevent such unfortunate happenings and further losses I should place trackers in all my belongings."

He watched her as her face muscles palsied.

"Mr Stone, I..."

"Please, Patsy. I do not wish to dignify this topic any longer. I know there has been... some playing. If you have any troubles, I can offer some advice as a friend. I'm never fond of whisky, and I don't wish to become a drop of whisky in a winter night and bring any poor souls to ruin."

"Mr Stone." She sat up straight, took a deep breath, and turned to look at him. "It would only be fair if you allow me to state my case." Then her tone softened, "Yes, I do play, but I play responsibly." She sighed. "On the first day I started at this hospital, there was a patient who had acute asthma and diabetes. His doctor was a junior doctor. He had prescribed some steroids, but he had forgotten to adjust for the diabetic conditions, so I didn't pay much attention to the patient's blood glucose level. Another nurse found out in time. I'm forever grateful. But recently, there've been some missing medications. It's hard to believe the same person who...but NHS staff are not paid well, at least not in line with our work at the coalface. I knew it must be...must be...so...when your wallet. I saw it when she ditched it. I made a blind bet. I'm sorry for what I did..."

Their conversation continued until nightfall.

CHAPTER 8

1st February.
Monday afternoon.

He arrived at the hair salon five minutes before his appointment. The receptionist received him and asked him to wait on a settee.

There were some fashion magazines stacked on a lounge table. He chose one and flipped through. He found an article on a celebrity filmmaker advocating her blood donating experiences and tips on maintaining a healthy lifestyle.

He closed the magazine and took out his phone.

Catherine's flight was on schedule, and the weather at both airports was good. She had called earlier saying that Melody would drive them back to the flower academy and that she expected to meet him later in his flat.

He messaged Turner not long before the receptionist introduced him to Jule, his stylist for the day, a spirited lad in a check shirt and jeans.

He changed into a black cape and followed someone's lead into the area with sinks, then settled down on a black chair as instructed.

"Is the water temperature alright, sir?"

"Yes. Thank you." He closed his eyes then overheard someone else talking.

"Where are you from?" he heard a voice asking.

"Earth."

The other giggled. "Yes, yes. I'm from Earth too. But *where* on Earth?"

"China. Why? Do I get a discount or something?"

"No, sorry, but your hair's beautiful. It has a beautiful gloss."

"Thanks. I always eat sesame."

"Oh, yeah. I have some clients who treat their hair at home with sesame oil. It's funny, you know, but we've had several Chinese clients making appointments this week. Getting your hair ready before the Chinese New Year celebrations?"

He listened on as they talked about why it's taboo to cut your hair anytime during the first month on the Chinese lunar calendar...the best places to get bubble tea...the scenery in Derwent Valley...some celebrity plastic surgeries gone wrong...and how raspberry leaf tea can help relieve menstrual cramps and period pain.

He made a mental note to do some shopping later.

***

She heard Orla calling as she stepped out of the lady's room.

"Cat, will you please handle this customer for me? I need to call my sister."

Catherine emerged from the basement and found Felipe standing among the flowers in a glitzy outfit. If there had been bees in the shop, she wondered if they might buzz around him instead.

"Hi, Cathy, how was National Tulip Day? And tell me, do tulip bulbs indeed look like onions? I've heard a story of how an unfortunate sailor mistook a rare tulip bulb for an onion."

"They do look alike," she said as she put on her apron. "The owner of the tulip farm where we stayed told us that the Dutch ate tulip soup during World War Two when food was scarce."

"I wonder what it tasted like." Felipe looked down at her hands. "Oh, look at you. You've got the hands of a proletariat. Your fingers are so tempered. You should ask your favourite partner in crime to buy you some nice hand cream. Have you enlightened him on your favourite *passatempo* yet?"

"No, not yet."

"I don't think it would make his blood curdle." Felipe thought for a few seconds. "How about if I send you some hand cream from the Farmacia Santa Maria Novella?"

"Thanks, Felipe, it's really alright." She checked the almost healed cuts on her fingers, "Every profession comes with some occupational hazards...so long as my feet are not killing me. How can I help you today?"

"Well, I'm going to a rave for a bit of exposure. I'm taking a risk subjecting myself to more light, like a vampire. *Jaja.* At least vampires can turn people into immortals, but I know people who suck and bleed others to death. Anyways, I am thinking of a boutonnière."

Catherine thought for a while. "How about a Checkmate rose?" She pointed it out for him. "It would go well with your tux."

"Something simple like a white rose would do. I don't wish to over-egg the pudding even though I'm always dressed to kill." He talked as she worked. "Tomorrow I'm going to Italy to visit my friend Roberto Cavalli. I always find he can make me look more result-driven and unflagging. Him and Jean Rousseau. Then I'm jumping off the Siberian Express and heading to Canberra. I have a merger to see through."

"Oh. I was thinking of inviting you to celebrate Chinese New Year with us. Thank you for everything."

"Not at all. I'm exceptionally good at matchmaking. I once even made a couple out of a consigliere and a carabiniere. Goodfellas, they were. You have your fun and give me a bell if things go well so I can finally put a wedding on my iCal. Oh, and please tell him that I'd still like to meet his stepmother."

She smiled, dismissing it as another joke. "Still looking for people to fulfil your imagination?"

"I've got no more tricks up my sleeve because you know them all."

"Here you go. Have a great night and safe travels."

He took the boutonnière and placed it on. "Thanks, you take care. Well, I really need to find a McDonald's and go Operation CICO. It's the only value they add to society. I guess this is where we say goodbye then. Pip pip."

Felipe paid and left, and Catherine felt that his shadow looked a little lonesome.

She knew that Felipe was no heartbreaker.

Hope someone would appreciate the wuthering winds, she thought.

***

Night.

He was checking the news when the door opened. Catherine came into the room with her signature winning smile.

"Miss me?"

"Very much."

He wore the same turtleneck he had on the New Year's Eve. She found it quite pleasing to her eyes.

"Someone's got a new haircut, I see." She took off her scarf and gloves. "It's freezing outside." She took out an envelope from her coat pocket. "I've collected my receipts; can you shred them for me later?"

"Yes."

Catherine placed her suitcase by the door and went into the washroom. By the time she came out, he was looking at something on his tablet.

He seemed mesmerised by it, and he had such a dreadful look that if Catherine didn't know better, she might think that he had just witnessed a crime scene.

"Cecil agreed to take care of Mr Darcy for one more day. I would have gone back home if I wasn't so knackered and I do have an early morning tomorrow."

She sat down beside him on the sofa and stole a quick glance at his screen. It had a news item on two Brits who had gone missing while scuba diving in Colombia.

How fragile life is...

Catherine remembered how she had lost her parents in one night...

"Mick called," she said, oblivious to his inner turmoil. "Good to know that you rubbed along quite well. And what a small world, isn't it?

Sam's so happy to learn about us. Says it's serendipity. Sam remembered you. Oh! An asked me if we would like to have lunch with her tomorrow. She knows a great vegetarian curry place in Covent Garden called Sagar. And we should definitely plan something for the Chinese New Year! An says she has a special pot for hot pot. How about a hot pot party at my place? It has two sides, I've heard. We can do a veggie side and a meaty side. We can invite Cecil, Lynette, my uncle.... He is trying to win back Valerie, so we should invite her as well."

He looked at her blandly and turned off the tablet.

Curry and codeine...rats and rivets...

He decided to push aside those thoughts and put on a smile. "Sure, why not? And it's tradition to have dumplings on Chinese New Year's Eve. We could make some. Does carrot and cloud ear fungus filling sound good?"

"Yes, I had it once when I visited my uncle in Xi'an. Oh, and Felipe came to the academy earlier for a boutonnière. He said he won't be joining us for Chinese New Year," Catherine said regretfully.

"Felipe...Felipe," he murmured. "He's..."

He wanted to tell her that Felipe Kazama was a dangerous man. How you could only believe a tenth of what he said...no, not even a tenth.

"Yes?"

He shook his head in resignation. "Nothing. Umm...did you ask him about the paper shredder?"

"No," she said, "I decided to trust you, Mr Yang."

"Thank you."

They cuddled together like two lazy cats, then he said, "I think we should have dinner with Orla someday."

"Umm?"

"I want her to take a very good look at me with my new haircut. Just in case."

"Don't be so difficult," she cooed.

"Don't you approve of it? The haircut, I mean."

"Fishing for compliments?"

"No." He gave her a wink. "Just angling."

She loved their repartee. "Hmm, yeah, I do like it. And you smell nice."

He smelt faintly of mandarin and lemon.

Catherine pulled him close for a kiss.

"I have good news…" He punctuated his words as he planted kisses on her face.

"Do tell." She found out that his lips had taken particular interest in her eyelashes.

"The new bed is ready," he said as he nuzzled her neck. "Someone accused me of lacking bodily desires. I should remedy that, shouldn't I?"

Catherine laughed. "How foolish of me. Now I know better than to make false accusations…though my Aunt Flo has visited."

"It's something we can look forward to. And there's no need to speak in riddles." He looked at her with all sincerity. "I'm perfectly fine with the language of menstruation. And I do believe there are more aspects to bodily desires than the carnal ones. Would you like a hot water bottle or a foot bath? Or we can banter while having some tea?"

"Tea with salt?"

He laughed. "I don't drink all tea with salt. Only black tea. Would you like some raspberry leaf tea? I've heard that it's nice. Oh, and Catherine, if you need any pads or tampons, you can find them behind the mirror in the washroom. We haven't talked about this yet, and I'm not sure if you use a Mooncup or not."

"Thank you. I used to, but sometimes I got very bad cramps so I stopped using it. But many of my uni friends like them. I might try it again some time. I will keep you updated."

She had never felt this comfortable talking about menstruation with anyone other than her pen pal.

The tea made, the hot water bottle filled, the candle lit, the accent lighting on, they talked as they sipped their drinks.

"So, no dinner with Orla?" he asked as he linked his fingers behind his head.

"Now, you are *trying*, Mr Yang."

"Fine." He collected their cups and put them on the countertop before settling back on the sofa. "I'll overlook her case this time. It is not as though Orla is the only one who mistook me for someone else or the only one who did not recognise me."

Catherine thought for a few quick seconds. "A comment like that invites another question: who else did not recognise you?"

He gave her a knowing smirk.

"No way!" she exclaimed. "You are jesting, for sure?"

He smirked again.

She decided that it was time to find out where he was the most ticklish.

Her plan failed miserably.

It did not take long for him to find out where she was the most ticklish.

"Okey dokey, let's try this." Catherine stifled more giggles. "Tell me now, so you don't need to sleep on the sofa tonight."

"Is this how you treat Mr Darcy when he misbehaves? The silent treatment then this?"

"Sometimes."

"Alright." He looked at her. "I'll give you a hint. Glasses?"

"Glasses? As in...spectacles?"

"Yes."

She ruminated for a while. "Sorry, doesn't ring any bells."

"Very well. Another hint?"

"Yes, please."

He smiled and said, "Push or pull?"

So, she remembered.

Once, when she had visited Sophie at Imperial, there was an unlabelled door. She pushed it open, hitting the person on the other side who had tried to pull it. The impact was so bad that his spectacles bent. They even had a heated argument over who was to blame.

"You had a single braid and you slanted your shirt into your skirt like a diagonal, so I remembered."

Catherine suddenly felt that she had known him for a long time. Mirth bubbled in her eyes as she mused. "The first time my father met my mum was at the British Embassy in Rome. She spilt coffee on his favourite shirt. I guess I followed her example. Serendipity it is."

He held her tenderly. "Happy today?"

"Inexpressibly."

***

7th February.

Chinese New Year's Eve.

An followed her phone's instructions and found Catherine's house without too much trouble. She leapt onto the steps and pressed the doorbell.

"Hi, An!" Catherine opened the door. "Happy Chinese New Year! We're still preparing. Come on in."

She went in and hung up her coat, changed into slippers and followed Catherine into the living room.

A ginger cat yawned on the sofa.

"Must be the famous Mr Darcy," An said as she observed the cat.

"Or the infamous Mr Darcy." Catherine held her cat up and the green jingle bell on his neck shook. "Who's Mr Darcy when he's at home? Just a little kitty. And the cutest mischief-maker."

"I had a cat when I was little," An said. "One day my dad was talking to my mother on our landline phone and my cat pressed a button and cut the call. She wanted some attention, I think."

"Mr Darcy loves attention. His nemesis is Bob the Street Cat. He cannot stand his face in this house." Catherine put her cat down. "Why don't you sit for a while and play with him? My uncle and my godfather and Lynette should be here any minute. Help me with the door, will you? I'm going to check on the kitchen staff," she joked. "Oh, would you like something to drink? We've got homemade juice, hot drinks?"

"I'm fine for now, and you do just that."

Catherine put on her favourite earrings, the ones with ceramic bees, strolled into the kitchen, and found her Mr Yang slicing stem lettuce, white radish, ginger, tomatoes, and preparing assorted condiments.

She washed her hands and made some juice with apples, passion fruits, chicory, and a whole grapefruit. It was a recipe she had learnt from her pen pal.

"Do you cook well?" she asked casually, eyeing the cooking books on top of her fridge.

"I get by."

"Tell me more about it."

"Well. One thing with hot pot is that it takes time to prepare but minimal effort in cooking," he said as he soaked and washed a handful of spinach, rocket, coriander, celery, and crown daisy. "When we were little, I once cooked some soup noodles for An and her friend. I improvised and added ketchup, a little fermented red bean curd, and black vinegar into the soup. They decided they would rather skip lunch than eat it, though I thought it was good. Shanxi vinegar is an important item in our families; we always have it with dumplings, noodles, and cold dishes. I've managed to get some from Seewoo."

He retrieved the bottle of vinegar and gave her a warm smile. "And in Chinese if you say someone is eating vinegar, it means that person is jealous. Do you like to eat vinegar?"

Catherine remembered how unhappy she was when she mistook An as his girlfriend and how she wanted to devour Lynette in the first few minutes they had met. She decided to dodge the topic as she observed the pre-made dumpling wrappers. "Do you know how to make dumplings?"

"Yes," he said as he peeled a few peanuts. "We used to put coins in New Year's dumplings, and whoever got it would have good luck. Peanuts serve just as well."

They prepared hot pot dipping sauces with chopped coriander and spring onion, fermented red bean curd, and sesame paste from Wang Zhihe with a side plate of Laoganma, a chilli sauce, for Lynette. She helped him place the vegetables on large melamine plates and then held up a celery stalk. "Mr Yang, you may well know someone who likes to eat her vinegar, but I know someone who needs his five a day. And you know what else we should do? We should tour the Jubilee Walkway."

He took the celery, stole a quick kiss by her ear, and whispered in a silky voice, "I'm sure that she has had a fair share of sourness so far, and I hope to bring her only sweetness from now on."

Catherine blushed a little as his warm breath tickled her.

Felipe is wrong! He's definitely no taciturn fella!

And wasn't she supposed to be the expert in their flirting?

Then he took out a box of freshly cut pineapples from the fridge as he munched on the green stalk. "Would you like to have some?"

She shook her head in frustration. "I don't like pineapple; it irritates my lips. What's your favourite fruit? Mine is dragon fruit."

"I like watermelons." He tilted his head, "When I first came to the UK, it surprised me that people didn't wash peaches with salt, and they don't soak pineapple with salt water before they eat it."

She laughed. "Salt again?"

"Salt is a perfect remedy for this. Wait and see." He took a large bowl, poured the pineapple chunks into it, then filled it with some water, and added a generous pinch of salt.

They waited for a minute or so before he drained the water and rinsed off the remaining salt. He grabbed a fork, took one moderate chunk, and handed it to her. "Trust me?"

Catherine looked at him dubiously, and took a tentative bite. The fruit tasted sweet and a little salty, but did not sting.

"Hmm. It tastes very enjoyable!"

He asked, "Happy for now?"

She put down the fork and declared, "I'm going to ask An if she knows where you are the most ticklish."

***

The dumplings were made, the guests arrived, and the feast started.

To Catherine's surprise, her uncle did not bring Valerie, but Cecil brought a friend along.

Her name was Patsy, whom Cecil had met at the hospital and who grew upon Catherine during the celebrations that night.

Lynette was happy to see Chance with his new haircut, and she marvelled that her brother would love to know that someone was still concerned for his health and safety.

They had a pleasant evening talking, eating, and preventing Mr Darcy from jumping onto the table and joining them.

Cecil was most fortunate to find several dumplings with peanuts. Catherine had remembered when her godfather told her that he was very lucky to still be here.

After dinner, they chatted over spicy mixed nuts and *chenpi* tea with fresh longan, and Patsy asked a quiz question on whether you should give a drop of whisky to someone with hypothermia.

An said no. She recalled a children's story she'd read in which a boy had to catch some fish for his ill father. He drank some alcohol before diving into the freezing sea so his body heat would attract the shoal. She was not sure if the story held up, but it moved her somehow.

They talked about the Chinese Zodiac. Chance was born in the Year of the Tiger; Catherine and An in the Year of the Goat. Alexander Roxborough showed off with a tale about why the Chinese Zodiac did not include cats; Mr Darcy was not too impressed with it.

Catherine talked about how to tell *rosa rugosa* and *rosa chinensis* apart and the histories of those flowers. An told them how her best friend from childhood had once ignited a firework that landed in someone else's kitchen. Luckily no one was hurt. Lynette said how an Iraqi friend who visited Yiwu with her during the Chinese New Year had nightmares: the sounds reminded her friend of gunshots and depleted uranium bombings.

The hot pot was feasted on, the pot cleaned, and the guests left.

The couple watched a movie, *Man Up*, and Catherine's cat was happy to be the third wheel.

The film ended and they cuddled for a while. He used the guest washroom down the hallway, then said, "I better get going."

Catherine considered. "I can think of better ways to spend the night than being stuck in traffic."

He turned to look at her with inviting eyes. "You do?"

"Yeah," she teased him. "We can play Chinese checkers. What do you say?"

"If permission were granted…" Amusement flickered in his eyes as he licked his lips. "I'm thinking of doing your lips a service."

She blushed scarlet.

"Hmmm…that is very slippery of you, Mr Yang." Catherine smiled impishly. "I happen to know other places where…such a service might be needed."

"You do?"

"Oh, yeah. And I have lovely batiste bedding from Liberty." She took his hand and purred, "I think it's time that we found out."

***

Morning.

He awoke from a calming languor.

Catherine was still asleep, one of her hands placed awkwardly above her head. He moved it gently back into their cocoon. There were newly added cuts on her fingers.

He watched her as she slept soundly in her lovely bedding.

"Has that ever happened to you? One day, you discover a small cut on your right hand. You have no idea how it happened. Then two or three days later you find another cut on your left hand. You promise to watch out. Then you have another cut…"

Better not go down that route.

A patch of skin on his neck itched. He touched it and found slight dents.

The memories from last night put a smile on his face.

He had discovered that she liked to bite.

He knew that happiness is also a bonfire; without the chilling nights, you would not learn to appreciate its warmth...

Mr Darcy, the attention seeker, crept onto the bed, kneaded a while, and snuggled in between their warm, spooned bodies.

Catherine had an afternoon shift that day and he was about to drift into sleep again when he heard the doorbell ring downstairs.

EPILOGUE

Somewhere in Heathrow Terminal 5.

A man stood by a window as he watched aeroplanes taking off and landing.

He raised the volume of his Jabra wireless earphones. "Good to know that he had nailed his colours to the mast. It's time when push comes to shove. Did they rub shoulders? And did he tell my favourite assistant 'Happy Chinese New Year?' They didn't talk for long? Well, let's see how it goes. Me? I've just had my daily dose of caffeine. *Et toi?* Still drinking a bottle of Coke every day? In North Korea this would be considered a luxury lifestyle. Do you know that you can more easily find Coke than life-saving medicines in many LEDCs? Money works, and it does work wonderfully. At a decent price, I can get you to compromise a Vanguard."

The other end laughed.

"Yes, babe, tell me, and I will give you the world. You don't want a Vanguard? Do you want a Borei? No? You want a Zephyr S? Hmmff, very nice tastes, as my friend would say. Or would you prefer d'Estaing's *chaîne en or*? Just remember not to put it in your blazer pocket and send it to the dry cleaner. Well, a socialist would never have enjoyed ortolans. No, I delayed my departure. I'm always sentimental when I go away

on sorties. You know how racist everyone is in New York...even the
Oak Room and the Tribeca. *Jaja.* Haven't you heard that two-thirds of
America's criminals are roaming the streets? I wonder what that figure
would be in the UK. I'm down and out in London and Paris."

He turned, walked to a waiting seat, sat down, and crossed his legs.
"You can easily manipulate people if you know their interests. Incentives
are like potty training. Even the word 'conscience' breaks into 'con' and
'science'. Maybe I've pioneered a new profession called a 'con scientist'. If
there's a con artist, there should be a con scientist. Uh-huh. Before I craft
a demise, I always give some false promises. I like to kick them upstairs
before letting them crash and burn."

He watched as a BA aircraft landed. "If all men are angels, we'll have
really messy air traffic control problems. I do feel human beings of all
living things are the most biologically incompetent and ill-organised.
Now you are titillating. Do you? A gentleman always waits to be
invited... Well, I was given to understand that I had been invited. No?
Well. I'm certainly no gentleman and now you know all my sensitive
spots. Perhaps next time we can have some unprotected sleep. No pun
intended. As Seneca once said, friendship always benefits but sometimes
love injures."

Felipe listened and continued, "You saw them together? Good
for him. Not often that you find wimps taking initiatives. If you lose
something, be very sure to not go to Jonathan Wild's Lost Property
Office. If you go to a hair salon, never go to Sweeney Todd's. Yes. Let's
hope our gormless Cecil does not mistake a tsetse for a firefly and an
onion for a tulip bulb.

"Do you know that the word 'tulip' comes from the Turkish word for turban? Well, sometimes things are better left unsaid. Fiction's best served with partial facts and some room for imagination. Who doesn't like a fish in silk for dinner? Cecil has feet of clay. He's so used to playing by the cab-rank rule that he cannot think otherwise. Well, I guess he's absolutely zonked of waiting after a binder. The Law is not the only reality in a lawyer's life. Pettifoggers have rent to pay, status to achieve, and heights to scale*. Me? I never play by anyone's rules. I don't even play by the Queensberry rules. I only play by the Minecraft rules... Well, did she place a flutter on the horses? Let's hope that she takes him to the cleaners. Cecil needs a smarting lesson. I've infinitesimal tolerance towards double-dealers and double-standarders, but I bear no one any malice today. I'll be home and dry soon. Oh, and I've decided to hold Lewis' feet to the fire. It would make a lovely bonfire with their tender mercies. He won't get off scot-free."

He stretched and yawned. "Everything is working like a Swiss clock. Everything's in shipshape on my end. Yes, I believe that the best way to protect a lamb is to place it beside a well-fed tiger. Let's hope the tiger stays mentally sound. Percipience is both a blessing and a curse. It's often with the best comedians that you find the worst cases of depression. And yes, 2016 is the Year of the Monkey. In Japan, people say that even a monkey can fall from a tree. Whether we choose to save the lady or the tiger, that's an entirely different question. The ball's in his court now. I think the job would suit him down to the ground, nonetheless. He's a perfect choice to rub something out. And I'm the perfect choice to rub someone out. Horses for courses and don't leave grenades in pockets. Well...another meeting? Fine. Maybe you can tell me next time how many toilets there are in Parliament? And the awful backrooms of power and powder... Gun powder. Of course not! I do think that the bedroom's a proper venue to conduct such business. I meant reading, of course. It seems that I've planted too many ideas in that adorable head of yours. The British have a very visual language. For example, I love the phrase 'all fur coat and no knickers'. No, no, no...I have no proclivity. I'm not the one who has been sharking around. And do you know what's even more visual? Here's my version: all body bags and no knickers."

He listened attentively. "Some people deserve a body bag; some don't even deserve that. I have my own ways to pull a blinder. They'll be FUBAR BUNDY in my hands and they'll be missing till the cows come home. I can make something gone with the wind, and I can conjure it up again. Just like I did with little Sophie's suitcase. Good that you didn't acquire your Equity card in vain. Oh, you didn't like performing my skit? What's so wrong to call Sildenafil a nutritional supplement? It's a type of spiritual nourishment for sure. Do you really have to go? Fine, fine, I'll belt up. Just give me a holler anytime you want to collar anyone. I hate to sit in boooored-rooms. No pun intended. If you miss me, send for me. I remain your humble servant."

The call ended, he pocketed his Jabra and felt eyes watching him.

Felipe turned and saw a little girl, aged no more than seven or eight, staring at him.

"Can I sit here?" She gestured to the seat next to his.

"Sure."

She put down her Dora the Explorer themed backpack and climbed on the seat. "What are you doing? I heard you talking about tigers."

"Oh, nothing. I'm just enjoying some bird watching." He pointed at the planes.

"I saw some beautiful birds at London Zoo."

"London has a zoo, alright. But I'm here to see the gardens. My favourite one is called 'Crossbones'. It's not too far from the Shard."

"Mummy says that the Shard is an ostent...atious symbol of ugliness. She wants the UK out of the EU so it'll no longer be the tallest building." The girl eyed him. "Are you a zookeeper? Do you take care of tigers?"

He grinned. "Yes, I'm a zookeeper, and I'm just waiting for some accidents to happen. Maybe a fight between donkeys and elephants, or a quarrel between owls and crows. Or we can kill some chickens to scare the monkeys and see how they ostracise their shrewdness. Do you know what the word 'shrewdness' means? It means a group of apes."

She gave him an incredulous look. "But you don't look like a zookeeper. And why would you want accidents to happen?"

"Haven't you heard? The best cloak of invisibility is a three-piece suit. Scudder said that."

"Who's Scudder?"

"He's another fellow zookeeper. But his pay is probably not as good as mine. And if all the animals behaved, the zookeeper would lose his job. It's in times of crisis that people learn to appreciate the emergency forces."

"What's your favourite animal? Mine is the Senegal Bushbaby."

"That's quite a name. My favourite animal is rats. Never underestimate them. I like rats better than I like people. Do you know why the rat is in the Chinese Zodiac, and the cat is not? Even though cats are considered to be tigers' maestros?"

"No."

"Go and look it up. Though I wonder if rats like curry..."

"Of course they like curry! I saw them gobbling it once in our bin."

He nodded. "Good to know. I'll soon verify your observation. Do you know that even Aristotle made wrong observations–"

"Elzbieta, Elzbieta, quickly, we need to go onboard," a woman urged.

"I'm here, maman." The girl jumped off her seat and hoisted her backpack. "Tell me if the rats like curry, zookeeper."

"Off you go now. Live life while you have it and always listen to your mother while she's still here."

The girl had gone, and Felipe contemplated his life.

He had missed his *toshikoshi* * soba once again; his mother always liked it.

His flight would not board for another hour. Maybe he would go to the Gordon Ramsay Plane Food and have a bowl of chicken katsu udon.

Or maybe some curry at Wagamama. Maybe.

The Learning
Curve of Pain

CHAPTER 1

2016.
8th February, Chinese New Year.
London.
Holland Park, Kensington.

"I won't be long," he told the driver as their car stopped in a no-parking spot.

"Aye, sir," the young officer in his shabby uniform responded as he rubbed the bags under his hooded eyes.

He opened his suitcase, retrieved his delivery, tucked it in his coat pocket, and got out, jolting the BMW's suspension system.

The brisk weather had sprinkling rain and passing clouds. He eschewed an umbrella and darted to the Grade II Listed building across the street.

A smart doorbell welcomed him distantly.

Eh, technology... He rolled his eyes at the device.

But then, he mused, if every household in London had a smart doorbell, it would probably make his line of work much easier. And now they were hacking the CCTV budgets again.

A crow watched him as he approached the door.

"Do you know what a flock of crows is called? It's called a 'murder' and sometimes a 'congress'. Do you know what a group of owls is known as? They are known as a 'parliament'. Isn't it funny that you can't stand for MP as a police force member, but a tried criminal can?"

He remembered Felipe Kazama's words.

To the general population, Felipe Kazama was a finance professional with a flamboyant dress code, a galling mouth, and a Harvard Business School MBA degree who sometimes called 'smuggling' involuntary export and import.

To him, Felipe Kazama was a dangerous and resourceful man.

Some had found it extremely lucky to have Felipe as a friend and some worried for their lives if they had him as a foe. But what was scary was that they would never know in what regard Felipe held them.

A car passed, blasting *'California Dreamin''*.

He put his reflections aside as he climbed up the stone steps, his knees jerking. He pinged the doorbell once, twice.

He waited for a minute, and the door opened quietly.

"Hi, erm, morning. How can I help you?" a medium-built Asian man said with a cut-glass accent; his eyes were bleary and his red jumper hung on his body a little awkwardly.

"He doesn't smoke. He doesn't drink. He doesn't even watch Netflix. He's been trained for too long to strive and thrive and not to enjoy. Although he does not say, but by my reckoning I sense that he needs some diversion. When you meet him, you'll know that Chance Yang is damn good at worming information out of people. He has the common touch and hence is a hard act to follow. The job would suit him down to the ground."

He suddenly understood what Felipe had meant.

He remembered how his son once described his best mate from school: 'He's the kind of person you could trust with the name of your crush and be sure that he would safeguard that secret...'

"Excuse me?" the man at the door prompted.

"You must be Chance Yang." He cleared his throat, opened his frayed coat, and pulled out a stack of envelopes. "Give them to Catherine, will you? If she asks, tell her that I got them from the Lost Property at TFL."

The man took the envelopes after a pause. "And you are?"

"See you around."

He ran down the steps and got back to the car. His driver was perusing a copy of *The Sun* from last week.

A dirty object...

He hoped he could find a dirty object this time.

***

Catherine woke from a pleasant lethargy and stretched languidly before opening her eyes.

Her swain was nowhere to be seen, but the other side of the bed was still warm: Mr Darcy, her cat, occupied it.

The memories from the evening before put a smile on Catherine's face; she had discovered that he wore red boxer shorts.

She was silly to let titbits get the better of her and tittle-tattle had nearly scuppered their budding relationship, but they had overcome mistrust. And now, everything was coming up roses.

They did have chemistry; sparks, at least. Catherine smiled as she recalled that once a static had shocked them both on their lips when they tried to kiss.

She got off her bed as she heard faint noises and snippets of conversation from downstairs. She relieved herself and checked her dishevelled hair in the bathroom mirror. She prinked a while; it was tousled in a good way. She looked at the empty bottle of L'Air du Temps on her vanity set.

Mr Darcy, her cat, meowed impatiently, seeking attention.

Her toilet complete, she put on a plush hooded bathrobe and followed her cat into the kitchen downstairs.

He was making tea.

"Morning," she said lazily.

He turned and gave her a warm smile. "Did I wake you? Sorry. I rushed to get the door."

She looked at his cowlick and smiled broadly. "Oh, I can see *that*."

Catherine hummed a song as she fastened her coral-coloured hairband before preparing food for Mr Darcy.

He recognised it as the theme song from one of the *Twilight* films.

"Did Cecil drop by?" Catherine asked, thinking that her godfather who lived down the road had paid an early visit.

"No." He hesitated before pointing to some envelopes scattered on the kitchen table, "Someone came. I don't know him. He told me to give you these."

Catherine recognised her handwriting on the envelope as she cleaned her fingers on a washcloth. "Oh, these are my letters! I have a pen pal that I always write to. How strange...." She winced. "This person, what's he like?"

He recalled as he put down a steaming mug for her. "He's about 5 feet 8 and he had a Barbour coat and shirt, but no tie...unshaven...for three or four days at least. And he has a mole in his left eyebrow. He came in a BMW and he parked it where no parking is allowed."

"Do you have a photogenic memory or what?" she half-joked as she picked up her mug and warmed her hands with it.

He smiled. "Not really, but I do have a photo of him from the doorbell if you need it?"

She thought for a few seconds. "From the way you describe him, he sounds like my uncle's friend Nigel. He's a Detective...Detective Chief Superintendent for the Met. He once went for training at the FBI Academy. I rarely see him these days. But he did offer some advice on the 'stalker' last time."

"He said that he got them from the Lost Property at TFL."

Catherine shrugged. "It must be him then. Nigel once found my uncle's student's bag. It had her thesis. It was when they still used paper submissions." She checked the envelopes. "After uni I wanted to become a police officer, but my uncle argued against it vehemently. Then I thought about becoming a Special Constable. You know, as a volunteer, but he wouldn't have that either..." she trailed off.

He watched as Mr Darcy finished his food and licked his paws contentedly. Then he considered, with a sad musing gaze, "Has your uncle's friend ever worked for the Vice Squad?"

"Yeah." Catherine pocketed the letters. She yawned as she eyed her clock; it was still early morning. "I only wish he'd visited in more sociable hours."

"Would it make you happy if we had breakfast in bed?" he offered.

"Living up to your promises?" she questioned, raising her brow. "I'd love that."

He opened the fridge and said, "We can each have half an orange and I'll join you in bed shortly."

"By the way, Mr Yang," she purred, "I've noticed something."

"Yes?" he asked. "Do you think that I have cute morning hair? Because you do."

She raised her hand and summoned, "Closer, and I'll tell you."

"Hmm?"

"C'mon. Are you once bitten and twice shy?" She had a side of her hip perching on the table and gestured, "*Closer*, please."

He moved towards her with an orange in his hand.

"Mr Yang, it seems that..." She waited as he approached, enough for her breath to tickle him. "You're wearing your jumper back to front!"

Catherine escaped, giggling, before he could grab her and kiss her.

***

They had their breakfast in bed, canoodled for a long time, and barely managed not to ruin Catherine's lovely bedding.

Later, he drove her to work and found his way back to his rented flat at Kean Street.

He parked his Audi not far from a modern furniture store, got out, went in the glass door using his key card, and retrieved his mail.

There was an ad for house appraisal, another from Thames Water.

He waited for the lift, wondering about the contents of Catherine's letters. The lift arrived, its door opened, and his neighbour, Hannah

Robinson, greeted him eagerly with her tongue almost hanging out. "Happy Chinese New Year! Eddy and I are off to Chinatown tonight for some tasty dim-sum. Why don't you and Catherine join us?"

Hannah had moved to London from the US with her husband Eddy, who worked as a legal counsel for a Fintech.

He kindly declined her invitation, and after an exchange of pleasantries, he went in the lift and pressed '9'. As he found his way to his flat, he saw Sarnai, the Robinsons' cleaner, wiping their kitchen windows.

She nodded to him, and he nodded back, before smoothing the Spring Festival couplets taped on his door, and he went inside. The curtains were open, and he could see St Clement Danes Primary School students capering about on the AstroTurf of their school's rooftop playground.

The BT Tower stayed still afar.

It was a lovely penthouse he had rented with a panorama of Covent Garden, despite the fact that its former tenant had passed away in the bedroom upstairs.

He changed his clothes, and went out again to Catherine Street hoping to discuss his joint venture with his business partner Dominic Turner.

He got to the newly furnished jazz bar. Turner was there, orchestrating his latest social media campaign to drum up customers for their new business. Turner had copies of *Bar Magazine* and a bag of Bombay Mix in front of him.

"Chance, the gentleman there has been waiting for you," Turner said to him as he approached the bar counter.

Chance turned and saw the man from that morning standing up from a barstool.

He moved closer, and the man reached out his hand. "Nigel Weatherby. I believe that Catherine has told you about me."

"She did, yes." He sat down. "She's happy to get her letters back."

"I thought so. Well, I don't wish to stall so I'll cut to the chase," Nigel said. "Felipe Kazama referred me. I've a situation; a knotty problem where your succour might be greatly helpful." He continued, "I have a friend who works for a think tank in Brussels. His neighbour recently passed away. She had pizza delivered to her semi, and the deliverer was a former workmate of hers. They had some foul work-related trouble and in the heat of the moment the man lost the plot and attacked her with a kitchen knife and escaped on his scooter. He must have been agitated, as he crashed into a lorry. They both died."

Nigel gave him a meaningful glance. "It's a straightforward enough case, but what we don't understand is that she didn't order the pizza. We checked—we checked all over the shop and..." He shot a look at Turner and lowered his voice. "My friend does not wish to make this known; you must understand—we found cats in her house. Lots of dead cats. *Sous vide* cats skinned like rabbits in Tupperware buried in her backyard. And here comes the baffling problem. My friend has adopted an orphan girl from Sudan. She used to be a child soldier. When the neighbour was attacked, the girl was downstairs in their house listening to music, as she told us, while their housemaid hoovered upstairs. The problem is..." Nigel stopped to collect his breath as he took out a photo from his shirt pocket. "You know what this is?"

Chance recognised it as a remote control for a Sony portable digital audio recorder whose production was discontinued.

"It's a control for PCM-D50."

"My fellows could hardly tell a floppy disk these days," Nigel said plainly. "We've found the carry case, the USB cord, the wind screen, the power adapter, and even the operating manual. But not the device. It's conspicuous by its absence. According to our bloodstain pattern analysis, it should have been there at the scene. Someone took it. Mr Yang, you see, my friend's not entirely certain of what happened in there, in his neighbour's house and his place."

Nigel sighed. "We found hair samples in the Tupperware containers: not from the cats, but from the girl. My friend is cheesed off with the whole thing. He wants answers. His wife was raring to adopt the girl, but he had his reservations. He's a frequent traveller, and now he dreads that he has invited hazard into his household. He wants to enter politics next year and he doesn't wish to draw excessive attention, so I cannot help him more than I have done. His wife's considering hiring a private Maths tutor to help the girl. That's where I think you can come in."

He primmed up his lips before speaking. "I've never considered myself a part-time fixer. I did what I have to do. It does not mean that I have to continue doing it sub rosa."

Nigel looked at him, solemnly. "You ought to know now that sometimes there's evidence but not enough evidence and other times there's interference but never lawful interference. Sometimes, even solved crimes remain unsolved. Sometimes we close cases simply because of resource constraints. I've got problems here and there and all over the place." He paused. "Joyce Peng and Emma Milken are dead and buried. This is in the here and now. You might be able to prevent something wicked from happening."

He didn't say anything.

Nigel breathed deeply and spoke gruffly. "Do it for Catherine's sake then."

"What do you mean?" he demanded. "What's Catherine got to do with this?"

Nigel's mouth twitched. "The deceased was a pen pal of hers. I only found out recently."

He thought for a moment. "I'm on an intra-company visa, and I'm afraid that I cannot help you."

"As a 'Special Advisor' to Jayden Peng, who doesn't even know you exist? Trouble may not be your business, but trouble does seem to like you." Nigel took back the photo and took out a slip of paper. "The job closes in a week, on the 15th. Reach me here if you change your mind." He stood up and said, "So long then."

***

Chance talked briefly with Turner then returned to his flat.

Sarnai had finished cleaning the windows, and was dusting the Robinsons' doormat.

He shredded his receipts then settled on the sofa with his tablet in hand and ran some searches.

The two Brits who had gone missing when scuba diving in Colombia remained missing; an update from *The Evening Standard* informed him that their relatives had made their way to join the search. One of the mothers said that it was 'heart-breaking news'.

It didn't take him long to find the unfortunate incident that had happened in mid-December last year in a house near Primrose Hill. However, there was one discrepancy between the media report and Nigel Weatherby's version. The attacker and the deceased, Daniele Vidas, worked at a market research firm; they not only had work-related trouble but the victim had filed an 'unfounded harassment complaint' that drove both parties into exile.

An article in the side bar featured a piece on the infamous Croydon Cat Killer.

He discovered that the aggressor had used a classic Wüsthof chef's knife obtained from the victim's kitchen. The injuries caused were fatal and instant, and it was the neighbours who had discovered the 'horrific scene'. The aggressor crashed at a junction near Adelaide Road.

No mention of cats, dead or alive, was made.

By the time he put away his tablet, he realised that Catherine's shift would be ending soon.

Catherine worked as a part-time florist in the floral academy in Slingsby Place.

A pigeon watched him on the balcony and made a dropping as he tried on another jumper.

Was he really going to be a stool pigeon and sleuth for Scotland Yard?

He did not wish to think so.

It drizzled as he made his way to Catherine's workplace. Many parents crowded the pedestrian road on Drury Lane as they waited to pick up their primary school children.

"If we all enjoyed a happy childhood with happy parents... If our

neighbours, friends, and families all lived contented lives, wouldn't it be likely that prisons, barracks, and asylums would be empty? Wouldn't it be the case that the herd is kinder, society wiser, and cosmopolitanism achieved more efficiently? Given the right time and location, anyone could kill. Not mentioning a less suitable milieu."

He made his way through the milling crowds as he reflected on Felipe's words. He listened as a girl played 'I spy with my little eye' with her nanny and turned onto Long Acre. The leather goods shop where Joyce Peng once bought her belt was rolling out their latest Valentine's promotion. A deliveryman exited Pho, a Vietnamese restaurant, in a hurry.

"Better keep an eye on everything. Even an errand as simple as ordering delivery can lead to a camel's nose under the tent. It's all chaos out there. Chaos not ciaos."

He chewed on Felipe's words once again.

Two fundraisers from Save the Children loomed ahead; he dodged them with dexterity. A ticket counter near Covent Garden Station advertised discount packages for the *Wicked* musical.

"Joyce Peng and Emma Milken are dead and buried. This is here and now. You might be able to prevent something wicked from happening."

He shed those thoughts as he remembered what Felipe once said about Catherine: 'She shares one common hobby with me. She likes to read and watch thrillers'.

It was an odd enough comment, he thought; he'd never seen any book or thriller DVD in her house. Catherine had several films of Jane Austen adaptations, some BBC dramas, and movies featuring Harrison Ford and Simon Pegg. He had never seen any R-rated content in her house—unless Felipe considered *Fifty Shades of Grey* a thriller, which was unlikely.

As he passed the tube station, he overheard a couple chattering: 'Everyone has secrets, and the people in that house are no exception. That house is not sacrosanct'.

CHAPTER 2

"An orphan has no past, and a widow has no future."

Orla, another assistant at the flower academy, murmured beside Catherine at the till.

"I'm sorry?" She was a little startled by this sudden observation.

"Oh, sorry!" Orla realised her slip-up. "I didn't mean...sorry, Cat." She qualified, "I was helping Melody with our promotion ballyhoo for Valentine's. She kept on nagging on how Word won't allow her to move a paragraph into a new page so I told her to use the 'orphan and widow control' when formatting. I didn't mean to...sorry..."

Orla cleaned her garden snips with the soft edge of her apron. "Then I remembered what my ICT teacher used to tell us, that 'an orphan has no past, and a widow has no future'." She wondered mischievously, "Do you s'pose that Melody has had a thing with the owner of the tulip farm where we once stayed? For one, she loves to go to My Old Dutch. They have pancakes to die for. Next time we should visit Meijer Roses–"

"Orla, dear!" their floral design teacher called from the basement. "Be a dear and help me with the mailing list, will you? Technology's not my thing, and the computer glare gives me a headache that dulls my eyes."

Orla left on this summons, and Catherine thought about her life after she noted down two orders for bouquets on Valentine's Day. Then she remembered a conversation she had had with Felipe:

"Have you enlightened him on your favourite passatempo yet?"

"No...not yet."

"I don't think it would make his blood curdle."

But...

She didn't want to pour her heart out only to be mocked and scolded. She had had a fair share of that.

He did say that he had no right to comment on my reading options, in or out of my house. And he does know that reading is one of my favourite pastimes...

And the letters...

They were well preserved and kept with care. How did Daniele lose them?

And what would Catherine herself say if he ever asks about the letters?

She looked up and saw him waiting on the bench outside. She decided to ease into the topic at hand, starting from tonight.

They had an early dinner at Pho, went back to Kean Street, and drove back to her house in Kensington.

Mr Darcy, her cat, idled on the sofa and played with a cushion with a cover designed by Nathalie Lété. He jumped off the sofa and held his tail high in greeting.

They had some homemade juice and shared a celery stalk with some pineapples; then he reminded her that they had a double dinner date with her best friend Mick and his spouse Sam on the 12th. They decided on the Palomar in Soho, where she had once dined with her uncle.

Later, they watched a film that Catherine had chosen: *The Remains of the Day*.

He followed her through the film, the deleted scenes, the making of, the cast interviews, and finally, Catherine said, "*The Remains of the Day* is such a sad story that I only dare to watch it once every year." She turned to look at him. "You do know what fanfiction is, right?"

He nodded. "Yes."

"Do you know what a 'ship' is?"

"Like a couple in the story?"

"And do you know what 'canon' means?"

He thought for a few seconds. "What happens in the story?"

She nodded approvingly. "Then you know what 'headcanon' means?"

"What you wanted to happen in the story?"

"A bit like that, yeah," Catherine said, hugging her cat. "Miss Kenton and Mr Stevens will always be my favourite headcanon." She sighed slightly. "I used to write fanfiction about them. It's a bit of a niche ship, but there's a writer on Dreamwidth who writes beautiful stories about them." She hesitated. "Do you know what my favourite ship is? Has Felipe ever told you?"

"No, he hasn't." He decided on an easy answer, "Umm...from *Twilight*?"

Catherine shook her head. "I do ship Bella and Edward. I ship a lot of pairs. I also ship Mac and Gin from *Entrapment* and Erik and Christine from *The Phantom of the Opera*, but..." She cast down her eyes with a sad smile. "My favourite ship is a bit taboo. I won't tell you yet."

Days passed as they settled into a comforting routine.

He would spend the night at Catherine's place, drive her to work, attend his own business, and pick her up from work. They would dine out, or he would make some simple dishes with rice, and they would watch a film or two after dinner.

They had watched *Howards End*, *Shadowlands*, and *Surviving Picasso*. He had learnt that Catherine was a great fan of Sir Anthony Hopkins, but he felt as if she wanted to send him a cryptic message with her choice of films.

One night, after watching *Entrapment*, she asked him, "How do you feel now that the FBI agent ran away with the criminal?"

"It's none of my business, really," he said as he held Mr Darcy on his lap.

"But do you approve of it?"

"Well. I cannot make decisions for others. And I don't care if they ran away or not. But...if you want them to elope, then why not?"

Catherine considered his responses and then asked, "Do you spook easily?"

Yes, he wanted to say, he was spooked easily by household items such as curry, rats, codeine, and strong rivets.

In the end, he only said, "It depends."

Catherine questioned with a half-raised eyebrow, "Do you like to watch horror films? Thrillers?"

"I've seen a few, yes."

The truth was, he never liked movies that made death an entertainment.

Catherine considered for a moment, went upstairs and retrieved a large aluminium storage box.

She placed the box on her lap, cleared her throat, and took a breath.

"Do you know Hannibal Lecter?"

"Hmm…the TV show?"

"No, not quite." She seemed somewhat dismayed. "The books and the films." Then she declared, "I'm going to show you my favourite ship."

***

The next day, they had dinner with Catherine's best friends Mick and Sam.

Mick was a choreographer who occasionally taught at the Pineapple Dance Studios in Covent Garden; Sam was a musician who sometimes taught vocal training at the Actors' Centre not far from Seven Dials.

They rocked up at the restaurant, the Palomar in Soho, at a quarter to seven. Sam was already there, idling with a glass of cucumber water in a boisterous background.

"Coo! I'm dead chuffed for you both!" Sam greeted them and asked him, "When you came for the singing taster, did you know Catherine then?"

Catherine gave a radiant smile and recounted how they'd met the first time seven years ago on less friendly terms when she had visited Sophie, her godfather's daughter, at Imperial College where he was studying for his computing degree.

"Oh, and how is…" Sam recalled. "How's your friend Joyce, by the way? Is she about? I haven't seen her lately. Tell her that I'd love for her to take more lessons with us."

He hesitated. "She went home."

"To celebrate the Chinese New Year?"

"No. She won't be back."

"Such a pity." Sam continued recounting episodes about their honeymoon in Bali.

Catherine excused herself to use the washroom while he chatted with Sam on the best ways to make a scrapbook. Sam told him of the London Graphic Centre in Covent Garden with its ample art supplies. They had also talked about the London Bass Guitar Show that was scheduled to take place in mid-March in Olympia.

Mick arrived shortly after, running a little late, and they ordered.

Catherine had a salad with farmhouse bread and aubergine. He ordered a chicken dish and a sumac tart for dessert. He didn't drink, but the rest of the group shared a bottle of Krug Grande Cuvée champagne.

After dinner, the four of them strolled to Carnaby Street, where Catherine and Sam indulged in a bit of shopping and window shopping. Later, they went to Anthropologie on Regent Street, with a brief stop at Prowler.

"So," Mick said as he vaped outside the store, "did Cathy tell you her hobby yet?"

"Fanfic?"

"Uh-huh." Mick thought for a while. "She had a short period of anorexia after her parents passed away. I think she blamed herself for not going with them that night. She'd lost interest in all things: she even stopped dancesport and riding."

They made way for a family carrying large bags from Hamleys.

"I was the one to blame, actually," Mick said. "I visited her with some flicks but I mixed up some horrors that I borrowed from a friend. By the time I found out, she'd already watched a few of them. Her uncle was angry at me." He smiled bitterly. "Apparently, Cathy had asked for some fava beans and that's when she decided to become a vegetarian. I think she does it to punish herself."

He concurred secretly, drawing a parallel with his own lifestyle choices.

Mick continued, "I think she's had a shock. It was such a shock to lose her parents so suddenly, and she needed a bigger shock. Before they went away, she was a teenybopper, very into the Spice Girls, *The Parent Trap*, and *The Princess Diaries*." He paused, "Her uncle didn't understand her using fanfiction as a crutch and obviously Cecil didn't find the notion that a cannibalistic serial killer who breaks free with a special agent that agreeable. Naturally, these topics were banned in her house." He took a drag. "That's when she started finding pen pals. They exchanged correspondence like a sort of...ritual." He gave a small laugh. "At least one good thing *The Silence of the Lambs* did was to persuade Cathy to continue with piano, and I guess part of Pierre's allure was that he knew all the fancy vintages."

They stood in silence and watched as cars roamed by. Then Mick said, "Even if you don't share the enthusiasm, don't judge."

"Aha, so here you are, still chin-wagging?"

They heard Sam's calling and entered the store.

***

Later.

They got back to Catherine's house shortly before ten.

"Did you know that Mick and Sam first met at the Fopp in Covent

Garden?" she said as she put away her shopping. "Wasn't tonight splendid?" Catherine decided to broach the item that had been niggling her for a while. "Perhaps next time we can dine with your friends? Like... Joyce perhaps?"

She was a little leery in asking him, but she did.

He heaved a heavy sigh, "Catherine, I..."

I have something to tell you...

I have a confession to make...

I want an out...

Her mind predicted his responses like annoying search engine auto-suggestions.

He looked at her with a sombre expression. "She's..." Then he trailed off again.

His ex...

His ex-fiancée...

His ex-wife...

His dalliance...

Her imagination sometimes went haywire.

"Yes?" Catherine settled on the sofa beside him and pretended to busy herself with combing Mr Darcy.

Finally, he said with a furtive look in his eyes, "Joyce Peng was the former tenant of my flat."

"Oh." She felt as if she was in a hole. She thought for a few seconds. "The one who passed away during the Holborn fire?"

"Yes."

"But...she was not your friend?"

"No. I never met her..." He let out a breath. "I thought it would be easier to say she was rather than explaining the whole thing to Sam."

Catherine pondered, "How did she pass away? I know that it was a suicide."

He decided to tell her as much as he could, even if it was only the tip of the iceberg.

"It was a codeine overdose induced choking."

"Sam would be so sad to hear about this," she reflected.

"Then don't tell them, please."

"I feel very sorry for her. I only wanted to...know more about you. You know about Pierre and it seems only fair if I..."

"If you insist..." he smiled a little. "She read law. She liked Silk Cut. She wanted to become a pro bono lawyer. "

They looked at each other for long seconds with palpable tension.

Then, he turned his head and sniffed around. "Why do I sense some sourness in the air? Has someone been eating vinegar tonight?"

Catherine shied away from the innuendo and held up her cat. "Yes, definitely Mr Darcy. He's grumpy that we didn't bring him on the date."

Mr Darcy meowed, as if in agreement or disagreement.

That night, they watched *Hannibal*, and then the alternate ending, the deleted scenes, the making of, and finally the cast interviews.

He observed Catherine as she immersed herself in the scenes that flickered on the screen.

He once told her that he liked to know a different side of her.

It seemed then that he was slipping into a bittersweet learning curve: the more he learnt about her, the more he cared for her, and the more he found himself undeserving.

This is here, and now, he reminded himself.

***

14th February.

Sunday.

Valentine's Day is a great day for everyone except florists, Catherine decided as she wrapped up another bunch of vibrant red roses and checked the newly added plaster on her finger.

It had been a hectic morning.

She had risen with the lark to join the crew at the New Covent Garden Flower Market in Vauxhall to prepare for the shop's major sales event of the year.

Melody had arranged for lots of quality coffee to be delivered from the Monmouth Coffee Company as the shop staff worked their way through the pre-orders and the special deliveries while exchanging private florist jokes.

By midday, Orla had complained that her hands were already sore from writing so many personalised message cards.

Catherine had made delicate plans for their first Valentine: they would have dinner at their favourite restaurant, and then go to the Prince Charles Cinema for some classic romance...and then...

But she had some serious second thoughts. It seemed that their first Valentine would turn out to be pear-shaped.

Her Mr Yang dropped by after lunch with a thermos of burdock root and cinnamon tea and a bag of flying saucers.

"Is there anything else that you might need?" he sensed her predicament and asked.

"Do you know how you can make me happy today?"

"I'm all ears."

Catherine smothered a sigh, "Here's what I want you to do. I want you to cancel the reservation at Vanilla Black. Cook dinner for us and get me a surprise."

He thought for a moment. "That can be arranged."

"Very well," she said, "I'll see you later at your flat."

By the time she left, it was nearly seven.

Melody was still at the shop, saying that some customers, *ahem* men, tended to pluck up their courage or remember the occasion at the last minute.

Catherine put on her tam o' shanter and left Slingsby Place, turned onto Long Acre, and headed down Drury Lane.

She was tired from all the caffeine. It was in times like this that she appreciated him living so close to where she worked. Cecil, her godfather, had agreed to check on Mr Darcy after his dinner with Patsy, someone he had been seeing.

Catherine was glad that her godfather had now recovered.

She found the deserted Kean Street and the entrance to the building, remembering that Mick had once said it was 'a doable place for an ambush'. His flat now felt like a home from home. She laughed in the lift, recalling the reason for their first argument and his cast iron alibi and felt truly happy that it had only been a mistake.

The Robinsons were having a night out, Catherine observed, as she passed the open-air atrium and opened the door with her set of keys.

"Dinner's ready," he said as he garnished two plates with heartsease.

"I'll be with you shortly." She took off her serge coat, washed her hands, and laid the table for their meal.

A small candle burnt with a zippy, citrus scent.

"Well," he explained, "the surprise is that I've used edible flowers in all the dishes."

"Oh, that sounds wonderful!"

He brought out two shallow porcelain bowls. "Let's first try this porridge with mum."

Catherine had a spoonful; it was slightly sweet but easy on her palate.

"My compliments to the chef," she said with delight.

He flashed her a mischievous look. "I'm sure that my rice cooker would be very happy."

They had some fried cauliflower with truffle and black sesame sauce; a cold dish of daylily, ceps, and spicy tofu; a casserole of lily bulbs and finally, *tangyuan* with osmanthus flowers as they chatted with a pot of rose tea.

"My compliments to the chef again," Catherine said. "I'm sure that your rice cooker wouldn't be able to make all those delicious dishes." She tilted her head. "Or, if I'm mistaken, tell me where you got it, and I'll get one for myself as well. It seems a terrific bargain."

He smiled. "I'm glad that you enjoyed it."

"Did you make do with what was in your fridge?"

"No, I went to Whole Foods and Seewoo." He hesitated. "Catherine, I'm no gourmet by any standards."

"The food was lovely. Thank you."

They finished dinner, put away the dishes, and settled on the sofa.

Then Catherine decided to tease him a bit. She pouted, "I saw you gawking at Orla today."

"Did I?"

"Uh-huh," she joked. "You stared at her as if trying to say 'You better take a good look at me in my new haircut; otherwise, I'll invite you to supper'."

He laughed a bit. "I'm sure I can cook something to her disliking."

They cuddled together, then she said, "Sorry that we missed Valentine's Day."

"That's okay." He mused, "There's a Chinese song that says that 'If you find the right one, every day's Valentine's'."

"Oh, that's sweet. What's it called?"

"Hmm... Are you sure you want to know?"

"Do tell."

"It's called 'Happy Breakup'."

"Ha-ha, very funny."

He shook his head slightly, "Ask An next time if you don't believe me. Now, how'd you like a sensual experience?"

"As in?"

"As in a rubdown?"

"It sounds charming."

They went upstairs, and she settled comfortably on the king-size bed as he drew her a bath and removed her socks.

She had a pair of socks with happy parrots on and he saw the slight indent marks the socks had left on her skin from standing too long.

The bedroom was where the former tenant had passed away. Catherine reflected on what Hannah Robinson had told her: Joyce Peng had passed away on her own bed, a bed that had long been removed, and no blood was involved...

How fragile life is...

Her mind drifted to the recent news about two Brits missing in Colombia and why suicide rates always soar on Valentine's Day.

Catherine observed the room and its high ceiling, then felt something wet moving against her feet.

"What are you doing?" she half raised herself and inquired.

"Did I startle you?" He had a wet tissue in his hands. "I thought that maybe you wouldn't want to share your bath with the fluff from your socks?"

She bobbed her head. "You're very right."

The bath was ready. She got up, and white rose petals welcomed her into the water.

***

By the time the rubdown ended, she was dog tired.

Catherine could do nothing but snuggle under the duvet.

"Let me see..." He took out a small velvety jewellery case from the nightstand on his side. "I happen to have another surprise."

She took the case and opened it. It was a necklace featuring a porcelain bee from And Mary that matched her favourite earrings. Catherine put away the box carefully and murmured, "I have a surprise for you as well...but I'm too tired to put it into action."

"Tell me."

She laughed. "I happen to have some lingerie from Agent Provocateur that I'd love to try on...but it'll have to wait. It's my belief that a gentleman should always unwrap his present by himself."

"I can wait." He settled beside her before lowering the brightness of the lamp. "It's something we can look forward to."

"Uh-huh, all good things come to those who wait. But you know what we can do now?"

"I can think of some possibilities."

She raised herself and tried not to laugh out loud as she exclaimed. "We should put our *tu-lips* together on this Valentine's Day!"

"Oh, yeah," he said as amusement flickered in his eyes. He leaned close, "We are *mint* to be."

"Hmm," Catherine laughed, "I'd very much like the chef's kiss now."

They had a brief kiss, then Catherine remembered something. She purred by his ear, "Now, tell me, Mr Yang, before we got together, did you ever imagine things between us? Scenarios and exchanges? Have you ever imagined me in a bodice or a waspie? Or...*nothing* at all?"

"No," he said, "I had no right to imagine." He sounded sincere.

"And now?"

"Now," he looked at her, "you fulfil my every imagination."

She tittered, "Do you know Felipe's classic pickup line?"

He nodded unwillingly. "He would say to someone that his girlfriend was in another nation and then when they asked him where she was, he would say, 'She's in my imagination, care to fulfil it?'"

Catherine laughed like a duckling. "Felipe seems to like white roses as well. Last time he asked for a white rose boutonnière although a Checkmate rose matched his tux better." She continued, "Where did you learn to give massages?"

"Well, I've had some sports massage before, and I picked up something along the way."

She reflected, "I'm glad that I didn't scare you off with my literary pursuits. See, I'm not the goody-two-shoes that you might think, Mr Yang."

"If you want to scare me off, petal, you must try harder."

Catherine basked in pleasure with this term of endearment, yet she sighed, "You know, Felipe's the only one who didn't disdain my hobby. He once told me that people can have so many off-colour hobbies, writing a few words hardly counts." She giggled. "Once my uncle tried to cut me off from our WiFi and Felipe helped me to spoof my laptop's MAC address. I'd pretend to go to sleep early every night but in fact, I was secretly perusing the LL archive. Now that you know something about me, tell me a secret about you."

"A secret?"

"Yes, a *dark* secret that only a few know, or preferably no one."

"Well..." he hesitated, "I *really* don't want to scare you off."

"Try me."

"Fine," he said. " Let's say that there were two children, X and Y. One day, X told Y that someone had done something horrendous, so they decided that they'd take revenge. It was a great success, and afterwards they had the tastiest Kentucky Fried Chicken they had ever had in their lives."

"Oh," Catherine reflected. "What did this person do to receive such harsh treatment?"

"What Mason Verger did to children before he was immobilised. And what was most unforgivable was that the person was a teacher."

"How terrible! I know very well that childhood traumas can have a long-lasting impact." She eyed him. "I knew that you're not as harmless as you might look. But I understand. I do. Revenge is sweet, like how Clarice enjoyed a certain dish the Oliver Twist way." Catherine shrugged. "When I gave you the silent treatment, Mick said that, 'Kean Street sounds like a doable place for an ambush'."

"He did warn me, yes." Chance smiled warmly. "It's nice to have a good friend like Mick. Someone you can lean on..." He paused. "Mick is a dangerous name for me, though. I used to read this detective series called *Matthew Scudder*. It made me feel that New York was a very dangerous place. There's this character called Mick Ballou who has a farm and hogs..." He rubbed his brows. "And there's a serial killer who played with people's lives..."

"You know, among us Clannibal writers we always say that rule number one is never to forget who he is..." She turned to look at him again, her eyes beaming. "You once said that you and Felipe tracked people down. What did you mean?"

"Sometimes, before a major case, we would make some confidential inquiries and talk to ex-lovers of the owners or ex-employees of a company to see if the management had tampered with the accounts or if there was any pump and dump, and to investigate the case's worth."

And sussing out dodgy suicides and snooping about missing persons...

The night grew dense, as did their conversation.

He thought for a moment. "Catherine, can I ask you something?"

"Yes, now you know the rules, Mr Yang: *quid pro quo*."

"Can you tell me more about your pen pal?"

Catherine recalled, "I know her name's Daniele but I'm not sure if that's her real name. She says that her parents are from Lithuania. They passed away as well, in a double suicide. Do you know that Lithuania has one of the highest suicide rates in the European Union? I do feel for her, and we all feel for Clarice. We both shipped Clannibal and Miss Kenton and Mr Stevens with a certain fervour. They have so much UST! Daniele says that the Good Doctor is the world's most famous Lithuanian. And we used to write quite frequently. We would send the letters to a PO box and make it all mysterious with anagrams and puzzles."

She gave a mournful moue. "Sometimes she whinged that there was this *blasted* bloke in her workplace who always rattled her. His family owned a pizzeria, and he would always have pizzas delivered to the office as petty perks." Catherine stopped to gather her thoughts. "She sent her congratulations on my engagement. What with one thing and another, I don't think we communicated again after I set off for India."

Catherine had volunteered to teach English in India for a year after discovering her unfaithful ex-fiancé's doings.

"And I've given up on my hobby for a while. If I read smut, it reminded me of how lonely I was and if I read a story that ended sadly, especially with a major character's death, it made me a whole lot sadder, so I decided on a writing hiatus."

He looked at her. "But now you are happy?"

"Yes."

"Then maybe you can pick it up again?"

"Maybe. I do have a work in progress for *The Remains of the Day*. I once went to read the film files at the British Film Institute's archive and I shadowed a butler. I even asked my uncle to pull some strings so I could visit the houses where they shot it. Oh, I actually met a butler from a hotel today at the Flower Market. He was there to get a bouquet for a couple staying at their suite. He had to get up at three! I guess I need to dig up my notes." She looked up. "Now, tell me something about you."

"I think when you evade life, life evades you."

"That's a very philosophical observation."

He thought for a long time. "There's a time when I locked myself up in my room for a month. I was very into a computer game. My dad always smoked under my window every night before I went to sleep. I finished the game and repeated it a few times even. And one day, I decided that I had had enough. Guess what my dad did?"

"I hope he didn't hurt you," Catherine offered tentatively.

He smiled, "No, no. My parents never laid a finger on me. Nor did An's parents. My dad bought me the sequel."

"I like games too. I liked to play Neopets. There was supposed to be a *Hannibal* PC game that I so looked forward to playing, but it was never released. My uncle's always busy with teaching and his 'European relations', and Cecil with work. At least Felipe's fun. He even accompanied me to the Castle of Threave and we picnicked on the River Dee. He told me the difference between a *kimono* and a *yukata* and a *nagajuban*'."

Catherine smiled as she recalled, "Now, we can have a lot of rollicking fun together. And high jinks for the two of us only." She sighed and continued with a tone of worry, "I know quite a lot of fanfiction writers, and sometimes, they stop responding to messages or drop their stories out of the blue. You only hope that they're too busy enjoying life than seeking solace in a fictional world. With some writers, their works can be stand-alone books and their language is so touching."

After a long pause, he said, "Catherine, I've been thinking about applying for a job as a private tutor."

He told himself, if Catherine expressed any form of disagreement, even the slightest resistance, he'd discard the plan at once.

He hated the word 'plan'.

"You've made me very happy lately." Catherine held his hand delicately as if she were holding a dove. "You've always encouraged me to do what I liked. If you do what you like, you'll be happy. I enjoyed teaching, and I hope you will as well."

Later.

He slipped off the bed after Catherine had fallen asleep.

She slept soundly like a kitten who had played all day, and her hands settled above her head. He noticed that she had a newly added plaster on her finger.

"Has it ever happened to you? That one day, you discover a small cut on your right hand..."

He moved her hands under the duvet, and ventured downstairs.

The brutalist Space House glowed an eerie blue and he felt a twinge of fear.

"Do it; do it for Catherine's sake, then. You might be able to prevent something wicked from happening."

He picked up his phone and dialled Nigel Weatherby's number.

The call connected, and he said, "I want a taser. The girl...what year is she in?"

CHAPTER 3

*T*he next day.

Catherine was roused by the sounds of cooking. She checked her phone; it was nearly nine-twenty.

She got up, put on a dressing gown, drew open the curtains, opened the door to the balcony to let in the air, went downstairs and found him in a charcoal grey suit and a matching tie and black-rimmed spectacles.

She had never seen him in a suit and tie. He used a Balthus knot and looked dapper.

"Breakfast is ready, and you look surprised," he said. "I have an interview at ten-thirty."

Catherine recalled their conversation from last night.

"Aren't you scrubbed up all lovely? What subject are you going to teach?"

"Maths. If all goes well." He stepped forward. "How do I look? Do I look like I'll land a job?"

"Nothing short of perfection."

"Really?"

"Yea, Mr Yang, you look impeccable."

He smirked. "That's a pity. I was hoping for someone to give me a peck."

Catherine laughed heartily. "You're *impossible*, you know that? And very demanding."

She bussed him lightly on his right cheek.

"That I do know," he said as she helped to straighten his tie. "What I don't know is why you put up with me."

"*Alas*, don't be such a smart arse. Look smart and get to your interview now." She walked with him to the door and handed him his umbrella.

He put on his shoes and a down jacket and took the umbrella and picked up a briefcase. "There's nothing smart about me except for my smartphone."

She helped him with the scarf. "Well, Mr Yang, we can banter all night after you land the job. I'm sure you'll ace the interview."

"Only bantering?"

"Maybe we can play cat's cradle. Who knows; all good things come to those who wait."

"I'll message you later then. A proper good morning kiss?"

They kissed and parted. She had a nice breakfast with a kale and dragon fruit smoothie, got dressed, and decided to slack away her day off.

She spent some fifteen minutes in the furniture store downstairs, placed an order for a corduroy donut cushion, and made her way out of Kean Street towards Aldwych. Then she saw An, Chance's cousin, sitting on a chair outside the counter at the Delaunay with a cup of coffee.

"Hi An! How was your Valentine's Day?" Catherine sat down beside her.

"Like any other day." An smiled nervously. "Catherine, please thank your uncle for driving me back the other night after we had hot pot. I have his lecture this afternoon. It's a bit awkward; I've heard that he likes to cold call people."

"Just look him in the eye when he asks questions then he won't pick you. Trust me; it's a tried and tested method. He calls it playing academic chicken: the one who looks down first loses." Catherine mused, "So, no dates?"

An laughed a bit. "I've been single since the day I was born; it won't hurt to wait longer."

Catherine was a little surprised, as they were the same age. Then she remembered something. "Tell me, An, is there a song in Chinese called 'Happy Breakup'?"

"Uh-huh," An nodded. "It's by a famous Malaysian singer called Fish Leong. She's known for love songs and sad love longs."

"I see." Catherine looked at the teeming street. "By the way, when you were little, did you and your brother like to eat Kentucky Fried Chicken?"

An thought for a while. "Hmmm, I don't think so. There was a KFC in our city, yes, but it was rather far downtown, and I don't remember ever going there." She held her chin with one hand. "But in China, KFC is a lot more popular than McDonald's."

"We've got great fried chicken in Charlottesville! Eddy and I'd love some chicken with ramp butter now. We'll be back to the stompin' grounds and enjoying the mountains in Easter if the creeks don't rise. But we won't be staying for frog gigging, though."

Catherine recognised this jovial voice and turned; Hannah Robinson flashed a Duchenne smile. "G' morning ladies. I've always found that fries could make or break a meal. I have a hankering for Maccies because they have crispier fries."

"Morning, Hannah. You're as fresh as a daisy."

"Just had my morning spinning workout. I hope you all had a great Valentine's Day?"

"Oh, it was great..." Catherine said sarcastically as she rotated her shoulders. "I feel like I got hit by a lorry."

"Sore day, hey?" Hannah Robinson gave her a knowing smile. "I'm worn slap out as well."

"Nah." Catherine squeezed the stiffened muscles in her neck. "It was like Piccadilly Circus at the shop. I got up at four and we worked like billy-o, and by the time we closed, I was too tired to do anything other than hit the pillow."

"Oh, poor darlin'," Hannah Robinson said compassionately. "Eddy and I went to make chocolate at Hotel Chocolat, and we went to their restaurant, Rabot 1745, in Borough Market. They've got great dishes made with cocoa beans. We had a great night and we hit the hay quite late."

Catherine smiled inwardly at the memories of the pièce de résistance of her dinner.

"Won't you introduce us, honey?" Hannah Robinson gestured.

"Oh, yes. This is Chance's cousin An, spelt AN. She's reading for a Master's at King's College London," Catherine said. "And this is Mrs Hannah Robinson, his neighbour."

They exchanged pleasantries and talked about the Magic Lantern Festival at Chiswick House Gardens and then the Caffè Florian in Venice. Then Hannah left because she said her eyeballs were floating.

After a pregnant pause, An said, "Catherine, please say 'I take it back'."

"I'm sorry?" Catherine did not quite understand.

"You said that you feel like you got hit by a lorry...please say 'I take it back'."

Catherine hesitated for a beat. "I...I take it back."

"Thank you." An led out a deep breath. "I'm very cautious about these things...slip-ups. I have a friend who had an accident; she's a great violinist but now she..." An considered, "And my brother as well...he's very superstitious."

"Is he?" Catherine hadn't noticed.

"He never shares a pear for one, because it means to 'separate' in Chinese and he dislikes the number four to an extent." An mused, "Once I saw him writing an email and he waited for the time to turn to fifty to send it. Sometimes even when he drinks water you'll see that he takes gulps of three or five."

Interesting...she thought.

"Oh, I have to go to my seminar now." An checked her phone. "Have a great day."

They parted, leaving Catherine with much food for thought.

***

He left the flat, passed the half-face of a clown on a red brick wall, and went onto Kingsway while basking in their morning bantering.

A sports shop promoted winter golf apparel in its windows, and he remembered something Felipe had said.

"Better than being hit by a golf club, heard that they hurt like hell."

He did wish that it would hurt like hell.

His thoughts drifted to the ambush that X and Y had staged on a sultry summer night...

He did what he thought was right then, but was he doing the right thing now?

A car horn brought him out of his reverie, and he followed the commuting gaggle to Euston, took the Northern Line from there, and got off at Camden Town Station.

According to Nigel Weatherby, the Edens, his would-be employers, lived in a triple million property on Gloucester Avenue. Amani, his student-to-be, was at sixth form at a co-educational academy in Marylebone.

The Edens had no children of their own.

He found the address and circled the neighbourhood as he observed a newly vacated semi-detached house.

A couple jogged by while discussing Daniel Craig's former residence by Regent's Park.

A dog barked somewhere, and he saw a nondescript van parked in front of Daniele Vidas' house. A young lad in dungarees got out of the vehicle and went inside, followed by the driver. It seemed that Daniele's relative had hired the transport service from Man and A Van.

He watched as they moved dozens of cardboard boxes and large shopping bags, a few bottles of wine, a ruby ball cactus, and one rolled-up mattress into the vehicle, then he walked up and caught a glimpse of the contents in one package. It had a broken dream catcher and a pile of A4 print-outs with a railway gothic font heading of...

The lad swayed in his path, and Chance saw a part of the title that said: '-arlington Mystery'.

The van left, and the deserted house now looked like a forlorn, bare barn. A house that made you wonder if you should light up a candle to see if there was enough oxygen in there before entering.

He checked his watch; it was time to meet the Edens. He passed the well-fenced gate, rang the bell, and waited.

"Yes?" A demure, matronly woman in her mid-forties opened the door.

"Good morning. My name is Changxi Yang, and I am here for an interview as a private Maths tutor."

"Oh, yes. Mrs Eden has informed me." The woman made way. "I'm the housekeeper, Geraldine Parker; please call me Gabby. Follow me, if you please."

He removed his jacket and umbrella, followed Gabby into the drawing room and observed his surroundings.

There was an Arflex sofa, an intricate model of the Sagrada Família in a glass case, and a chess set with pieces resembling the London Skyline. A pair of large porcelain vases stood apart on the floor.

He took in these details, then heard someone bellowing somewhere inside the house with a harsh tone of condescension.

"That queer fish! That turncoat! You know who that rotter reminds me of? He reminds me of a Putin—not in the Russian sense, in the French sense! And Callanan...you can't expect much from someone who attended a poly now, can you?"

Chance already disliked Ambrose Eden.

Yes, Felipe sometimes spoke out of turn, but he always had a wisecracking twinge. But this? This was true codswallop.

"He'll be here for a while, as long as the Lord doesn't call for him. He'll make his stance clear soon, he's jerking the rug out from under–"

The noise suddenly halted, and he heard a door shut.

"I'm Amani's mother, Georgiana. Thank you for coming on such short notice, Mr Yang."

He turned, and a woman in a Juicy Couture velour tracksuit stood there. She was emaciated.

"No...no worries at all."

"Felipe has spoken very highly of you. He recommended you to my uncle." She gestured for him to sit down.

"He did?" he murmured. He knew that Nigel Weatherby would give him a potted history.

"Said that you were his favourite assistant of all time and very capable."

Gabby came in with a tray with a fine china tea set and Di Leo biscuits. She put down the tray but did not pour tea for either of them.

"Which made me wonder–" Georgiana Eden looked at him as his English teacher in middle school would. "Have you had previous tutoring experience, Mr Yang?"

"Yes. I taught Maths and sometimes programming."

He opened his handbag and took out his CV in a clear file folder with his enhanced DBS check certificate. "For your reference."

The woman flipped through the pages. "Impressive. You speak Spanish as well."

"Well," he offered, "My stepmother is Mexican."

"Oh, I see." She winced slightly. "You speak *Mexican* Spanish then."

He felt annoyed. "Mexico has many renowned mathematicians, like Victor Neumann-Lara, like–"

"Yes. Of course." Georgiana dismissed him with a brusque tone. "Amani has been learning Mandarin in school, so we thought it might be helpful if you could help her to improve her Mandarin on the side?"

"That I can try. But…" He paused. "I have had no training to teach Mandarin, and Maths will be my priority." Having said this, he scolded himself quietly. His priority, it seemed, was everything other than teaching maths.

"And what is your teaching philosophy, would you say?"

He considered, "My teaching…well…" He pointed out from his CV. "I worked briefly for a gaming company, so I suppose that my approach is to try to turn learning into a game. How would you design the levels and encourage the players to continue with it and thrive? Gamification helps to inspire them to use creative and divergent thinking. The learning curve, I think, is the key, and I endeavour to help them move down their respective learning curves as fast as possible."

The lady of the house seemed delighted with his answer. "Yes, and we've been trying very hard to support our little girl. Amani studies biology, politics, drama, and maths at school. And she struggles most with maths. Indeed, she does like games and she likes to play *Angry Birds*. She needs at least a B for her AS exam." She paused. "What's your favourite animal, Mr Yang?"

He took a moment. "My favourite animals are bees. They are hardworking, and they have strong teamwork. They are loyal and very productive. They are inseparable to how nature functions."

"Very well." The woman nodded slightly. "Is it Yang as in Yin and

Yang, by the way?"

"No. It means a poplar tree."

"I see; like *Binsey Poplars*. Are you married, Mr Yang?"

"No."

She hesitated. "Felipe said that...please understand that if we take you on, you'll be required to sign a confidentiality agreement. Whatever you hear in this house, whatever you see in this house, stays in this house."

"I'm aware of that, Mrs Eden."

"Call me Georgiana, please." She then went into a long rigmarole about the terms of his employment. She also asked him to complete a detailed questionnaire asking about his favourite music, books, films, memoirs, and mathematical formulae.

After he had completed the questionnaire, she said, "Amani finishes school every day at three, and we'd expect you to teach from four to seven on weekdays and ten to three on weekends, starting today. Gabby's our in-house maid. If you need anything, just tell her."

"Starting from today?"

"Are there any difficulties?"

"I...I suppose not."

"Any more questions that you'd like to ask, Mr Yang?"

"Hmm...has Amani had any previous tutors?"

"Yes, she did. They're all first-class graduates, but they didn't stay for long. They left in various circumstances."

"I see."

"But I'm certain that you'll be most helpful." She eyed her Cartier wristwatch. "Any other questions?"

He brought up the topic of parking, and then they decided it would be best if he didn't drive to work.

"Very well, now, if you'll bear with me one moment," Georgiana said after their stilted conversation, and left.

He stood up and looked at the untouched tea tray.

A minute or so later, fragments of arguments came in again.

"Stop setting my teeth on edge!"

"For pity's sake, for once let me decide!"

"You always decide without considering! Why do you always have to be mardy?"

"Don't get shirty with me and stop rabbiting on–"

Ambrose Eden's remarks confounded Chance. Either he was putting up a show, he thought, or the man didn't want him in the house at all.

The argument continued, and it took them a while to thrash out their decision.

Georgiana appeared again with a trace of victory in her guttural voice. "I'll get the paperwork ready, and I'll see you this afternoon at four."

"Of course."

"Come on, let me show you out. I need to have my nails done for an event with Jim Mellon tonight." She grabbed a Herno jacket, and they left together.

After they got onto the streets, she said, "Gabby's a good cook but if you want anything different, there's a lovely bakery down the road across the canal. They have wonderful cupcakes."

"Thank you. I'll keep it in mind."

Before they parted, he caught her, in his peripheral vision, staring at her neighbour's newly vacated house.

***

He called Nigel Weatherby, and they decided to meet up for lunch at the Chicken Shop at Holborn.

A black cab passed by and brought him to the place before Nigel arrived.

Adjacent to the restaurant was a salon named Cheeky Nails. He watched as its neon signs flickered a pink hue.

Two girls sat, facing the window, and facing him, and talked. They might even be laughing at him for looking too intently at the shop's opening hours scribbled on the glass door.

He knew that Catherine didn't have her nails done often because of her work as a florist—she had once complained about the scratches. His cousin An kept short nails to play her *pipa*, a four-stringed Chinese instrument. He was not familiar with the beauty treatments regarding nails.

Perhaps he could ask Felipe next time; Felipe was the omniloquent metrosexual who knew it all.

"Do you know that pâtissiers and nurses can't have their nails painted?" a voice said.

He turned: Nigel stood there like a working-class Poirot with a paper bag from Pret a Manger.

"Uh...no, not really."

"Well, now you know." He pulled open the glass door and offered. "Let's crack on. I've a meeting later."

They walked down the stairs, and a porcelain Rooster of Barcelos greeted them on the till. A waiter led them to bolstered seats at the counter, in front of the iron racks that roasted and rotated oil-dripping whole chicken. One chef chopped a cooked bird with a cleaver on a wood stump, and another rubbed spice onto a raw one. They gabbed as they worked and fado played in the background.

"How are we doing today? Would you need help with the menu?" A short-haired girl pointed to the menu on the wall and took out a few items of enamelware.

He had a brief look and decided, "I'll have a quarter of chicken and coleslaw, and a lemonade, thank you."

Nigel ordered half a chicken with fries.

"Your requested item." Nigel handed him the bag from Pret a Manger. "You know the rules: don't harm peaceful and honest citizens."

He took the bag under the counter, eyeing its contents. "I'm not sure if you are being honest here. I don't want some potted version of the story. If there's anything that I should know, it's probably better if I know it now."

"Three things you might need to know: Ambrose likes to cop off with new talent. Georgiana is a social butterfly who likes to buy her reefers from Amsterdam. Her uncle sits as a Crossbench Peer in the House of Lords. He's the one concerned. If you mistreat a pet, the pet bites. If you mistreat a child, the child no longer acts like a child."

He took in the roaring flames in the oven in front of him. "Tell me about Daniele Vidas. Had she been living in that house for long?"

"She had both ends of luck," Nigel said. "She hit the jackpot in '13, and the windfall gave her enough financial independence to rattle around and quit her job. On the day she was killed, we confirmed that she was at the Zoo and had a walk later in Regent's Park. She then bought some food items from Starbucks, and took an Uber from Baker Street back to her house. The Uber driver confirmed that she didn't call for a pizza delivery during the car ride. We've no leads of her calling the pizzeria. And for your information, she seemed to have an aversion for pizzas. We found her ordering Chinese and Thai food, but never pizza. No one ordered from there in the near vicinity, so it wasn't a missed delivery. We traced the call back to the pizzeria to a public phone in Dagenham. Still, we cannot rule out it being *casu consulto* and a staged accident."

"We can trace the payment information."

"No payment was involved. The caller redeemed a free pizza coupon. The only thing we know about the caller is that he doesn't speak very good English."

"How was the coupon circulated?"

"It was given out as a Christmas promotion. The owner of the coupon said she'd lost it."

"If anyone knew about Daniele Vidas' trouble with her colleague, they could..." He stopped. "But the connection seems quite ostensible and random. Who discovered the body?"

"Georgiana Eden, the girl, and the maid. Everyone in the vicinity had gone on holiday. Georgiana said that she saw the front door was half closed and there was blood on the doormat. She went in to investigate, then she sought help from her own house."

"So, any one of them could have taken the voice recorder...even the attacker. When did Daniele Vidas move into that house?"

"In October 2014. According to our analysis, the device was taken after the assailant had crashed."

"I see...and before that? Who lived there?"

"The house was unleased. It was on the market for some while."

He looked at the roasting chicken once again. "And the cats...how many were they?"

"Twenty-five. Only two had microchips. Two were euthanized and put down by injection, some were drowned, and some were strangled. Whoever did it was a neophyte at the beginning. The fur didn't break off cleanly."

"The girl, what do you think of her?"

Nigel hesitated. "My officers on the scene told me that of the three of them, only the girl did not panic. I think she carries a heavy burden on her shoulders. Playing house is usually a mug's game; but playing house in a hellhole is a torture."

Their food came, and they ate quietly as soft music played and flames burnt.

***

Later.

He went to the Robert Dyas on the Strand, bought a large thermos and a lunch box set, and went back to his flat. Catherine was not there.

He messaged her about the upcoming changes to his routine, printed out some pure maths material, prepared some food and tea for himself, and left again at three twenty-five in an Uber.

As the Camry approached Primrose Hill, he received a message from Catherine with congratulations and asking if she could use his tablet to read some fanfiction. He texted back with the passcode and its location, then Catherine replied with a sour face emoji:

'Be very careful what you concede to, Mr Yang. I don't want to find anything in there that might make me sour.'

He smiled; her insecurity was, in a way, winsome.

'Go ahead,' he replied.

He arrived at the Edens' house at a quarter to four. Gabby was surprised to see him so early, and so 'eager to get on with work'. She informed him that Amani was not back yet, and he was glad to hear that Ambrose Eden had left for a one-week trip to Brussels.

He signed the paperwork and Georgiana invited him into the dining area and asked him if he would mind teaching with a nanny cam.

"That's fine." He set down his bag and set up his laptop.

"Oh, and Mr Yang, do you know how to play Mahjong?"

"No."

"A pity. I was hoping that you could teach Amani. I've heard it's good mental stimulation."

"I know how to play Guandan. It's a card game with four players; it's similarly stimulating and good for teambuilding."

They then talked briefly about the girl and her past.

Soon, he heard footsteps, and then Gabby shrieked, "Oh, my!"

They rushed into the parlour, and he saw Amani, his student.

She wore a navy jumper over a white shirt and dark grey trousers with smart black shoes – and a newly shaved head.

"Amani, what on earth happened to your hair!?" Georgiana demanded as her face registered terror.

"The cats were stored in Tupperware containers, and we found some hair

samples—not from the cats, from the girl." He remembered what Nigel told him days ago.

"I did it to support children who are battling cancer," the girl said as she shook off her backpack and patted off some hair clippings from her shirt collar.

"Oh, you're such a doll! But next time you must consult us first." Georgiana checked the child's somewhat ragged hairline, "Whoever did it did an awful job. Come, let's clean you up, and we can share your kind act on Instagram." She turned. "Mr Yang, would you mind waiting a bit?"

"No, not at all."

He waited in the dining room and checked the model of the nanny cam sitting on the Colonial Cream kitchen countertop.

Georgiana soon entered, followed by Amani holding a pencil case and a bag of Monster Munch.

"This is Mister Yang, and he'll be helping you with Maths from today onwards. Now, if you'll excuse me, I still need to figure out which outfit to choose for tonight's event." She left having said this.

"Hi, Amani."

He smiled a bit, and the girl smiled back tentatively.

He had learnt from Felipe how to tell lies with a smile, but he had yet to learn how to tell apart smiles from lies.

"Please have a seat," he gestured. "I hope to make Maths fun. But before that, I think it's important for you to get to know me a little."

He took out his CV and handed it to her.

The girl took it and scrutinized the pages for long seconds.

"Sir, you are smart," she said. "Maths makes my head boil. Especially Calculus; it grills my mind."

"Well. Many people have told me that I'm smart–" he paused. "And far more have told me that I'm not. It's all about learning the right techniques. And there's no need to call me 'sir'."

She put down his CV and sighed. "It's crazy that they make me learn the language of a country that I've never been to and yet they forbid me from speaking Arabic in the house." Then she asked, "Can I call you 'lao-shi'?"

It meant 'teacher' in Chinese.

He hesitated for a bit. "Yes."

"Yang lao-shi. Is it Yang as in Yin and Yang?"

"It means a poplar tree." He wrote it down on a piece of paper.

"Chang-xi. How is it intoned in *pinyin*?"

"Well." He checked mentally. "First tone and first tone."

"And what does it mean?"

He considered, "It means to make the west prosper."

The girl lifted a side of her brow. "Not again?"

"No." He smiled. "My...a friend said the same thing, but when my parents decided on my name, they had western China in mind. The relatively poor provinces."

"It's a very thoughtful name then." She then said mildly, "Yang lao-shi, have you ever fired a gun?"

He took a moment. "Yes. Air rifles. There were air rifles in our parks when I was a boy that you could shoot balloons with and you got all sorts of prizes if you did well."

She laughed quietly. "You had a very happy childhood then."

Her comment stung him a bit.

"Amani, may I ask what your favourite subject is in school?"

"Drama," she said. "Because I don't have to be who I am."

"I see." He paused. "And what might be your least favourite subject other than maths?"

"Politics." She added, "Because people talk about who I am."

"And what papers do you take in maths?"

"Core Maths and Statistics with Edexcel."

They sat down around a long dining table intended to seat more than ten. He asked her about her school progress then she showed him her recent test paper, and they identified a few weak areas.

He said, "There's a learning curve for everything, and so it is with maths. I've heard that you like to play *Angry Birds*, so let's try to make learning maths like playing a game. The more you practise, the better you get. The more levels you unlock, the more badges and trophies you'll collect."

He took out a problem set. "I've prepared some materials that we can start with." He looked around. "You have a calculator? The type that is approved by your examination board?"

"Yes, I'll go and get it."

He waited, and heard the front door open and close.

He dismissed it as Georgiana Eden leaving the house, then he took out his thermos and poured a cup of jasmine tea for himself.

They worked through a problem set and familiarised themselves with her calculator's functions. They wiled away the hours quickly, and he left in another Uber before bidding goodbye to Gabby.

His car arrived quickly. As he clicked his seat belt in, he saw Georgiana Eden leaving the house in a fur coat and a Bentley.

Chance got back to his flat around seven-thirty; he could see warm light seeping from under the door.

The Robinsons were away, it seemed, and the moon shone a quarter.

His door swung open before he could bring out his key.

Catherine flashed her winning smile and declared, "I've missed you, Mr Yang. I've been waiting for my Valentine."

He went in, closed the door, and took off his scarf. "Did you find anything on my tablet that failed to live up to your expectations?"

"Not really, but I did find that you like to go *incognito*. That in itself is telling." She took his briefcase and her hand brushed by his trousers slightly. "Umm...someone's happy to see me?"

"Yes, well..."

She crowed by his ear, "Do you know that I can make you very *sour* in an all-different way, Mr Yang?" She reached her hand into his trouser pocket. "I can give you some vinegar stro–"Then her movements froze. "Wait, what's this?"

"It's a taser."

"A taser, you say?" Catherine sounded perplexed. She took the device out, inspected it, gave him a sceptical look, and lowered her voice. "Why do you go around with a taser? Is it even legal to carry one?"

"Hmmm...London streets are quite dangerous." He hurried to explain, "You know, with all that knife crime. Turner fought with someone on the Tube the other day." He took the taser gently from her hands.

Catherine eyed him with her chin up. "Well, Mr Yang, I know from that time when you asked me about planting tripwires around my house that you have something fishy going on."

"Oh, yes." He tried to keep his tone light. "I intend to fish for some compliments tonight."

"Meh. Now you're pulling my leg, and I know that it's a different kettle of fish we are talking about...maybe even a finer kettle of fish." She helped him with his down jacket. "But if you're fishing for compliments, be a good boy now and earn them. Or I'll put you on the naughty step. Who knows what you might be hiding in *this* pocket?" she joked, and reached her hand inside his jacket pocket.

In a split second, he sensed her tensing up.

"Catherine?" he asked with concern.

She took out something that was wrapped in tissue paper and held it in her palm.

He opened it cautiously. There was a dead slug.

A beheaded slug.

CHAPTER 4

A famous Chinese story goes like this:

Once, a man buried three hundred taels of silver in the corner of his house. He worried that someone might steal it, so he found a piece of wood and wrote on it: 'There are no three hundred taels of silver buried here'.

Chance dismissed the dead slug as a prank, yet it was like the piece of wood that stood out like a sore thumb.

Like having a loudspeaker boasting about a 'zero crime' community, yet you see lynching in front of everyone's house...as Felipe once said.

He reflected as he watched Catherine put on an apron and start cooking. He then remembered the photo of the Milkens.

"We're having pasta tonight because I don't know how to operate your rice cooker yet. It has a Chinese menu." Catherine brought two plates onto the table. "And I've reset the time on your oven. It was ahead by ten minutes or so. I hope you don't mind."

"Not at all. Ah, speaking of rice cookers–" he decided to keep their conversation light for the night. "Once my aunt sent An a rice cooker from China. When it arrived, UK Customs kept it in bond and sent her a letter asking her to pay the duties. She did some calculations and found out that the tariffs were higher than the actual price of the item itself.

Then she decided to return it. When it arrived at my aunt's again, she discovered that the socket was not compatible for use in China...it was a Korean rice cooker."

"My uncle would love to use that as a globalisation pratfall case study," Catherine said. "I saw An today in the morning. Then I went to Somerset House for their latest exhibition, and I went back home to check on Mr Darcy." She opened a cupboard to retrieve a bottle of olive oil and then marvelled, "What's this? Why do you keep a jar of garlic and...is it vinegar?"

He got beside her and held up the jar. "Yes. It's called Laba garlic; you make it before the Chinese New Year and use it for New Year's dumplings." He shook the jar slightly. "And the garlic turns green when it's ready."

"Can I have some?" She looked at the turquoise-coloured garlic.

"Of course." He poured a small dish for her; she dipped into it with her fork, tasted, and claimed, "It's a little bit sweet and spicy. Vinegar is made by converting sugar compounds, right?"

"Yes, you could put it that way. Fermentation of carbohydrates."

"See, you can't fool me. I took GCSE Chemistry."

They had dinner and settled on the sofa with their panorama of Covent Garden.

He wondered, "What does it mean if you say someone likes to cop off with new talent?"

"It means that this person pursues new sexual partners." She decided to tease him, "Having second thoughts already, Mr Yang?"

"No." He gave her a look. "I'd very much like to be yours only."

"Your student..." Catherine asked with a tinge of worry, "What's she like?"

"Her name's Amani, and she was originally from Sudan. Her parents passed away in an attack by a rebel group. She was then recruited...forced to become a child soldier...and she was adopted five years ago."

It was the capsule story that Georgiana Eden had offered to him.

"I don't think it's usual for slugs to be around at this time. In winter, I mean," Catherine suggested.

They fell silent for a while, then he said, "Amani's been learning Chinese for some time. And she decided to call me 'lao-shi', which means 'teacher' in Chinese." He squeezed out a thin smile. "But when she says it, she makes it sounds like 'lao-shu', which means 'rat'." He considered, "And she thought that my first name meant to make the West prosper, just as someone did..."

"Mea culpa and there's no need to rub it in." Catherine pondered, "But isn't it sad that so many people are still enmeshed in warfare, and so many children are still suffering? I'm grateful that my uncle did not send me off to a boarding school. My mother went to Moreton Hall and she didn't like it there. She always missed the time with her family. My uncle's always there for me...and Cecil, Sophie, Mick, and Aunt Liz." She decided to change the topic. "Today I managed to recover my password for my account on FF.net. My pen pal hasn't been updating her stories but she did message wishing me a Merry Christmas last December. I've PM'ed her."

He remained quiet for some time, then said, "Will you tell me more about your stories?"

"Well. My debut piece is called 'Darlington Mystery'. It's about a masquerade where two guests are murdered. Daniele's my beta and she proofread my stories. And my handle is 'C. Catling'." Catherine smiled, "I won't give you any spoilers. The suspense is always better if you read it for yourself, but you must read the book first. The film has some parts that are quite different from the book."

"Can I borrow your book?"

"Sure. I'll bring it over tomorrow. And the Lecter tetralogy: don't knock it until you try it. And we can discuss them later." She thought for a while. "I've installed a pet camera at home so I can check on Mr Darcy. Now that you have started tutoring, we better stay over here for more nights."

"That won't be necessary. We can still drive back after dinner."

"No, I don't want us to drive at night."

They stayed silent for a moment, then he said, "I met a housekeeper today."

"No butler?"

"No."

Then he said, "I told you this morning that there's nothing smart about me except for my smartphone. I meant it. My dad started as a factory worker after high school. It was a job handed down from my grandpa. One day we were in a diner, my dad and I, and one of his superiors got drunk and told him to his face that when his stripling grew up, he'd go to university and have all the good prospects. His child would eat lots of chocolate while I could only drool on the side. I think his words gave my dad an epiphany of a sort. The next week, he enrolled in a night school offered by a Polytechnic in our city. He decided to learn programming. No one around him knew what it was. They thought it was some odd form of weaving. He finished the course and began a distant BA program in Computing. My parents divorced when I was very little, so my dad did many things in between to support us.... He sold digital watches, hardwood flooring, and flared trousers. They were a fad at one point in time."

Catherine took his hand. "Tell me more about your childhood."

"The winters were quite cold, in the range of minus ten and twenty Celsius," he said. "The shop owners would put heaters in their fridges, so the drinks wouldn't freeze. I was never...umm...I never..." He sighed. "There was a time as a boy that I...I had this 'ailment'. I would always have a headache whenever I needed to do my homework."

"Who hadn't?" Catherine gave him a light squeeze.

"When we got to the US, I hardly spoke any English. I didn't even know that you need to use the word 'are' after plurals...and my English teacher told my dad once during a parent-teacher conference that 'Your kid isn't so bright'."

"Oh." Catherine patted his hand. She noticed that he had a large writer's callus. "All that is just fiddlesticks."

He smiled faintly. "There was also once I thought that I was colour blind. My dad was too busy with work and his studies and I didn't want to trouble him. Do you know why I thought I was colour blind?"

"No."

"We used to play in cornfields, An and I. And I knew that corn flowers were a pale yellow. But then I read in my textbook that 'cornflowers' are blue!"

Catherine smiled understandingly.

"I asked our local librarian, and she was kind enough to explain to me." He reflected, "I told her that we used to hunt this harmful fungus growing on corn ears that looked like grey marble, but she said to me that they grow corn in Mexico to harvest that mushroom. They call it *huitlacoche* or black gold. Anyway, corn is how my dad and Lynette met."

"Perhaps I can get you some cornflowers tomorrow to brighten your study, Mr Yang," Catherine mused. "How long did you stay in the US?"

"About two years. We left after my dad completed his Master's. He was a very good role model. He gave me a window on the world." He stopped to collect himself. "Catherine, I once suffered from imposter syndrome very much. I came to Imperial, prepared to fail the whole degree. I always thought, what if I'm not good enough? What if they find out that I'm not good enough? And what if the offer was made in mistake? I was always chasing and catching up, and unknowingly, I got ahead of the curve. I got a First."

"Well." Catherine cuddled closer. "I think you're smart because you've earned it, and I think you deserve *all* worldly goods."

"That I don't know, but," he clasped their fingers together, "I do know that I already have a treasure."

***

The next day, he told his student, "Amani, do you know that I didn't grow up in big cities, let alone urban areas? In the summers, we would have this one-of-a-kind schoolwork to collect longicorns, vermin that damage tree bark. In springtime we raised silkworms and noted how they turned into moths; and there was a year when we had a plague of locusts. My cousin and I were sent out to collect them with large, empty glass bottles, and we would collect full bottles of them. Then we would feed them to my grandmother's chickens. I've never been a city slicker and I've never been afraid of creepy-crawlies."

He watched his student intently as he reminisced.

"Once we had some termites in the house and Mrs Eden screamed. Gabby's brave enough to take them out and contact the pest control. I've seen tewwibe tsetse and onion thrips." She continued, "Lao-shi, do you know that chickens tend to bully an injured chicken? If a chicken's injured or ill, the rest of the flock will peck at it. Sometimes they will peck at its anus so badly that its intestine leaks so it dies."

"I know that they tend to do it when the coop is crowded."

"Have you ever been bullied?"

"Yes."

"How did you deal with it?"

"I moved to the US, knowing very little English. Missing stationery, name calling, no one ever wanted to work with me on group projects... At first, I just tried to stand it and hoped it would end one day, but it never did. And one day...it happened to be after a Maths class...one day I decided that I'd had enough. And I fought with the bully."

"What happened?"

"I lost, and I cried very hard in the washroom. Then I had an epiphany." He looked at the problem set that Amani had just completed. "I decided that if I could not beat him up, at least I could beat Calculus up."

"You are lying," she stated simply.

"Yes," he admitted. "We were not learning Calculus by then, we were learning trigonometry, but the sentiment is the same."

"That's okay." She looked him in the eye. "Because I lied too."

He waited.

"I didn't shave my head because I want to support children with cancer. People have been…saying things about me, and I don't like it. I don't like it anymore, and I've decided that I've had enough."

He waited some more.

"Lao-shi, do you know why they adopted me? Why they chose *me*?"

"No."

"Because my name starts with the letter 'A'. It's that simple."

He did not know what to say.

Amani continued softly, "When was the last time that you had a haircut, lao-shi?"

"Last month. Mid-January."

"My Mandarin teacher said that it's taboo to have haircuts during January on the Chinese lunar calendar because people believe if they did their uncles would die. And that people dislike the number four because it sounds similar to 'death'."

"Yes."

"It wouldn't matter so much for me, though." She cast her eyes down. "My uncle's already dead. So are my parents. Pretty much everyone I know back home." She then added, "You feel numb when you see so many deaths."

He decided to navigate to another topic. "I have heard of the terrible incident of your neighbour."

"Oh, she was a lovely lady," Amani said haltingly. "Once it lashed it down and I forgot my keys. Gabby was out, so Daniele invited me in for some juice. It was delicious. She said she put chicory in it. She also gave me a huge lolly from the Zoo that said 'Conservation is Sweet'. She had lots of books and she had this wonderful writing desk with hidden drawers. She said it was a butler's desk that she bought from an auction. We chatted and she said she grew up in a bedsitter and her parents would use an ironing board as a makeshift desk for her to study. If I could choose, lao-shi, I'd rather live with my parents in a shanty town in a war zone than playing dolls in this grand place for strangers."

Having said this, Amani excused herself to use the washroom.

***

When she got back, he gave her a piece of paper, on it a maths question.

"After I lost my fight with the bully, I decided that I didn't want to be looked down on again. Maths is wonderful. It doesn't require too much vocabulary, and it allows you to think so you will no longer be fooled by what others have to say. I became very good at maths because of the learning curve. It is very rewarding if you can turn something you were not good at into one of your fortes. Many people have told me that I am not smart, Amani. I wanted to do well in my exams, not because I wanted to prove that they were wrong but because I wanted to do well for my own account."

He showed her the question. "Here's a homework problem that you can consider."

She took the paper and read it out loud:

$$x^2+1+x=0$$

Divide both sides by x, then

$$x+1+1/x=0$$

Rewrite the original equation and you have

$$1+x=-x^2$$

Then you get

$$-x^2+1/x=0$$

$$x^2=1/x$$

$$x^3=1$$

$$x=1$$

If x=1, then

$$1^2+1+1=0$$

$$3=0$$

Where did it go wrong?

"Interesting...like a magic trick." Amani tilted her head, "Let me think about it."

"When you find it out, you'll know that maths can be a game where you play detective."

He stood up, arranged his things, and made to leave.

Georgiana was away for another event. He waited for his Uber and listened as Gabby chatted with a plumber about some university students who had rented the newly vacated house. They didn't seem to mind; they were quite happy to get a large cut on rent in this neighbourhood.

Chance felt he had got something dense off his chest on his car ride back home. For a moment, he wasn't entirely sure who was helping whom...or if he needed someone to talk to more than Amani did.

His Uber driver made a fuss about the 'fart and farce of Brexit' as he sent a message to Nigel Weatherby asking if they had checked Daniele

Vidas' writing desk's hidden drawers. Felipe always liked to debate with taxi drivers, and he only listened. Nigel replied saying that that was where they had found Catherine's letters.

He got back to his flat. The Robinsons were still away, it seemed; a gull squawked somewhere in the rows of large terracotta flowerpots that belonged to Hannah Robinson.

He double checked all his pockets before entering the flat; nothing seemed amiss that day.

He went in and saw Catherine sitting with her elbows on the dining table and her fingers steepled. A vase of cornflowers garnished the table.

"Now, tell me, Mr Yang, what's your best childhood memory?" she asked.

He said resignedly, "I just played *quid pro quo* with my student; why do you think I'll play along now?"

Catherine was miffed.

He moved closer. "Fine, I'll play this game of yours, little catling. My dad and I loved hot soup noodles. There was this couple in our neighbourhood who made great noodles, but they couldn't afford to rent a place at first to start a business. You know what they did? They bought a scrapped bus and turned it into a diner. They would cook where the driver's seat was and sometimes, when people paid, they'd drop the coins. They'd run all over the place. I always helped them to find those coins and they would praise me, saying that I was a good boy and doing the right thing instead of pocketing the money. They managed to get a place eventually, and we ate there always."

He opened the fridge and took out a bottle of mineral water, opened it and took some hasty gulps. The cool liquid slaked his thirst. "We lived in a very kind neighbourhood. Even my dad's superior showed support for him and he often asked his relatives in Shanghai to help him get books on programming languages and TOEFL."

Catherine looked at him. "An was right."

"Huh?"

"She told me that you disliked the number four to such an extent that you drink water in three or five gulps."

"Analysing me now?" He smiled. "I thought that by now you would have noticed that I like my darling to have three or five..." He mouthed the 'o' word.

She blushed and then burst out laughing. "You're a big tease, you know?"

"Yes, yes. And impossible and *very* demanding."

"And a braggart!"

"Now, there's no need to be rude." He teased her, "How about we have some soup noodles for dinner? We'll just have to make do with what's in the fridge. Oh, and we can have a side dish of fried *fava* beans."

"That'd be nice." Catherine was glad that he plumped for playing along.

He put a pot on to boil, took out his thermos, opened it, and was about to clean it when something pricked his finger. "What..."

He moved under the accent lighting and saw blood rushing through a deep cut on his index finger.

They found glass shards in his thermos.

***

Later.

"I'm worried about you," Catherine told him before they went off to Bedfordshire. "I've asked Cecil, and he says it's not alright to carry a taser...not alright at all. He knew someone who got into trouble with a Leatherman. It's one thing to read about crime stories, and it's another when you have to... I shudder to think–"

"There's no need to worry about me." He planted a kiss on her hand and assured her, "I'm not as harmless as you might think. And I don't think it will be necessary for me to carry it. I'll leave it in the flat." He raised her hand. "Look, now we have matching plasters."

"Your student...what did you discuss today?"

"You want me to teach you Calculus?" he joked, tilting his eyebrow.

"Just tell me the small talk."

"I think she's a kind girl and she seems to be in great pain. And everyone has secrets, naturally, so the people in that house are no exception."

"They don't have a butler?"

"No."

"Then we can't blame it on the butler and say the butler did it."

He sensed that Catherine was still unsettled. "Enough about me, little catling, you know the rules: it's your turn to tell me things. How was your day?"

"I went back home in the morning to check on Mr Darcy. I've brought the books; I put them in your study. And I had lunch with my uncle in a restaurant on Aldwych. Then I went to work my shift at the flower academy after lunch. Orla and Melody were...boy, they were in a pretty pickle."

"What happened?"

"Someone brought a thumb drive that had some malware and the computers at the shop were affected and so was the point of sale. We had to reboot the whole thing, and we lost some transaction records. Melody's trying to figure out Valentine's sales now."

He thought for a while and swung his legs over his side of the bed. "Give me a second."

He went to the study, opened a drawer, took out something, and returned to their bedroom.

"This is something that we call a 'USB condom'." He held it up and showed it to her. "It helps to prevent malware and other unpleasant possibilities. This one's new. You can take it to the shop and use it there."

"Oh, thank you. That's very thoughtful." Catherine took it and put it on the nightstand.

They snuggled together, then she said, "I can feel your eyes moving over me, Mr Yang. Do you like what you see?"

"I like to watch you sleep. You sleep very soundly, like a kitten who has played all day."

Catherine nuzzled him, "If you don't like your job, you can quit anytime."

"Don't worry, kitty cat." He grinned. "I intend to do some fishing starting from tomorrow."

***

Days passed and the annoyances continued.

On Wednesday, a drawing pin was taped on his umbrella handle, the sharp end up, on Thursday there was a bag of dog poo in his coat pocket, and on Friday, his teaching materials were superglued together.

He stayed quiet to keep Catherine from worrying.

Saturday came. He arrived at the house at five to ten, and saw a moving truck in front of the newly vacated house.

The students were moving in.

He listened as they shared stories of haunted houses and plans for the weekend and then rang the bell. Gabby opened the door, and he heard Georgiana Eden yelling. "GABBY! GABBY! GET MY PEANUT BUTTER AND PICKLES UP HERE NOW!"

"Sorry about that," Gabby apologised hurriedly, "I presume it's a bad hangover."

He went in. There was a strong smell of cannabis smoke drifting in the air.

A few moments later, Georgiana yelled again: "She's a Peer, SO WHAT! You can't possibly think that she's haute with her Croydon facelifts: Lady Muck drinks *bloody* Armand de Brignac, for God's sake! She's so tacky!"

He sighed, set his bag down on the dining table, and opened his laptop. Amani joined him shortly afterwards.

"Lao-shi, I finally figured out your trick," she said with a wide smile and showed him a sheet of a notebook.

"Very good! Now you know how to play detective with Maths."

He opened a booklet containing her syllabus. "I doubt that the priority of the exam setters is to fail people. They need to balance out the questions: there'll be some easy ones, and there'll be some relatively difficult ones. But you know, you get questions from each type. You'll have Calculus, Sequences and Series, Algebra, Trigonometry. The trick is to get right all the questions that you can get right, and to practise the wrong ones with laser focus."

"I do have a notebook in which I collect the questions that I got wrong, but it takes a lot of time, and it annoys me so much that I made so many mistakes."

He smiled faintly. "It's okay to get them wrong now." He took out a pile of past papers. "The aim is to get them right during your exam. Make good use of your formulae sheet, statistical tables, and your calculator."

He wanted to say 'that's half the battle' but decided against it.

They worked through a set of past papers. Lunch hour arrived. He left his bag and declined Gabby's invitation to taste her roasted chicken and gravy and ventured out down the road across the canal to have a bite at the Primrose Hill Bakery.

It did have wonderful cupcakes.

He checked his phone, sent a couple of emails, and after lunch, he strolled by the canal and made his way back to the Edens'. The house had a fair garden with a patio swing under a white canvas cantilever umbrella and a pergola. The weather that day was enjoyable with tenuous clouds and occasional sun.

He went in and retrieved *The Remains of the Day* and settled on the swing to read.

A few minutes later, Gabby saw him and urged, "Oh! Mr Yang, you mustn't let Mrs Eden see that!"

"I'm sorry?"

"The book! You mustn't let Mrs Eden see that!" She moved closer and warned, "She absolutely abhors that book because she is related to

Lord Rothermere on the distaff side."

"Oh, hmm, I see. I'm sorry, I wasn't aware that–"

"It's fine." She considered, "I just thought that you seem to get on quite well with Amani, and you shouldn't be dismissed for something that...trivial."

He thanked her again and went back to the house. The smell inside still lingered.

Amani was already sitting by his laptop with her headphones on, listening to music.

"When the neighbour was attacked, she was downstairs in their house listening to music as she told us, and their housemaid hoovered upstairs."

He remembered what Nigel Weatherby told him, so he asked her, "Amani, what songs do you like?"

She pulled off one side of her headphones. "Mis-Teeq, Matibeye Geneviève, Busted, Ariana Grande, and McFly."

"I see." He thought for a few seconds. "What books do you like to read?"

"I like the *Hunger Games*. I saw the films," she said as she took off her headphones altogether, "but they forbid me to read it because they say it's too violent." She gave an insouciant shrug. "But life's a million times more violent than the books. I don't think that people can ever make dolphins eat leaves."

He reflected and watched her clear eyes, "That's a very philosophical observation."

"Do you know that, lao-shi, dolphins may appear to be cute and clever, but they can be very mean," Amani said. "Daniele once told me that she understands how detrimental war can be to a child. She'd asked me if I underwent any therapy. She said that someone called Tony Jude or Judt said that it's one thing to live in war and another to live in peace."

"My grandad fought in the war against the Japanese invasion," he said, "and he would always say to my dad that 'We fought the aggressors off so you can study in well-lit classrooms and yet you only like to play marbles'."

"I don't quite see the difference between war and peace," she said. "People hurt me then and people hurt me now."

He thought for a while. "Amani, have Mr and Mrs Eden or Gabby ever mistreated you?"

"No." She seemed to be telling the truth. "They treat me well. I mean...yeah...they treat me well."

He waited for some more.

"Lao-shi," she asked, "what's your stance on nootropics? There are people in my school who take Modafinil."

"I'm against all forms of drugs and substance abuse. I've lost friends because of it." He hesitated and continued, "Last time, I only told you half of the story. There was another boy in my school, he was Malaysian Chinese, and we were the easy targets in our class. His parents worked as physical therapists for a golfer and we always played together. After I fought with the bully that day, I was very weary. I saw the bully and his lackeys pestering my friend and I didn't do anything. The next day, I heard something terrible had happened."

She waited.

"They made him ate shrooms. It's a kind of mushroom that gives you hallucinations. And he thought that a demon was after him and so he ran onto the highway and had a terrible car accident. He was hospitalised for a month, and I locked myself up in my room for a month. One day, I finally worked up the courage to say sorry, so I went to see him. And you know what he told me? He said to me: 'Why are you so stupid? I only did it as a dare, because they said if I did it, I could join them to harry you!' He didn't have to tell me the truth, but he did. In the end, he didn't make it through."

Then he excused himself to use the washroom.

When he came back, Amani asked: "Lao-shi, can you keep a secret?"

"Yes," he offered with all his sincerity.

"So can I."

***

Later.

Their session ended earlier that day because Amani had to attend a volunteer session with her schoolmates.

He arranged his things and found that his mechanical pencil was missing. It was one of his favourites that he had brought from China.

He gave a laboured breath, checked his phone, then found Gabby. She looked out of the window and watched as a black pickup truck took away some furniture from the newly occupied house.

"They are selling Daniele's things," she mulled.

"It seems so," he agreed. "I have a friend who works for the Met and I've heard that the police searched her backyard and found dead cats. "

"Oh...."

He observed her and then said, "Gabby, could you help me with the nanny cam? There's something I would like to check. My mechanical pencil is missing; I must have misplaced it in the dining room. Sorry for being so heedless."

"No, no problem at all." She led him back to the room and held up the camera. "There's an SD card in here that stores all the videos."

He took it out, inserted it onto his laptop. The folder was empty.

"Oh! How very odd!" Gabby exclaimed. "Maybe Mrs Eden did not activate the filming options?"

"Or maybe someone erased them?"

"I don't know anyone who would do that."

"Could it be Amani?"

"I...I wouldn't say so, not quite." She wrung her hands.

"Mrs Parker, has Amani ever misbehaved? Has she ever clogged up your washrooms with water beads? Or put glass shards in your tea? Dog poo in your handbag? Drawing pins in your shoes? Some minibeasts on your scone maybe? Or inside your Dundee marmalade?"

"No. It's...it's not for me to say. It's not my place to say," Gabby said reluctantly as she bottled up.

"That's okay." He stood up and took his bag. "As a tutor, Mrs Parker, one has to prepare for all sorts of situations. I have a friend from Imperial, Julian; he once tutored a girl who took a liking to him. He told me that to avoid unpleasant possibilities, he always had a backup camera. He always carried his clunky video recorder around campus."

He unlocked his phone and found a video clip. "And technology has certainly advanced. You can now hide a camera even on a bag strap." He showed it to her and observed her as the videos played out. "Mrs Parker, I thought that we had a good rapport, and it seems that I'm mistaken. If you wish to make my life and my work difficult, then I have *every* intention to return the favour. And indeed, you don't wish to be dismissed on such a trivial matter now, do you?"

After a leaden pause, she shook her head and said in a feeble voice, "No."

"What happens in this house stays in this house, but I would appreciate it if you let me do my job."

"Yes."

He pocketed his phone and retrieved his mechanical pencil from a chest of drawers.

***

She sat quietly behind the toilet partition and waited until all the twaddle had died down and finally gone.

"I lost, and I cried very hard in the washroom. Then I had an epiphany."

He had shown her brutal honesty, and yet...

If she could choose, she would rather live in a shanty town with her parents in a war zone.... But she could not.

She saw what Georgiana did. She saw her taking Daniele's voice recorder.

She'd seen them arguing.

And she remained silent.

Was she to throw away the roof over her head?

She came out from the partition, washed her hands, splashed her face, and dried off with a paper towel. As soon as she walked out of the washroom, someone called her from behind.

"Amani! It is Amani, isn't it?" She turned and saw Ethan. He wore a dust-tainted pullover and a pair of black trousers.

"Yes." She tried to recall what she knew about him: he was their Head Boy and he was popular. His father worked in the Civil Service or the government or something like that.

"Did you enjoy our event today? I have to say it's the first time that I've ever seen a price gun..."

Oh, boys with their guns, she thought. They wouldn't be so interested in them if they saw how much damage guns bring.

Ethan continued his attempt to engage in small talk. "How did you do on the last Maths mock? They said that Mrs Lehre used past papers from CIE and the questions were really difficult."

"I did alright. Much better than last time, actually," she responded. "I have a new tutor, and he's very patient and encouraging." They talked as they walked out of the second-hand bookstore.

"Which way do you go?" Ethan asked.

"This way." She pointed in the direction of the canal cutting. "I'll walk."

"Oh, I'm heading that way as well." He cleared his throat and added, "I'm going to the Vaughan Williams Memorial Library to see their folk music archive. It's my EPQ project."

A poster of the *Hunger Games* hung in the bookshop's window. She stared at it, perhaps for too long.

"Do you like the Hunger Games?" Ethan asked.

She found him a tad annoying. "Yeah, but I haven't read them..."

"Well, just your luck then." He took off his backpack and took out a copy of *Catching Fire*. "I just finished this. You can borrow it if you like."

"Oh, I don't think that..." she hesitated.

"Come on, a lil extra reading won't take a jiffy." He produced a receipt from Tesco's from his trouser pocket and scribbled with a pen. "Here's my number; tell me if you liked it."

"Hmmm, sure." She took the receipt and the book. "Thanks a bunch, Ethan."

"No biggie." He checked his phone. "Oh, I've got to hurry; need to get there before they close. See you on Monday then. Have a nice weekend."

"See you, you too."

He dashed a short distance, turned sharply, and shouted, "It's Nathan. My name's Nathan!"

Chapter 5

Time plodded its way into March, and he was relieved to see the days getting longer.

The three puzzles revolving around Daniele Vidas' death remained: if it was planned or unpremeditated; the twenty or so dead *sous vide* cats skinned like rabbits buried in her backyard; and her missing voice recorder.

Ambrose Eden was still away and Chance's neighbours, the Robinsons, had returned from their trip to Monte Carlo. There'd been some good news too: Cecil, Catherine's godfather, had been awarded an honorary Doctor of Civil Law degree from Oxford.

Gabrielle Parker had ceased all her misdeeds, and Catherine was a lot happier when he stopped bringing 'foreign objects' back home. He decided to keep quiet about his episode with the housekeeper and instead told her that his student had begun to behave since he had given her a challenge.

He showed Catherine the same question on Mothering Sunday. She willingly accepted it as a challenge, and it took a week for her and her colleagues at the flower academy to figure out the trick. When she found out, she decided to spend a morning finding out where he was the most ticklish. In the end, he had to beg her to stop.

It occurred to him when he drove past the Harmony store on Oxford Street that Catherine had read *Fifty Shades of Grey* under cover of a magazine. He wondered if he had secretly expected or hoped for any punishment.

If only he could shed the past like a snake sheds its skin.

The two missing Brits remained missing, and he still took an Uber to and from work.

Ever since Boris Johnson had made a U-turn and declared he would back Brexit in late February, he had had the chance to sample the mixed views of Uber drivers.

One told him that he wanted to 'twat that bastard' and another said that 'it's time to stop hugging the skirts of nurses in Brussels. If they cannot stop the influx of asylum seekers...at least Britain needs to fend off the refugees...regain decision-making power from the bliddy Romans, Vikings, and Normans and their wild orgies...and end the limbo that they are in'. Another driver, citing Hannah Arendt, said that Brexit was 'a temporary alliance between the elite and the heavy mob'.

Another expressed her frustration because her sister had lived in Lisbon for more than fifteen years, which deemed her unqualified to vote in the Referendum. 'But', his driver added, 'Brexit may not be all irksome. There's an irony of sorts.' She explained how female drivers used to pay low insurance because they tend to be more careful and hence have fewer accidents. But the EU intervened and ruled this as gender discrimination, and the resulting equalization meant that now female drivers paid higher fees, and male drivers slightly lower ones.

Weeks passed. Amani gradually caught up with Calculus, and

she seemed to move down the learning curve just as he had expected. They worked hard to ensure that she could attempt all the questions in the given timeframe. Sometimes, they would watch a video on MIT's Integration Bee or solve a puzzle from the Royal Statistical Society's previous Christmas quizzes.

He kept on reading, and he had finished the books *The Remains of the Day* and the Lecter tetralogy. Then he finally understood Catherine's previous references to the Castle of Threave and Oliver Twist. He had also read her and Daniele Vidas' fanfiction stories, and he had found that they wrote touchingly and lovingly.

He had also learnt of Catherine's other ships. Her favourite pairings include Mrs Bradley and her chauffeur George from *The Mrs Bradley Mysteries*, the policeman that Harrison Ford played and the widow in *Random Hearts*, Margaret and Thomas from *Lark Rise to Candleford*, and Miss Audrey and Edmund Lovett from *The Paradise*.

Catherine asked him how he found the Lecter books, and he told her that there were some words in there, like 'chifforobe' that he couldn't visualise and some religious allusions that he didn't understand. Still, he had found an excellent source online called *A Connoisseur's Guide*. He told her that he could see where the allure of the story was and yet he wondered what had happened to Lecter's other victims, to the nurse he attacked, and to Chilton, as he recounted one episode that he had had with Felipe:

One day, they had been out for lunch in Osaka, and Felipe, an avid mystery reader, made his way through a book as they ate. Suddenly, he rushed out of the room and almost knocked over a waiter. When he returned, he looked disturbed. Chance showed concern for his boss and asked what had happened. Felipe said that he had thrown up because the book was too vivid and excessively descriptive. Chance didn't believe him, so he took the book and flipped through it roughly, and that alone made him queasy.

The book, which was called *The Disease that Leads to Killing*, was by a Japanese writer named Takemaru Abiko, who drew intricate details from the real case of a serial killer who targeted young girls aged four to seven in Saitama, Tokyo, between 1988 and 1989. The offender abducted, tortured, raped, and killed his victims, ate their bones with soy sauce, never repented, and never apologised to any of the victims' families.

In the end, he and Catherine agreed that what had not been written was most scary.

***

Time passed as his Uber fare accumulated.

In early March, Lynette, his stepmother, had stopped by briefly and had a lovely meal with them and An at the Palomar.

On 10th March, the Dragon Heads-raising Day, he had another haircut.

He and Catherine sometimes talked about World War Two, Clement Attlee, Lord Halifax, and how Churchill had compared Labour to the Gestapo. He had seen her grandmother's Defence Medal and her grandfather's George Cross.

Catherine reflected that she and her pen pal decided that Hitler was to blame after all. She continued, "If there was no war, then Miss Kenton would probably never have left Darlington Hall...or Lecter's family would never have died such a tragic death." She moved on, saying that Hitler had planned the assassinations of Sigmund Freud, Virginia Woolf, and EM Forster.

They also talked about courtesy and dignity. He said: "People respect you or disdain you because of the schools you went to. It's not right, but it's often the case." He'd also told Catherine what Felipe once said to him: "if everyone had a happy childhood, we would not have such crowded prisons, barracks, and asylums".

They now spent the nights at Catherine's house and would always watch a film after dinner. Mr Darcy continued to play the third wheel contentedly. Sometimes, he would step on the piano keys as Catherine played a vignette by Harry Warren called 'Just Love'.

One night, after watching *Sabrina*, some eye candy for a change, he asked her if she wanted to go to Paris for the Easter holidays. Georgiana had told him beforehand that they were going away to Northumberland. If Catherine did, he would need to apply for a new Schengen visa.

The truth was, he wanted to escape the first week of April when Joyce Peng had died in his flat last year.

He wanted to bring up the topic of Catherine's now-deceased pen pal numerous times but could not bring himself to break the news.

One day, after dinner, he had a shower. Afterwards, he saw Catherine perching on one side of their bed, sniffling, her eyes red and her hand clutching his tablet.

"What's wrong?" he sat down on the bed and asked with concern.

She shook her head in resignation, and her voice strained. "Nothing, really. I...I read a story, and it made me sad. And I could not stop thinking that sometimes people say goodbye not knowing that they will never see each other again. I wish for all my ships to live to a hundred and fifty years old. You must think that I'm really silly."

"Of course not," he said. "These are sincere and genuine emotions and I respect them." He paused. "If you would permit me one observation?"

"Hmm?" she sobbed slightly.

"Your parents. I think you want them to live forever."

"That I do." She snuffled.

He took the tablet and had a quick scan. It was a fanfiction story about how Miss Kenton's daughter, Catherine, breaks the news of her mother's passing to Mr Stevens.

He thought for a moment and said, "We can come up with alternate endings. Let's see... how about that Miss Kenton was an agent from MI5 sent to spy on Lord Darlington?"

"Then why did she leave?"

He considered for a few seconds. "I believe that they had already told us the answer. 'Sally'—it's their secret code name so Miss Kenton knew it was time for her to embark on a new mission. And now after her retirement, she needed Mr Stevens' help to locate lost Nazi gold in Buenos Aires. I can think of a road film and an adventure... For safety reasons, they needed another cover, so she became Mrs Bentley travelling with her chauffeur and solving mysteries across the Americas."

"Then she must have got into the wrong set..."

"Well, I do believe there is something called 'role reversal'?"

"I do appreciate your effort, Mr Yang." She looked at him, her eyes still dreary.

His fingers brushed her cheek lightly. "You know what your problem is, little catling? Your problem is that you're a yes but-ter, and I'm a why not-ter."

She laughed a bit.

"Come here." He hugged her. "I'm here to buck you up. I've promised to make you happy every day, and it wouldn't do if we went to sleep without a smile on your face."

"Maybe you can come up with some...scenarios of the kitchen scene?" she requested.

"That I can do." He thought for a few seconds. "Here are my takes. How about if she asks him, How do you say, 'I'm looking at what I want' in Italian?' Or she says to him, 'You're a well-read man, but have you read any racy books?' Or he tells her that 'I have had you up here under false pretences...'"

"Good stuff," Catherine mused. "They sound very out-of-character, but I like them. One thing I liked about *Sabrina* is that it mentions *The Remains of the Day*. I even acquired a Remains of the Day lunchbox from *Waiting for Guffman*."

"I'm glad you think so," he added. "How about she says 'Let's meet under the Swiss Glockenspiel in London a year from now? Be there or be square'. Or 'Now that you're here, I would very much like to keep you in my sight'."

Catherine breathed profoundly and gave a straining smile. "Stop it. Now you're just *ruining* my favourite lines and my favourite memories."

They got into bed, and he used an eyedrop. Then he said, "I read some research by UCL the other day saying that declining eyesight can be improved by looking at a deep, red light."

"Another perk for Clarice, then."

"I guess that Anthony Hopkins must have had very dry eyes when he played Lecter without blinking most of the time."

Catherine recalled, "Do you know that he wrote a sequel script to the *Hannibal* film? He has his own favourite headcanon. He said in an interview that he believed that they'd become lovers! And there's a rumoured third ending that was filmed but never shown. Oh, and they say that *The Remains of the Day* has a three-hour director's cut version. I hope they release it sometime soon; I'd love to read the scripts as well."

He thought for a moment. "In Chinese when we say that someone has red eyes, it means that they are jealous."

"Not eating vinegar?"

"'Eating vinegar' is more for couples and lovers. In Japanese, they call it '*yakimochi*'. And 'red eyes' are more like green-eyed monsters in that they feel jealous over others' possessions."

"It reminds me of alexandrite. It's a gem that appears green under daylight and red in artificial light. My mother has a necklace of it."

He recalled, "Did you wear it on New Year's Eve?"

"Yes, I did. And no wonder," Catherine reflected. "Felipe once told me that of all of the *mochis*, his least favourite one is *yakimochi*."

"I wonder if Mr Benn...I hope he's a decent feller. And if he had feelings for Miss Kenton when they worked together...Maybe Miss Kenton is Mr Stevens to Mr Benn, emotionally."

"Oh, I hadn't thought about it like that..."

"No, never mind. I just remembered my parents. They didn't seem to be very close. We had a small allocated apartment and my dad always slept on a single camp bed next to mine. He told me he didn't want to wake my mom up after his night shifts or before his early mornings.

He always smelt like tobacco, soap, and motor oil. Why don't you tell me something about your parents? I know that they loved the Chelsea Flower Show."

"They loved the arts. Theatre and opera and musicals. They went to Glyndebourne and Garsington all the time. Once they went to see Mark Rylance acting at Shakespeare's Globe. A mob of motorbike riders came and started to shout. Mark Rylance was on stage, and he responded to them in his Shakespearean dialogue, and their conversation continued somehow miraculously for ten or so minutes. My parents always marvelled at this. I don't think I ever saw them have a row. My father had a full twelve years on my mum.... They always pampered and cherished me. My mum called me her lamb..."

She continued, "Father was quite busy working for the Foreign Office, and sometimes he'd go abroad for long trips. My mum wrote for *Granta* occasionally and she made wonderful pickled walnuts. She had two Worth dresses passed on from her mother. Maybe I'll show them to you tomorrow. We can't have Mr Darcy near them just in case."

"Pickled walnuts?" he asked. "With dry walnuts?"

"With fresh walnuts when they are still green."

After a while, he said, "I don't quite remember my mother in much detail. In China, we say that children tend to lose their memories before changing teeth after they shed their deciduous teeth. If we crossed paths on the streets, I don't know that I'd be able to recognise her. Those hazy memories...I remember that on the night when they told me they were getting a divorce, I cried myself to sleep, and I woke up crying. She remarried shortly afterwards. We're quite distant now, but she keeps in contact with my aunt."

Catherine decided it was time to put a smile on his face. "Do you know that there was a musical production of *The Remains of the Day*? Mick and I went to see it. It was good, and it gave me inspiration to write a few songfics."

"A musical? I can't quite picture Mr Stevens singing."

"What were you like as a boy?"

"Very naughty. My aunt told me that I'd grab a spider and put it on An. Luckily, she doesn't seem to remember it now. She only remembered my good qualities after she changed teeth. In summer, we'd buy watermelon in sacks. They were very cheap, like two pence for a kilo. We'd eat them, and I'd make helmets out of the rinds. Ah, and I liked to mend my pen."

"You what?"

"Mechanical pencils and fountain pens were a rarity then. It was tough to save up and buy another if you broke one, so I always fixed them with some extra springs and metal tubes. My dad was a fitter and a crafter."

"Oh, sorry," she said, "I thought you meant 'mending pens' in Mr Darcy's way."

"I'm not quite sure that I follow you, Catherine."

She explained the innuendo of mending pens in Jane Austen's novel.

He gasped. "I'm glad you told me. I could have told my student without knowing it."

They stayed silent for a while. Just as he thought that Catherine was asleep, she crooned, "But do you watch erotica, Mr Yang? Don't lie, or I will know."

"Well, I cannot say that I've never watched any, but I can say that

I've not watched any since we got together."

"Hmm...You do know how to put things. Felipe's wrong: you're definitely no taciturn fella."

He turned to face her. "Do I get to ask questions?"

"Go ahead."

"I want to know when did you first develop a liking towards me?"

"When do you think?" Catherine tantalised.

"When I massaged your ankle?"

"No."

"When our fingers touched at Ladurée?"

"It was dreamlike, but still no."

"Tell me. Tell me *cuando, cuando, cuando*."

Catherine laughed. "Fine, I'll tell you. I'll put you out of your misery, Mr Yang. It was when you told me that you enjoyed listening to my childhood episodes that time when we met under the Glockenspiel."

"I see."

"But do you know what I thought when you cared for my turned ankle?"

"No."

She sighed slightly. "I wanted to tell you that I had another bruise on my hip needing attention, but I didn't because I didn't want to be too forward, and you were leaving."

"I appreciate your reticence, but I'm not trained to read people's minds." He mused loudly, "Anytime you need anything, you must tell me, and I'll try to deliver."

"Now I know, and I will."

They cosied up for longer, and he asked, "Enough questions for tonight?"

"No," she responded defiantly.

"Go ahead."

"I want to know what's in your pink pouch."

"My pink pouch?"

"Yes. You use a green pouch with a tiger avatar to collect your receipts so you can shred them. And you have this mysterious pink pouch with a panda avatar that you always bring into the bathroom."

"Are you a curious catling with twenty-one questions? Hold on for a sec." He got off the bed and found the item in question. "How'd you like a sensual experience, Catherine?"

"As in?" She sat up eagerly.

He unzipped his toiletry bag or the so-called 'pink pouch' and took out various nail clippers, nail files, and earpicks.

"As in for me to pick your ear?" He raised one bamboo earpick with a white plush end.

"I don't recall the last time anyone ever did it for me," she said hesitantly.

"Would you like me to?"

"I guess it won't hurt?"

"No. I'll be careful." He asked her to lie down in his lap. "Don't talk for now."

*Having your ears picked by someone is a very sensual experience, unlike any other...*she thought as excitement, fear, and a tickling sensation whirled around her head.

He picked her left ear, then used the soft plush to clean the remnants, and finally an alcoholic cotton swab to finish, and then repeated the process for her right.

"Coo." Catherine sat up. "Now I know how it feels for Mr Darcy when I clean his ears." She tilted her head. "I feel like a cat in Copenhagen."

He smiled. "I had a cat once. His name was Sonic, after Sonic the Hedgehog. He was an American Curl. He was very naughty and inquisitive, opening drawers here and doors there. He was always like a kitten. I think you're like him, in a good way."

"So, you just want me to be a *naughty* kitten then?"

He put away the pink pouch and returned to their cocoon. "I think I have a high tolerance for naughtiness. You bite...misplace my car keys... give me the silent treatment.... Oh, let's not forget that you also once attempted to break my spectacles."

"But you like me heaps?"

He smiled. "Yes."

"How much?" she questioned with a lifted brow.

"No limits whatsoever." He said, "You're most welcome to spill coffee on my favourite shirt. Should I bring it out and lay it on the bed tomorrow morning? Or you can maul it."

She considered with certain intimations of seriousness, "There's an Italian café around the corner that I like to frequent. Maybe I can get some quality coffee from there."

"Sounds nice."

They settled down. Just as he thought she had drifted to sleep; she breathed a question: "How much?"

"I love you, Catherine."

CHAPTER 6

The Sunday before the Easter holidays, he went to work as usual on an Uber.

It was a misty day.

As he was about to ring the bell, the door opened, and Georgiana Eden rushed out. Her eyes were red, and her hair matted.

She saw him, and croaked dejectedly, "Mr Yang, are you married?"

"No, Mrs Eden, I'm not."

"Good for you," she spat out and left.

He went into the house. There was mess everywhere.

Stains on the wallpaper in the drawing room indicated someone had puked there; a dozen Riedel glasses were shattered on moquette carpets; raw eggs were dripping down the banister; fragments of uncooked spaghetti flooded the London Skyline chess set; the glass case of Sagrada Família toppled over, and damask cushions were pierced with a replica set of Wiener Werkstätte cutlery.

Gabby and Amani were in the kitchen, apparently recovering from their shock.

"Lao-shi," Amani said when she saw him; she was still in her pyjamas. "What do you do when you are angry and sad? I play *Angry*

Birds."

"Well," he said, "I shred paper or I buy crisps and crush them."

"Oh, good Lord! But you wouldn't waste food, would you?" Gabby said, holding an empty bag of flour, watching its contents clogging the sink. A broken pot of Kimberly Queen fern lay beside her feet.

"No, I make fried rice with them." He wanted to find a clean spot to place his bag, but he could not. The Edens had a good collection of Joseph Joseph kitchenware, now bestrewing the floor. Their Gaggenau appliances were no longer shining.

"I feel sinful to throw away all this food," Gabby said as she looked down at the floor scattered with mung beans.

They spent that day cleaning the kitchen. When they finished, he noticed how Gabby kept on staring at the heap of mung beans that they had managed to collect. She looked as if she were standing on a precipice and would collapse and fall at any moment.

So, he offered: "Mrs Parker, do you perhaps know how to grow bean sprouts?"

The housekeeper pulled herself out of her musings and looked at him with a puzzled face. "I'm sorry, Mr Yang, you've lost me for a moment."

He turned to his student, "Amani, perhaps we can do a biology experiment? Why don't we grow some bean sprouts, and you can record their growth and make some line graphs?"

Amani nodded.

"When I was little, we always grew bean sprouts in winter." He rolled up his shirt sleeves while trying to keep his tone cheerful. "We grew them to add a bit of flavour to the table. It's effortless. You only need a big, clean bowl, and some unskinned mung beans, or black beans or soybeans work as well, and water. Some even make them with raw peanuts." He took a porcelain bowl and moved the beans in there.

"Amani, could you help me with the beans?" He handed her the bowl.

"Sure, what should I do?"

"Pick out those with broken skin and incomplete ones," he said and turned to the housekeeper. "Mrs Parker, could you help us boil some water?"

"Of course." Gabby rose and put the kettle on.

Amani did excellent work in screening the beans, and the kettle sang just as she finished.

"Now-" He went into the drawing room and retrieved a fork from a cushion, cleaned it, and handed it to the housekeeper. "I'll pour hot water and please use the fork to spin the contents clockwise."

Gabby took the fork and did as she was told.

"Why do we need to use hot water? Wouldn't the heat cook them?" Amani wondered.

"Hmm...I'm not sure why. My dad told me that we need to use boiling water to wake them up. Do tell me if you find a more scientific explanation."

Gabby continued to spin the contents. After a while, he took the fork and caught a few broken beans that floated on the water.

"What do we do now?" Amani asked.

"Now, we wait," he said. "We wait for the water to cool down. And tonight, Amani, pour it out and replace it with cold water. Tap water will do. Wait for a bit and then pour it out again." He looked at the kitchen cabinets. "Mrs Parker, do you have any gauze for cooking?"

"I have some cotton cheese bags...not sure if they will do." She stood and took one out. It was almost the size to cover the porcelain bowl.

"That should work. So, tonight, Amani, replace the water and pour it out. Then wet a cotton bag and place it on top of the beans. If you want, you could find something heavy to put on top of the cotton bag. The heavier the weight, the faster the beansprout will grow."

Gabby thought for a while. "I have a mortar and pestle set... It's granite. I suppose we could use that."

"But please remember not to get any cooking oil inside the bowl."

Amani asked him for the instructions again, noted them down, and clarified a few points. Before leaving, he saw his student still had a long face, so he asked her why.

"My friend Nathan," she said, "he lent me his *Hunger Games* books and Georgiana found out. She reproved him for giving me 'twaddle to read', and she took away my phone and banned me from the WiFi."

He waited.

"He's been very helpful, and sometimes I ask him Maths questions. I don't understand why it's not okay for some extra reading. Everybody in my class reads the *Hunger Games*."

He considered, "Amani, would it make you feel better if I help you with this matter?"

"Help me how?" she asked with a curious tone.

"How did she ban you? Did she change the password of your WiFi?"

"No, she used an app on her phone to block my computer."

He inhaled deeply. "There's something called a 'Media Access Control' address, or a MAC address associated with each device. We might be able to spoof it, so the router mistakes your device as another so we can bypass the ban."

"Can we please try? I'll bring my laptop down now."

Amani came back with her laptop, he tried it, and it worked.

"Thank you, lao-shi." She held her computer. "Thank you."

"Just be careful not to let Mrs Eden find out."

Later, Gabby saw him to the door.

"Mrs Parker–" he paused. "I sense that you are afflicted. If there's anything that I can help with, please don't hesitate to ask."

"Thank you, Mr Yang." She gave him a wistful smile. "I'm grateful to have my job, and I don't want to lose it."

"Of course." He nodded understandingly.

"I hope–" She spoke as if she had a frog in her throat. "I hope for Amani to do well in her exams so she can leave this house."

***

He got back to his flat at three-thirty, feeling shitty.

Catherine was reading on his tablet by the dining table and scribbling at times.

"How was your morning?"

"It was alright."

He washed his hands, drank some tea, and still felt disconcerted. Then he decided to shred some paper.

He went to his study, took out his green pouch where he collected receipts from daily spending and grocery shopping, had a quick look through, and noticed that Catherine had added in her portion as well.

He turned on his shredder and fed the receipts in one by one.

"Bad day, huh?" She moved beside him like a cat.

"No." He decided to shed his misery and squeezed a smile. "Valentine."

Catherine smiled at him then said worriedly, "Mr Yang, there seems to be some... eggshell and flour on the back of your shirt. Are you keeping another naughty cat somewhere else that I'm not aware of?"

He turned and kissed her hard. "I already have my hands tied with *one* naughty catling. And I very much prefer to keep it that way."

"Good-o." She giggled and patted the mess away. "I'll spare you the handcuffs then. But...what happened?"

"There was a hoo-ha in their kitchen. Oh, we're also doing a biology experiment to grow some bean sprouts. Amani seems very interested in it."

"Bean sprouts, you say. Maybe we can grow some as well?"

"Uh-huh. It takes some time and care. Let's wait until we get back from Paris."

"Oh, An told me yesterday that she's organising an event with her society on Chinese musical instruments and asked if we'd like to go?"

"When is it?"

"Later at six."

"Sure, why not?" he said. Then he remembered something. "Have you ever brought up the topic of fanfiction with An?"

"Not really, no. I don't think so."

"Do you believe in telepathy?" he asked. "The other day, she told me an episode from her translation class. Her professor used the Lecter books to illustrate how hard it is to translate novels. She said that if you don't know that a starling is a type of bird, you won't understand why he tells her to fly back to school. And in some Chinese versions, they translate 'Starling' and make it sound like 'Stalin'."

"No..." Catherine made an awful face. "That's why I always read in the original language whenever possible to make sure that nothing is lost in translation."

"Now that she ended up in South America, I hope they don't play 'Macarena' that often." He fed some more receipts into the machine; its destructive buzzing was somehow soothing. Then he noticed something strange. "The Italian coffee place around the corner that you mentioned the other day...is it the one next to Adecco on Kingsway?"

"Yep."

He held up one receipt and examined it. "That's weird, I go to that place sometimes, and they charge me £3.75 for a salad wrap. Why is it only £3 for you?"

"Oh." Catherine smiled ruefully. "There's this time that I didn't bring enough change and the couthie chap at the till told me it was alright. And whenever I go, he would...you know, it's like sometimes you get a free cup of coffee at Pret."

Why do I sense something fishy going on?

He put away the shredder. "Let's go down there now."

Catherine smiled wittily. "Why in such a hurry, Mr Yang?"

"I haven't had lunch, and I guess I'd like some salad wraps very much." He made up a ready excuse.

He grabbed his overcoat, waited for Catherine, and they ventured downstairs.

In less than five minutes, they entered the café.

"Hey, pet, how's your day? All right?" the guy at the till simpered.

"Not too bad. Just grabbing a snack." Catherine lingered at the food shelves, "Hubert, what would you recommend?"

"We got some great swede gnocchi today," Hubert offered. "I can heat it up for you in the oven. Got any plans for Easter, Catherine? My sister's planning a knees-up at her gaff, and I was wondering if you might fancy coming? You've got a lovely necklace there. I love nature, and I love birds and bees."

"Ta. I got it as a wonderful Valentine."

"Oh, you seeing someone?" The guy seemed upset and took up his phone with a grunt.

"Yeah, he's the bee's knees."

"Noice..."

Chance watched them interact with rapt attention like a vigilant cat.

"I think I'll have some of those gnocchi," Catherine then said with a tone of desperation. "Dash it! I forgot to bring my purse, look at me."

"No problem," Hubert offered, "Put it on our tab." He added, "You're our regular."

"Thanks a million." Catherine smiled and shrugged. "That won't be necessary though."

"I've got it covered." He stepped forward and put a salad wrap on the till. "Sorry for troubling you *always*."

"No worries, matey," Hubert answered with a swing of his hand.

They got back to their building. During their ride in the lift, Catherine said. "Is that why?"

"Why what?" he played his card of innocence.

"Is that what I think it is? Can it be that our Mr Yang shows his concern for his nearest and dearest a little *too* attentively?"

"I just don't want people to harbour false illusions. That's all." He shied away.

"Mind you." Catherine pinned him onto the lift mirror and purred, "Now that I know where you are the most ticklish don't make me force it out. Huh?"

"Are you attempting to distress my second favourite shirt with gnocchi, kitty cat?" he countered jocularly.

Catherine sniffed around his face like a frisky cat. "Why do I sense some sourness in the air? Especially around here. Has anyone been eating vinegar today?"

"Oh, *yes*, I'm very, very sour right now." He held her tight. "You know what I'm going to do with you when we get back?"

"Are you going to put me on the naughty step? Or are you going to do my lips a service again?" Her lips quirked.

"I'm having some sweetmeat."

"Will that be me? Seems that someone will be in for a treat then."

"You know the rules. Never ask–"

'Ninth Floor.' The lift door opened and their neighbour, Eddy Robinson, looked at them wide-eyed.

"Oh, sorry, Eddy, we're just fooling around." Catherine peeled herself off him and laughed.

"Good to see you guys dancing cheek to cheek." Eddy gave a big, aw-shucks grin. "Reminds me of the days when we're palsy-walsy...and you know, the barn stories."

He stood aside with his luggage and umbrella; his face frazzled.

Chance felt himself blushing like a flamingo as they stepped out of the lift, "Sorry about that. Travelling again?"

"Yes. The Hague. Is it raining?" Eddy Robinson asked, his voice gravelly.

"A bit drizzly. Safe travels," Catherine said.

"Cheers. G'day," Eddy Robinson replied as the lift door closed.

***

They got back to their flat, feeling a bit exhilarated.

The sky was overcast. The drip-drip had turned to a downpour in an instant. Rain splattered on their glass balcony door.

"Hannah told me about this spinning class near the London Transport Museum. Perhaps we should try it this weekend? She vouches for it," Catherine suggested.

"Sure, why not?" He put down the food and set the table. "And afterwards, you'll for sure sleep like a kitten who has been playing all day."

"We shall see." She smirked. "You remember what happened when we toured the Jubilee Walkway? Perhaps next time we can walk to Poplar, and I'll show you where they filmed *Call the Midwife*. They say that Stalin lived there briefly as well."

They ate their late lunch, discussing their travelling arrangements for their upcoming trip to Paris. Afterwards, Catherine stretched. "Now, Mr Yang, we might as well continue our *tête-à-tête* from the lift. What was it that you were proposing?"

"I've had quite a sour day today, and I hope to have an exquisite dessert. And I've heard that if you indulge in the afternoon, you can burn off the calories more easily." He stood up, opened the fridge, and took out two Braeburn apples. "Would you like to cook it with me? I've noticed that you have a copy of the *Joy of Cooking* in your kitchen on top of your fridge. Cooking can be a sensual experience at times."

"What are we having?" She joined him by the countertop.

"Candy apples, Chinese version." He took out a shallow plate, dropped a thin layer of flour, and made some batter with water only. Catherine helped him to wash, pare, cut, and core the apples.

"I saw you gawking at a girl's candy apple the other day," he said light-heartedly.

"Did I?"

"Yes," he said. "And I thought whatever my kitty cat wants, I must deliver."

"Are you planning to dote on me?" Catherine said with amusement.

"Do you want me to?"

"It does have a certain appeal."

He dipped the apple wedges in the batter, making sure to cover all sides. Then he took out a frying pan, a bottle of peanut oil, and a bag of table sugar.

Catherine watched as he heated the pan, added oil, and fried the apples until they turned golden. Then he placed the wedges on the plate and re-battered them and fried them again. He then put them on a kitchen towel to remove the residual oil.

"Will you prepare a bowl of water? Mineral water," he instructed.

Catherine took out a large bottle of Highland Spring and did as she was told. Then he poured a generous pile of sugar into the pan, turned the heat to medium, and simmered it until the sugar turned into a glow of orange syrup. A few seconds later, he put in the apple wedges and rolled them in the pan.

Catherine passed him a large plate where he let the apples fall.

He took out a fork and handed it to her. "Try it before it gets cold."

Catherine took the fork and picked up a wedge. Traces of the sugar coating drifted in the air in long, transparent threads. "Wow," she said. "This is new."

He offered the bowl of water. "Put it in, so the sugar solidifies."

She did and the fruit wedge now looked candied. She took a bite. "Umm...it's a performance of a sort."

"I'm glad you like it." He took up a pair of chopsticks and tasted it. "In China, cooking sweet potatoes this way is a famous dish."

They shared the dessert, standing. Then Catherine said, "Are you trying to woo me, Mr Yang? Maybe I should make you sour more often."

"I don't mind being sour at all, if it's lemony," he smirked. "Do you want me to show you?" He slunk by her and kissed off some sugar on her lips.

"Hmm. I would love to, but–" Catherine eyed the oven timer. "First things first. We have an event to attend. An's waiting. We might still make it on time."

***

The next morning, they slept in and had a late brunch.

Catherine said with a hint of annoyance, "Mr Yang, it seems that my life has been too sweet recently and I've developed a toothache. I have this molar that always gives me trouble." She pressed her left cheek gently. "Maybe I need to go to the dentist before we take off for

Paris." She added, "Mick trained as a dentist, but he decided to become a choreographer. There's a dental practice on Long Acre, and one of his classmates works there. I might make an appointment before work today."

They parted. He got to the Edens' and heard touches of laughter coming out of the house.

Ambrose Eden was back.

'Yes, we have ambitious plans for our girl,' he heard him saying.

The couple were posing for an interview with a philanthropic cause that they supported.

Chance went into the dining area. Amani stared at the bowl of beans. He had a look: the beans had already soaked up water and shed their husks.

"If we can remove all the husks, then change the water and wait, by tomorrow, they should be growing." He settled and opened his laptop.

Amani took the bowl, filled it with water, and used a slotted spoon to scoop out the husks. "Lao-shi, are you married?"

"No."

"But you are seeing someone?"

"Yes."

Amani washed the spoon, poured out the water, replaced the wet cotton bag, and put on the granite mortar. "I saw you and your girlfriend last night." She dried her hands. "Nathan likes folklore and folk music. We saw you last night at King's College London. Your girlfriend, is she a musician? She had this large case for a slender guitar."

"Ah," he said. "That's my cousin An. We are as close as siblings and she helped to organise that event. And that's a *pipa* that she played. But my girlfriend was there as well."

The word sounded foreign to him; Catherine meant so much more than that.

"What's she like?" Amani sat beside him and asked.

"Well..." he mused. "She's a florist, and she's really sweet, and she's a cinephile, a book worm...and a..."

Gabby came into the kitchen bearing a tea tray. She hiccupped all along. "Yex. So... ye...sorry."

"She's a cinephile and an ailurophile," he said intentionally.

"What's an 'ailurophile'?" his student asked.

"Just a fancy way of saying a cat lover."

"Oh. I'm more of a dog person." Amani smiled. "Nathan has a beagle. He's so cute. His name is Sherlock."

"Do you like *cats*, Gabby?" he asked.

"No! Yex, well...yex, no," the housekeeper replied too quickly and coughed. "Yex, it's, yex, so, Oh! I've...yex..."

He took a bottle of untouched mineral water that he had brought, opened it, and handed it to Gabby. "Try to take some water and swallow it very slowly, maybe in seven sips?"

She shot him a tentative glance and tried.

It worked.

"Ugh." Gabby recovered herself. "I don't know what to say."

"As they say, there's more than one way to skin a cat." He added, "I've heard that holding your breath works as well."

"Speaking of cats," Amani dropped in casually, "Nathan told me that in medieval times, people would use sheep or horses' intestines to make strings, but they called it 'catgut'."

Gabby gave a slight tremor. "Oh, I better bring them their tea." She refilled the teapot and left in a hurry.

Amani showed him her latest Maths mock papers. She had got the Calculus question correct but not the hypothesis testing one, so they spent their session that day on using the STAT function on her calculator to find the Z value quicker and later discussing the taxicab number. He also showed her how to use Wolfram Alpha to check step-by-step integration and differentiation problems.

By the time they had finished, the interview crew had gone.

He said goodbye to his student and the housekeeper, wished them a good Easter holiday, and went outside to wait for his Uber. Ambrose Eden was out as well with a set of luggage.

"Travelling again, Mr Eden?" he asked.

"Huh," Ambrose gave a terse and peremptory reply. "How's the girlie doing?"

"Well," he said. "She's doing well. I think she would secure a B and we can hope for an A. There are still some weak areas that–"

"Don't expect too much from her," his employer said with a snap and answered his phone with a vitriolic tone. "Yes, I'll be back tonight. Meet me tomorrow at the Karsmakers Coffee House. Right. My comment? He has underwhelmed. You think 'underwhelmed' is a strong word?" He laughed. "The Johnny-come-lately is a moron and an oxymoron. He's enjoying his pumpkinification. He's no maximalist. He's a sciolist. It's pure theatre and complete hogwash! We shall expect foreign policies that harm our economic policies and economic policies that mar our social policies. They'll swat everyone with the invisible slapping hand. Both are unpalpable and unacceptable. No, no, no. Budget fraud is not pertaining to the EU Commission only. I'll not be surprised if those scaremongers and their cabal don't spend a *penny* of that trousered money on the NHS. It's a feat to turn a fish tale into an extravaganza that goes down the back of our sofa. No, I won't lower myself to the oik's level and punch below the belt. He'll only be a pork barrel of laughs. Do you know how to raise hell? You have a Tory panel and a Labour speaker. Let's put those three on a hot air balloon and see who survives!" His cab came, and he left without saying goodbye.

A moment later, Chance's Uber arrived. As he was about to get into the car, Georgiana Eden bawled as she hastened out of the house. "Mr Yang!"

He turned. Her eyes were bloodshot and she clenched her teeth and twisted her jaw a bit too frequently. It was apparent that she was under another set of influences.

"Yes, Mrs Eden?"

"Did you or did you not TAMPER with the WiFi setting in my house!?"

"Well...yes. I did. I thought–"

"You thought, you thought! I did not pay you to think and do whatever you wish to interfere with my affairs! Do you have any children, Mr Yang? Do you know about parenting at all? You're not doing us any favours by allowing her to access disturbing information! I'll not allow my staff to get away with cheeking their employers! I'm sorry but Mr Yang, I shall not tolerate such contumacious insolence! I thank you for your help, and your service is no longer needed!"

"Very well, Mrs Eden, if that's what you wish," he said. "Please tell Amani that if she has any problems regarding Maths, she can reach out to me anytime."

"That won't be necessary!" Georgiana Eden spluttered abrasively and turned back, swinging her capelet.

His Uber driver honked, and he left.

He got back to his flat with a heavy heart. Catherine was making juice with chicory.

"Felipe called today, said he might come to London over Easter. He got a promotion," she said as she cut some celery stalks.

"I see." He felt reassured that they were going away to Paris. He didn't want to know any more crinkum-crankum about the Sancho Panza of Boston or how Felipe aided and abetted with its disappearance.

"Anything bothering you, Mr Yang?" She seemed to sense his dismay.

He sighed. "I got the pink slip. I've been dismissed." He told her what had happened and how his employer had told him off.

"Oh, knickers to them! Take heart, it's their loss." Catherine diced an apple. "You need a good holiday now and a new lease of life."

He leaned on the sofa arm and rubbed his temples. "Amani asked me about you today."

"Me?"

"She saw us last night."

"And what did you say?"

"All good things, I promise."

Catherine joined him with two glasses of juice. "Do you want me to tickle it out?"

He smiled a bit. "I told her that you're a cinephile, a cat lover and very sweet."

"Sweeter than candy apple?"

"Yes."

"Not cloyingly like treacle or...claggy like electuary?"

He knew that she was only fishing for compliments.

"By no means. I have a gusto for sweetness." He sipped his juice appreciatively. "And I do indeed prefer the scrumptious afters with my sweetnums." He looked at her. "Catherine, you are nectar for me."

Catherine flashed a beaming smile then said worriedly, "I went to the dental clinic today. They said that there's a bit of inflammation. And I need to wear my retainers more often."

"No more flying saucers for you then, kitty cat." He smiled wryly.

Catherine made a face. "Hey! That's not fair. I can still have them if I take good care of my teeth."

He looked at her pityingly. "Maybe I'll boil you some mung bean water. It's good to treat inflammation."

"Melody asked me today to train for First Aid at Work and Photoshop. She's booked me for a training course after Easter for Photoshop. She wants me to teach our floristry tasters starting in May."

"I'm happy for you." They clinked their glasses.

"Thank you, Mr Yang, for everything. I do believe that this occasion calls for some celebration." Catherine smiled. "I've already dropped off Mr Darcy at Cecil's place. And I've booked us a table tonight at Rabot 1745 in Borough Market. Hannah told me that they use cocoa beans for cooking, and I think we'll have a lovely time there and some lovely afters to perk you up."

They had a sensate meal, marvelled at the napkin provided at the restaurant with illustrations on the anatomy of a cocoa bean, got back, and spent some time sorting out their luggage while discussing a film to be released soon, *Zootopia*, which was renamed *Zootropolis* in the UK, and that they would watch once they returned from their trip. Catherine was exuberant as she told him about the nuances of the animation and her favourite ship.

They had a lovely evening, oblivious to what would happen the next morning.

CHAPTER 7

22nd March 2016.

He woke up early as he always felt agitated before flying. Catherine was still asleep. He scrambled out of bed and ventured downstairs.

The thrum of rain from last night had washed the balcony clean not long before a pigeon landed on the railing and made a dropping.

He opened his phone and drank some water as he checked the weather forecast—there was no rain predicted on that day in London.

A message from DPD informed him that his parcel had been despatched and would be delivered by 9th April.

He took some time to clean the kitchen, made sure that no perishables were in the fridge, arranged the twill sofa cover, double-checked their ticket and hotel confirmations, unplugged the Bloomberg Terminal in the study, lowered the heating by a notch, and made breakfast.

Just as he was about to go upstairs and wake Catherine, he heard her cry out: "Oh! No! God no! This is terrible!"

He rushed into the bedroom and found Catherine on the phone with Cecil, her godfather, mumbling in desperation: "But how far is her hotel from the EU headquarters? I've called but...Yes, I've messaged...no replies..."

His phone buzzed. There was a news alert: two bomb attacks in Brussels, one at the departure hall at Brussels Airport, the other at a metro station in the city centre.

He recalled that Cecil's daughter Sophie was attending a research conference at VUB and Ambrose Eden was planning to meet someone at a coffee house in the morning.

Catherine clutched the coverlet and her knuckles whitened. Her lips quivered. "I can't...my calls won't connect..." Strands of her fringe were stuck with sweat and tears onto her forehead.

"Maybe she's on the phone with someone else." He held her. "Maybe she's talking to Brendon...she's telling him that she is *safe*." He tried to soothe and smooth her ruffled skeins of hair. "Or that she lost her phone...It's possible. It's likely. Or she cracked it. We all know how easily phone screens crack these days."

Catherine took a moment to gather herself. "We can't go to Paris." She jumped off the bed. "We must get to Cecil!"

They arrived at Catherine's godfather's place in forty minutes. It took him an effort not to run any lights. The morning radio programme did nothing other than updating the latest casualties.

Patsy opened the door and wailed. "Catherine, oh, Catherine! What should we do? Sophie has not called!"

Chance made tea, and they waited as Cecil spoke to his grandson, Brendon, on the phone and reassured him that his mother would be safe and sound. The TV in the living room flashed CCTV footage of the attacks, and he took the liberty of turning it off.

Karsmakers...

He checked the coffee house's address on his phone and found its location was just across from the EU Parliament. He called the Edens' house number and the call connected. Gabby said: "Whoever this is, I can't keep this line occupied!"

"Mrs Parker, it's me. Have you heard from Mr Eden?"

"No, no... We are waiting. Thank you for your concern. I...Lord have mercy! I must attend to Mrs Eden now."

"I hope him saf–" The call ended before he finished his sentence.

***

Shortly before noon, they heard from Sophie.

She had no severe injuries except for a deep cut on her right arm, a small piece of shrapnel in her left shank, and a slight shock.

They were so relieved, and Cecil was so frayed that he almost cried.

Patsy worked as an Acute Admissions nurse and she still had to go to her hospital in the afternoon. They drove her there, got back to the flat, and warmed their untouched breakfast for lunch, even though none of them had any appetite.

After their light meal, Catherine decided to retire to the bedroom. They'd had some exhausting hours that morning.

He cancelled their flights and the booking at Le Meurice, made a mental shopping list, and called the Edens' house phone again. Amani answered and told him that Ambrose Eden was fine, and had decided to come home soon.

They talked briefly on caring for the bean sprouts, then he checked on Catherine. She was having a bath. She asked him to join her. He lit a candle and told her that he would need to do some grocery shopping. He then took the taser, and went to the M&S Simply Food on Long Acre. He remembered to make a stop at the candy stall, 'Toffee Nose', in Jubilee Market and bought all the flying saucers available.

He got back to the flat, checked his mailbox, and called the lift. It seemed to be stuck on the ninth floor.

He waited for a minute or so and decided to take the stairs.

Chance went upstairs with his heavy groceries, remembering to notify the front desk of the lift problem. When he reached the emergency door on the ninth floor, he found Hannah Robinson in her gym outfit half-lying half-slumping in the lift, crying, her legs protruding out, preventing the lift's door from closing.

"Mrs Robinson, are you alright?" He dropped his shopping bags at the scene.

She murmured something.

"I'm sorry?" He squatted down beside her.

"Eddy...Eddy," she murmured again. Her hands were wet from her tears and nasal mucus. "His company called. He's in Brussels."

"Oh! I'm so sorry to hear this, is he..."

She looked at him with void eyes and said, "He had a stroke...the ambulance couldn't make it on time because of the attacks..."

"Oh." He was left speechless. "Mrs Robinson, I..."

She ululated, her body shaking like a punctured jellyfish. "What the hell!? He's not supposed to be there! Eddy's not supposed to be in Brussels! He can't be! We still have a Jools Holland gig to go!"

It seemed that, indeed, everyone had secrets.

He got back to the flat. Catherine was writing by the window. She was calm but still dewy-eyed.

He regretted breaking the news about Eddy to her, but he did so without preamble.

This time, he had no choice, nor could he stall anymore.

Now, he thought, whenever they used that lift, they would remember Eddy Robinson and his stricken face and grizzled hair.

He used the washroom and then asked Catherine to lend him a hand with Hannah. They managed to get her back to her flat, and a moment later, Sarnai, the Robinsons' cleaner, arrived for work.

They spent the afternoon with Hannah, not saying much, and not knowing what to say. None of them could answer her most urgent question on why her husband had gone to Brussels. Hannah was prostrate with shock and sadness.

Gone like clouds, he thought as he drew the curtains after sunset. The Robinsons had a view of the Thames. Once they had invited him and Catherine to watch the New Year's Eve fireworks.

Sarnai had offered to keep her employer company for the night after her ex-husband agreed to take care of their daughter.

He and Catherine got back some time after eight. The BT Tower shone from afar.

They sat down on the sofa in darkness, the light pollution in Covent Garden providing just enough illumination for them to navigate around the room.

He could do nothing to make her happy that day, not even with the flying saucers, and he regretted not buying any crisps earlier.

They sat for a long time in silence, and suddenly Catherine snivelled,

"I...I take it back."

"I'm sorry?" He was so lost in his thoughts that he barely heard her.

"I take it back!" she said firmly. "I take it back; I take it back!"

In broken sentences, Catherine retold him how once she assumed that he was having a fling because her workmate, Orla, mistook someone going into a hotel for him. And later, An told her to be careful with slip-ups.

"I wished you unwell. I thought very lowly of you. I, I cursed you! I wanted to damn you to hell forever! But I take it back now! I take it all back," she wailed.

"Catherine, I'm not going anywhere." He offered his arms. "I'm in for the long haul, and I don't intend to make promises that I can't keep."

"Once, after my parents passed away," she stifled. "Once I had a big row with my uncle, and I shouted at him, 'I don't want you in my house! Why can't you just leave me alone!?' He was in a hurry to get to work...he taught at UCL then. That day...was the 7th of July 2005."

He only waited.

"I can forgive myself for not going to that restaurant with my parents, but I would never have forgiven myself if I had lost him that day. One of his students died, and Nigel found her bag. It was covered in ash."

He felt tears searing and scalding his shirt and skin.

He could offer nothing in return other than his honesty, so he told her why he had locked himself up in his room for a month.

"He didn't make it through, and his parents gave his golf bag to me after his funeral. Then my dad asked me, 'If you like games that much, why don't we move to Japan?' I know he was offering me a way out.

Lynette had a job offer from Yiwu and we moved back to China. But there was this one...one night after school, I was at a junction, and there was a motorbike speeding. It ran the light and walloped me. Come to think now; I don't know if I didn't see it coming, or that I saw it but didn't want to move out of its way."

It was a *quid pro quo* of pangs and tears they exchanged that night.

They talked for hours and found that they had each lost; they had lost family and friends, and they had lost a part of themselves and found it in each other again.

***

April.

Verdure had returned to the plane trees on Aldwych but spring had yet to enter the passers-by's hearts.

Catharsis on stage may be relieving, but catharsis in life goes hand in hand with long-lasting grief. He remembered Felipe once said that the art of distraction was always better than lies. He did everything he could to distract himself and Catherine from their gloomy thoughts.

They spring cleaned the flat. He managed to find a damp spot on the ceiling in his study and a minor clogging problem in the balcony's gutter, and he used them as a feeble excuse to hire maintenance so he could stay in Catherine's house during the week when the Holborn fire happened the year before. On the night of 4th of April, Tomb-Sweeping Day, he got back to the flat and burnt plentiful joss papers on the balcony.

He made her more candy apples...chilled bottles of sweet mung bean water...searched for a mouthwash that didn't leave an irritating aftertaste.

He told Catherine how An had a cat who liked to destroy potatoes and how he used to fall from his bike as a child whenever he passed a house that had a wolfhound and that barked only and always at him. He told her how he once read about an experiment from a children's science magazine: if you put a raw egg inside a bottle of vinegar, seal the bottle, and wait for a month, the egg would turn into a bouncy ball. He'd tried the experiment every year, but never succeeded. Years later, An admitted that she was very curious every time so would break the seal and check on the egg.

Catherine liked plants and flowers, so he taught her how to grow bean sprouts. He told her his childhood episodes on how the locals thought a viny plant, *Cuscuta chinensis*, was the landline phone network connecting lacertids or that burrs from *Tribulus terrestris* always found their way into his vest. And how he would use green foxtails to weave a bunny for An.

They did an awful lot of childish things. He sometimes read fanfiction of her comfort characters to her before bedtime, they had popping candies, and even blew bubbles in Catherine's garden, and Mr Darcy chased and pierced the bubbles ruthlessly. On April 1st in the morning, she passed him a note with instructions to mutter 'white rabbit' three times before speaking to her so they'd have good luck for the whole month.

Hannah Robinson had gone to Brussels and returned.

She was adamant in finding out why her husband had ended up in a wrong location at a wrong time and without even telling her. She had asked for Chance's help with her husband's digital trail. In no time, they had discovered a Eurostar booking that led Eddy to Brussels on the night when he said he was travelling to the Hague.

Eddy Robinson's last known whereabouts was in a hotel lobby in Alhambra in Brussels, a red-light district known for street prostitution. They found previous train ticket bookings to Brussels, luxury hotel bills, and account statements with frequent cash withdrawals in the past year. Hannah finally decided to give up her quest when they stumbled on some links in Eddy's browser directing to blurry but explicit videos on niche websites featuring her husband and various females.

Chance had recalled that Felipe once said if he were to die, he would leave detailed instructions on how to destroy all his electronic devices and wipe out his online footprint. Walking briskly under the plane trees on Aldwych, he dwelled on how Eddy Robinson might have reacted had he known that his nearest and dearest realised this hidden side of him.

One balmy afternoon, he heard Sarnai sighing in front of the plants now with chocolate spots in the open-air atrium. Sarnai told him that it was surprising how little refuse a single person could generate; she spent more time talking to Hannah than carrying out the chores. All the toilet rolls that Hannah had stocked up a year ago after the Holborn fire, Sarnai didn't know when she would use them all.

He and Catherine had learnt more about their newly deceased neighbour. Eddy was a foundling who had been adopted by a millwright and grew up in New Hampshire. He had met Hannah during a summer break when he worked on her parents' farm. Her folks had supported him through law school. They pondered about what was more shattering to Hannah: how she had lost her partner in such a sudden, harsh, and unexpected way, or that she had been living with a stranger for years...

Hannah had had insomnia for a while, and Catherine was kind

enough to buy her a vial of remedies to roll from Neal's Yard. He got Catherine one as well, for he knew that she had identified extensively with their neighbour, and he had learnt that too much empathy could cause great pain.

One day, he got back on foot in heavy rain and caught a cold. Catherine asked him why he hadn't taken the Tube. He told her that he was worried about manufactured risks.

The two missing Brits remained missing and the days grew longer every day, and people lived on, bearing their secrets.

***

The Saturday morning after the Easter Break, he drove to the Printek store on Burleigh Street to collect his delivered parcel. Later, he decided to get some stationery at the London Graphic Centre.

He got to the place, spent some time perusing the store's mechanical pencil collection, looked at the binding material and equipment, selected a set of ink cartridges, and paid. He left the store, secured his bags in the trunk, and then he heard someone calling: "Lao-shi?"

He turned, and Amani waved at him. She was there to buy iron-on transfer paper sheets for a school project.

They talked for a while, and he asked her about the bean sprouts.

She cast her eyes down and told him that they had died one night after Ambrose Eden had kept the kitchen tap running and drowned the newly sprouted beans. The next morning, when Gabby found them, they had already turned sour and mouldy, ruining her cotton cheese bag.

Amani told him, in low spirits, that she had a new tutor and Gabby had allowed her to use her phone so she could keep in contact with her friend Nathan. She expressed that she desperately wanted to do well in her exams because she had eavesdropped what Ambrose Eden said to his wife after returning from Brussels: if Amani were to get an A in her AS Maths, they would not divorce.

Chance was angry, but he didn't show it.

They walked for a short distance from Shelton Street and went to Slingsby Place through Mercer Street. Catherine had an early shift that day, and he introduced them. Catherine was working on a vase of orchids for a ballroom event, and she explained the basics of floristry to the girl.

They talked for a bit more, then his cousin An came into the flower shop. She had been invited to a dinner party that evening and wanted to order a bouquet as a token of appreciation.

"You should never bring a bouquet to a dinner party," Orla told An at the till, "because the host needs to find an appropriate container, or they might be allergic, or they might not want to take care of it. Trust me; they would appreciate a bottle of wine or some *hors d'oeuvres* or some dessert."

An thanked Orla for her advice and decided to visit the Majestic Wine store on Drury Lane.

Before parting, Amani asked An about her 'slender guitar' and how she played it.

"I use fake nails, and you wrap them on your fingers with tape. Then you practise," An explained. "Like Maths, it's all about practice and daily effort." She smiled. "Do you know that if you calculate 0.99 to the power of a hundred, you'll get 0.366, but if you calculate 1.01 to the power of a hundred, you'll get 2.70? A small step every day will get you very far.

Hard work pays off."

He brought up that Amani was learning Chinese and An asked some questions about her studies and learnt that she was planning to take her HSK Level 2 exam later that year.

"Good for you!" An said excitedly. "Do you know what my professor says about China? That the most common three-word phrase in the world is not 'I love you' but 'Made in China'. I'm a volunteer at the Language Resource Centre at King's College London, and we have ample resources on learning Mandarin; do pop in one day."

Amani saw that An had a book in her shoulder bag and inquired about it.

"This book is called *Mr Ma and Son*. It's a novel by a famous Chinese writer and playwright called Lao She. He taught Mandarin at SOAS for five years. I'm doing my dissertation on him and comparing the TV adaptation and the novel. The story is about a Chinese father and his son who lived in London in the 1920s. They rented a place, and the father fell in love with their white landlady while the son fell in love with the landlady's daughter. But sadly, neither relationship worked out for various reasons such as discrimination and cultural differences. In the end, the son decided to go back to China, and the father stayed. Later, Mr Ma junior died on the battlefield fighting off the Japanese invasion, and the senior Mister Ma died in London alone."

He listened as An explained the heart-rending story and watched as tears welled up in Amani's eyes. Then he asked, "Amani, are you all alright?"

"No," she said, her face lugubrious. "I have an awful headache."

They parted with An and found a wicker table at the café by

Ladurée; he ordered some sweets and hot drinks and tried to keep the conversation light.

"As a child once I was hungry at home, and I saw the bean sprouts that we had and decided to have some. I added vinegar, chilli oil, some salt, and Sichuan peppercorns, but it tasted terrible. In the end, I found out that I had forgotten to boil the sprouts first. I didn't know you need to blanch them." He tried a smile.

Yet Amani seemed disturbed and sad still.

He only waited as he watched kits of pigeons and teams of shoppers circling the rumbustious piazza. After a moment, Amani asked, "Lao-shi, what happened to your bully?"

"Well." He thought for a while. "I'm not sure, I haven't heard about him."

Amani sulked for a long time, and she let out a deep breath and told him the cause of her distress. Once, in a Politics class, she debated with some classmates on war, aid, and conflict resolution using herself as an example. She'd won the motion, and some people from her class started to call her names afterwards. Worst of all, they called her a 'comfort woman'.

CHAPTER 8

G abby was kind enough to fetch Amani, and he found his car and drove back to Kean Street. He took the lift and thought about Eddy Robinson and his frazzled face, and Amani and the cause of her distress.

The open-air atrium had lost its liveliness, as Hannah Robinson had stopped caring for her vegetables and red pelargonium. Sarnai did a thorough job of keeping them alive, but the plants seemed to comport telepathy with their dispirited owner.

Catherine was back as well. She was on her laptop, preparing for her Photoshop training commencing the next week.

"Oh, what did you get?" she asked when she saw him with his unwieldy delivery box.

"Just some things from Farmacia Santa Maria Novella, I thought you might like them." He put down the box, opened it with a cutter knife, and removed the bubble wrap. "I've bought some *Carta D'Armenia*. Perhaps we can give some to Hannah, to help her sleep better."

"That's very thoughtful of you," she said. "But Hannah left for the States today. It was a hasty decision. She messaged me. She needed to make funeral arrangements and sort out her finances. And she needs her family for support more than ever. She's not too familiar with her...with Eddy's 401(k) plan."

"I see."

"And..." She hesitated. "She's given away all of his possessions, his clothes, his books, and all his CDs and records to the Oxfam Store on Drury Lane. She told me that she finds them as filthy as a shit shovel. She's been eating her heart out, and the only thing that she couldn't bring herself to throw away is their fridge magnet collection. They'd buy a souvenir fridge magnet whenever they visited a new place on their hiking trips. They were planning to go back to the States over Easter and hike at the Bighorn Mountains. We played 'Cheek to Cheek' today in the shop. It made me think of Eddy."

Strands of cloud drifted across the leaden sky, and he turned on a side lamp so Catherine could read better.

"What did you think of him?" he asked. "Your first impressions?"

"He struck me as simpatico and canny. And he looked hale and hearty." She reflected. "But I remember how he smoked on their balcony on New Year's Eve when Hannah discussed the US presidential election with their guests. I felt that Eddy had some...private affairs that perturbed him. He looked preoccupied."

He put away the hand creams and home fragrances and noticed a newly opened bag of sanitary pads in the washroom. He washed his hands and made a cup of raspberry leaf tea for Catherine.

"Would you like to use the study?" he asked her.

"No. I like this view. And...there's something that I meant to ask you," she said as she warmed her hands with the mug.

He sat down across their dining table. "Yes?"

"Have you been carrying your taser around?"

"Yes." He added, "I won't when things quieten down a bit."

She nodded lightly and resumed her reading. After ten or so minutes, she said, "We've never talked about these things."

"I'm sorry?" He put away his phone; he was messaging Turner.

"We've never talked about our finances." She winced and chewed the inside of her lip. "If we're in for the long haul, we need to be prepared, and we need to prepare well."

"I have a good financial standing if that's what you are asking. Nothing opulent, but comfortable, yes." He explained, "I have a few software patents still valid for some time."

"These are the things that I treasure the most and I treasure them alike," she listed: "my family and friends, my cat, my house, this relationship, and my job. I have some savings but nothing astronomical. And now that we've chosen each other, I want to make this work and make it last."

"How about if we open a joint account?" he suggested.

Catherine considered. "Let me sleep on it. I don't want us to make any rash decisions."

"That's fine."

"You are upset. I know you are." Catherine made two of her fingers tap-dance across the table and held his hand. "It's not that I want to pussyfoot around or that I want to be avoidantly attached, but life's not all hearts and flowers and a bed of roses. There are unpleasantries like toothache and Brexit as well. Or are you upset because I compared you with Mr Darcy? Mr Darcy's my doudou and you've been my ballast."

He squeezed her hand softly. "I'm upset, yes, but not because of what we've been discussing. I'm upset because Amani told me that she's having a difficult time at school. Catherine, I do appreciate you taking consideration of us." He checked the oven timer. "Shall I make lunch now? How would you like some bean sprouts?"

"Yes." She smiled faintly, then she remembered, "Oh, Felipe called; he invited us to dinner tomorrow. Cecil and Patsy are going. I'd told him that we'd go."

"Of course." He stood up. "Let me charge my phone, and I'll set to cooking."

He sent Turner a message before charging his phone in the study.

***

Dinner with Felipe Kazama was always trying.

They got to the Ivy Market Grill in Covent Garden at five to seven, and Felipe was already there. He wore a flannel, bespoke three-piece by Thom Browne and a pair of John Lobb shoes.

"Oh, Cathy, aren't you a vision tonight? Mwah!" He strutted towards them, air-kissed Catherine on her cheeks, and shook hands with Chance. "Good to see you so bubbly, stranger! One more point for the matchmaker. What gives, buddy?"

"Thanks, Felipe." Catherine smiled. "I hope you had a nice trip to Canberra?"

"Yeah, it was lovely. I love koalas. They taste a bit minty, though. And Caramello Koalas aren't bad either. Isn't it nice to have some local signatures? I can't resist simple pleasures. As Freud would say, I permit no philosophic reflection to spoil my enjoyment of the simple things in life.

Tut. I didn't acquire a sophisticated palate growing up, and I've found all the Michelin restaurants that I've been to *way* too salty. But I do think that caviar is heavenly; it's heavenly food for a cats' heaven."

Catherine laughed heartily. "I'm not sure if Mr Darcy would agree with you. Cats can't have too salty diets and all aging cats eventually die of kidney failure, or so I have heard."

They chatted a bit and then Patsy arrived.

"Oh, you must be Patsy the Nightingale! It's great to put a face to a name. You look like an ape—oops, my English is a bit rusty. Sorry for the *lapsus linguae*. I meant to say a babe from a beauty shop! What a joy to behold for my sore eyes! Your smile could certainly launch a thousand Titanics!" Felipe bent down and kissed her hand. "Ooh! Lovely French manicured nails. A lacquer, I presume?"

Chance sensed that Felipe was in his unctuous mode again.

"Y...yes." Patsy retrieved her hand nervously and smiled weakly. "Hi, hello. Actually, it's Patsy the Bennett. And I usually don't wear nail products."

"The call of duty, right?" Felipe flashed his teeth. "Good to know that Cecil the curmudgeon is in a nimble-fingered pair of hands. Allow me to introduce myself. The name's Felipe Kazama. I have a nice little ice-breaker for self-introduction, but I don't suppose it's appropriate for dinner time. Suffice to say that my mother named me after the then Prince, now King, of Spain."

They made their way to their table, ordered some drinks and starters, browsed the menus, and Cecil arrived shortly after.

"Ha, here comes our intrepid Serjeant-at-law! Cecil!" Felipe feigned a harsh tone. "You mustn't make the ladies wait for you. You know, as my buddy would say," he thumped Chance on his left shoulder, "early is on time and on time is late."

They ordered. Catherine asked for a sweet potato curry with jasmine rice, and Chance and Felipe ordered the lobster dish. Cecil had the shepherd's pie and Patsy sole meunière.

"Nice choice, Miss Bennett," Felipe commented. "Who doesn't like a grunter for dinner? *Fisch am End.* I've had a difficult time deciding between the two—lobster and sole. Do you know that soles have migrating eyes that move to the other side of their body when they mature? Might be useful for a pub quiz night. I hope you didn't mind my choice of restaurant. I guess I've missed British cooking. Meat and two veg. Rustic-style."

"No problem at all and just call me Patsy, please; all my friends call me Patsy." She sipped her sparkling wine. "So, Felipe, what do you do? Consulting, is that correct?"

Catherine whispered with Cecil about Sophie and her recovery, and Chance listened as the two interacted as he drank his 'Beet It' juice.

"Yes, more precisely, I'm in the killer acquisition racket," Felipe said with a fish-eating grin. "We acquire targets and kill them."

"Oh, it sounds quite...aggressive." Patsy arranged her napkin. "Do you just drive them out of business or out of the boards?" She quickly covered her mouth. "Sorry if I'm asking too much."

"Not at all. I love shoptalk. Yes, and no. It depends. An acquisition can be a kill or a cure, but we kill them stone-dead most of the time." Felipe smiled meaningfully. "There's nothing magical about what I do. Just like healthcare provision, you need to have your finger on the pulse of the ailing lame ducks." He cleared his throat. "I'm very good with numbers, and I used to work in auditing. Once I needed to cross-examine some figures, and it pissed off my boss, his boss, and the bosses of his bosses. It didn't work out, so I fetched up where I'm now."

"Speaking of which," Patsy recalled, "wasn't there a recent scandal in the City with someone named Milken? They've said that his alma mater was too ashamed to accept his donations and his children have disowned him."

"Yes," Felipe nodded, "Lewis Milken, I know him. His family and friends fled like rats abandoning a sinking ship. And the Nikon choir, they nearly drowned him in their feeding frenzy."

Patsy moved on to tell how a colleague of hers always liked to drop acronyms into their meetings. Instead of saying 'The Rapid Assessment and Treatment in Hospital Emergency Liaisons and Leadership', he would say 'Tell me more about the RATs in HELL'. Some had complained about this inappropriate backronym.

"I've made an interesting observation recently regarding rats," Felipe said with a toothy grin. "That rats don't like curry with organic turmeric, especially when they panic. They twist, they turn, they burrow holes in certain objects, and they try to hang tough, but in the end, they suck it up."

Chance nearly choked.

Patsy tilted one side of her brow. "Cecil told me that you went to Harvard Business School?"

"Uh-huh. I didn't like it there. Universities in the US and the UK are only private clubs. The school of life teaches valuable lessons for no costs. Every university has a notable alumni list; every university should also have a notorious alumni list. The question with the whole ropy kit and caboodle of financiers, you know, Patsy, is not who's had shenanigans but who hasn't had any hanky-panky scandals yet, and to my knowledge, none of us survived. Do you know what cabbies call the London Stock Exchange? Den of Thieves. I think it was wise of me to switch track." Felipe laughed thickly. "Are you from around here, Patsy?"

"Uh-huh. I was born within the sound of Bow Bells. And where are you from, Felipe?"

"Oh. I'm from a humble background." He gave a vacuous smile.

Catherine cut in excitedly. "He's been promoted to the position of Managing Director of the EMEA region of his company."

"Oh, my sincere congratulations!" Patsy raised her glass in reverence. "So, will you be stationed in London?"

"Yes. I'm tired of being a bird of passage moving restlessly from pillar to post. I'm looking for accommodation at the moment and I'm as busy as a beaver. Pure drudgery. And I still need to figure out what to do with my apartment in Osaka. I don't want to flog it."

"Perhaps you can lend it out on Airbnb."

Felipe spurned that idea: "So that strangers can wear my underwear? I don't think so, Patsy. Whenever I wake up every morning, I treat myself as a work of art. As David Ogilvy said, image means personality. After all, form follows function."

"Oh, I see. Power dressing, right? You do look very impressive, Felipe." Patsy nodded in approval, "But as Ovid would say, ladies are *always* advised to avoid those men who profess to looks and keep their hair carefully in place."

"Well." Felipe slicked his hand through his coiffed hair. "At least I've got something to keep in place, unlike Cecil. I envy him. I do. What a time saver when there's no mussing."

Chance looked back and forth between the two.

"How old are you, Felipe, if you don't mind me asking?"

"Trust me, sweeting; you can ask me anything. I was born the year of the assassination of John Lennon."

Patsy did the maths. "You certainly don't look like your age. You look quite...worldly-wise."

"Well, I'll take it as a compliment, though I do prefer the term 'raffish'. Patsy, scalpers are a trying profession," Felipe continued. "Some say that trading is no different from gambling, except you don't get free drinks but direr Vegas odds. When I worked in trading, a fellow trader who made a loss decided to blame it on me. I was saved by the bell. Luckily, we had well-developed CCTVs and I came up smelling of roses, or else I might be behind locked doors now, so I always keep a low profile, and I always keep GPS trackers in all my belongings so that if I lose anything, I won't need to go to Jonathan Wild's Lost Property Office. I always watch out for myself. There is a 'hell' in 'Hello'. There is even a hazard in 'Thank you'"."

Patsy nodded understandingly. "I see. It's a pity that not everyone has such concern for themselves."

"And I take pride in my metier; it does have its perks, like the opportunity to dine at upscale establishments with charming and not-so-charming individuals and sometimes invitations to literally *mind-blowing* events." Felipe scratched his angular jaw and asked, "Nursing seems to be a rather busy occupation. Do you still have time for recreation?"

"Oh, yes. I like to read and bake, and London has a lot to offer...the exhibitions and the shows. Felipe, you are half Nikkei, right? I've recently read *The Hare with Amber Eyes* by Edmund De Waal; the *netsukes* are wonderful."

"I like to read, as well," Felipe concurred. "I like Japanese *yokai* stories—supernatural sightings and folklore. My recent favourite is a *yokai* called 'Todomeki'. It's about a girl with a hundred bird eyes on her body as a punishment for stealing. She finagles kind passers-by on worn-out pathways into giving her pelf. I also read of murders, wars, bankruptcies, jackpot winnings, and Shakespeare*."

"It reminds me of Argus from Greek mythology. What's your favourite Shakespeare then?" Patsy inquired. "If you read the sonnets, I recommend the Penguin book edited by John Kerrigan."

"My favourite is *Titus Andronicus*. I've never liked his other treacly pieces." Felipe paused. "I once met a man with a lobotomy. He had acalculia and he was as complacent as an oyster. It made me think that whoever wants the world to be an oyster must have very evil intentions. I've heard that a bowl of Jell-O emits the same brainwaves as adults."

Chance noticed that Catherine pricked up her ears upon hearing this episode.

"Well. I can't say that I've seen too many patients with a lobotomy," Patsy grimaced, "But I do know the research nurse at the Cambridge Brain Bank. What work! Speaking about oysters, though, the Wright Brothers at Borough Market have marvellous oysters."

"I always rise early to go to Billingsgate Market for my oysters, but I'll remember to put it down on my to-eat list. Do you think that the gut is the second brain? I'm pedantic about dining. Patsy, do you mind if I pick your brains for a minute? Do you have any local favourites or must-visits that you'd recommend?"

"Oh, Billingsgate...I haven't been there for donkey's years. Well, you could visit the Prospect of Whitby. It's London's oldest riverside pub."

Felipe tilted one side of his eyebrows. "Patsy, I'm not sure if you have ever noticed this. One particularly interesting observation I made in England is that there ought to be somewhere sticky in an English pub. The counter, the seat-top, the back kitchen...and some other times, people have *sticky* fingers."

"Or you can try...Rules in Covent Garden? It's London's oldest restaurant."

"Oh, I've been to Rules. I like their games. The olde times...I've heard once that pickpocketing was rife in Victorian times and the punishments were quite severe."

The diners at the adjacent table were discussing a horrifying incident that happened recently. A former City banker who took meth had killed a police bobby and practised cannibalism on him.

Felipe looked at her with gleaming eyes. "Patsy, I suppose that you haven't had any authentic blood puddings?"

"Well, you can buy Stornoway to eat at home. But I eat it less frequently now; sometimes I feel it's too high in suet. I've had patients who suffer from gout. And personally, I like Vienna sausages more."

"Now, now. Who doesn't need some decadent comfort food? People's tastes can change. I can see that now you prefer fish over fur and feather, maybe? And Vienna, what a place, I was there for the New Year's Concert. They do have wonderful sausages. I like the *käsekrainer* the most."

"Lucky you!" Patsy exclaimed. "I wish I had more time for travel."

"I don't believe in luck, but planning I do." Felipe said. "Besides reading, Patsy, what else are you into?"

"Hmm...sometimes I play a bit. You know, betting, mostly with Ladbrokes. And I do believe in luck: every time I play, I knock on wood subconsciously."

"Sounds exciting. You're not a high roller, I suppose?"

"By no means." Patsy shook her head slightly.

"Here's a game I heard about from a professor at Yale. You have a deck of cards: twenty-six black and twenty-six red. You can draw one card at a time. If it's black, you'll win a quid; if it's red, you'll lose a quid. You can stop the game anytime. How would you play?"

Patsy gave it some thought. "I'd draw a card. If it's black, I'd stop and if it's red I'd stop as well."

Felipe looked at her. "Folding so quickly? That's hardly the optimal strategy."

Patsy responded wittily, "I've no time to strategise when I need to attend to my patients. I can stop playing anytime, right? I play responsibly. It's no different from the lottery."

Felipe clucked his tongue. "I do think there's a difference. If you play the lottery and lose, the money goes to some charitable funds, and if you bet and lose, the money goes to a private company; who knows how many Hermès Birkins you've helped to buy for the executives' WAGs and HABs. Is there any bang for your buck?" He winced. "And I don't think I'll ever play with Ladbrokes. It sounds like a bad omen: lads who are or will be broke. Technology is great. You can now access a gambling account on your tablet, on your phone, on the high street. Not very helpful for anyone who's addicted, right? I've heard that they call roulette machines the crack cocaine of gambling. You can never outsmart the house edge, Patsy."

She laughed. "I think it means for them to be brokers, but everyone has different interests. I've had a patient who liked to collect cat stickers. What do you like to do other than reading, Felipe?"

"Sometimes I golf; golfing is a business essential in Japan."

"I heard there is an underground golf course at The Vaults underneath Waterloo. Maybe you should try it there?"

"I like to do it in the open air and it's okay if you don't know how to read the accounts or tell apart ROE and ROCE, but it's a big no-no if you can't hit a nice tee shot. At least it's not a brutal sport."

Patsy nodded. "That I do agree. I once attended an in-patient, a fly half, because of hospital passes in rugby. Do you go to the gym often, Felipe? You seem trim."

"Not really." Felipe adjusted his cuffs. "I've worked very hard to escape manual labour, and I don't find it appealing to use the kale I earned with brain work and spend it on manual labour again. I'm very good at digging up dirt, Patsy, and gym memberships are higher than a cat's back! Correct me if I'm wrong: I've heard the treadmill was invented in Brixton as a punishment for prisoners."

"Yes. I've heard that too."

"Oh," Felipe considered, "when I was in Vienna, a friend told me that according to local lore, the first translator of Sigmund Freud's work made a terrible mistake when translating it into English. The translator had translated the German word *trieben* to 'instinct'. Instinct is biological, but the actual word, meaning 'drive', is not." He laughed. "And she told me that every time someone uses the word 'subconscious', she knows that this person has no idea of psychoanalysis. The *Young Dr Freud* film is good; you should watch it, Patsy."

"You seem to know your onions." Patsy added, "You don't strike me as an *arriviste*."

"Thanks. At least I don't speak with a plum in my mouth. I hope I'm not acting like a punchable *besserwisser*, because knowing too much may not be a boon." Felipe sipped his drink. "It may eventually cause people to alienate family and lose friends."

"But I think you're quite witty; you can make people laugh."

"I'm glad that I'm no dolt." Felipe grinned. "When I forget my scintillating wits at home, I make sure to bring my wildest imagination." He eyed Chance. "I know your tricks well enough. Whenever you don't want to talk, you pretend to drink water. I hope you've kept up with the news?"

He ignored him and filled his glass with sparkling water.

Felipe then asked Catherine, "Cathy, how's Alex, the celebrated roué, been? Still on the rebound?"

"He's quite taken up with work. He has a new book with Routledge."

"If I have a niece, I'll make sure that I place my family first. A professorship is only a form of life. Not the lowest, but tertiary education is only there to meet the ugly needs of industrialism by putting bums on seats. Does he know that one in ten students in London drop out during their first year due to financial hardship? All that money he gifts to the Royal Opera House as a patron, and now he doesn't have a date to bring on the First Nights. I prefer to take my dates to Row Zs than the loges. Even if the show's not up to standard, you'll have an alternative entertainment to distract yourself."

"Do you like fine arts, Felipe?" Patsy asked.

He returned his attention. "Of course I like fine arts. I'm a patron at *yokai.com* and I frequent the West End bohemia and the Albertopolis regularly. And I have another hobby. I like shopping, but sadly I'm too busy for it lately so these days I shop online, Amazon and the like. One drawback is that I can't try the clothing items on."

"I shop online too. I've got an Alexa," Patsy said. "Before Cecil and I met, I would talk to it sometimes. How desolate I was! Do you have anyone waiting at home, Felipe?"

"No. It's just me, my lonely eyelashes, and *Emmerdale* at home."

"Do you know that feeling lonely is as detrimental as smoking fifteen cigarettes a day? Why don't you host some parties?"

"There's no party culture in Japan. Yes, people hang out with friends, but more often they get drunk by themselves. Did you know, Patsy, that someone wrote that soap operas are a form of voyeurism? And Alexa, what a wonderful device. Maybe I should get one so I don't spend my spare time doomscrolling," Felipe mused. "Ah, do you know that Amazon is planning to roll out a microwave?"

"I haven't heard." Patsy popped an olive into her mouth.

"Yes. When you buy a bag of microwaveable popcorn online, Amazon knows that you bought it, but it doesn't know what you did with it. You might keep it in your house, or you might eat it, or you might poison the pigeons. And it seems that they are not so pleased with this situation. But if you buy their microwave, they will know what you did with it. The digital trail is the new gold. Speaking of which," he paused, "I've a friend who works for Operation Falcon, the Fraud and Linked Crime Online response force from the Met Police. He tells me that there have been cases where people steal information from smart assistants.

You *must* be careful, Patsy."

"I see." She nodded.

"Who knows? Maybe one day they will roll out a smart toilet that analyses your stool. But I haven't been shopping on Amazon recently. You know *why*, Patsy?"

"Why's that?"

Felipe flinched. "The last time I shopped, I got into a triangulation fraud. You know what that is? When you buy something from a seller, the seller buys it from another seller on the same platform and sends it to you. It made me feel that e-commerce platforms, in general, might be a good tool for racketeering. I've heard that the fraudster often uses *stolen* payment information for cat in the sack."

Patsy took a sip from her glass. "I think sometimes it happens if you're not careful enough, so I always compare the ratings and examine the reviews. At least no party is hurt; the customer still gets the parcel. Some of my colleagues in paediatrics wards complain that when family and friends visit the children, they bring toys and all sorts of jollies, but when they leave and the nurses take them away, the children always cry and their conditions worsen."

"Very well, Patsy. You don't live up to your name; you're stunning, more's the pity." Felipe smiled. "I hope the muggins never finds it out and files a claim." He tapped his finger on his glass in an excited tattoo. "I'm thrilled to be here tonight, and I'd like to propose a toast." He rose and raised his glass. "To Cecil; to your health and financial health, and down with the Rump!"

Their food came, and they waffled on as they dined.

***

Halfway through the meal, Chance excused himself to use the washroom.

He heard someone come in and use the urinal and heard Cecil and Felipe muttering by the washbasin.

"You've been gammoning too much tonight," Cecil upbraided in a low voice.

"So what? Are you going to read me my Miranda rights or are you going to cant me the Riot Act, *barrister* Stone? Can't one show concern for an old friend?" Felipe singsonged glibly. "I've tried my very best to scrape acquaintance with her in the last painful hour and I don't think that she's remotely good enough for you, but who knows, a hole in the wallet is better than a poke in the eye. Are you sure you are *compos mentis*? That when you collapsed, you didn't ding your pate or lose some of that brain down the drain with your memory like a sieve? My advice is always to sign a prenup and never die intestate, and you're no longer a spring chicken, Cecil. Indeed, you have more legal bog and dad bod than I do. If you strike a deal with the devil, please first check the terms and conditions in the small print. Do you know that people only spend, on average, forty-seven seconds on Google's privacy terms? Or do you need more eyewash? You need to go to Specsavers, man. I've learnt a new Latin word recently: '*captator*'. If you think that she's a nice catch, then I have a bridge to sell. I think you'll buy it in a poke. You can enjoy a view from the bridge, or you can burn it. But be careful not to fall into deep water—the Thames, in my opinion, is too thick to drink and too thin to plough. I'm worried that you might not have both of your oars in—"

Cecil warned, "I'm not as gullible as you might think, so I'd kindly ask you to *refrain* from overstepping!"

"Aa-ha, the thick plottens!" Felipe delighted. "The many faces of Cecil Stone? I hope I don't see an unhinged and a foolhardy one. I dare to say that you fool yourself with all the malarkey of the Eloquence Stone at Blarney with brass knobs on! Fine, I'll keep my mouth shut. I do know how to read the air. Though I'm surprised that you didn't call out 'Order!'. Even a fish wouldn't get caught if he kept his mouth shut. Oh, no, I won't. Do forgive me if I keep my mouth shut; I won't be able to eat. But I'll say less and talk more from now on. I understand, I do, who doesn't have some side hustles? I won't be a killjoy. All is fish that comes to your net? Cecil, you have no compunction whatsoever. I don't know who's shanghaiing whom in the coop. If you're so hot-headed, I won't pour cold water on you. Just remember: don't get your fingers burnt. Life is too short, ugh, Earth is too dangerous for honest dwellers like me. It's all chaos out there, chaosmos."

Chance heard a door shut, someone washed his hands, used the hand dryer, and then went out. By the time he returned to the table, Felipe was not there, and Cecil had said to Patsy, "I've been on the trot all day, would you mind if we retire early? I'll call the driver around now."

"Oh," Patsy said. "But I've promised Cathy that we'll visit the Pylones shop later. She needs to get her colleague a birthday present."

Cecil rubbed his brows. "I feel a bit unwell. I'll go back now. I'll call a cab."

"No, I'm alright. Take the car, please. You haven't eaten too much," Patsy said with concern. "Cecil, do you feel any pain or any tightness in your chest? Any palpitations?"

"I'm only a bit tired, that's all." Cecil stood up. "I'll take a cab, and I'll ask Eamonn to wait for you. Call him when you finish?"

"Well. If you feel peckish at home, there are still some hot cross buns I baked the other day. "

Cecil left just as Felipe returned to the table. "Did Cecil leave already? He ducked and dived faster than I thought." He sat and arranged his napkin. "I hope you don't mind, but tonight's on me. I'll treat you all to the VAT part." He fleered at his own joke. "No, no, just joking. Don't be scared off by my token gestures, Patsy. Tonight's on me, and I've already settled the bill to celebrate the World Haemophilia Day."

She shot him a sharp look.

"Please don't feel bad; I have a corporate account to squander anyway. It's good to be a butter-and-egg man once in a while. And I ordered desserts for us. Pity that they don't have any pudding tonight."

"Oh," Catherine said ruefully. "That's very kind of you, Felipe, but I really can't have more sugar tonight. I've had a little inflammation in one of my molars."

"Not a whit, I'll have it then, I hate waste."

Patsy looked at Cecil's half-eaten shepherd's pie. "Perhaps, Felipe, if it's not too much trouble, can I have mine and Cecil's to go?"

"Of course. My mother always scrimped and saved, and I think it's a virtue. Though I'm not sure: when it melts, you might find yourselves in the soup."

"Then I'll have it here. To avoid the hassle."

They waited for the desserts and chatted more.

"Cathy, did you go to the dentist yet? Pericoronitis can be persistent, and if left untreated, it could cause infection under the jaw and tongue," Patsy explained.

"Yes. I've been to the dental practice in Covent Garden. They said it's fine, but I need to have a better hygiene routine, especially after sugary food. Too much of a good thing can hurt." Catherine shot an amused glance at Chance. "I know who to blame."

Patsy clapped her hands lightly. "Oh, I know someone who works there: Prateek."

"Prateek's my dentist," Catherine recalled. "Do you know that he has a twin brother who's also a dentist? I saw him another time, and I greeted him, but he didn't say anything, and I was so vexed; I thought how *rude*."

"No, I wasn't aware he had a twin brother. Prateek is our hospital consultant and once we had a patient needing urgent jaw surgery, so we worked together."

Catherine talked with Patsy about her First Aid workshop and how she met an employee of a football star's wife's fashion brand who said that it was not uncommon to have people's fingers transfixed by the ball point needles on sewing machines and bodkins in their factories in Jordan.

Felipe said to Chance, "I've been to the new jazz bar. It's nice. But I have to say the names of the drinks on offer aren't so creative. Do you know that there is a pizzeria called 'Clubhouse' on Earlham Street that has a menu of names of games? You should have some menu innovations. How does 'Choking Devil' sound? Or 'Eschew Evil'? Or 'Santa's Incarnate' and 'Fallen Angel'? And tell me, when you mark questions, do you use checks or circles?"

"I'm not tutoring anymore." He briefed him on what had happened.

"I see," Felipe said. "But the puzzles remained, right? Why don't you come to my room later and we can put our heads together? Nigel's coming as well."

He reclined in his bolstered seat. "I met Ambrose Eden once over brunch at Duck and Waffle. Oh, boy! What a mouth! I'd kill just to shut him off. He only blusters and riffs on with no substance. What difference does it make between him and the Mayor and others of their ilk? Pointless conversations, blank verses, and broken vows only. He spends more nights at the Sofitel in Brussels than at his house. Oh, it's his wife's house. Better to be a dead economist than a not much cop one." He smiled. "On another note, I watched the last ounce of life leaving her. Interesting, isn't it? That you can measure life's weight. No, scientifically speaking, its mass."

"Wait." Catherine frowned. "Who are we talking about?"

Felipe looked Chance in the eyes and grinned. "My mother."

He then turned to Patsy. "Miss Bennett, do forgive me if I've spoken out of turn tonight. My mother died of a 'patient safety incident'. I believe this is how your NHS calls it. Since then, I've held a dubious attitude towards medical professionals. Have you ever heard of this joke regarding medical ethics and legal ethics? A Crown Court's judge might feel hideous with the indictable offences that people committed and want to strangle the convicted, but there isn't a doctor on the other side trying to kill the patient. But hell, who knows? I've known many doctors, and none of them were good. My friend told me that 'honour' is the keyword in fin-de-siècle Vienna. I do hate quacks and pettifoggers very much. I do mind the Ps and Qs."

"Oh, I'm so very sorry to hear that," Patsy looked away and spoke softly. "I share your sentiment, Felipe. My old man died young. Did your mother pass away in the UK?"

"No, she passed away in Peru. The NHS values hospices, right? But I wished I hadn't seen her passing. It's hell to see it when you're very little and very angry, and no mother's lips to kiss you anymore*."

Their desserts came. It was fig and pistachio feuilleté with yoghurt sorbet. Chance had no appetite, but he still ate.

***

They left the restaurant, went to Pylones, and waited with the ladies for Cecil's driver.

The Bentley came and they parted ways.

The sun had long set. Covent Garden remained as lively as the time they had discussed wasabi and Victorian folklore. They made their way to the Savoy, where Felipe was staying.

"Everything alright with your plumbing? You heard us, didn't you?" Felipe asked as he lit a cigarette while they waited for a pedestrian light in front of Kimchee.

"Bits; here and there," he said. "You seem to be rather pointedly at Patsy tonight."

"It's Patsy who was barbed at me. Never mind. I haven't had a neat bunfight in a while." He swung his hand like a baseball player who's angry at the umpire. "Did Catherine tell you her favourite pastime yet?"

"Yes."

"Very well. Then I dare to say that Cecil fools himself with all the malarkey of the Eloquence Stone at Blarney." He laughed with his teeth showing. "It's a line that I've borrowed from one of Cathy's stories." He cleared his throat. "The first time we met at Le Méridien in Phuket, I was with a date, and I made my date an origami rose with a napkin. Then I saw this girl beside our table looking at the rose, so I asked her if she wanted one as well. She asked me if I knew how to make an origami chicken that jumps. I told her I could make a frog that jumps, she said she'd like one. So, I made her one. I hope Cathy kept it."

They proceeded over the crosswalk. Felipe took a drag. "I'm sorry about your neighbour. What can I say? Never die intestate, I guess. Tell me about Georgiana Eden. Does she buy the *Big Issue*?"

He told Felipe what happened, the cause of Amani's distress, and how the Edens carried themselves around the house, the pranks by the housekeeper, and the lady of the house's aversion to *The Remains of the Day* and *The Hunger Games*.

"*The Hunger Games*, huh?" Felipe mused. "It's hardly *The Turner Diaries*. But I know what this is about." He moved out of his way for a couple with a baby cart. "This is about power and control. Your student might as well read the *Magna Carta*, and she'd stop her to boot. She's gotten her claws into the girl already. One historian has an interesting theory: if Hitler had had his own children to torture, many more lives could've been saved."

They'd passed the food shop on the Strand, Viandas de Salamanca, that installed no more mascots in front of the shop.

Felipe looked at the whole Iberic ham legs hung in the window and asked, "Do you know the differences between the sheep and the goats?"

Chance considered, "Goats have goatees, they are smellier, and they have horns, which are uncommon in lambs or sheep. I once read goats like to eat the tops of plants and lambs like the grass at ground level; not sure if that's true. Oh, you need to trim goats' hooves, and sheep take more time with shearing."

Felipe stopped before the Savoy's driveway and smoked. "And you know what happens when you piss them off? The goat attacks, charges, and bunts you, whereas the lambs take to their heels. Rams attack, but lambs don't."

A group of students passed, canvassing AI, predictive modelling, and how an Artificial General Intelligence would wipe out the human race. Felipe listened and laughed. "I know several folks from the FBI who are scatterbrains. Humans profile and blunder; humans make computer programs and AIs that profile and blunder. After the Centennial Olympic Park bombing, the FBI profiled Richard Jewell, the guy who found the bomb, and alerted others, as an unmarried, frustrated white male living with his mother, obsessed with guns and desperate for a soupçon of glory. They tried to pin the blame on him."

He took a puff. "What I don't like about *The Silence of the Lambs* film is that if you don't read the book, you don't know what made the killer a killer. People only scream at a man in a dress who kills and skins young women; they don't think why and they don't care to know why."

An ambulance sped by. Chance remembered Eddy and his frazzled face.

"A longitudinal study of 323 child soldiers in Sierra Leone finds that," Felipe said, "forty-seven per cent experienced anxiety and depression; twenty-eight per cent had PTSD, and eleven per cent had attempted suicide. I wouldn't be surprised if one or two of them experienced traumatic decrees that transmuted and *drove* them to engage with animal torture." He took another puff. "Surprisingly, the children have a very pro-social attitude, but they experience stigma on a daily basis. You know what the difference between a scapegoat and a sacrificial lamb is?"

"Yes."

Chance had thought about this possibility: if Georgiana Eden had not adopted Amani as insurance to rid herself of her peccadillos when the need arose; if Daniele Vidas had discovered the cats and assumed the most obvious culprit...

"Good to know that you're on the same page. It's cheap to frame someone. Now, the silence of the goat has a less juicy ring to it, doesn't it? And who's the real patsy? Whereof one cannot speak, thereof one must be silent." Felipe took one last puff, snuffed out his cigarette and said sternly, "Thanks to you, the figurative black leather notebook that Lewis Milken left has an interesting entry: that in the not-so-wholesome London circles, there's a book club...a coterie where instead of turning the pages, people skin felines. And guess whose name is under 'G'?"

***

"Why do they do it?" he murmured to himself as well as Felipe.

"Ah, think of it as a novel form of urban mojo. They do it to save their failing marriages. Will felicide bring felicity?" Felipe clucked his tongue. "You'd expect these people to know better. I wonder what they learn at school other than Shakespeare. *Parliament of Fowls*, maybe? And there are rules to this deadly game that they play; they can only bury the carcass within proximity of their house. Handy, isn't it? Silly girl: if there were no cats, there wouldn't be a British Empire. It must be awful to work in that house twenty-four seven."

They entered the Savoy and stepped on the black-and-white chequered marble floor in the lobby. Nigel was waiting on a plush filemot armchair under a bright chandelier. He looked as though he hadn't slept in the last seventy-two hours. They joined forces and talked as they got back to Felipe's suite on the sixth floor. Felipe opened the door, then he said, "Oh, I have to make a call. Be my guests."

They entered the room; the curtains were open, and they could see the illuminated London Eye and the riverside scenery. There was an orange sofa large enough for fifteen. A bottle of Slivovitz sat on the glass table with a leather beavertail sap, a fountain pen, some hand cream from Captain Fawcett, a box of Incasur Quinoa cereal, two éclairs from the Melba at the Savoy on a small plate, and a few books: *Fatal Lies* by Frank Tallis, *The Lord Chandos Letter: And Other Writings* by Hugo von Hoffmannsthal, *Young and Dangerous: The Backgrounds and Careers of Section 53 Offenders*, and another called *In the Sea There are Crocodiles*.

Nigel settled himself comfortably on the sofa and browsed through a magazine on hounds.

Chance heard Felipe talking merrily on his phone: "Kawamura-san, *ohisashiburidesu*. Oh, I'm older than you? Am I? Age is only a number that I hardly remember. Today's me is the youngest. I'll call you Asahi-kun then. How've you been? Are you moving house? Really? To Singapore? Do they need more industry transformation roadmaps? And are you escaping the purge or escaping Brexit? Do I have time tomorrow night? It's a complicated question... No! No! It's just me and my square eyes at home." Felipe brayed with laughter. "I've got this sofa set in my room big enough to host the Red Devils. You did work with the DCMS? No? Ah, with the NHS. The NHS is better without you, I think. You think so too? No wonder they say great minds think alike. A jack-of-all-trades means a master of none. Multitasking means screwing up several things at once. You should never have consulted for Oxfam, the IMF, and the NHS at the same time."

Felipe listened and responded. "Uh-huh. Let me put it frankly; I have time tomorrow for dinner. I have no time to spare for the Blair Last-ditch Project. He had already burnt all his bridges between the old and new worlds. Does he know 'My Number'? All tragedies are alike, and all project management failures run in parallel. He only had one blue-collar in his cabinet, and they dare to call themselves Labour? Government by the rich, for the rich. Life is so rich, and it is in a rich text format, three times underlined. That's an in-joke, by the way. Have they ever composted manure? Have they ever mucked a slot of land? Do they even know how to shop on Amazon? I don't want to dine with anyone who eats a club sandwich with a knife and a fork. It hurts my class consciousness, and I don't do God."

He turned and gestured for Chance to wait a bit longer. "Well, he's not French, is he? Whenever I'm invited to a dinner, I make sure that it's not a Black Dinner and not a rubber chicken dinner. Politics is not for gentlemen amateurs but professional hypocrites. Scottish Devolution is a project management failure, and who spies with his little eyes? Andrew Fulton. Authorities know, and subjects obey. Brexit is just *kabuki*. Who doesn't like a ride on a gravy train? Yes. I see. Are they making a documentary? The killing... Oh, quite a provocative name, I have to say. Yes, yes. Let's not forget that not long ago, every theatre script was checked by the office of the Lord Chamberlain before it reached the public. I think censorship is great, and we should have more of it. Five per cent gross profit gives the media audacity. Any publisher with a morsel of conscience would never publish any books by Issei Sagawa. Don't you know who he is? Good for you. No, no, no, don't look it up. I don't want you to ruin your appetite for tonight."

He paused. "Umm…I think I know her. Did she work at Saatchi and Saatchi? Ah, yes, then we've been introduced. She told me: 'Let's all go down the Strand'. Then she said something about bananas and I felt offended. No, we parted ways and went back home to get our beauty sleep separately. I better not kick against the pricks. Golf? You know I always have time for golf. Where? Royal County Down? In Northern Ireland? Sounds enticing? Uh-huh. Ranked first on the World's 100 Greatest Golf Courses? No wonder Ireland wants it back. Celt, Briton, Roman, Saxon, Dane, and Scot. Time and that island tied in a crazy knot. No. I didn't say that. John Hewitt said it."

Felipe looked in the direction of Nigel. "That's right. If you tell a devil that he's as close to human as any devil could get, will that be an insult to the devil? Now, I have guests… No, I don't want to go to the American Workhouse. What do I want? Nothing fancy: rice with garlic butter, *shibazuke*, and pulpos*. Do they have it there at L'atelier De Joël Robuchon? No? I thought so. Nah, Ikeda is okay and boring. The Japan Centre? Fine, I'll let you decide. *Ja na**!"

Felipe dropped his phone slapdash on the sofa. "Phew! Does every Eton boy like to palaver? Now that I have some disposable resources to apportion, everybody wants to wheedle a donation from me. They eye my treasure like someone who wants to marry into money." He took off his jacket and leaned on the sofa. "Nigel, you must tell your officers to be aware of anyone who watches *Breaking Bad* and takes meth. If everyone blames their problems on Satan, where should Satan go and file a claim for libel? In East Asian countries, they consider being anti-drug as a collective social responsibility and a sine qua non. In the US and the UK, you think being pro-drug is a collective self-deception to freedom. Ho! The legal cannabis production in Colorado emits more greenhouse gases than its coal-mining industry. Some people die because it's necessary, and I hate to see unnecessary passing."

Nigel put down his magazine. "Shite happens."

They fell silent for a while, then Felipe asked Chance, "But you haven't found out anything about the recorder? I wonder what's on there." He moved his fingers as if he were counting. "The kitchen is the most dangerous place in a household. No one should ever leave knives out in the open air."

"Daniele Vidas was making juice," Nigel said. "But I don't think Georgiana would lead the hunters right by her house."

"Everyone must treat data backups as a lost art form. One pizza drop-shipped and two people died. Someone must have lied. I don't believe that no sharp practice was involved. No pun intended."

The phone in the room rang, and Felipe leaped up like a fish. He picked up the receiver. "Uh-huh. Please put it through. Thank you, but there's no need to make a fuss. I've never eaten pizza with cutlery, and I don't think a Margherita would go well with champagne. It goes well with moonshine and sundae. Sure enough. Or you can get me a Moonwalk by Joe Gilmore. Well, no one can bring back the dead. I won't bother you then."

Felipe put down the receiver and turned to look at them. "None of you cared to order pizza from that place? The UK population is rather forgiving now, I have to say. If you're in Japan and run a snack place and your family members kill someone, it's improbable you'd keep it running. The local community kills it softly and socially." He looked up at Nigel. "I guess that you have moved on from your Criminal Tribes Act mentality?"

He walked to the glass desk and moved his books. "I've been ordering their pizzas and tipping generously, and I've learnt that on that day, the guy only filled in for a sick part-time." Then he said, "The stories that move me the most are always inadvertent."

The pizza delivery arrived. They shared it with Felipe scarfing down three slices. Chance made to leave. Felipe saw him to the door and he said, "I think 'The Remains of the Day' is an awful title for that book. If I were to name it, I'd call it 'James Stevens and the Haunted House'. There must be something in that house that cozened them, maybe a *sakabashira*. To make him see, you need to bring him out of that house and see what life has to offer. That's exactly what I plan to do with our lady of solitude."

"What do you get out of this?" he asked sceptically.

"Can't one do some good deeds?" Felipe smiled. "Just to balance things out a bit? I've not always shown disinterest in others' suffering, and I don't make chump change out of this."

Chance exited the lobby and hopped into the first black cab in the rank. He had remembered that Felipe once said: 'Someone I know has a smart way of dealing with his anger. Whenever he quarrels with his wife, he goes out and drives for Uber, so he can stay away from her and make money at the same time'.

Was it an inadvertent accident or did someone lie?

He thought about the possibilities that bounded thunderingly in his head, then he initiated a talk with the cabbie and asked about life as a cab driver as they drove down the Strand.

CHAPTER 9

13th April.
Wednesday.

*A*ll love stories end with cheating partners or major character deaths...or *both*, Catherine clutched her sunglasses and thought pensively as she moved through the open atrium.

Hannah Robinson's plants had begun to wither and mildew. Sarnai was kind enough to care for them once every few days.

Catherine sighed as she opened the door.

The weekly routine fire alarm test sounded as she got in. She put away her sassy boots and changed into her kitty-faced flats, used the washroom, and crept upstairs on her pointes. Maybe she could catch him napping, then she could make some pasta for lunch...The study door was ajar, and she had a peek. He was in there, on his laptop and earphones, watching...

Yikes!

Catherine was stupefied by what she saw. She bit her lip, retreated a few steps, then left quietly.

A moment later.

He finished his business, closed the laptop, and went downstairs to refill his thermos. He saw Catherine sitting by the balcony window, looking at the view and wringing her hands.

"You're back quite early today," he said.

"Umm." Catherine couldn't bring herself to look at him. "I changed shifts with Orla so she could have tomorrow off for her birthday. And I thought..." she trailed off.

"I see." He checked the timer on the rice cooker. "Should I make lunch now?"

She ummed again, downheartedly.

He made a simple lunch with brown rice, a cold dish of bean sprouts, and stir-fried pak choi with crushed walnuts. He set the table, and they ate silently. He glanced at Catherine from time to time and found her emotions hard to gauge that day. He could not put his finger on why.

All of a sudden, Catherine's eyes opened wide, her jaw clenched, and she cried, "Noooo!" There were tears in her eyes, and she held her chin as she rushed to get a cup of water from the tap.

"What's wrong?" he asked as he rose.

She rinsed her mouth then said with watery eyes, "I've chewed on something...it made my mouth tingly and numb."

"Ah," he reflected. "Must be the Sichuan peppercorn. Sorry, I'll use ground powder next time."

They resumed their lunch without saying much. Afterwards, Catherine planted herself on one side of the sofa, looking lachrymose. He decided to sit on the other end, with her handbag and sunglasses in between them. He sat there as if sitting on tenterhooks, then he finally mustered up some courage for small talk. "I like your sunglasses. I remember the first time I saw them, and they were quite...unique."

"I must be a barrel of laughs at the Chamber," she mumbled tersely. Her expression was inscrutable.

He walked his fingers across the sofa and held her hand. "You are upset. Please tell me why. I promise I'll only use ground condiments from now on."

Catherine breathed harshly. "I saw you watching...erotica." Her tone suggested that she'd caught him out.

His brows creased. "You saw me just now?"

"Yes."

He shook her hand gently and said, "Welp, would it make you feel better if I tell you that it might not be what you've assumed?"

Catherine pulled a face. "It's okay, it's really okay. I hadn't expected you would be watching that today. Not when we re-met last year today."

He stood up and offered, "Come on, let's go upstairs, and I'll show you."

They got into the study, he turned his swivel chair around and patted his donut cushion. "Take a seat?"

Catherine ignored him and dragged the ladybird-themed beanbag in the corner beside his chair. She settled down and hugged her knees.

He sat on the chair, opened his laptop, maximised the webpage he was browsing, muted the video, played it for a few seconds and paused it. He'd noticed with his peripheral vision that Catherine had looked away all the time.

"Please have a look," he pleaded.

Catherine turned and raised her head. The video frame showed a modest hotel room and a middle-aged white man sitting on a double bed with a towel around his waist...

The man was Eddy.

"Bah! Why would you want to watch *this*?" She snubbed him a little too impatiently with her arms akimbo. "I feel awfully sorry for Hannah, but of all the videos out there, you have to watch this!" She crossed her arms.

"Catherine, I...I hope you can think more highly of me," he bemoaned. "What I'm trying to say is, do you think this man is Eddy? I mean, could it be possible that it's a deep fake and someone blackmailed him? Or a...sextortion scam?"

She balked at the idea. "Even if you try to absolve him, Hannah won't feel any better." She looked at the man on the screen once again. "He looks like a different person." Her thoughts drifted to her fickle ex-fiancé.

"I feel sorry for Eddy if he was a victim, but now everyone thinks he's a cheater. There's a number that always called him in Brussels. It's from a payphone. I've tried to contact the uploader of these videos...."

"Sextortion...don't they do it with Bitcoins and all that? How realistic can a deep fake get?"

"Some appear quite real; that's what makes them so socially destructive."

"Do you like to play detective?"

"Well," he hesitated. "Perhaps...life is not like debugging; knowing where something went wrong won't make anyone happier. But sometimes, the bug is too obvious to be ignored. And I'm doing myself a favour. I feel what transpired between Hannah and Eddy had made you lose a little confidence in us."

Catherine leaned forward to scrutinise the screen. "Sophie once tried to solve the Zodiac Killer's cypher. I'm not sure if Hannah would be happy knowing where this went wrong. Promise me: if you find any more bad news, don't tell her."

"Alright."

They stayed silent for a few seconds, then a pop-up from the website caught Catherine's attention. It said:

Nudge Nudge, Wink Wink. New Badge Unlocked: Completed a Daily Hot Premium Video for a 19-week streak~

She narrowed her eyes at this message. "Mister, care to *explain*?"

"I..." He blushed like a ripe tomato. "The links that we found on Eddy's computer only provided previews. I needed a Gold account to watch them and you need to be a member on this site for at least a year, so I borrowed Turner's account."

Catherine took a deep breath. "Come off it!" She looked askance at him. "Your explanation does sound a little fishy, Mr Yang. I might as well ask Felipe about the paper shredder. There's no way that I can ask Turner about this."

He let out a soft sigh and grabbed his phone on the desk. "Fine, if you don't believe me, I can show you our chat history." He unlocked it and handed it to Catherine.

She took his phone and checked; their chat lent colour to his testimony.

"I'm not sure if I should be annoyed about your lack of trust in me, or I should be glad that you care for my affairs so attentively." He turned to face her. "But I've decided to make the grand gesture."

She put down his phone and leaned in. "No, you did not."

"Huh?" Doubt registered across his face.

She sat on his lap and pulled him close for a quick kiss. "This is what you call a grand gesture."

"I like it. You should definitely make it more often."

"Well, Mr Yang, today you remain as *taxing* as when we met last year."

"But you fancy me very much?"

"Mm-hmm."

"How much?"

"Huh...pasta spoon one portion?" she quipped.

"Pasta spoon one portion..." He looked at her then tickled her fervently. "Pasta spoon one portion... pasta spoon one por–"

"Alright, stop! I'm having second thoughts!" She burst into gales of laughter. "Well, Mr Yang, I fancy you this much." She gestured with her arms open.

He murmured by her ear thickly, "Little catling, do you know what's the most often said three-word phrase?"

"Uh-huh."

"Tell me."

She nuzzled him and said, "I..."

"Yes?"

"I think, according to my uncle, it's 'Made in China'!"

Catherine escaped, giggling.

***

His phone buzzed just as he wanted to chase after his naughty catling.

He picked it up grudgingly. It was Felipe. He let the call through.

"Hel-lo! It's time to fish or cut bait! Clear your calendar for this weekend, for we are going on an escapade!"

He sat there and listened as Felipe explained his plan.

"Pack light. And let's spin the roulette of fate! Over and out!" Felipe exclaimed briskly and hung up.

He shut his laptop, came downstairs. Catherine sat by their dinette.

She looked at him with amused eyes. "Heh. Heh. Mr Yang, I've no time for trysts now. I have a Photoshop certification exam to prepare for."

She opened her laptop and cranked her neck a bit; the table's height was suboptimal. He went back to the study, removed his laptop stand, and installed it for her.

"Thank you," she said. "That's very considerate. Or are you trying to woo me into saying a particular three-word phrase?"

"No, I'm only trying to keep you sweet."

"It does have its charms."

He sat down across the table. "Catherine, when does your shift end tomorrow?"

"It's an early shift, so noon."

He nodded. "I'm going away for the weekend."

"Oh." She seemed a bit surprised. "Where are you going?"

"I'm going to Windsor," he explained. "Felipe's company organised a weekend leadership bootcamp as an outreach effort, and he wants me to help him out."

"I can't go." Catherine thought for a while. "Fine, at least if you're with Felipe, I know that you won't be fooling around."

"Catherine, *please.*" He gave her a frustrated look.

"I know, I know." She stood up and walked to his side. "I should think more highly of you. I do like you *very* much, Mr Yang. I think the world of you. And my world is so much more interesting with you close to my heart."

They held hands. He noticed that there was a newly added plaster on her hand, and he suggested, "Perhaps it's time that we discuss your birthday plans. It's less than two weeks away."

"My birthday plans," she murmured. "Time flies, doesn't it?"

Catherine had mixed feelings about celebrating her birthday. Two years ago, she had called off her wedding scheduled on the same day because of a cheating partner.

"I don't want anything extravagant," she said. "Well, I want to invite friends and family. Patsy said that she'd bake me a fancy cake. Let's gather everyone and we can slop around, talk bosh, eat flying saucers, host a Murder Mystery Party, and stop Mr Darcy from dancing on the table."

"That can be arranged." He added, "I can make something for you; something sweet with honey."

She smiled back. "I have to say, Mr Yang, that your candy apple offerings are growing a little tedious."

"I'll make you a new dessert tonight." He smiled. "How'd you like some mango sago with coconut milk?"

"Why not?" She sat back with a flourish. "It's always important to try new things." She looked at her screen then said, "Mr Yang, if you could enlighten me on one issue."

"Yes?"

"Are you familiar with Photoshop?"

He nodded. "The basics, yes."

"Might I prevail upon your kind intentions and ask how many shades of grey there are under the Grayscale mode?"

"Well... I think, if I'm not mistaken, you can use up to two hundred and fifty-six shades of grey."

"That's right." She checked with her digital operating manual. "And do you know what makes you as *frustrating* as Photoshop?"

He puffed a bemusing laugh. "Am I as frustrating as Photoshop?"

"Uh-huh."

"Perhaps you would be so kind as to tell me why, Miss Roxborough?" He looked at her earnestly.

"Well." Her expression softened into a pleased grin as she saved her work. "You both have too many layers on."

***

The next day.

Catherine got back to Kean Street shortly before noon. As soon as she stepped inside the flat, she recognised a foreign object by their dining table: a piece of furniture that was not there when she left for work that morning.

It was an antique butler's desk.

The flamed mahogany item was in relatively good condition. It had four conforming graduated drawers, standing a little taller than the escritoire she had at home. A small, white envelope adorned a corner of the desk, together with a set of miniature silver keys. Catherine opened it and recognised his round, block handwriting:

Dear Catherine,

Amani's neighbour was selling this butler's desk, and I thought you might like it.

I had intended to present it for your birthday, but it seems that our dining table is too uncomfortable for writing and learning Photoshop. I hope this gesture is to your taste.

I have heard that the previous owner was a writer as well.

Catherine tucked the message away, feeling like a cat that got the *crème de la crème.*

She then took a chair, sat down, and examined the ogee-feet desk on the edge of her seat. There was a fair bit of wear and tear and a nice gloss patina that reflected its age and use. The bronze pull handles were cold to touch as she unlocked and flipped open the top faux-front drawer. The fall front moved smoothly, and the hinges were quiet. A braw baize lining embellished the writing surface. She opened one of the marquetry inlaid wood compartments, and traces of rose greeted her. She'd linked that scent to a wax tablet from Farmacia Santa Maria Novella.

Catherine wondered about the previous owners of the desk and what their stories were. Someone sitting in his parlour, writing to a former member of staff with a cup of cocoa... Or someone who was writing to her pen pal, cavilling on the nuisances of life with a glass of juice...

"Do you like it?" All of a sudden, a voice startled her, then a hand touched her shoulder.

She almost jumped, recalling where she was, then she felt safe in an instant. "Oh, sorry, I was...I was a bit lost in my imagination. Yes, I do like it very much." She stood to face him. "Were you upstairs?"

"I just got back. I went to have a chat with Turner." He gave a faint smile and shrugged. "I haven't been to the jazz bar that often."

She swept her hand softly against the satiny green lining. "Sometimes I have a feel for things and seeing this desk makes me warm-hearted. I feel a connection for reasons unknown. Whenever I see that beanbag upstairs, I feel sad, and I think I'm at a loss... Perhaps it's because I know what happened with the previous tenant. Anyway–" She turned to show him the secret cubbyholes. "I think this part is perfect for storing my letters from my pen pal."

His lips moved as if wanting to say something, but he remained silent.

"More brownie points to you, Mr Yang," Catherine said in an uplifting, mellow tone. "I think you've done a wonderful job in making me happy. And I...I..." she faltered.

"Catherine, I don't want you to say it because you feel that you're obligated. I want you to say it when you mean it."

"But...I want you to be happy."

"Oh, I am happy," he said. "I'm happy every day being here with you."

She nodded. "Let's open a joint bank account then."

"Now, shall we have lunch? Then we can go back to fetch your letters and you can tell Mr Darcy about your present. Then we can go to the bank. After that, we can go and watch *Zootopia*."

"Yes, let's do that." She pecked him on his cheek. "But if you're amenable, I'm cooking today."

He gave her a cheery smile. "I hope my cooking has not grown tedious for you."

"Not at all," Catherine said with a coquettish grin. "And Mr Yang, don't think that I'll let you idle around. You have to muck in and plan our dessert. I've heard that you can burn off the calories more quickly if you indulge in the afternoon."

"Very well," he lit up. "I can think of something new and sweet."

Chapter 10

The next day, he packed a duffel bag, made sure he had everything he needed and that Felipe required, and left.

It rained quite heavily when he walked across Waterloo Bridge. By the time he arrived at Waterloo Station, it was raining stair rods.

He checked his watch: ten to three. He was early.

He waited as he checked the offerings at Lola's Cupcakes and then the ads from McDonald's, listening to a hodgepodge of various tannoyed information on signal failures and observing the bustle. Shortly after, he saw Felipe in a La Martina sweatshirt slinging his leather Bennett Winch weekender bag on his Palladium boots, chatting with two other people.

He was quite certain that when Felipe had referred to 'our lady of solitude', he had meant Amani. Now Chance was not so sure.

He waved and greeted them. "Amani, Mrs Parker, how have you been?"

Amani waved back. "Lao-shi! I didn't know you were going to the bootcamp as well!"

"I'm helping out." He smiled. "If you have questions, you can always ask me."

"Mr Yang," Gabby said as she clinched the insulated picnic basket in her right hand and a greige holdall on her left elbow, "I didn't expect the rain this morning."

"One thing I didn't miss about London was rain. It never rains, but it pours," Felipe exclaimed with a wince.

"Well, Mr Kazama," Gabby said, "April showers bring May flowers."

"Guess I'll just acclimatise. Perhaps it's time that I loop 'Rainy Blue'," Felipe exclaimed. "I'm infinitely obliged to Georgiana for being kind enough to send us in her car. Public transport here's so expensive! Pity that she couldn't extend her courtesy to the rest of our trip."

They chatted a bit more and bought tickets for a fast train to Egham. They found their platform, train, and seats within minutes and settled sitting face to face in their table seats—he and Felipe on one side, Gabby and Amani on the other.

"The rest of the group will join us there," Felipe explained. "We have eight participants in total." He smiled a bit too phonily at Amani. "So, are you looking forward to the weekend? I always got myself into panic stations before exams."

"Not really." Amani bit her tongue. "Why does everyone on this bootcamp have to come from our school?"

"Aren't you the future leaders?"

Amani's mouth twitched. "But my friend Nathan's not selected. He's...he's more of a leader than any of the others."

"Well." Felipe crossed his legs. "If he's already a leader, he doesn't need any more leadership training. I'm here to teach what they cannot learn from the books and what their parents have neglected."

Chance knew why. All those selected were the ones who gave Amani trouble at school.

They sat for a while in silence and watched as rain splattered on the window and as open fields interspersed with buildings as the train passed through the London conurbation. Chance felt hot despite the cool temperature inside the train. He went to the washroom, took off his sports jacket, then his turtleneck jumper. He got back to his seat and tried to squeeze his jumper inside his duffel bag.

"If you don't mind, Mr Yang," Gabby offered, "I can keep your jumper in my bag. I don't wish to see the material suffer." She gestured to her greige Boston bag.

"Thank you." He folded his jumper carefully and handed it to her. "The weather is a bit volatile these days." He eyed the insulated picnic basket on the table. "I hope the weather will be nice enough over the weekend for a picnic."

"Oh." Gabby held the basket. "Just something I brought in case Amani doesn't like the food there. Mrs Eden has been adamant about her nutrition. Exam seasons can be very trying and tiring."

"Yes." He nodded. "I'm not sure if they have a fridge inside the rooms. Perhaps you need to speak with the kitchen staff and store any perishables if needed."

"I will." Gabby patted her basket softly with her gloves on. "I have some pickles, cheese, and cold meats here." She remembered, "We've been growing a new batch of bean sprouts. It's a success this time."

Amani cut in. "Lao-shi, do you know how to make pickles? Gabby is a master at making them."

"No, not really."

"Well, Mr Yang," Gabby said. "Since you offered us the recipe for bean sprouts, I can give you some insights for making top-line British pickles."

Pickles...

He thought for a while. "Mrs Parker, do you happen to know how to make pickled walnuts? From fresh walnuts?"

Gabby clapped her hands lightly. "You are asking the expert, Mr Yang. You see, to make them right, you must use the unripe fruit; that is, before the shell has formed. Pickled walnuts are known as the 'King of Pickles', and Mrs Eden particularly fancies them. I have some here; maybe you can try some later."

"I see." He nodded. "If it's not too much trouble, can you teach me the recipe?"

"Yes," Gabby said, "I always buy the fresh walnuts from Potash Farm in West Kent. There is a short window in July when you can order them online. And the farm has a nice recipe on their website that you can use."

"Thank you." He took a mental note to check the farm's homepage later.

"I make stellar duxelles and ragouts," Felipe said. No one responded.

Their journey ended after another twenty minutes. They got off the train and made their way to the taxi rank at Egham Station. Amani and Gabby took one car, and he and Felipe took another.

It was still raining, and Felipe complained as the windscreen wipers moved frantically. A moment later, he asked, "Do you know that Johnson's sister-in-law works for the Crown Estate?"

Chance had worked briefly with Johnson from Mercury's London Branch last April.

Felipe mused, "Cumberland Lodge...I think the Brits should do something with their naming. The other day I met with someone from Slaughter and May. The name itself is ominous enough. Cumberland Lodge…" he murmured again and laughed wickedly. "I hope it's not an insinuation to anything. Anyway, it might just fit the bill. I hope it's not a hard row to hoe. It might be too *cumbersome*. Ah, Nigel once attended a police conference here and listened to Theresa May. Every cloud has a silver lining; every copper pot has a tin lining. Most of all, them gumshoes like to talk about old cases they'd solved. They never spoke about the cases they'd failed. Now we have the May, and where's the slaughter?"

Chance observed the driver. It seemed that Felipe's flippant remarks had fallen flat.

Felipe harped on, "Say, Mister Driver. I've heard that for legal reasons, GPS and SatNAV systems don't work within Windsor Great Park? Is that true?"

The driver did not respond.

"No comment? Well. I'll take it with a pinch of salt then. Or maybe I can try with Google Maps later. I once stayed at Frogmore House. Isn't it a flower frog by another name? Perhaps I should trudge my way there and try to catch an old friend for dinner. Sorry for the mouth. I'm always grumpy when I don't sleep well, and there's been some biological construction work and noisy tumbles and sweet nothings in the room beside mine. Pure acoustic terrorism!"

Felipe had recently moved into an apartment at the Cheval Three Quays near the City.

"Delicious single blessedness doesn't sound so blessed for me now. I do miss those torrid salad days of my youth with my Lady Mondegreen and my age of innocence." He turned to Chance. "Egad! I could never think about platform envelopment in its proper meaning having read the Lecter books. It's a rather titillating image, wouldn't you say? Perhaps I should say some tongue twisters to distract myself. Seth at Sainsbury's sells thick socks. Zoe at Zozotown zips *zozobra**. Or I'll just recount the elements between iron and lithium on the periodic table."

They arrived at their destination, Cumberland Lodge, in less than ten minutes. Chance now regretted that he didn't drive. With a car, he could leave anytime he wanted without waiting for train connections.

Amani and Gabby were already there waiting, together with a few others.

Chance got out and unfurled his umbrella as Felipe tipped the driver. Then he heard a boy bawling: "I don't want to come to this *stupid* bootcamp! Stop driving me bonkers!"

He turned and saw a gawky boy struggling against a burly, finely dressed adult, presumably his father.

"Wilfred, don't talk such drivel and don't make this difficult!"

"Let go of me!"

The man dragged the boy aside and gave him a dressing-down in a raspy voice. In the end, the boy retrieved his suitcase half-heartedly from the boot of an Aston Martin and stepped away in a downtrodden manner. He looked as if he couldn't live after tomorrow.

"Mr Kazama, welcome to Cumberland Lodge."

Chance turned back and a stocky, tweedy fellow greeted them as the children gathered and the cars left in the fuming rain. "We've prepared some refreshments. Could you follow me for a brief orientation?"

"How very considerate of you! I hope you're not a few sandwiches short of a picnic? I'm famished already."

"Hmm. Not really." The man seemed slightly confused. "This way, please."

"Great! We'd love to have some *amuse-gueule*."

They entered the hall and shut out the incessant rain.

***

Built in the seventeenth century, Cumberland Lodge was once a royal residence to the Rangers of the Great Park and was now a charitable foundation that hosted residential conferences and programmes to 'exchange views and inspire minds', the fellow, Peter, explained as they filled registration cards, collected electronic passes for their rooms, and took a moment to learn about the domestic arrangements for the weekend, the no-go areas, and the dos and don't-dos. The children eagerly asked for the WiFi password.

Then Felipe told them, "Let's take a group photo so I can hang it above my bed."

The children laughed lightly, and Peter helped them to stage the photo. A few quick snaps did the job.

The staff had prepared a temporary office for Felipe on the first floor. He dumped his weekender bag and had a quick look at the business amenities, consisting of a photocopier, a printer, and a scanner.

Chance took the stairs covered in wall-to-wall red carpets and found his twin-bedded room that he was sharing with Felipe. He opened the door and was met with a faint waft of burnt firewood and a strong fust. The dank room was spacious with en-suite facilities. It also had a chintz-covered easy chair, a small wood writing desk with a black lamp, heaters, blue-dandelion-patterned curtains, and two paintings of flowers on the wall. The single beds had white striped linens and he was glad he had brought his own sleeping bag.

He put his duffel bag down and went into the small washroom to wash his hands and face. There were white towels that he decided against using and waited for his face to dry.

The rain had lost its momentum and turned to drizzle. After ten or so minutes, he took what he needed, went downstairs and found Felipe by an unlit fireplace talking to a boy.

It was Takashi Kawamura, the one who had initiated Amani's distress at school.

"Takashi," Felipe said, "I know your dad. I've heard that you're moving house?"

"Yes, sir," the boy said as he read a book on Winston Churchill. "We leave this summer."

"He told me that you wish to read History at Oxford? Perhaps you can visit the Kranji War Memorial there." Felipe checked his Panerai Tourbillon. "It's time that we gathered the sweetie pies."

They waited for a few minutes as the children gathered again and moved into a conference centre called The Mews situated next to the Main Lodge. According to Peter, it once hosted the most famous racehorse of all time, Eclipse.

They went into the Hodgson Room—a brightly lit, medium-sized conference room with cream-coloured walls, a projector and screen, a small whiteboard with flipcharts for brainstorming, some refreshments, and chairs arranged in a circle.

The children sat down, each immersed in their phones or tablets. Gabby came into the room to give Chance his jumper. Before she left, Felipe called out over his shoulder: "Señora, sorry that I only ordered sunshine for tomorrow but you're welcome to stay. I don't mind having another audience, and I usually charge ten thousand dollars for what I have to say. Crazy, isn't it? If you stay, think of it that you made ten thousand dollars."

Gabby hesitated. "Well. Perhaps I'll sit for a while, and then I'll have a stroll in the park." She took a chair and settled in a corner.

"Wonderful. Without further delay, we better start now." Felipe clapped his hands. "Shall we start?" He waited as the children pocketed their phones and shut off their other electronic devices.

"Okay. I'm not walking out of the door and emptying the chair. I'd appreciate it that you look at me other than with your black mirrors." He paused. "Some housekeeping rules. The first and only rule is that there are no rules." He stated firmly, "There are no social mores in this room. I don't like to hew to others' rules; I like to bypass the rules; I like to play around the rules, and I like to make others play by my rules. I don't go by laws, I create bylaws." He glanced around the room. "Let me introduce myself first. The name's Felipe Kazama. Kazama is a Japanese word that means the time when wind passes—not passing wind, mind you."

The children laughed.

Chance saw that only the boy, Wilfred, remained as jumpy and on edge as before. He looked as if he had a wasp in his pocket and his eyes were glazed.

Felipe continued, "No rules, but let's show some respect and remember that I have zero tolerance for drugs. You can call me by my name but never call me names. I'm a Peruvian citizen and here I am today. Why am I here today? I always ask myself this question. Why am I here today instead of hoeing maca or guiding people to Machu Picchu or shovelling bullshit or selling some two-bit souvenirs? I'm here because I'm the brand spanking new Managing Director of the EMEA region for Mercury Investments and Securities. We are a global firm, and we always go after global talents. Mercury welcomes talents from all over the universe. We've been running this leadership bootcamp for some years. They always invite Lord this or Lord that or some Rhodes scholars or the Right Honourables, the Left Honourables, and the bald, blandiose Honourables. I've told my team, a new man in charge, new rules. A new broom sweeps clean. I'd very much like a one-man show. We can divvy the money we pay to the moonlighters as our bonuses instead. So why am I here? Why am I spending this weekend with you noughties and not with me, myself, and I at my place?"

He looked around. "Some say that growing up is a learning process. I'm here to teach you what you cannot learn from books and past papers. So, who the hell is Felipe Kazama Infante? I used to be a mouseburger and a nobody. But the twists of life brought me here. Besides my undertakings at Mercury, I've served in a paid and unpaid advisory capacity to the Tata Sons, the Mulliez family, the Omidyar Network, the Inter-American Development Bank, and the four houses in the past decade. Namely, Chatham House, the House of Commons, the House of Commons-but-they-don't-think-they-are, aka Lords, and the US House of Representatives. I'm a Fellow of the American Association for the Advancement of Science, the RSA, and the Royal Anthropological Institute of Great Britain and Ireland, as well as a member of the Bretton

Woods Committee. Now, as for why you're all here. Perhaps you are
not aware yet, but the thing for sure is that you're all here because your
parents are all leading lights in their various fields and wish you to extend
their success. You're not here to play patty-cake and I'm here so you can
benefit from my pearls of wisdom. Frankly speaking, this'll be a pilot run,
and you're all laboratory rats. I've prepared no PowerPoints. PPTs make
me sound like a dull and unadventurous person."

Felipe glanced around the room. "I can assure you all that I'm not.
No one likes to read off from a hundred-page PPT. Everybody wants
to listen to more from Russell Brand. Well. We haven't got the budget
to hire him, so you have to make do with me. If you liked this weekend,
please tell your family and friends; if you didn't like it, please keep it
in the inner sanctum in your heart. I'm a strong advocate of word-of-
the-mouth marketing only when my clients say good things about us. I
suppose there's one rule that we should all remember. In that case, that'll
be the Chatham House rule."

He stood still to face them. "And I believe that you're all old enough
for civic conversations, so don't go home and cry and tell your parents
that Mr Kazama says there's no Santa Claus or that the World Bank
does not always do good deeds. What happens in this room stays in this
room."

The children tee-heed once more and nodded.

"There might be some optimal frustration. I know my forthrightness
will offend some people, and there'll be others who think that my words
make sense, although they have to pretend that they are offended by my
remarks. I'll not apologise for whatever I have to say, but I thank you for
your time in listening. Now, is there anyone who does *not* wish to engage

with our feast of reason? Please raise your hand."

The room went quiet, then Wilfred raised his hand limply.

"What's your name, kid?" Felipe asked.

"Wilfred Perry," he said disconsolately.

"Do you feel unwell?"

"No, not really." He paused fretfully and looked around. "I mean. I'm well but–"

"Well. Wilfred. If you don't want to dive into our interminable discussions, I'll give you a way out. I'll ask you one question. If you can answer it, you'll get a personalised recommendation letter from me, and you can leave, do whatever you want in your room, or play with your phone as long as you don't belt out 'God Save the Queen' and faze others from listening."

Wilfred nodded feebly.

"The question's simple," Felipe said. "Which company initiated the first genocide as a multinational?"

"Which company..." the boy bumbled.

"Do you know the answer?"

"N...no."

"Sorry then. You'll have to put up with me for the rest of the weekend." Felipe then said, "Because you all know each other, we'll skip self-introductions. Let's start our programme today with a little game called 'Helicopter Surgery'."

***

'Helicopter Surgery' was a team-building game that used the LEGO

City Ambulance Helicopter kit. Chance took out the kits and gave out the instructions. The game was simple: in teams of four, each player was assigned a role. The Nurse can only pass the parts; the Surgeon wears a mask and tells which pieces go where; the Anaesthesiologist only assembles the miniature figures and keeps time; the Resident receives instructions from the Surgeon and assembles the parts handed by the Nurse. No one can speak except the Surgeon.

The game progressed at a lick, and Felipe asked the group for their feedback.

One Surgeon found that speaking through a mask can be difficult for others to listen to; a Nurse said it was frustrating knowing what to do but not being able to voice it. And Amani, who played a Resident, reflected that it was stressful to work under time and peer pressure.

"Talking is easy peasy lemon squeezy," Felipe said. "But it's hard to be in someone else's shoes. What I'm going to tell you today is that you already have these skills. Many of you are already fully versed in horsemanship and sportsmanship and penmanship with your airs and graces. You go to a leading school, you have no three hots and a cot to worry about, and you all have a competitive edge and the ability to deal with crises. Arty-farty talking is easy. I talk all the time. The hard part is listening. Active listening. Listening's great tool. I have a friend who runs a homeless shelter in Johannesburg. Sometimes they have visitors... people taking refuge in the middle of the night. They won't say anything. Then he tells me that they listen to what they have to say by looking at their pulse rate and their irises. If you're a good listener, you don't have to wait for people to open their mouths to know that they are sending out an SOS. You can sense it from their body language, pulse rate, behaviour, or anomaly in their behaviour. You can be a behaviour detective! Now, let's play another game. You probably are familiar with it. The game is called 'AMA'—'Ask Me Anything'. Anyone can ask questions, but not everyone can ask quality questions. Do we know how to ask good questions?"

Someone raised her hand. "Is it to do with the open and closed questions?"

"Could you elaborate on that?"

"Closed questions often start with is, are, did, will, would, can, was, were...and open questions start with what, why, and how?"

"Very good. You'll find most of the time people ask these questions in interviews." Felipe sat down. "I want each of you to ask me a question, preferably an open one. Let's dial... 'W' for Wilfred."

Wilfred was lost in his own world and jumped at his name. "Yes? Sorry, sir, could you repeat that?"

Felipe said, "Don't call me sir; that makes me feel old. The question is, I want you to ask me a question. Ask me anything."

"Well...yes," Wilfred hesitated. "Which...which company initiated the first genocide as a multinational?"

"Ah. Interesting. I might as well tell you. Who knows, it might be useful for a pub quiz. The company that initiated the first genocide as a multinational was the Dutch East India Company, and the slaughter took place at the Banda Islands in Indonesia. They wiped out about ninety-three per cent of the indigenous population, and you know why they did it? They did it so the Europeans could enjoy nutmeg. As they say, variety is the spice of life. Maybe life is the spice of variety as well."

Felipe turned to the next child in the circle. "Now, ask me another question."

The girl said, "Felipe, what do you think your leadership style is? Do you think that it's important to have a fit between one's leadership style and the company culture?"

"Well, to answer this question, we need first to distinguish between a manager and a leader. A manager does things right within the boundaries, and a leader does the right things. Managers have subordinates, while leaders have followers. A company's culture is the CEO's culture, and a company's brand is the CEO's personality. Most of the time, I lead with laissez-faire cos I trust my people. And I'm an expert at delegating." He paused. "And yes. People always talk about a product-market fit or a strategic fit. It's equally important to have a personal fit with the company. A couple of years back, I was tabbed by an Asian business tycoon. He's in the top quartile of Forbes' richest. He brought me to Tokyo on his private jet from the US and showered me with all the worldly goods. I was touched and moved to the point that he even treated me better than my dad did. One morning, I went to the gaffer's office. A huge calligraphy work hung above his desk said: 'Even the CEO's fart is an order'. That made me think. Did I really want to work there? I haven't conducted my reconnaissance, and I didn't even know if he had any leaky gut syndromes. In the end, I decided to stay with Mercury. It's better to be the head of a mouse than the tail of a lion."

He stretched. "And culture is something you feel, but you can't easily replicate it elsewhere. A finance official from Mongolia that I met at the World Economic Forum told me that he envisions turning his country into a global financial centre, and this very same person told me that it's no use to have a pair of new shoes in Mongolia because they'll get ruined on their first day. You can imitate something beautiful, but you can't prevent something dreadful. Peter Drucker said that culture eats strategy for breakfast. There's a great film called *Trading Places* featuring Eddie Murphy that I like. It tells about the craze of pit trading and the pitfalls of capitalism. A friend from the DoD in the US tells me that they have two hundred and ten Chief Information Officers. What a maze! And when we talk about failed companies and corporate culture, we must speak of Enron. The scam and scandal of the century. Some say that Enron failed because its management had become a cult group. Jeff Skilling would lead his executives on thousand-mile bike trips with enough risk that someone might die. The snowball problems began to roll when an accounting professor gave his students an assignment to analyse Enron's financial position. Enron had some great people, the Ivy Leaguers, and none of them noticed anything fishy? I don't think so. I think they all had vested interests, or they had no psychological safety to voice themselves. It's a toxic culture. If you work for a toxic employer, you choke in the rarefied air. If you work for a great employer, you feel like you're a fish in the water. Do you know what the people at Land Rover told me when Tata acquired them? They said, 'Thank heavens and hell! We finally no longer need to worry about bottom lines! We finally don't need to save on costs!'"

Felipe waved his hand. "If any of your family or friends bought a Land Rover or a Jaguar before the sign-off, I'd recommend a full-course overhaul. Oh, here's another piece of trivia that you can boast during school hours. When people train AIs, they often train them with Enron emails. Scary, isn't it? You'd wonder if it learns the language of integrity or dishonesty. Next question, please?"

A boy asked, "Mr Kazama, what do you think is the top quality of being a leader to have your life in the fast lane?"

"I don't think that my life is in the fast lane. I feel I'm like a bird in a gilded cage. It's tiring work that I do, so don't think that I live on the pig's back. The only secret I've got is damned hard work, as J. M. W. Turner would say. And I did work my fingers to the bone. And we are talking about working eighty, ninety hours a week." Felipe clucked his tongue. "Anyhoo, I think the primary qualities are curiosity and eagerness to learn. If you don't want to be fooled by others, you learn. Do you know that Maslow never drew the pyramid of needs, and he was against putting them in a hierarchy because he knew that different people would value different things? Once, a US client invited my buddy here and me to his house for dinner. He had this Chinese artefact that he called a traditional Chinese enamel fruit basket that he had bought at auction. My client thought it looked so marvy that he used it as a champagne bucket. My buddy," he gestured at Chance, "was secretly amused that evening, so I asked him why afterwards. And he told me that it wasn't a fruit basket at all; it was a chamber pot."

The group cackled.

"Perhaps it's ominous to drink champagne from a chamber pot, and the client ended up having a pot to pee in. My mentor once told me, if someone invites you to dinner, make sure that it's not the Black Dinner. If people extend you an olive twig, make sure it's not poison ivy." He crossed his legs. "I was not a precocious child. As a kid, I grew up in the boonies and I didn't like school at all. And I was brainwashed about the concept of God. I had learnt the Bible by rote. Then I lost my mother as a teenager. And so, I asked the Lord or the Holy Moly Mother, or the José Santa Maria out there. *Por qué?* Why? Why did they take Felipe's mother and not Alberto's? I asked every day, but there was no answer. Then I decided that I'd have a slightly better chance to hear back from extra-terrestrial creatures than from God. I learned that life would be brutal, cruel, and short if I didn't change myself. Then I wanted to become an astronomer, and later I had this opportunity to spend an exchange semester in the US." He looked across the room. "I have a confession to make now. I'm an alien, truth to be told. I'm a man from Mars. Do you believe me?"

The group shook their heads in amusement.

"Well," Felipe said. "The term 'alien' means any person who's not a citizen or national of the US. The first time I went to the US, I was an alien, a flat-footed dweeb, and a shit-kicking wonk. My English was very rusty." His forehead crinkled. "And my roommate, my chum, he was studying at the Gordon–Conwell Theological Seminary. He *suggested* that it'd be best if I could practise English with native speakers and strangers or, you know, talk to people in different places. In the parks, at department stores, so on and so forth. I thought his advice was great." Felipe stood and poured a cup of coffee. "So, you would find me, every day after my lectures, at the train station asking people for one-night stands."

***

Upon hearing this, a few boys giggled, and some girls winced.

Felipe sipped his coffee slowly, put down the cup, and continued without inflexion. "One day, a police officer stopped me and told me not to mess around. I told him, 'Señor, my roommate tells me that I need to practise my English and I'm here to get an overnight ticket standing—a one-night stand. What's so wrong with that?'"

He scratched his brow. "He was kind enough to tell me the...nuance. As Heinrich Heine would say, experience is a good school but the fees are high. I was not only the laughing stock at my dorm, I was the laughing tap, the laughing fountain that they could just turn on and off. And that really was my own school for learning. Some lessons you can never learn from books." Felipe sat back. "I didn't become an astronomer, but there's a UAP seminar group in Kyoto, and I'm a member there. UAP stands for 'unidentified aerial phenomena' or, in lay terms, UFOs. Their catchphrase is that if you join them, there's a ninety-nine per cent probability that you see one. I guess I'm the unfortunate one. I've been with them for ten years so far, and I've not seen one yet. If anyone of you is interested in joining them, talk to me later." He gestured. "Let's continue the meat of this talk, please."

Someone asked, "Felipe, I interned for UNDP last summer and there were some reports on Mercury's lack of corporate social responsibility. What do you think of that, and how are you going to change the *status quo*? Will Mercury set up something like the Gates Foundation maybe?"

"I think we have oodles of great CSR initiatives. We sponsor many knowledge exchange programmes hosting visiting academics from the Global South."

"But that is just all hypocrisy! Your company doesn't even join the Earth Hour movement!"

"Yada, yada, yada. I'll tell you what hypocrisy is. Hypocrisy is

Lockheed Martin having a Sustainability Director for Missiles and Fire
Control. We don't do Earth Hours, so what? We keep our lights on
in case some passers-by or some colleagues have lygophobia or fear of
darkness. Mercury's been a 'Best Employer' for decades in a row because
we care for our people and planet Earth." Felipe mused aloud, "Now, did
you play 'Nurse' just now?"

"Yes."

"Well. As a nurse, would you cut a patient off oxygen for an hour?
Or someone with severe Thalassemia off their blood transfusion? A small
downtick in electricity consumption won't mean that less energy is being
pumped into the grid. It won't help at all. In some cases, it might hurt
the grid. I don't like British education because it's too narrow; you choose
subjects too early, limiting what you learn and what you see. For example,
those of you who study and don't study Geography, do you know that
Lima is twice as large as New York City? But suppose you wish to set
the world to rights today, write a missive *en masse* and petition to end
the travelling circus of the EU Parliament and its cadre of farraginous
politicos. Please do it now while you still have a say in EU affairs."

He laughed. "When you read a news article, you need to figure
out what has not been written. An Austrian saying has it that paper
is patient, but it does not show you the real world. If you help others
to spread lies, you are morally beyond the pale. Be a leader; don't be a
ninny! And the UN needs to have a meeting with the ILO on decent
work. It doesn't even pay its interns. Now, what can we expect from their
quality of work? If you want to get into a good school, donate money.
If you want to sound nice, found something. When you donate money
and let the whole world know, that's not philanthropy; that's marketing.

Genuine good deeds stay unknown to others. We all know that the non-profits are not here for a profit, but are they loss aiming? It's no secret that there is a culture of denial and avoidance and short-termism among those Astroturfers."

Felipe leaned by the window. "The richest man on planet Earth may well tell you how many good deeds he has done, and he deftly avoids talking about how they transported an entire sand beach from the Caribbean on a barge to his new house in the US. Now, how many emissions would that create? How much damage would that do to the local ecosystem? I was once at a high-end wine-tasting event in the Dürkheimer Wurstmarkt. What they did there gave me a shock. People had a sip from a glass, spat it out, and repeated it for six hundred bottles of wine in a day. I mean, can't they use that time to meditate or pray? Research says that in Germany, people waste fifty kilos of food per capita. Fifty kilos of food!"

He picked up Chance's jumper and swirled it in the air. "Don't take your clothes for granted. Don't take your underwear for granted. Don't take anything for granted. If I tell you that it takes as much water to make one organic T-shirt as you can drink in three and a half years, and the T-shirt travels across the five continents before you see it in-store, what do you think? Everything that is labelled 'organic' is not necessarily sustainable. You use all the water for cotton farming, and you leave the land parched for other food production. The per capita consumption of milk, eggs, and meat are pretty low in Less Economically Developed Countries and Newly Industrialised Countries. Instead of telling these populations to eat less meat, you should say to your parents and your school to throw fewer parties and waste less. Ah, I was speaking of the importance of learning. Once, I met some people advocating for the ethical treatment of animals at a sumo event. You know what 'sumo' is, right? It's wrestling, basically, but the players have to undergo training where they add weight and they have big paunches. It's a bit like the force-feeding that the goose for *foie gras* has to go through."

He stopped and mused, "I wasn't sure if those people were there to have fun and watch the show, or to advocate for the unethical treatment of the *rikishi*, the wrestlers. These people had some dodgy advertising practices, and they've lost several lawsuits for fraud and violations of advertising laws. One thing they did was to frame a promo on how people skinned sables alive on fur farms in Asia."

Chance observed Gabby. She seemed fraught, as if she might vomit and swoon any moment.

"Now, perhaps none of you have had any experience on a fur farm. What's the best way to skin an animal? If you skin them alive, the animal, of course, twists and turns and may even burrow holes in certain objects. They might damage their fur. The industry standard is to use an electric probe in the rectum. It's a quick way of doing things. At this sumo game, I raised as a joke that I have some evidence of Japanese businessmen torturing mammoths and eating their meat like they would eat whales. I told them that 'They're having a whale of a good time!' And the next day, the organisation reached out to me, wanting to know who were the torturers. Was it trophy hunting? Did they skin them alive, or did they slaughter them ruthlessly? Hell, it seemed that they still lived in the Ice Age. Interesting, isn't it? I think I've missed out on something important. Children, if there's ever a session to torture a mammoth one day, remember me and sign me up!" Felipe grinned. "Next question,

THE LEARNING CURVE OF PAIN

please."

"That'd be like saying that you support capital punishment!" someone shouted.

"Of course I support capital punishment. An eye for an eye, a pie for a pie. And a 'ta' for a lion. I think capital punishment is a significant deterrent to crime, and we should have more of it." Felipe cleared his throat. "Once, there was a Japanese serial killer who did awful things to young girls. I'll spare you the details because I don't want you to lose your appetite for dinner. We called him the Albert Fish of Japan anyway. He was caught, and the whole of society was shocked. An urban legend says that the head of a gang was so furious that he sent out hitmen to kill this bastard. But the police did a good job at protecting the killer—perhaps a bit uselessly good, I have to say. He was only executed in 2008 after lengthy protests and lobbying, and some of the victims' family members died before him. I think there's something wrong with the whole rickety system. People with no vices are going to have some purty annoying virtues*. Your countryman Sir Robert Anderson puts it quite well. He wrote, the humanity-mongers are so lavish in their pity for criminals that they have none left for the victims; none for outraged society; none for the children they beget and rear to follow in their evil ways. Some people deserve a bullet and a body bag, some others don't even deserve that. But what's happening now? You keep them in prisons so they can play World of Warcraft and study political science? And hoosegows and jails are dangerous places, really—especially the private prisons in the US. Once, I bought some lingerie for a girlfriend from someone's secret. And, children, before anyone tries on new lingerie, you know what the first step is?"

Some said to wash the garment.

"Yes. Personal hygiene is essential. Before or after you wash it, here is my secret in relationship building: you should always cut off the label because it brings discomfort to the wearer. Now we don't want that in the middle of...important learnings that come with strings attached. So, as I was about to cut off the label, and I discovered a note pinned on the label that said: 'Help! I'm enslaved in the White House!'"

Felipe stopped and walked around. "Well, I thought. It seems a likely and compelling story. It's no secret that enslaved people built the White House. Maybe they procured some more for its daily maintenance? But how did this garment get to the store and then me? I didn't know. Then I began to cotton on to the problem. Maybe someone had a fixture with an intern, and things got mixed up and someone decided to flog them after a woeful press conference. Anyway, I always liked doing a good deed every day. Better safe than sorry, so I brought the garment back to the store and complained about their quality control on the side. After a thorough investigation, it was a relief to find that actually, someone in prison in the Palmetto State did it because she didn't enjoy her compulsory work. What can I say? It's hard to believe that there's still slave labour in the world's most developed country, right? But the truth is harsh to the ear. Talking about coerced labour, did you know that many food items in the US are from prison to plates? The largest egg company in the Southwest contracts with the Arizona Correctional Industries. The big suppliers in mozzarella buy buffalo milk from Colorado Correctional Industries. The US ratified only two out of the eight core ILO conventions. Even Libya beats them in this regard. Americans have always marketed itself as the leading light. One interesting observation

I've made recently is that it's always pitch-dark directly below a lighthouse. Perhaps one day, a great force will finally set them free."

He looked out of the window and observed the tranquil cottages. "You're all still yoof, and I hope you'll never have the chance to find out what it feels like to be victims of crime. But life is like a box of chocolates, and you'll never know if you'll have KitKat, Cadbury's or Snickers. Hmm...I wonder if Muhammad Yunus drinks Activia yoghurt. Does he know that the yoghurt containers people throw away would end up on a beach and rot there for who knows how many years? To give more emphasis, people's perspective can shift with time. If you ask Saif al-Islam Gaddafi, would he rather be Prince Charming or Prisoner Garbing? Perhaps he has new world views now. Or maybe he likes to keep his charms in prison. If he seeks asylum in the UK, would you have him? I've heard he's on friendly terms with Prince Andrew. How long is a piece of string?"

He sighed. "Such a pity that asylum seekers don't have a work permit, so he can't put his diplomacy skills to use. Maybe he will be granted with exceptions? But if he has any wits, he might not come if he'd heard about the CIA torture flights and the UK's role of complicity. Do we have any aspiring legal professionals here? Anyone who cares to explain the meaning of extraordinary rendition? Even if he did come, the Home Secretary might not welcome him as she had shown her hostile approach to others. We'll see how things turn out. Next question, please."

Someone asked, "The World Economic Forum predicts that it's going to take two hundred and three years to reach gender equality. Felipe, how do you think we should tackle this problem?"

"Wow. I wonder how they figured that out. With a time machine maybe? And it's a tough task. When we talk about levelling the playing field, I do feel that sometimes all-gender-except-male candidates have lower self-confidence in their abilities. And I think there's built-in prejudice and basis for discrimination in our socioeconomic systems. Many of the so-called 'founders' of social sciences were eugenicists, misogynists, racists, and rapists. For example, even the Bible would say, 'Wives, submit to your own husbands, as to the Lord'. I know a feminist, and she asked me if I thought the Bible was scary. I asked why. She said that you could think of the Virgin Mary as the world's first surrogate mother. Another friend of mine is working on his latest book and he asked the question, why do companies keep on promoting incompetent men? He asked me this question on the very first day I got back to London. I don't know if it's an insinuation to anything. I hope not."

They laughed.

Felipe continued, "Sometimes I ask my people, do you want to join the marzipan layer or why don't you apply for this and that. And some people might say that they are content listening outside of the boardrooms or the charrettes. They told me that we always have manels anyway. Shirley Chisholm said, if they don't give you a seat at the table, bring a folding chair. I think people need to have thicker skins. Fake it until you make it, right? Bring a folding chair, bring stilts, bring a jetpack. Slip a note under the door. Smash the glass ceiling and burn the bamboo ceiling. I know a woman who's a Formula One driver. I know someone who's an astronaut."

He thought for a while. "Is there any occupation that one gender cannot take on? There is. If you are a pilot and you gave birth through C-section, there are certain altitudes at which you can no longer fly, because the scar will burst under pressure. Why don't we design better planes and vehicles instead? Get in, get ahead, get the things that people ignored done. All humans have to be involved every step of the way. I hope I'm not quoting the UN. No one is a born leader. And that's why sometimes I promote people by tossing some dice. There are some people, if you put them under pressure, they'd do well, but if you attempt laissez-faire, they'd burn their laptops and have a field day. I think gender equality is difficult to attain especially given the various conditions and cultural and religious contexts in different countries. Someone I know, her family moved from Venezuela to Saudi Arabia to escape the US sanctions. Her mother wished to land a job as an engineer, but she couldn't go to the interview by herself. The dad had to accompany her and he had to answer the questions on his wife's behalf. She got the job, but commuting was another hassle. She couldn't use taxis alone because being with an unrelated man in a public area wasn't okay. People always say that the feminist movement is quite successful in the West, in the US, in the UK. I have a different opinion. I mean, now in China and South Korea, when women marry, they rarely take on their husbands' last names. Talking about female emancipation, I had this client from South Korea, he travelled to Canada with his wife and they were stopped at Border Control or whatever they call it there. The officer suspected that they weren't husband and wife because the wife's last name was different from the husband's. I mean, talking about social progress, there are a lot of things that you can learn from the—"

"What, learn how to bind our feet?" Someone laughed.

"Ah. Binding feet. Let me remind you that not so long ago, European women suffered in their whalebone corsets. There were girls who had deformed ribs because of that evil item and died because their bones punctured their internal organs. Not so long ago, the aristocratic ladies in Austria, when they went hunting, they often sat on the horseback with two legs on the same side out of propriety. Many fell, got hurt, and even died. This world is a ghetto. We are but one of the multitude, in no respect better than any other in it'."

Felipe said airily, "I was in Vienna a month ago, and I visited quite a lot of museums to enhance my cross-cultural competencies. There's this famous painter called Egon Schiele. Some museums that host his work would note that he was charged with sexual misconduct. And some people think he was unfairly branded because you cannot judge the situation in early twentieth-century Vienna by present-day standards. It was an age when Austrians married young girls of fifteen or sixteen. I think this is regressive thinking. We still have derogatory words like 'femme fatale', 'damsel in distress', 'trouble and strife', 'tiger moms', 'dragon ladies', 'Xanthippe', 'Grimalkin', 'SOBs'. And the dress code. A friend would sometimes complain about how wearing heels hurt her feet. She calls them 'atrocious torture instruments'. We don't have a dress code at Mercury. In business we always talk about learning the best practices, but have you ever heard people say that we should learn from each other's worst practices? I think there are lessons to be learnt around the globe. Next question, please."

Someone asked about leadership in crisis.

"Leadership in crisis..." Felipe mused aloud. "I once dined with the man who saved Japan. Gee. It sounds like a film title. I should definitely put it down on my LinkedIn, and after tonight, you can post on Instagram that you all dined with a man who once dined with the man who saved Japan. For your record, I'm not the one who said that this person saved Japan. It's Junichiro Koizumi, the ex-Prime Minister of Japan, who said it. Where do I start?"

Felipe thought for a moment. "Let me lay the background. In March 2011, Japan experienced a severe earthquake and tsunami. I was in my apartment in Osaka. One night, shortly after the earthquake, I got an urgent call from a friend who worked in the Cabinet asking me if I could get him a concrete pump truck asap."

He paused. "For the poets and quants in the room, a concrete pump truck is a truck that has a pump mounted on the back to transfer liquid concrete. It's widely used in the construction of high-rises for the concrete jungle." Felipe gestured. "A concrete pump truck has a very long placing boom. That's the word. You can think of it as a giraffe's neck. And people normally use the height to describe it: for example, a thirty-metre-tall concrete pump truck." He cleared his throat. "My friend told me that he'd offer two-hundred million yen if I could get him a sixty-metre-tall concrete pump truck."

Felipe sighed. "He was overwrought. So I asked him, why did he need a sixty-metre-tall concrete pump truck? I could get him a UFO sighting for no cost if he was interested. And he told me not to joke because it was a matter of life and death! Well. I was a bit drunk that night. So, I asked him again, what did he mean by a matter of life and death? Was Godzilla coming or what?"

Takashi giggled.

"For those who don't know, Godzilla is a monster dinosaur. A mutant icon created on the big screen after the nuclear bombings in Japan because people feared the deadly effects of the radiation."

Felipe expounded, "My friend told me, 'Felipe, if you don't help me out, Godzilla might come true!' That was a scary comment. I mean, my favourite music band from Japan is called Dreams Come True, and simply, he told me that my worst nightmares might come true." Felipe chewed his lower lip. "Then I asked him what was wrong, and he told me that because of the damage caused by the tsunami, the units of the nuclear reactors at the Fukushima Daiichi nuclear power plant were overheating, and if the problem was not solved, a meltdown was inevitable, and God knows what would happen! It's a secret that they could no longer keep."

Felipe stopped to collect his breath. "Then I realised that was *why* my boss flitted to Singapore that morning. He didn't want to give remote working a try at all. He could have brought me. I foolishly revelled in my joy of becoming the chargé d'affaires. I thought that my inning had finally come. You know, every dog has his day." He raised one finger. "So, lesson number one for leadership in crisis: always bring your most faithful employee."

The room fell quiet, then Felipe continued. "I asked my friend, if the problem is overheating, why don't they cool it down? He told me that the cooling systems inside the power plant were *out of power* because of the tsunami. They'd been using helicopters and fire engines to pump cold seawater to reduce the temperatures, but the fire engines could not reach that high, and the helicopters could not descend that low. That's why they needed a sixty-metre concrete pump truck."

He looked around. "I pulled some strings, and I understood that the tallest functioning concrete pump truck in Japan at that moment was a German-made fifty-metre one and it was too short." Felipe showed them his hands. "Leadership in crisis lesson number two. Always lead yourself before leading others, and always save yourself before saving others. So, I made to pack." He patted his hair. "In the morning, my friend called again, telling me the offer was off the table. I told him that there's no way I could get him a sixty-metre-tall concrete pump truck anyway, and I told him my new address in Kuala Lumpur. He told me that they'd found a sixty-two-metre concrete pump truck, and it was on its way to Osaka Port. Guess how they found it?"

Felipe stopped to drink his coffee. "There's a Chinese man who went to Japan to study and later stayed for work. He's the general agent for Sany in Japan. In case you've never heard of Sany, it's a Chinese heavy equipment manufacturing company headquartered in Hunan Province. Hunan is where James Cameron set his planet, Pandora, in *Avatar*. This man, this general agent of Sany in Japan, knew a sixty-two-metre concrete pump truck that Sany made in China for a German client, and they were exporting it to Germany via the Shanghai Port. The Tokyo Electric Power Company heard about this, and they said they didn't mind paying a premium for this as it was a matter of life and death. The general agent delivered this message to the Sany headquarters, and guess what the chairman said? He said they wouldn't sell."

Felipe waited for a few suspenseful seconds. "Was it because they didn't want to breach their contract with their client? Was it because they felt the price was unsatisfactory? No. The chairman said they wouldn't sell because they were going to donate it to their neighbour in need."

He let out a breath. "It turned out that I didn't have to move house at all. The sixty-two-metre giraffe arrived at Osaka Port, and the Japan Red Cross coordinated, so it got to Fukushima on time." He took another sip of his now cold coffee. "I don't think I'm qualified to teach leadership in crisis, and I think the title of 'the man who saved Japan' is not an entirely accurate one. He was, after all, only one of the hundreds of thousands of humans who saved Japan. The NHS promotes something called 'collective leadership'. Everyone can be a leader. All those people who went to support, who went to rescue, and who evacuated their homes, were all leaders in their own ways. And let us also remember the staff at the Ministry of Foreign Affairs, those who designed, built and tested that concrete pump truck. If we can give all those people who deserve more credit their portion, the world would be a better place." He announced loudly, "And I think the Chinese are terrible at public relations. If it were the US, they would have made three films out of this already."

The group laughed warmheartedly; only Wilfred did not join in.

"How many tonnes of water did they use to cool it down? It's Japan's top national secret. The Tokyo Electric Power Company had stored all the water in large tanks for now. If the management think that these tanks take up too much space and that the forgone opportunity cost of rent is too high, I shudder to think what might happen. Anyway, I hope my nightmare won't come true and that Japan would only be exporting Godzilla culturally and not physically." Felipe clapped his hands. "Next question, please."

Amani asked, "Mr Kazama, do you think that Brexit will happen?"

"Good question," Felipe said. "A better question might be *when* will it happen. This year? Next year? In 2019? In 2099? That's the question. If we consider your friends from across the channel, they think you don't have the guts to do it. The Europeans have not yet learned their lesson to discuss power using the language of power. They only use the power of language. Treaty, agreement, protocol. In conclusion, EU conclusions are just paper wasted. But hey! Everybody plays multiple tables. There are some decisions that you cannot keep on the back burner always as they have been brought to a head. The Kingdom's no longer united and even London is a vast and fragmented city. My London is very different from your London; your London is very different from your maids, servants, au pairs, and chauffeurs' London. Brexit will tell us what's fallen through the cracks of all this–"

"If you think that Brexit will happen," someone asked, "do you think that Donald Trump will be nominated for the presidential election? If he did, do you think he'd win?"

"I think so, yes."

Someone put in, "But the polls–"

Felipe smiled. "If you ask the motherhood and apple pie Americans on the street about some policymaking agenda. They'll only say that they don't care or they don't know if they are competent enough to make a decision on this or that. But if you give them a poll item, ask should they do A or B, they'll say, 'We should definitely do B'. But if you ask them, are they sure? They are not so sure anymore." He turned and wrote a word on the whiteboard: 'Psephology'.

"The first time I saw this word," he said, "I pronounced it as 'piss-phology'."

The children burst out laughing.

"Now, 'psephology' means using statistical tools to study elections and voting trends and patterns. Twenty or thirty years ago, you could randomly dial a number and reach out to people and ask them to do public opinion polls. Now, under forties mostly have cell phones, and public opinion is a hard thing to determine. Most surveys don't give people an option of 'I don't know'. It's costless for the parlour patriots to say that they hate blablabla in a survey. As David Ogilvy said, people's problem is that they don't think how they feel, don't say what they think, and don't do what they say."

"Do you think he'd be a good president then?"

"Ah. Now, one difference between Gordon Ramsay and me is that he can cook a lobster and I can eat one. Is it a big difference? Is it a small difference? I might buy it if you told me that someone who has never acted before might be a great actor on his debut, but if you have never swum before, will you drown?"

"He'll have a professional team," a boy urged.

"If I put you in the cockpit of a bomber and give you a team of engineers and pilots on support, will you fly the plane for me? If I give you a fully equipped kitchen and ask you to make me Beef Wellington from a live cow, would you know where to start? Do you think you could manage? Do you even know how to kill a cow? Where to aim with a gun? For those who have never killed a calf and are interested, never aim the gun in between the eyes. You'll miss the brain and leave it to suffer."

Felipe paced around. "I have a good friend who always says that 'Not all birds are meant to be caged'. She's right. Some birds are meant to be consumed. There's the 'capon' in Spain, a neutered cockerel fattened by forced feeding. The French have this delicacy called 'ortolan'. It's a songbird and when people snare them, they either blind it or cover its cage with a black cloth, so the bird thinks it's night-time. The bird asks, 'Is it daytime? Is it daytime?' And the human says, 'It's time, it's dinner time!' When people cook it, they feed the birds Armagnac and when people eat them, they cover their own faces with a napkin and they don't even spit the bones out. Sarky, isn't it? François Mitterrand enjoyed his last meal with the birds. It's outlawed, but people do it anyway. Money can get you anything. Now, as for the king of birds, might Trump be an ill bird that fouls its own mew?"

He considered, "When was Donald ever held accountable for the things he did? When journalists interviewed him after 9/11, he laughed because Trump Tower would become the tallest building in Manhattan. Didn't he say that he's so popular that he could shoot someone on Fifth Avenue and not lose a single voter? That's a bold statement. A teacher from the US I know tells me when students make mistakes, they'll not say that they were wrong. They'll use sugar-coated gentle correction. This sounds like a cosmetic product. A saying in the US Congress is that 'the authorisers think they are God and the appropriators know they are'. Even a layperson can cook a bird, but no one can revive a cooked bird, not even God. That's the US quandary in the twenty-first century."

The group nodded and Felipe continued.

"And you know what's the worst-kept secret in the US that no one wants to admit? Having a fractious committee tussling on how to best revive a cooked bird. The truth is that it's easier to live in lies. Maintaining the status quo uses no effort. You can't reason with unreasonable people. It's a Sisyphic condition and it's going to be a smarting lesson. A football legend, Johan Cruyff, says that football is a game of mistakes. Whoever makes the fewest mistakes wins matches. All leaders make mistakes. Sometimes they do it to take advantage of certain situations. For example, there's a *remarkable silence* in the US over Obama turning a blind eye to what the Saudis did in Yemen. Someone said...I better not mention who. You know, the Chatham House rule. Someone from your Ministry of Defence said that 'Russia is the acute threat, China is the illusory threat, and the US is everybody's bloody threat'. The ten most terrifying words in the English language are: 'I'm from the US government, and I'm here to help'."

Felipe roamed around the room. "One thing that Donald got wrong is that China is not a threat to the US. China is a threat to US dominance in today's monopolar world. Breaking the US supremacy in the world order for the Global South's benefits has been a long-term endeavour. The US cannot play the silverback forever with its fool's gold and it cannot always roust in the catbird seat." He smiled. "But let me get one fact straight. Those who support Trump are also human beings. I'm not saying that Donald is a man without qualities. He golfs better than Abe Shinzo. I've golfed with them both on different occasions. Donald has more...down-to-earth tastes, and he supports domestic firms by walking the walk and favours Big Macs daily. One thing about good golfers is that they all have great lies. No pun intended."

Felipe clapped his hands. "Now! If someone says he's going to modernise the WTO, he really means that he wants to limit the power of that agency. Some politics give a warm inner glow, and some raise a furore. What the US and the UK need now is politics that make you feel good, not something you won't regret later. Let's see if Donald brings a Hollywood ending or an imbroglio. What can I say? Perhaps the tinderbox would favour a short fuse? If no one has any burning questions, let's stretch our legs and take a fifteen-minute break. We can continue our constructive, courteous, enjoyable, and productive debate later."

***

The afternoon passed quickly with Felipe's ripostes and anecdotes and they concluded with a human rock-paper-scissors energising activity after watching a TED Talk, 'Do schools kill creativity?' by Sir Ken Robinson.

Before dinner, Chance saw Wilfred, still bottled up, approaching Felipe. Felipe was scrutinising a mounted and framed letter written by the Queen Mother to celebrate the Lodge's fiftieth anniversary as an educational foundation.

The boy tiptoed and was startled when Felipe suddenly turned around. "Perhaps you are interested in UFO sightings, Wilfred Perry?"

"Mr Kazama, I..." the boy stammered glumly, shuffling his feet with his hands clasped and unclasped. "I wonder what's your stance on... Bitcoin. Do you have any?"

"Ah. Bitcoin. I don't trust it."

"I see," Wilfred said dejectedly.

They chatted as they moved to the dining room. Dinner that night was Scotch eggs with mustard sauce, French beans, boiled potatoes, baby carrots, and cherry tomatoes together with a selection of desserts and soft drinks.

Gabby seemed pleased with the menu. She reminded Amani not to eat with her elbows on the table, then she offered Chance some of her tip-top pickled walnuts. He found it tasted like mushy aubergine with Worcestershire sauce. Gabby told him that it went well with salad dishes, particularly asparagus and parmesan and mesclun salad.

Felipe commented, "Did you know that potatoes only arrived from the Andes to Britain in the sixteenth century? You'd wonder what people ate before that. And did you all know that once Europeans thought that tomatoes were poisonous? The acid in the fruits' juice reacted with the lead in their pewter plates, causing lead poisoning. Who knows, might be useful for a pub quiz. In the old times, they were also called 'love apples' but in 1893, the US Supreme Court ruled to classify tomatoes as vegetables and not fruits."

Someone talked about the summer his family spent in Deauville and another time in Tangier. Another complained that there were no TVs in the rooms. Then someone asked, "Felipe, do you watch TV? What TV series do you like?"

"I have a penchant for detective stories. My recent favourite is *Sherlock*. I've heard that they've begun filming season four. Here's a topic that I've debated with some fans of the show online. If we ask Sherlock Holmes to solve the Hagley Woods Mystery, maybe he can solve it with all the fancy technologies and gadgets of today. But the tricky part is this: if we ask Sherlock Holmes to solve the assassination of the Belfast solicitor Patrick Finucane, perhaps he won't take the case. He'll say, 'We all know who did it, we all know why they did it, and we all know their methods, so why don't we just keep cool, calm, and collected and have our tea?' Or he might tell us to make some requests on *WhatDoTheyKnow.com*. Maybe he'll say that he doesn't want any contentious trouble from the MI5 and a particular No.10. Oh, and I also like *Miranda* and *The IT Crowd*."

He had a bite of food. "I used to like Bill Nye the Science Guy. I even had a photo with him. We were at an event, and he wanted some Fanta. The waiter was reluctant to give it to him because the function was almost over. I offered my secretary's to him. What a surprise! Bill Nye, the Science Guy, drinking fizzy drinks. No wonder child obesity rates are rocketing in the US."

They finished dinner with light chat. Before leaving, Felipe told the group, "Unless you are kin to the Royal Family, don't go running around after dark in the Great Park and don't go anywhere near the castle. I don't want to be anyone's whipping boy. And who knows, the woods might turn into Hagley Woods in the night. So, off you go and don't let the bedbugs bite."

The children giggled once more and spent the evening without causing havoc.

Amani shared a room with another girl, and Gabby had a room of her own. Chance and Felipe made sure that the children got back to their respective rooms and returned to their shared room after ten. Felipe saw his sleeping bag and various travelling accoutrements and winced. "I didn't mean for you to move house."

Chance arranged his bed as Felipe continued. "Did you know that they filmed parts of *The King's Speech* here? Brings back old memories, doesn't it? They filmed King George V's deathbed scene in the Chapel. Perhaps you can tell Catherine. Do you two love birds have breakfast at The Delaunay often? Hmm. Luckily there aren't any cookies to my eyes, or they would find my eyes drifting to the babushka all the time. Freud said that if their lips are silent, they gossip with their fingertips; betrayal forces its way through every pore."

Felipe moved towards the window and stood there for a while. "Every school should have a kid-free zone. What'd you say if we go for a walk now? I need to have a smoke, and I'm scared of whoever might haunt this place. Don't you feel that this estate exudes an air of disconcertment? The Castle of Threave gave me the creeps. Who knows, maybe I can finally see a UFO here." He drew the curtains.

They went downstairs; it was a clear and cold night after the rain. The air was crisp as fresh perilla and the moon was gibbous. The darkling sky glowed a violet blue like Concord grapes.

They rambled within the Lodge's perimeter, and Felipe chanted as he smoked. "It's time for my compline. Socrates says that to be is to do. Jean-Paul Sartre says that to do is to be. Frank Sinatra says *do be do be do~*"

Then Chance saw a silhouette by the woods. He first thought it might be one of the Lodge's staff. As they got closer, they found out it was Gabby.

She was looking down at something.

"Mrs Parker." Chance stepped forward and found her staring at a slug.

"Oh! Mr Yang... Isn't it a beautiful night?" she greeted him hurriedly.

Felipe joined them and said a bit too loudly, "Emil Cioran writes in *The Trouble with Being Born* that the only nights that remain in our memory are the ones when we couldn't close our eyes. I'd never wish insomnia on my worst enemy."

He looked down. "Mrs Parker, do you know that slugs have green blood? That's because, unlike us who have iron in our blood, they carry copper in theirs. A pest to gardens, aren't they? If you spray vinegar on molluscs, their bodies will dissolve. If you behead them, you can create a nice solution that glows under ultraviolet light with some alcohol. There are two species of sea slug that, when they discover that their bodies are infected with parasites, they decapitate themselves and regrow a new body."

Felipe took a meaningful puff and continued, "Once, a colleague wanted to challenge me. He put a skinned cat inside my bento box. I nuked it and ate it with some wasabi and *kaki no tane*. He took off like a scalded cat. No one gave me trouble again."

Gabby gave Chance a horrid look.

"Now, señora, no need to sweat. I was just joking. My buddy here will tell you that you can only believe a tenth of whatever I say. But I do recommend *cuy*. The tender meat goes very well with a white Châteauneuf-du-Pape." Felipe took a drag, "How did you find your room?"

"Oh. It's quite lovely. I have an entire suite to myself."

"Well. I'd find the coop itsy-bitsy. There's no room to swing a cat even."

Gabby responded with a careworn expression. "Mr Kazama... I...I've wanted to ask you," she voiced timidly.

"Yes?"

"Do you indeed charge ten thousand dollars for this course?"

"Not really. I charge nine thousand and nine hundred and ninety-nine dollars and ninety-nine cents. Marketing psychology says that prices that end in nine always work wonders. It makes the number seem less daunting. What did you think of this afternoon?"

"Well, you said some interesting things about business..."

"But?"

"I felt uncomfortable with some of your...blasphemy, if I may say so."

"Of course you can say so. We must treat enabling psychological safety at the workplace as an art form. You can call me a renegade but never call me names. I have a warped sense of humour, I know. I'm known for having more hide than Jessie, and I have no qualms at all and I have no faith in humanity. By the way, the folks at the Tedder Academy loved my jawing. But of course, I needed to drop in some racy tidbits and urban legends on the Royal Family."

He puffed, "If circumstance permits, I'd rather be a misanthrope. I don't want to go to heaven, for none of my friends are there. But isn't it nice to see that there are still *staunchly* devoted stalwarts like you? Ah, I think the Royal Chapel is having a service this Sunday. Perhaps you can join the bastion and get some spiritual nourishment? Will you trill prayers for deliverance or tender mercies or Turkish delight?" Felipe moved by a mature, sturdy tree. "Is this a common lime or a buckeye?" He then patted the trunk.

They nattered for a while, then Felipe said, "A group of bats is called a 'wisdom'. But bats don't even form groups in the wild. Tonight reminds me of another night in my now distant memory. It was a sleepless night. I guess saying it now won't cause any trouble because the persons concerned are all as dead as doornails. Once in Japan, the wife of a renowned figure passed away, and I was summoned to help out with the funeral arrangements. On the night of *otsuya*, or the all-night vigil, I saw the family's children—the elder son and his younger sister—for the first time. And throughout the vigil, I saw the boy. He must have been thirteen or fourteen. I saw the boy smiling all the time. I cried buckets when my mother died, and later I asked him why. He said to me, 'Kazama-san, smiles are easier to fake than tears'. I found it an odd comment, so I asked him why again. I understood that they were a strict and formal family. The boy was very hesitant at first. But by now, you know, Mrs Parker, I can be rather annoyingly persistent in some issues and, believe it or not, I can tell if a person wants to die or not. I wheedled a bit of information out of him. Everyone has secrets, and the people in that house were no exception. It happened that every day after school, he and his sister, who was two years younger than him, had to spend their nights in the basement of their house. And by midnight, two 'ghosts' dressed in various uniforms would enter the basement and chastise them and tell them that they had behaved badly. And these ghosts would then force them to do multiple bizarre sexual acts. None of the neighbours guessed what happened in there. None of their teachers noticed anything wrong. The servants knew, but they said *nothing*. The boy told me that he'd lost his ability to cry since the age of five. He told me it's like living in hell but only worse because at least in hell you are dead."

They remained silent as Felipe smoked, then he continued, "I told him that I couldn't imagine his pain, but I could help him to inflict some of that pain on his enemies. He turned me down. He said he wanted to do it by his own hands before it was too late. His sister had attempted suicide by cutting her wrists twice. If he couldn't save himself, at least, he wanted to save her. He told me, 'Kazama-san, have you ever heard of the balloon debate? Now, my sister and I and that beast are on that sinking hot air balloon. If I don't throw him out now, it'll crash, and we'll all die.' I then said to him, 'If you throw him out now, you'll all die a social death. Your so-called friends and family will burn your effigies. Who doesn't like a bonfire as long as they are not on the tripalium? And to exist is to be indexed by a search engine, no matter how much you hated it. There are terrible plans, naïve plans, and tragic plans. Think about your sister, please. I can help you if you allow me some time.'"

Felipe took another puff. "I thought that I had convinced him to put off whatever plans he had. Three days later, he stabbed his father to death and leaked the gas and died in an explosion. The sister couldn't stand the volleys of limelight and tried to cut her wrists for the third time and then there were none. Talking about the best-laid plans of mice and humans. Not a comforting bedtime story, is it?" He looked at the moon. "Mrs Parker, do you have children?"

"Y...yes. They are at university."

"How silly the way things are: you need a licence to drive; you need a licence to marry; you need a licence to busk, even James Bond needs a licence to kill, but you don't need a licence to parent. I think there's a hell of a difference between being good and being well mannered. Mrs Parker, I take it that you are familiar with the kitchen?"

"Well, yes."

"Are you one of those people who use napkin rings?"

"Of course not!" Gabby seemed offended.

"I use them and I do like onion rings. Do you know that when an onion rots, it often rots from the heart? Do you know what happens when you superglue wounds together? The wound may stop bleeding, but it festers underneath. If you don't do anything, the fur will fly. Your knowledge is sod all if no one else knows you know it."

They walked back in virtual silence.

Before they went to bed, Felipe said, "I hope my theatrical effect works."

"Umm?"

"Did you not notice? Your student, she's up on that tree." A minute later, Felipe said, "I'm more worried about that Wilfred boy. He gives me the willies. He looks like he might give up the ghost any moment."

***

Felipe's comment gave Chance the heebie-jeebies and left him tossing and turning. He finally drifted into a fitful sleep hours later.

In the morning, he woke up to find Felipe gone. He checked his watch; it was almost eight. He had a change of clothes, used the washroom, messaged Catherine who had an early shift, called his cousin An briefly, ventured downstairs and found Felipe by a magazine stand on the ground floor corridor, leafing through the latest issue of *The Economist*, a publication that he dubbed 'The Egoist'. He had a nifty black sweatshirt from Ragyard with a pair of embroidered parrots patched on the sleeves.

They greeted each other, then a student came in, picked up a copy of *The Times Literary Supplement* and asked, "Mr Kazama, what TV channels do you watch for information and news?"

"The usuals," Felipe said as he put back the magazine. "You know, the Blatantly Blithering Company, Gloomberg, and the Crappy News Network. Here's my secret sauce for making sound investment decisions: just do the opposite of whatever they tell you on the news. If they say that the Chinese economy will collapse, you invest in China. If they tell you that Brexit won't happen, you prepare for it. If they tell you that Trump won't get elected, you prepare for the good, the bad, and the ugly with equanimity. The twenty-first century is Asian; more specifically, it's Chinese. Whoever thinks otherwise is *sumamente tonta*. They deregulated their economy street by street, postcode by postcode. It's out of the common fashion, but it beats the shock therapy a million times." Felipe grinned. "Oh, you know what happens when you give a cold turkey shock therapy? It gets goose bumps. Not so funny, right? In China, they call it a 'cold joke'. A joke that's not funny at all. If you want to be the next Bill Gates, go and learn Mandarin."

"I don't want to be the next Bill Gates!" the girl said firmly.

Felipe feigned surprise. "You don't want to become the next Bill Sikes, oh sorry, I meant Gates? My English always gives me trouble if I don't sleep well."

"No, I want to be the next Elon Musk."

"Huh. You want to be the next Elon Musk? Well, then Mandarin is a must. Or else where would you sell your models A, B, and C? How many US cities have more than four million people? Only two: New York and Los Angeles. How many cities are there in China with more than four million people? Twenty, last time I checked. And here's advice from a top Silicon Valley unicorn hunter: if you're a high school student and you're highly technical, don't go to university. Start something now. And you know what you should never learn from Musky boy? Never acquire something maliciously, and then market yourself as the almighty founder and the world's saviour. Do you know how much emissions Bitcoin mining generates? Business is a grungy trade, I tell you. Whatever you do, remember to create solutions; don't profit from creating wicked problems for people and the planet. Innovation should not be theatre—"

Then, all of a sudden, they heard a string of noises from upstairs. Chance and Felipe sought its source. The rumpus came from the room that Takashi and Wilfred shared. They got there and saw a clarinet wrapped tightly in wet toilet tissues.

"Kazama-san! Look what the wally's done!" Takashi cried. "It's dreadful!"

"Now. I've seen horses who nap." Felipe picked up the dripping clarinet, which resembled more of a bludgeon that Yeti used. "Wilfred, would you explain this?"

"I...I needed to do it!" the boy stammered gingerly. His eyes were sunken and his hair looked like Einstein's. His pallor was paler than the wallpaper. "Or...or–" He clammed up.

"He even took photos of it and sent it to someone else! Who knows where he wiped before destroying my clarinet!"

"Well, well. Birds in their little nests agree. Why don't you go and have breakfast first, Takashi? We'll have a chat with recalcitrant Perry here."

Takashi left with a grunt. They sat down, Felipe on a bed, Chance in the armchair, waiting for Wilfred to explain. His face puckered, and his eyes were teary, but he didn't say anything.

Chance observed the boy. He vaguely recognised this behaviour. From where? he asked himself. Then he remembered: Hannah Robinson. Felipe was wrong, he thought. The boy didn't look as if he would give up the ghost. He looked as if he'd given himself up. Chance sensed that he wanted to tell them something, but the boy bottled it at the last minute and slipped into a state of obscurity.

Felipe did not give the boy a rollicking. He only said, "I won't send you packing because I feel that's exactly what you want. You still have to put up with us for the weekend."

Later, they took the woebegone lad downstairs for breakfast. The good weather did nothing to dispel Wilfred's downcast demeanour. He seemed as if his nerves were pulled tautly by a mysterious force, and he was nearing the end. Wilfred ate like a bird and remained quiet all along.

Afterwards, the group gathered again in the Hodgson Room at Felipe's behest.

Felipe stood and stared at the group for a long time. Then he finally said, "Anthropologists say that just by observing a culture, you can change it. But we can't say for certain the change is for better or for worse."

He then announced ex cathedra, "It's a lovely day today, and I was thinking of bringing you all out in the park for some fun and some sun. But Mr Wilfred Perry here pulled a prank that changed my mind." Felipe distributed a pile of blank A4 paper, making sure everyone got a sheet.

"What should we do with it?" someone asked.

"What do you see?" Felipe said strongly. "An artist might see a canvas. An engineer might see an aeroplane. The more poetic ones will see clouds. If there's no cloud, there's no rain, and if there's no rain, there's no rainforest. No forest, no tree, no lumber, no pulp, no paper. To be a leader, first of all, respect your paper! Yesterday, I told you not to waste. Now, I want you to hold this sheet of paper before your eyes, and I want you to sit here for an hour and imagine the trees' pains."

Chapter 11

Catherine woke up that Saturday morning and found Mr Darcy, her cat, observing her on the other side of the bed.

"Morning," she said lazily and petted him.

Her bed seemed too big to sleep alone now. She'd missed how they billed and cooed.

She got up, texted him, pottered around and prepared breakfast for herself and her cat, then got ready to work as the birds warbled.

Orla, her colleague at the flower shop, had been peppy and jolly the past few days, as her boyfriend George had proposed on her birthday, and she'd said yes.

"Ahhh!" Orla mused as they prepared a centrepiece for a nearby hotel, occasionally showing her elfin face. "Cat, I'm not sure if I should take his last name or if I should opt for double-barrelled. You know, keeping mine and adding a hyphen. It's long to spell out... I can't keep on putting it on the long finger."

They chattered and enjoyed the craic as they worked. Later, Orla said, "Have you heard of a new shopping site called SheIn? I've been browsing there. And I've read somewhere that with men who aren't bald, then their grandchildren aren't likely to be bald. Do you think...do you suppose you can ask your...partner if he knows something. You know, traditional Chinese stuff that prevents people from losing their hair? And thank him for the USB stick."

"Yeah. I can ask him."

They finished their shift, confirmed the details of their teaching sessions with Melody, and then Catherine got back to the flat on Kean Street.

She settled herself comfortably in front of her butler's desk. Then she remembered that she had gathered a handful of receipts. She ventured upstairs into the study; the 'Two-headed Monster' terminal greeted her together with his laptop. There was a digital device cleaning kit and a blower on the desk as well. Catherine found the shredder on the shelf beside some black and red faux-leather bookmarks from the Sherlock Holmes Museum and a battery organiser with a power tester. She took out the device and connected the cable. Then she noticed a small pale purple Post-it note on top of a pile of receipts and unwanted mail together with a staple puller. It said:

Do you know the rules?

No staples, no paper clips, and no pins.

Catherine was tickled pink.

She shredded her receipts as if they were tabloid, went down and retrieved her diary organiser, sat down in front of the study desk, and took out an engraved, gilt-bordered correspondence card with her initials that she recently ordered from the Carfax Print store and wrote:

My dear inamorato,

On this note, he called.

Catherine picked up her phone as she swivelled in his chair.

"Mwahahah! Miss me already, Mr Yang? I've found your Post-it. I have to say, I'd very much prefer messing around with you other than 'lorem-ipsum'. Photoshop, I'd rather bugger this for a lark!"

"I'll take it as a compliment then. How've you been?"

"Everything is tickety-boo." She sensed a foretaste of agitation in his tone, so she asked, "Anything bothering you?"

"Well. Yes, quite a lot." He hesitated. "Catherine, how's your exam preparation coming along?"

"Pretty well. I'm on it like a car bonnet." She stopped swivelling before it made her dizzy.

"I was wondering...do you think you can take some time out later? I called An earlier, and she didn't sound alright. I think she's fallen ill. Could you check on her for me?" he suggested.

"Sure," she said. "I'll call her now, and I'll message you how it goes."

In the background, Catherine heard Felipe whooping, "Go take the chequered flag!"

"Thank you," he said, "I have to go now."

"When will you be back tomorrow?"

"Around seven in the evening, I think."

"See you then. Don't miss me too much." She waited for the call to end and then he said, "Catherine? I'm waiting for you to hang up."

"Yes, Mr Yang. I've forgotten that you never hang up on a lady."

The call ended, and Catherine stretched in her chair. She had familiarised herself with the various Photoshop functions and the brushes, and she thought a visit to An would not harm her preparation. She called An, and she picked up on the third ring.

"Yes, hello?"

"Hi, An. It's me. I've heard that you've been a little under the weather? Would you mind if I visit you later? Say, in an hour?"

"No, not at all. I'll send you my postcode." She sounded fatigued.

"Do you need anything? Perhaps I can bring lunch. Say...some salad wraps?"

"That'd be great. See you in a bit."

Catherine went downstairs, shut her laptop, enjoyed the panorama view of Covent Garden for a minute and watched as tenebrous clouds gathered. Then she went to the Italian café on Kingsway and bought some salad wraps. Ever since they had been shopping together, she'd lost her discount.

She put the food items in her satchel and found a Santander Cycle Hire dock down the road. She checked An's address and cycled to the place.

Chance's cousin had rented a small studio apartment on Webber Street in Southwark. Catherine found the place, returned her bike to a nearby Cycle Hire, went upstairs, knocked on the door twice, and waited.

"Hold on for a sec!" she heard An saying.

A minute or so later, An opened the door. She had a wan expression and was wearing pyjamas. "Sorry to keep you waiting. Hi, Catherine. How've you been?"

"I'm well. How are you? A bit out of sorts, I've heard?" She followed An into the room.

It was a studio with en-suite facilities, a rumpled single bed, a wardrobe by the window, a study desk scattered with books together with a minifigure red telephone booth and a large bottle of coins, and a small kitchen area with necessary cooking amenities. There were coffee-stained mugs in the sink, a Tesco salad bag, and a tapered saucepan with chilli noodle soup. A small, white ceramic fan heater was off in the corner. A quilt shaped like a flying fox lay on the bed.

An sighed. "Nothing, really." She brought a chair for Catherine and sat on her bed. "Just this." She raised her right hand, and Catherine saw An's pinkie was all puffy and swollen like a sugar pine cone.

"What happened?"

"It's an allergy. I've always had mosquito allergies."

"Are mosquitos out so early?" Catherine asked as she took out the food items and placed them on the kitchen counter.

"I don't know. I went to the GP. The first time, she prescribed me Dermovate cream and some Ibuprofen. But it remained swollen. It's so difficult to type, and so annoying that I can't even play my *pipa*, so I went to my GP again. She referred me to a dermatology clinic on New Cavendish Street. A specialist examined it and said it's an insect bite. Maybe mosquito, maybe spider."

"I see." Catherine looked at An's finger again. "Did the specialist prescribe you something more effective? You still look a bit unwell."

"She told me to get some over-the-counter Ceti...rizine. It's a lot better now." She winced. "I'm having some terrible period cramps. I took some painkillers just now; they should work any minute. I didn't want the medications to interfere with each other."

"Well..." Catherine regretted not bringing some raspberry leaf tea. "I hope your finger recovers soon."

They chatted as they ate the salad wraps, then An reflected, "I never knew that the insects in London could be quite so harmful. Guess it's just my bad luck with Mercury in retrograde."

"Oh, there've been cases of ticks transmitting Lyme disease. And I've seen some tussock caterpillars in my garden."

An nodded. "Well, I have to say that I wasn't expecting so many rats as well." She tilted her head. "I'm not sure the last time I saw a rat in China. When I was small, once there was a rat outside our apartment, and we decided to put our cat out. You know, cats are supposed to hunt rats. But she was too scared to get close to it." An put away the wrappings and found her phone. "Let me show you my cat. My mom scanned some old photos and sent them to me the other day."

She found her photo album on the phone and showed it to Catherine.

It was a calico tabby cat with green eyes like jewels.

"And her name?"

"She's called Mimi," An reminisced. "She's very shy and flustered and she always hid away when people came to visit."

Catherine suggested, "I think some cat calming pheromone spray might work."

"Does it smell bad?"

"No, not at all. I mean, us humans can't smell it. Mr Darcy likes it. He doesn't respond to catnip at all, but he's over the top whenever I use the spray before vet visits."

"I wish I had a cat now. They say that cats can help people stay calm. I'm so strung out with my dissertation and everything."

"Well, you're welcome to visit Mr Darcy anytime."

"Thank you."

Catherine opened her pet camera's app on her phone; they waited for a while, but her cat was nowhere to be seen.

They talked about the Lady Dinah's Cat Emporium, a teahouse where you can play and interact with cats in London that An once visited. She said that the cats were so lazy that they only slept.

Then An, having spent an exchange semester in Seoul at Yonsei University, told her how Korean students, before a major exam, would ask to borrow a hair from the top performer and hide it in their pen, hoping they would do well. They also talked about the Waterloo underpass poem called 'Eurydice'. They went on to discuss *Zootopia*. An had watched it at an ODEON cinema with her classmates and she wasn't aware that it was renamed 'Zootropolis' for marketing purposes in the UK. Then they spent some time on Larry, the Chief Mouser, and why Mr Darcy might not be suitable for the job.

The painkiller seemed to have taken the edge off and An smiled faintly. "Catherine, I've always found that Mr Darcy looks a bit like the Merriam-Webster dictionary cat. If you go on their website, there's a cat with glasses on, looking very serious and very knowledgeable."

"Oh, I know that cat. Mr Darcy was a slip of a thing and a runt when I adopted him but look how large he'd got."

An swiped her phone and showed Catherine more of her cat's photos. Then she stopped at a photo showing two boys in front of a bulky cathode ray tube TV, playing *Tetris*.

"This is my brother and my best childhood friend." She smiled. "Whenever we visit my brother, he plays *Tetris* to show that he's above the other common games. But my uncle told me that he always played *Contra*."

"Yes. He told me how he liked to play games."

"Ah. This is my favourite photo."

Catherine leaned to look closer. It showed a sort of open circus. There was a tiger sitting down and a teenage girl in a fleece jacket beside it. "Once we were at our city park and they had this tiger on tour. They asked if anyone wanted to take a picture with the tiger and I said yes." An reflected, "There's a Chinese saying that you cannot touch a tiger on its butt and that's exactly what I did. I've read online that you can spend a night in a lodge with lions nearby at London Zoo."

Catherine did not know such an opportunity was available.

An showed her another photo. "This is my brother when he fell from a tree."

"Oh, right. He was attacked by wasps I've heard?"

"Yes," An said, "and here is when he's one."

Catherine looked at the photo and found a baby boy wearing a tiger hat. "He's born in the year of the tiger." She spoke softly.

"That's right. That's why his pet name's 'Dahu', meaning a big tiger. We all have a nickname of a sort. My parents would only call my name when they were angry at me."

"Oh, what's your pet name then?"

An thought for a second. "Catherine, do you know that my name's not 'An'? 'An' is my last name, and my first name is spelt 'XIN'. It's too difficult to pronounce for some people, so I go by my last name. 'An Xin' means to feel reassured in Chinese. My pet name is 'Xiao Xin'."

X and Y!

Catherine swallowed. "How were you as a child, An? Did...did you like school?"

"Well...all my teachers were nice." An showed her a graduation photo. "After we moved house from Inner Mongolia to where we live now, I had an English teacher from California." An laughed. "He had this fancy mountain bike that he loved. One day he went to buy groceries, but his bike wasn't allowed entrance. He locked it up on a tree. By the time he finished grocery shopping, the tree was gone."

"Wow. He must have been broken-hearted."

"I heard that he wanted to find his bike so much, then he had a fight with some people that he suspected, and he was hospitalised for some weeks."

Catherine considered. "An, do a lot of people's names start with 'X' in China? Or...or their pet names?"

"Yeah, it's quite common, especially with pet names. With children, you just add a 'Xiao', meaning 'little'."

At this, someone knocked on the door.

"Let me get that." An opened the door, and Catherine heard her conversing in Chinese.

A minute or so later, An returned.

"You know what I need most?" she asked rhetorically. "I need a good screw."

"Really?"

"Yeah." An held something up in her left hand. "One of the screws on the window is not working. You can't close it very tightly, and I think maybe that's why the insects came. I asked a friend to 3D print another. Do you mind helping me?"

"Sure."

An found a screwdriver, removed the old screw, and tightened the new one as Catherine held the parts. "That's better." She opened and closed the window.

"Oh, you've got a ladybird here!" Catherine marvelled at the insect that landed on the other side of the glass. She sang sotto voce, "Ladybird, ladybird, fly away home."

"I've remembered. Once I wrote in an essay that someone 'skipped like a magpie'. In China, magpies are considered auspicious. And my professor left a comment saying that 'magpies don't skip'. Then I learnt about the superstitions and how people dislike a single magpie in Scotland especially."

"Some people salute when they see a single magpie," Catherine said.

"Well." An tried the hinges of her window again. "At least I've solved this problem. Especially, you know..."

"Yes?"

An lowered her voice, "Have you heard about the terrible news on the missing police officer?

"Ah." Catherine nodded. "Scary."

She'd heard the story from Orla. It was a macabre occasion.

"The other day, I came back. It was a bit dark. Well, it was past midnight. Don't tell my brother, or he'd worry." She added, "I needed to pass this area, but it was all cordoned off. Is that right, 'cordoned off'?"

"Yes."

"There was this patrol car, so I asked what's wrong. They didn't say, but one of the officers told me, 'Don't worry, he's not after women'." An shuddered. 'I'm not sure if that's the best way to tell others not to worry. Anyway, scary biscuits. Drugs have a tremendous social cost."

An then told her that a man had tried to accost her one day after lunch in Covent Garden. He had followed her to the M&S Simply Food despite her saying no, no, and no. She finally shed him by pretending to go into the Underground. It was an unsettling experience. She regretted not bringing her specially made pepper and hot chilli spray.

They sat back and browsed more old photos. Then Catherine said, "An, do you have any photos of your cousin's mother in here?"

"My uncle and my aunt divorced before I was born. Maybe my mother kept a few photos of her."

They sat for a while, then Catherine asked again tentatively, "An, do you suppose...do you know about your brother's previous girlfriends?"

"Ah." An took a bated breath and said hesitantly, "I know this one person..."

"What's she like?"

"I'm not sure, but she passed away."

Catherine was speechless for a moment. "Last year?"

"No, no. Seven or eight years ago?" An sighed. "It was tough for my brother. And my uncle passed away a year later or so; I think it took the spark out of him." She rubbed her temple with her index finger. "It's good to see him truly happy again."

They chatted some more about An's dissertation, then as the clock approached one, Catherine made to leave.

An saw her to the door. "Catherine, my mother likes to study numerology and fortune-telling. She says that there are people with a... difficult life and who witness many passing around them."

It started to rain on Catherine's way back home. She walked to the bus stop on St George's Circus in the claggy weather, took a bus across Waterloo Bridge and changed on the Strand to go back to Holland Park.

She'd remembered that night when Hannah Robinson had lost Eddy and when they cried together.

"It really took the spark out of him."

Some of our pains are the same.

Catherine brooded over this realisation as she rested her head on the cold bus window.

CHAPTER 12

Catherine called him around one-thirty and updated him on An.

The group was having lunch: spaghetti Bolognese with garlic bread, a vegetarian option of risotto, and chocolate mousse.

He left his seat to take the call. Catherine told him about An's allergy and cramps and told him not to worry.

Their call ended quickly, business-like.

He sensed that Catherine sounded as if she'd reached a major decision or even a conclusion.

He knew about An's insect allergies. Once, when she was in middle school, her left eyelid was bitten by a mosquito, and it was swollen like a rotten peach for days. He ordered some DIY mesh curtain screen for the windows and decided to return to his plate that held too much. He went back to the dining room and saw Amani down the corridor. He walked over. "Amani. Do you know if Wilfred has any family members that recently passed away?"

"I don't know." Amani looked out of the window; the rest of the group was playing. "He's a good friend of Nathan. Perhaps I can ask him if he knows."

"Yes, please do that for me. He seems rather disturbed."

Amani typed up a quick message on her phone. "I'll let you know when he replies."

"Right. And...there's one more thing." He hesitated, not knowing how to explain. "Later, Felipe will ask everyone a question. And when he asks you, here's what I want you to do." He told her what she needed to do.

Amani responded passively, "But do you think it'll change anything, lao-shi?"

"Well, Felipe is very good at..." he wanted to say 'intimidation' but decided against it. "He's very good at negotiations."

"Fine. I'll do as you said because I trust you."

"Thank you." He hoped that she hadn't misplaced her trust in him.

After lunch, he found Gabby in the oak-panelled sitting room. She was reading a book about the Lodge's history.

"Mrs Parker," Chance said, "I was wondering if you would be so kind as if to do me a favour?"

"What might that be?"

"Well, we are playing another game this afternoon, but we are one person short. Mr Kazama would like to know if you could join the group. We need ten."

"Another game?" Gabby questioned. "Is any sport involved?" She had not been very pleased when a boy almost knocked her over when they played merry hell earlier this morning.

"No. We'll still be using the Hodgson Room."

"May I ask what is expected of me?"

"Mostly listening with minimal interaction." He added, "And you'll be doing Amani a favour."

Gabby thought for a while. "Well, I think I can read in that room."

"Thank you."

His task completed; he went to the Hodgson Room. Amani was there already. She told him that Nathan said Wilfred had no family members that had passed away recently to his knowledge.

Later, Chance found Felipe smoking outside and told him this.

"Where's that Wilfred sprog? Still at lunch?" Felipe yawned. "He should be glad that I'm not out to lunch, for I always keep tabs on whoever is around me." He checked his watch. "Let's cross out the upcoming item, and we can deal with him."

The group gathered again at two p.m.

Felipe announced, "This afternoon, we'll play a game called 'Ten Questions'. The game is simple." He took out the same pile of A4 paper again. "There's one question on each of these papers. I want you to answer that question, and later I'll answer them in front of the class. As we are a small group, I've asked my buddy and Mrs Parker here to join us and to increase the anonymity," Felipe said as he handed out the questions. "These are easy, closed questions. If you don't want to answer them, don't."

They took some time to answer the questions and returned the sheets of paper. Gabby borrowed Chance's mechanical pencil and completed her part.

Felipe flipped through the sheets. "Let's start with this one. The question is, 'What did you dream about last night?' I'll read the response out loud. 'Last night, I dreamt that I didn't make it to my Physics exam because I'd fallen into a wormhole. I ended up in a world with Newton, and he had yet to develop his laws of motion. I woke up just as I was going to present my work to the Royal Society.'"

Felipe nodded. "I like this dream. Whoever wrote it, perhaps Newton had yet to come up with his laws of this and that, but did you hear about Hooke and Leibniz? Did they come up with their research yet? For those who don't know, Leibniz was the one who invented Calculus. Well now, Amani, we know whom to blame. He invented Calculus and published his works before Newton, but Newton's supporters accused Leibniz of plagiarising Newton's unpublished ideas. We can say that great minds think alike, or we can say that Newton knew how to run a beefed-up PR campaign, and people believed that Newton was the victim. But Newton had similar rows with Hooke, another mathematician, over the law of gravity. It's sad that Newton died like a statesman and Leibniz died like a lost man. No one went to his funeral, except for his secretary. I have a mathematician friend, and she said that Newton was such a bully that he'd intimidated all the prominent mathematicians in England of his time."

Felipe sighed. "Now, as for me, I dreamt of the Nazis last night. By the way, in case you don't know, Nazi was a pun and Bavarian slang meaning 'simpleton'. A reporter first used the word to make fun of the Nazi regime. I dreamt that the Nazis were experimenting on someone, and I was next in line. They were putting people inside high-pressure chambers, and they gradually increased the pressure until the subject perished. I was trying to find the remains of the ones before me. Not a very promising dream, right? I think it was because I had some 'day residues' as Sigmund Freud would say. Do you all know about the history of Cumberland Lodge?"

He walked over to Gabby and borrowed the book that she was

reading. "A remarkable woman called Amy Buller led some British delegations to Germany before World War Two. They talked with intellectuals and with citizens, and she recognised something dangerous with the whole Nazi regime. She got back home and wrote a book called *Darkness over Germany*. Someone recommended the book to the Queen Mother. She was very impressed, so she invited Amy Buller to Buckingham Palace and the author brought up her vision to have a meeting place where people, especially young people and students, could explore timely issues and have inspiring debates. In 1947, the King had offered Cumberland Lodge to Amy Buller to help her realise this vision. And now, here we are. Yesterday we talked about gender equality and diversity. I think we are prone to neglect those who have paved roads like Amy Buller, Leibniz, Lermontova, and Buzz Aldrin, and we only remember those who reaped the fruits like Churchill, Newton, Mendeleev, and Elon Musk. And perhaps to have gender equality, we need to acknowledge and recognise and remember the other half of the equation. The untold stories and the evidence unseen."

He shuffled the papers. "Let's move on to the next question. This question is, 'What is your favourite place in London?' The response is, 'My favourite place in London is the Ritz because that is where my husband and I met.' Well, Mrs Parker, it seems that you've given yourself away." Felipe huffed a laugh.

Gabby smiled faintly. "Well, the Ritz *is* my favourite place. It's magical."

"I think it's quite nice," Felipe said approvingly. "I've been to the casino. Alright, let me offer my response. My current favourite place in London is the John Harvard Library. Sometimes I go there to use their free WiFi. Just joking. John Harvard was born in Borough High Street in the early seventeenth century, and if you walk for about ten minutes or so, you can reach another site called the Crossbones Garden. It was once a mass burial ground for paupers and the destitute. By walking the walk, you can see the inequality and discrimination braided in the history of London. I'd recommend that you all go to the Garden and have a look."

Felipe moved on to the next item. "Here's another question, 'What is your favourite number?' The answer is, 'My favourite number is 'Lambda' for I've learnt to code with Lambda School.' I see. I might know who this is. Short answer short, my favourite number is pi. I've set the passcodes to my electronic devices with pi to a certain accuracy, and none of my previous dates have bothered to remember them. They always lost their patience after I typed the twentieth digit. It's a life-saving technique."

Someone butted in, "Can't you just use Touch ID or something?"

"I had a smarting lesson with Touch ID once," Felipe said. "One of my exes works in forensics, and this person managed to replicate a copy of my fingerprints using tape. It's effortless if you know how. The story didn't end too well. I've many secrets that I keep in my phones, and if they were leaked, I'd be in deep shit. Anyway, let's move on from this sorry episode. Why don't we stretch our legs, and we can continue after a fifteen-minute break."

⁕

Some went to use the washroom, and Chance made a cup of tea for himself.

"Such a pity that they don't have any salt here, isn't it?" Felipe leaned casually on the wall and commented.

Gabby stood in front of the refreshment cart and hesitated with choosing the tea bags. Felipe asked her some questions about the Ritz, and shortly after, the group returned and sat down again.

Felipe put down his cup of coffee. "Next question. Ah, here's one that I like. I've acquired much knowledge from games and *manga*." He raised the paper. "The question is, 'What is your favourite game?' and the answer is, 'My favourite game is Nintendo's *Super Mario Kart*.'" He put down the paper and looked around. "I like to play games as well. Games are amalgams of science, management, and arts. I used to love *The Sly Cooper* and my recent favourite is *Guacamelee!* It's an action game set in Mexico. You play a luchador to find a kidnapped girl."

He paced around. "Nintendo's success is a classic case study in business schools. They have a strategy that they call 'lateral thinking with withered technology'. It's not about how advanced or pioneering the technologies are; it's about applying relatively mature and well-developed technologies across products. One good example is the Game & Watch series. It was inspired when a game designer at Nintendo saw how Sharp used LCD screens on its calculators. There's a great book called *Super Mario: How Nintendo Conquered America*. It's an excellent read for anyone who's interested in the company's history. Of course, Nintendo had many failures as well. Once they rolled out this product called a 'Virtual Boy' after their Game Boy hit. Well, I think now the people at Nintendo know that girls game too. So, they invented this product called 'Virtual Boy'. It was a bulky headset, and to play, you need to jut out your neck. It gives you whiplash. And the display was all in this horrifying red and black that made people dizzy. And here's something that Miyamoto

Shigeru said, he's a director at Nintendo. He said that adults are only children with more ethics and morals. I guess that's why he thinks adults like to play games as well. Rumour has it that even Osama bin Laden liked to play *Super Mario Bros.* This reminds me, during the break, I had a friendly chat with Mrs Parker. She was deciding between black tea or green tea. So, I told her, you know, to show off a bit, I told her, 'Mrs Parker, do you know that all tea is the same? It's like wine grapes: you have different varieties, but all tea comes from the same plant called *camellia sinensis*. That's right. You didn't hear me wrong. All teas, whether they are black, green, white, oolong, matcha, Pu'er or lapsang souchong, are all the same. What makes them different is the processing methods— what happens after you harvest the tea. Some are oxidised, and some are not.'"

He looked at the group intently. "Going back to the adults are children statement, teas are like people. Tea is cultivated all around the world, and people live all around the world. You have short and tall, plump and thin, but all in all, there is only a 0.01 per cent difference across all humans' DNAs."

Felipe scratched his chin. "Why do I say that teas are like people? Because although all teas are the same when they are harvested, or all babies were the same when they were born, some teas grow up in cultivars and sell for an exorbitant price with all the overpackaging and marketing. And some other teas are left out in the wild, with no one caring for them. When I first hung out my shingle and entered M&A, I had very little confidence. I failed my first assignment miserably. It was a murder, literally. Many of my yuppie and Eurotrash peers went to good schools and had all these contacts. Them trust slugs know what caviar brand to order and where to find a chef in Paris that would cook ortolans for their clients. So, I told my mentor that I didn't think I was suitable for the job, and I tried very hard to find my entrée into the circles. Eish, they didn't write it in the job description, but everybody knows that it was no job for the proletariat nor for a mouseburger. I was Mr Irrelevant there. My mentor was a rocket scientist from a meagre background. He said to me, 'Felipe, go to any bank, and tell the clerk that you have a first from Oxbridge, or the Ivy League, or MARCH', and now ask them to lend you a million dollars. There are three situations in which they'd lend it to you."

Felipe turned, took up a marker, and listed them on the white board:

1. Your parents own the bank.
2. You know someone who owns the bank.
3. You have a gun in your hand.

He continued, "So, don't try harder; try different. Don't be rushed, don't be scared, don't mind losing face."

The group giggled.

"Don't try harder; try different." Felipe looked at the ceiling for a fleeting moment. "It's a life lesson. Be a 'purple cow', as Seth Godin would say. And it's a partial factor that made Nintendo a success story. Perhaps we can say that all successful firms are very good at creating legitimate market failures and achieving legitimate monopoly power. Good-value propositions and great designs made them different. Life needs design thinking, as well. Let's move on to the next question before you all fall asleep."

Felipe cleared his throat. "Ah, this is a cool one. The question is, 'If there was an opportunity for you to have a robot that looks exactly like you, will you take it?' The answer is, 'Yes, so I can put it here and hang out with my friends.'" He showed them a hurtful smile.

"Aiyo. Sorry, Feli," someone offered in a frail voice.

"*Pas de problème.* No hard feelings," he said. "If I have one, I'll put it in this room as well so I can go and play in the park." He thought for a moment. "Do you know what the term 'uncanny valley' means? It means the eerie feeling that you get when you see a robot that looks like a human. The theory suggests that the closer a robot resembles a human, the eerier you feel when you see it. I think our minds alert us that it's not a human, but our eyes try to tell us otherwise, and that's where the repulsion originates. Once, I visited Kawasaki. It's a Japanese company known for heavy machinery and motorbikes. I went there, and I found that they had named the robot arms there with human names. They called them 'Jiro' and 'Taro'. I asked them why, and they said that they felt better working that way on the production line and they can reprimand the robot arms if they malfunction."

He sipped his coffee. "I once dined with Mark Setrakian. He's the guy behind the scenes who made the robots for *The Terminator*. He apologised that the AI education delivered through movies aren't entirely accurate. And I know this roboticist at Osaka University. He likes to build robots that look exactly the same as real people. He calls his robots 'geminoids'. In Latin, '*geminus*' means twin. He created all these twin robots, each with a human owner. He had one for himself as well, so he could place it in boring conferences and grants meetings. I mean, how awful these meetings must be that he'd make a robot instead of attending them. I know how he feels. I do. Whenever I needed to go to some jejune boardroom meetings, I bring a drawing compass to jab it into my thigh to stay awake."

The group laughed as if in disbelief.

"Really, I'm telling you the honest truth. I once had some meetings with Jeff M. Fettig at Whirlpool. He favours these terribly long monthly meetings where people read a three-hundred-page document for an hour. But back to our story on geminoids. I asked this robot researcher once; didn't he feel weird and creepy looking at a copy of himself? He said that it's all part of his research and his research question is to know what *is* a human. Now, I thought the answer was obvious. Perhaps I don't know what a supernova or alien is, but what is a human? I told him that I know a thing or two about humans. Humans are mammals that eat, shit, and think that they are above everything else. Oh, and they practise procrastination as a lost art form that's unique to that species. He laughed uproariously, of course, and he asked me how I would react if I woke up in an apocalyptic world like *The Matrix* and saw all these human-like robots. They talk, they laugh, and they sling shit. How can I be sure which is which? Your life depends on how to tell apart a human and a robot. Any ideas?"

Someone said that you could ask the robots to go through the Turing Test. Takashi said you could stab the suspects with a knife, and those who bleed are humans and those who don't are robots.

"Bleeding can be tricky," Felipe said. "What if the robots all have synthetic blood or even chicken blood? Once, I heard an urban legend. Someone hired an assassin to kill his enemy's wife and children, but the hitman couldn't bring himself to do such a task, so he'd faked a murder scene using chicken blood. You know, all gore and gross. Then the boss came to inspect the hitman's handiwork. He stepped into the room and sniffed around, and shot the hitman on the spot. The hitman thought that he'd done meticulous work, and he didn't understand why. His boss told him, 'You think I'm a newbie? Human blood clots faster, and is saltier and stinkier than chicken blood.'"

Felipe reflected, "The other day I read a report saying that it won't take long for children and youth in OECD countries to be poorer than their parents. Many of them will be three on the hook and three on the book. Well, if one day we indeed end up in a world like that, at least you know how to tell apart chicken blood and human blood now. If you see someone all covered in blood, don't be fooled if this person tells you that a chicken was in their pot. Going back to my friend and his twin robot, I saw his geminoid once. It could barely move its eyes and lips, but it could output audio, and you could see through its eyes with built-in cameras."

He chewed his lips. "He told me about this interesting phenomenon. Sometimes he'd put his avatar in meetings or events, and people would kiss the avatar's cheek as a greeting. He says that when people peck on his avatar, he feels an actual connection as if someone had kissed his cheek in real-time. He could be a thousand miles away from his robot but still have telepathy with it. There's a synchronisation of feelings between him and his robot twin. You all know what sympathy is, right? When you see someone crying, it makes you want to cry; or when you see someone puking, you want to puke. I think that if there's a synchronisation of feelings between humans, if we can share our pain, if there's more sympathy, the world would be a better place." He sighed. "What do you all think? Do you think that I should order a robot twin from him and attend this bootcamp virtually next year?"

They had a show of hands. Most said that if they had an eerie robot as an instructor, they wouldn't join the programme.

"Perhaps I'll wait for the technology to advance a bit then. Shall we have another break? I'm worried that I've already exhausted your attention spans. Let's make it a thirty-minute break."

***

During the break, Chance observed Wilfred closely.

The boy seemed unruffled. He didn't use the washroom, nor did he have any refreshments. He appeared too stolid and he looked like death warmed up.

The break ended, and the group gathered again. Felipe took a chair and settled comfortably. "Let's have some mercy on my back and move on to the next question. 'What have you read recently?' The answer says, 'I read *The Remains of the Day*.' Do we all know the book?"

The group nodded, some citing it was a must-read in their English class and the film a must-watch for their winter assignment. Chance saw that Gabby had relinquished her book and turned her attention to Felipe.

Felipe's thoughts lingered for a moment. "The first time I read a Kazuo Ishiguro book, I read *Never Let Me Go*. I was alone in a new country, and after finishing it, I thought, hell! I must avoid this writer at all costs. The story made me so sad and angsty. So now, whenever I read a book, I always jump to the last pages and see if there's a happy ending. It's a nasty habit."

He shifted in his chair. "I'm very used to reading Japanese mysteries, so I hoped for a twist or a revolt but in vain. A close friend of mine would watch the film every year. After watching it, she'd watch *Howards End* to escape the schmaltz. In case you don't know, *Howards End* features Anthony Hopkins and Emma Thompson as well, and they played a couple, husband and wife, later. They shared a kiss in the film, and my friend would watch the kissing scene back and forth and in slow motion. And in *Howards End*, the role that Anthony Hopkins played did some beastly things and said some very hurtful words to his wife. So, my friend feels that because Mr Stevens had mistreated Miss Kenton in their previous life, he had to suffer, and he had to pine for her in their following life."

Felipe gestured with one hand. "It made her feel better this way. But I've always been the party pooper. So, I told her that 'constant conjunction' or a fake causal relationship is a dangerous notion. You will think, because I've behaved badly, so I deserve chastisements. Because I didn't listen to my parents, so they died. And because we are all barbarians, so we must be enlightened by the *conquistadores* as white as shrouds with blood. What's even worse? That we have to carry the burden of their dreams."

He continued, "My friend told me to give the book a try, and so I've read it to enhance my cross-cultural competency. I wasn't too fond of the twee film adaptation because, in the book, Miss Kenton cried because her aunt passed away, and in the film, Miss Kenton cried because of Mr Stevens' heartless words. I can understand that if Miss Kenton cried because of a passing family member, I know that Mr Stevens might wish to give her some privacy. Yet, in the film, he made her cry, and she was crying and he brought up something about cleaning the alcove. I mean, what a workaholic!"

Felipe crossed his legs. "Some things are better left unsaid. I'm buggered if I ever tell any of my lady friends that 'We may never meet again'. They'll slap me for sure, especially the spitfires."

The bunch laughed.

"What do you think of him?" Felipe asked.

Someone brought up how Mr Stevens is persistent with his notion of 'dignity' and even told the butler and the tiger's story. To Chance's surprise, Gabby also joined the discussion. She said that her husband, a member of *Les Clefs d'Or*, was the Head Concierge at a high-end London hotel. Mr Parker once said that 'the best butler serves you as if he does not exist'.

Felipe's nose wrinkled. "I congratulate the butler's shooting skills. But only the tiger's mother cries for the tiger. And I've read on *Nature* that India's tigers face inbreeding, so now we know at least one culprit." He straightened his posture. "I read somewhere that abjection is the passport for the despicable, and dignity is the epitaph for the dignified. I do feel for Mr Stevens. I do. He reminds me of a friend, an Enron employee. Once I almost slapped him, I shouted to him, 'Never use your money to buy Enron stocks! You need at least to diversify your life, get a family, get a hobby, fly a kite, go gamble even!' But he didn't listen. He threw in his lot with all he'd got and rallied around the flag like a shot. What can I say? At least he had the wits not to defend his manager? Ah."

He took a deep breath. "One fallacy with leadership is that if you think of someone or some group or some countries as a leader, you tend to be led. You become dependent on your leader. You tend to overlook your thinking duties. You'd rather believe in someone else other than your own judgement, like poor Mr Stevens. Thinking is an intellectual exercise. Maybe the brain is like any other muscle: if you don't use it, it degenerates. If you don't do your thinking, others will do it for you. Should we delegate the task of thinking to others and let them think for us? The answer is no. Yet, many of us still do."

He pondered. "Once upon a time, the UK's intelligence on the Middle East was top-line. One day, the US came along and said, 'Heya, why don't we share our intelligence on the Middle East? You know, I have troops out there, and a trouble shared is a trouble halved.' The UK government thought, 'This sounds like a modest proposal and seems to be a good idea'."

Felipe raised a finger. "I was the top of my negotiation class at Harvard, and one thing about negotiations is about people getting away feeling good. It's not about necessarily getting anything they want. Then what happened? The UK began to cut its spending on Middle East intel, they cut down the stipends for academics and researchers and then what happens? The US does share the intel, but they only share a pea of the whole story, and they were basically saying 'Just kidding' and the UK is now at the mercy of someone else. Similarly, with the EU, NATO's European Commander has always been a US General. They use terms like 'soft power', but the putrid truth is that the EU is the US's soft colony branded as a 'strategic partner'. The US tells NATO members to contribute two per cent of GDP, but it does not itself. And if these countries make this pledge, they would need to buy US weaponry. So, who's the winner who takes all?"

He stood up and stretched. "And I think Mr Stevens is a coward, and like every coward, he professed allegiance, he eschewed judgement, he feared passion, and he sought sympathy. Yesterday we talked about living in lies. It's much easier to say that 'I have served for a gentleman through and through' than saying 'I served for a Nazi who brought the air raids to London'. Is it so gentlemanly to make a lady cry? Is it so gentlemanly to appease? Is it so gentlemanly to support evil? And is it so gentlemanly to call another a 'half-naked fakir'? This brings us to another important question: when Adam delved and Eve span, who was then the gentleman? I do think that the 'gentleman' is a weird social construct and a Western, eccentric, industrialized, ragged, and disputable flock. And I think we should teach Mr Stevens about the perils of modern slavery."

Felipe sat back down again. "I've recently read *The Theory of Moral Sentiments* by Adam Smith. I think it's his best work, and it's a lost pearl. The book says, in a nutshell, that our nature as social animals drives our moral ideas and actions. Ask any Nintendo executive, and they'll tell you that storytelling is important. I'd remember that Kazuo Ishiguro noted that when he worked as a social worker, sometimes he talked to the homeless people, and he found that they would say 'I have a friend' to tell their own life stories. They mentally distanced themselves from their past pains. Einstein said that education is what remains after you've forgotten what you learned in school. If there is only one takeaway from this leadership Bootcamp, I hope that you can remember never to make any gentle man, gentle woman, or gentle human cry. Is there British-ness? Is there Chinese-ness? Is there Japanese-ness? Is there human-ness? We are all the same tea." Felipe refilled his coffee and took a few sips. "Let's move on to the next question to escape the schmaltz."

He put down his cup and picked up the pile of A4 paper. "'What is the most embarrassing thing you've done?'" He thought for a while, walked to the window side, and looked out. A half-minute later, he turned, "Rats! I can't even say now that I have a friend." He gestured to Chance impatiently, "Remind me to write up an aide-mémoire and change the question later to 'What is the most embarrassing thing your friend has done?'"

The children waited for his answer eagerly. They certainly expected another boffola.

"Well. I've promised myself to be sincere. Whoever had the question did not answer, and it's my turn...and I guess if I share my experience, you'll all learn." Felipe lolled by the window wall. "Once, I had a girlfriend. She was an English girl, and we had a row over some minor, everyday topics. Some disagreement... So, she gave me the silent treatment. I was completely wretched. I'd been looping 'Send for Me' every day, but she didn't. I wore my heart on my sleeve morning, noon and night, and it marred my productivity devastatingly. I was in a maudlin mood and on the bender all the time. One day I decided that enough was enough, so I summoned all my courage and called her in the evening. I told her that she was my favourite cucumber sandwich on the lawn, and she seemed pleased to hear that. Then I asked her if I could come around to her place later. She said it was not good timing because her Aunt Flo had come to visit. And, children, guess what I said?" Felipe left no time for responses. "Horror of horrors, I told her not to worry because my motto is family first. I told her that I'd be delighted to meet her aunt. We could show her around and have tea together at Harrods. Then she hung up on me."

The group giggled and Gabby cringed.

"Now of all the books I've read and all the TV programmes and films that I've watched, I can say that less than one per cent ever mentions menstruation, and I think that's very wrong. Oh. And yesterday, we talked about gender equality. You rarely find female sushi chefs. Why's that? According to a male sushi chef, it's because women have an imbalance in taste when they have their periods. I think that's bullshit. Who in the blazes benefits? I see it as a way of limiting the labour supply on the market. You know, higher quantity demanded, lower quantity supplied? Higher wages. I'll never live down that gritty gaffe. It felt like the same time when I first tried Marmite. We broke up shortly after. She must have thought that I was the most uncaring, dim-witted, two-legged man-imal on Earth."

The group nodded and laughed.

"Now, let's take another break so I can offer myself some tea and self-sympathy," Felipe said.

***

During the break, Chance saw Felipe carelessly knock on the small whiteboard in the room as if trying to determine the material before wiping it clean.

The group corralled again, and Gabby attuned her attention as well.

Felipe counted the sheets of paper.

"Three questions left. Let's see. This one, 'What is your favourite bird?' The answer, 'My favourite bird is grouse. It tastes...super... supercalifragi...listicexpialidocious.' Wow, that's a mouthful word to get my tongue around." He turned and sipped from his cup. "I've never had any grouse before. Maybe I'll have some after we get back to town. Is now the season for grouse?"

Someone said, "No, the traditional shooting season starts on 12th August. We call it the Glorious 12th. Oh, and Kazuo Ishiguro was once a grouse beater for the Queen Mother. They are to die for."

"How fascinating! I only know of a wife beater and a switch-hitter. If you literati can enlighten me on what a grouse beater is?" Felipe winced. "It does sound awfully like a job title for the proletariat. I'm still feeling my way in the local colours."

"It's someone who helps with the hunt. They have to walk for a long distance trying to flush out the birds."

"Then it's not as ruthless an occupation as I thought," Felipe said. "Hunting and horse racing are long and honoured traditions of cruelty in this country, right? Well, I have down-market tastes, and my favourite bird is chicken. There's a YouTuber that I've been following called 'The Chicken Connoisseur' who reviews chicken shops in London. Chicken is a common dish and has a lot of uses. Its feathers make dusters; its blood contributes to staging, its by-products make pet food, and its meat and eggs provide much nutrition."

He looked around. "But do you know that the chicken industry was not as developed and essential as it is today in ancient times? Chicken meat was once considered a delicacy and sold for higher prices than lobsters. Just as quinoa was only a cheap grain, but now it sells for the price of tea. Advancements in coop management and poultry care expanded the business's scope, but people soon found problems. For example, there's something called 'chicken bullying'. It happens for various reasons: sometimes the chicken is stressed with newcomers;

sometimes the chicken is simply bored, and sometimes the chicken sense a sick member in their group and try to drive it away. Chicken bullying is brutal, and some even call it 'chicken cannibalism'. These chickens would run amok and peck their peer to death. And sometimes they peck on the victim's anus and pull the intestines out."

"Yuck!" the group chorused.

"Of course," he continued, "this hurts egg production, right? Inefficiency is the nemesis of scientific management. So, people tried many methods, including beak trimming. It involves amputating a part of the beak with a hot blade at birth so the chickens can't peck each other, and when they do, it hurts less, but it didn't seem to work."

Felipe seemed to have realised something. "Ah. The last time I brought this topic up at a university, I got feedback saying that I supported animal cruelty. I think a disclaimer is needed here. I've never hunted any birds, and I've never trimmed any beaks in my born years. By the by, they do it with infrared nowadays. The worst I've done with the bird population was to collect some guano. These things are happening out there in the world. It doesn't mean that I support them. Right, so people tried many more methods to stop the chicken bullying, and some found that if the chickens are raised under a red light, they seem to be less aggressive. But, of course, it makes the human operators very difficult to see. So, someone came up with a brilliant idea: why don't we make chickens wear red contact lenses?"

Some tittered, and some baulked at this idea.

"Now, let's discuss this impartially. In the 1990s, there was a US businessman, and he thought this might be a good idea, so he started doing some experiments and even partnered with a university. And an

NGO called United Poultry Concerns investigated his case and found
that the contact lenses gave chickens eye problems and even made some
blind, so the project was halted. We should definitely be concerned
about poultry health. We should care immensely. Only in Germany,
forty-five million male chickens are killed every year directly after birth
just because they are male. But some people with very evil intentions
might try to over-egg the pudding and tell you that eggs are the
pullets' menstruation. Jeez Lewise! Shock, horror! Well, here's Biology
101. Chickens don't menstruate. They only gestate. Only mammals
menstruate, kay? Let's all have some respect for the broody chicken next
time we eat one. If you don't eat them, then when you see one."

"Next question," Felipe announced. "'What is the scariest thing for
you?' And the answer is, 'I'm afraid of water. Once, my cousin took me
Powerboating on the Thames, and our boat lost control. I fell overboard.
And now, I can't go on boats anymore'. Oh." He said, "I'm so sorry to
hear this. Everyone has their weak spots. I know people who fear driving
at night and some others who fear curry and *menudo*. And leaders,
of course, have weak spots as well. As a finance guy, I know very well
that what has not been written in the financial statements matters the
most—employees' morale, solidarity, and ethics. And a harsh reality is the
scariest thing for me. For example, do you know what's more hair-raising
than *The Shining*? The Shining Path. Do you know why this is scary? The
lights are on, but no one's home. For me, the scariest thing is one magical
sentence: 'This is based on a true story'. The dream I told you earlier,
the one where I was undergoing a Nazi experiment in a high-pressure
chamber: I'm not a historian by trade, but I know Sigmund Rascher did
this in Dachau concentration camp and it happened in Unit 731 as well.

That was a Japanese Imperial Army biological and chemical warfare unit that did many infernal experiments in China in World War Two."

Chance observed Takashi. He fidgeted in his seat and looked peeved.

Felipe stood up. "Now, what's not been written is most scary and what's not been taught is most important. Kazuo Ishiguro once wrote a screenplay for a film called *The White Countess*. It's a story set in Shanghai in the 1930s about a Russian countess who is also a refugee in the city, and a blind American diplomat. I think it was as close to a love story and a happy ending as you could get with Kazuo Ishiguro because they managed to escape at the end together on a sailboat and they were going to Suzhou, a city near Shanghai. The film tells this much but didn't say how or if they can survive the Japanese invasion. Maybe the crew wanted to leave the audience with some room for imagination. Maybe they couldn't bring themselves to describe how cruel the war was. Maybe they ran out of budget. *The Remains of the Day* tells us what happened after Lord Darlington's trial and supplies very few details about the time during his trial. Did Mr Stevens turn King's evidence? If he did, what did he say? If he didn't, why not? What happened to the Jewish maids? How did young Cardinal die? What happened to Charlie, Lizzie, and George?"

Felipe thought for a moment. "I told my friend, let's consider to what extent did Miss Kenton leave because Mr Stevens didn't return her feelings or because she had a conscience of some sort and didn't want to work for a Nazi sympathiser anymore? Now, they said in the film about reminiscing about what-might-have-been. I think we might also consider another what-might-have-been: if the Nazis had won, would Mr Stevens write to Mrs Benn and say, 'Look, I've helped to make history among these very walls'. And Mrs Benn would say, 'Yes, Mr Stevens, you've helped to make some horrible history'. Now, that'd be the optimistic scenario. A more realistic one would be that he had no one left to correspond with."

He cleared his throat. "The jest of appeasement is this. Some British and some French took pity on the Germans for they thought the Treaty of Versailles and the Locarno Pact were too harsh. And before that there was a twisted history of wars and conflicts in Europe that would make the world's longest telenovela. If you trace it back, you'll wonder why the Chicxulub Impactor, the comet that made dinosaurs extinct, did such a lousy job: if it had finished Earth, none of this farce would ever have taken place. So, my advice, for everyone here and every spirit present in this room: if you do a job, you should do it well. I don't expect you to do well in everything, but never be ne'er-do-wells. If you are a leader, you should shoulder some responsibility for the welfare of your followers."

Felipe gestured at Chance. "When people see him, they don't point their fingers at his back and say, 'Look, he worked with Felipe Kazama, the sod who supports capital punishment'. No. They'd say, 'Look, he worked with Felipe Kazama. The man who delivers. The man who made a trademark out of himself, the man who closes deals, and the man who get things done'."

Chance felt a bit uneasy as all the room's eyes riveted on him.

Felipe continued nonetheless. "I said to my friend that I think 'The Remains of the Day' is an awful title for that book, and if I were to name it, I'd call it 'James Stevens and the Haunted House'. Now, that spices things up, doesn't it?"

Someone snickered.

"Why do I say it's a haunted house? One of my hobbies is to collect supernatural stories. In Japan, there is a *yokai* or a supernatural being that's called a *sakabashira*. It's a wood pillar or a column, and when a house is constructed, this pillar was erected upside down. So, not in the correct direction as the tree had grown: the root was on top. And this makes this piece of wood angry, so it'll cast spells on the household and drag it into demise. An acquaintance that I know in Japan, their house saw three funerals in two months and an explosion, so the landowner sent an *onmyoji* to investigate why the tragedies had happened. And the exorcist said there was a *sakabashira sgangherati* in their house. If left unattended, the thing would cast spells until the owner of the house died. So, the grandpa decided to tear down the house to redress it. People can't be too careful, right? He decided to tour the Mediterranean while they demolished the house. The exorcist told him to wait, but he didn't, and he had a hot air balloon accident in Turkey. Tut-tut. Sometimes, children, you had better listen to others' advice."

Felipe stopped to drink coffee. "I've told my theory to my friend who loves *The Remains of the Day*, but she finds the concept of a 'sakabashira' difficult to grasp. So, I thought, is there a fitting figurative and literal translation for the term in English? There is."

He paused to gather people's attention as he shifted his weight onto his toes. "I think we can call it a 'fifth column'. You have a house, and you have four supporting columns shoring up the house; I shouldn't wonder that the left out one feels bored and sometimes goes to the neighbour for beer and Bratwurst."

The room laughed more.

"I think we cannot blame Lord Darlington entirely either. He had a group of intelligentsia that he looked up to and he had a bandwagon that welcomingly blinkered him. King Edward VIII had pro-Nazi sympathies. Maybe they both saw how cruel war could be, and they had no reason to object if Hitler only wanted to put a chicken in every pot in Germany." Felipe said in a solemn tone, "And you know what goes hand in hand with a fifth column? The fourth estate. For those who don't know, Edmund Burke coined this term to refer to the media. Now, the media, we all know what a destructive role they can play. *Daily Mail* was once known as 'Daily Heil'. American *Vogue* ran pieces praising great makers of foreign policies like Hitler and his *gemütlich* room decors that were 'characteristic of man and country'. Inflation is always and everywhere a monetary phenomenon. Adulation is always and everywhere a votaries' phenomenon. Can we say that the fourth estate didn't egg on the likes of Lord Darlington to go down the wrong path? Why did Lord Darlington read *The Foundations of the Nineteenth Century*? Why didn't he invite Amy Buller to his roundtable and have a constructive, courteous, enjoyable, and productive *tour d'horizon*? All we are asking is for him to have an open mind! Maybe we should say to Mr Stevens that 'idle hands are the devil's workshop; idle lips are his mouthpiece'. Perhaps we should also say to him: Mr Stevens, you are no different than a flunkey, a thrall, a scrubber, and a poltroon. You are no different than a spaniel with a white collar and they wipe the floor with you. And we should undoubtedly tell Lord Darlington, be very careful with well-wishers who don't slate you. You are only a useful idiot to them. They're hallooing you and giving you enough rope so you'll hang yourself down the primrose path. The road to hell, as they say, is paved with good intentions. Or perhaps we should advise them to get a good psychiatrist because I suspect they might have been suffering from *folie à deux*."

Felipe drew a quick breath and continued, "Storytelling is important. In the 1930s, all plays in England had to be checked by the Lord Chamberlain's office before they reached the public. And there was a guy called Lord Cromer who would send scripts to a German friend so the German Embassy could approve them. They were the anti-anti-Nazis. They were the dregs who supplied garbage to UK society with their Orwellian umbilical cord and they smeared Vaseline over the circuits on the sounding boards. Storytelling is important. You can make someone appear to be a saint or a sinner. You have all these films and books saying how gallant the US were during World War Two. They don't tell you that before the Pearl Harbor Attack, the US traded with both sides of the story and sold arms to both Allies and Axis as long as they paid in cash and didn't carry them on American vessels. Double-dealing has never been a modern phenomenon. They don't tell you that U-Boats were filled with American oil. What can I say? Either the Americans had strategic myopia and didn't see it coming or that they deserved it? Everyone makes mistakes, and everyone has strategic myopia. Emil Cioran supported Hitler and was fascinated with the Nazi regime, yet he recognised his failure. Lord Halifax tried to negotiate peace with Hitler, yet he realised how dangerous he was and adopted a firmer attitude."

Felipe paced around. "My friend would always watch the deleted scenes where Mr Stevens cries on the pier, and she thinks that Anthony Hopkins deserves another Oscar. Are we content with just that? Zowie! We drew blood from stone and tears from wood but now let's go home and play *Super Mario World*! Winner, winner, chicken dinner!"

He sighed heavily. "The world does not work in that way. Once, I was at a high-level function, and…a friend managed to offend *everyone* in the room. In front of a group of renowned British and Japanese business leaders, he said, 'Do you know the one common problem of you British and Japanese? You dish out apologies every day on trivial issues, but you scruple to talk about the dense matter at all costs. Two countries steeped in aggression. Isn't the British Empire the epitome of commerce without conscience? Slave trade, opium, smuggling of cultural relics to name a few. Each of them would merit a tome. The British should apologise for what happened at the Boer concentration camps, for what happened at the Parthenon, and for what happened at the Summer Palace. And the Japanese? You should wake up from your limbo and see reality. You say that the Nanjing Massacre is a lie. 'We didn't kill three hundred thousand civilians in Nanjing; we only slaughtered two hundred and ninety-nine thousand and nine hundred and ninety-nine and a half. Babies only count as half.' When Germans reflect, they think, 'Why did we start the war? How did we let Hitler come to power? Why did we fall for the banality of evil?' When the Japanese reflect, you think, 'Why did we lose the war? How come we lost? We lost because of our incompetent leaders. The fish stinks from the head down, and chickens come home to roost.' Balderdash! Everyone in the Japanese Imperial Army stinks, and every cell of them stinks. They were all willing executioners! And everyone who supported them and everyone who forgets and denies what they've done!'"

Takashi stood up abruptly and sputtered, "Kazama-san, how can you say this!"

Felipe fusilladed quickly, "Kawamura Takashi, *omae wa*

hajishirazuda'! Truth is harsh to the ear. Cowards live in lies, and the shameless live in anomie. Do you know that there were Japanese soldiers who fought in the Chinese Army because they knew they were fighting for the right cause? History is not for you to read by the fireside; the slaughter bench of history is for us to remember!"

Takashi was angered. He rose, his chair scraping noisily against the floor. He made to stalk out only to find the door locked. He kicked it hard.

The room fell quiet, and Felipe took a moment. "Then I had to deal with everyone pissed off in that room. There was a kahuna, a prominent member of our circle. His face looked like his father had just died a second ago. I walked up to him cautiously, not knowing what to say, and the Japanese in me made me apologise. He told me, 'Felipe. It's alright. I'm Irish, and I'm upset because your colleague didn't even bother to mention the Great Famine, which is pathologically ignored in my opinion'."

"Last, but not least." Felipe picked up the last sheet of paper as the sun began to set. "The question is, 'What is your least favourite word or phrase?' I want to start with my answer first. My least favourite word is 'bullying'. Bullying can be verbal, physical, and emotional. We've talked about chicken bullying. Bullying happens everywhere, just like tea is grown all around. Bullying is a grave problem in Japan. Japanese kids have top physical fitness but almost the poorest mental health. There's a high suicide rate among adolescents. An educator told me, 'Felipe, you can find bullying in almost every school in Japan. If you don't, it means they are either lying or they don't want to admit it'. Bullying is everywhere. I wouldn't be surprised to find bullying in Eton, in Harrow, in Westminster, Winchester, Wycombe Abbey. I wouldn't be surprised to find bullying in the Royal Family even. In fact, I've noticed that there's an inverse relationship between people's stature and their aggressive behaviour. I wouldn't be surprised if there's bullying in your school, your grade, and your class. And the question was, I repeat, 'What is your least favourite word or phrase?' And someone wrote–"

He took a red marker, and wrote on the whiteboard in capital letters, 'COMFORT WOMAN'.

Amani tensed up.

"Comfort woman," Felipe thundered. "What a *simplistic* term. I see the 'leisure' in 'leisure park', and I don't see the 'comfort' in 'comfort women'. Why stress the word 'women'? Is the phrase girls aged nine to twenty-five too much of a mouthful to pronounce? Some Japanese say that 'The Bible tells people how to rape women after a war, we've only done it during the war. What's so wrong with that? And oh! Which country didn't have prostitution? It's the world's oldest profession! In Victorian times, every one in seven households in London was a brothel. Comfort women were only prostitutes, and we treated them well. It was only a savage form of speed dating. We're all Dear Johns. It was so much more fun than *Tenko* the show! We kidnapped them, we tortured them, we gave them tattoos and STDs, we even kept a few of them a-li-ve!'"

Felipe stopped, looked around, and continued. "I know of another type of prostitution, and it's called 'academic prostitution'. Some historians who hide behind academic paywalls, they glamorise the stations where the Japanese Imperial Army kept those poor girls with so many rosy details that it makes you wonder if their fathers did not reside there. I think the problem with academia today is that they need more 'research', not in 'research' but 're-search'. If they did not misplace their conscience in the gutter and flush it away, or they didn't have too many mentos with coke in their brains? Idle lips are the devil's mouthpiece, and shit-puking lips are the devil's arsehole. War is cruelty, and no one can refine it."

Felipe stared at the posse for a minute, and then said curtly, "Mr Stevens is a chicken." He stared at them again. "If you're a human and your peer is hurt, you peck on their cheeks to offer solace and support, and if you're a chicken and your peer is hurt, you peck on their asses to *hurt* them more. If you want to be a leader, you *must* be human first. That's the pons asinorum. And those who peck on others' asses will find their mouths filthy, and they puke shit."

Suddenly, Felipe clouted the whiteboard strongly, snapping the panel and startling everyone in the room.

"My point is, hoity-toity posh gits," he gnashed his teeth irately. "When you've decided to let your mouths puke shit, that entitles peoples' savoir-vivre a *hi-a-tus*."

No one spoke during dinner.

CHAPTER 13

After dinner, Chance saw Felipe conversing in a low voice with Amani in the corridor. She nodded, then scampered away.

He went downstairs to the reception, where a small range of merch was on sale. There were some Cumberland Lodge logo mugs, guidebooks, prints, and also Great Park honey.

He bought a jar of honey and a few postcards and then asked if the staff had any envelopes that he could use and how one might send a letter. Later, he returned to his room and settled in front of the writing desk.

Night fell, and he turned on the side lamp. Then he wrote:

Dear Catherine,

I have heard some awful things. Perhaps what is most scary is that people still die in air raids every day today. Every day, some children are bullied, molested, and abused, and every day, some people get away with murder. It takes a lot of effort not to care, or perhaps in Mr Stevens' case, it takes a lot of effort to pretend not to care.

He put down his pen and looked at the wrinkled page, remembering that Lewis Milken once said they were so poor that they had to dilute the family ink, so all their writings were a paler shade of black. He'd remembered his promise to make her happy every day, so he tore the page and started anew.

Dear Catherine,

I have never written you a letter, and I thought, why not?

Do you miss me? I miss you an awful lot already.

I would have drawn you the local scenery if I had artistic talent, but this postcard will do a better job.

I hope I get back before this letter does.

He wished to see her and hear her at that moment so hopelessly. He thought about calling her just as the door opened and Felipe came in.

"Writing home?" Felipe asked ersatzly. Getting no response from Chance, he used the washroom briefly, then lay lazily on his bed and stretched. "I've nothing to write home about give or take the vapid coffee and the placid view from this crummy, boxy room. Not even a sausage. When the guy mentioned the racing horse, I thought that we'd be eating in mangers. It's been a while for me to go to bed with the chicken: new job title, new responsibilities. Tiresome work, really. Now that I'm in charge, I don't need to stay up late in anyone's good graces. Do you think

I should have my beauty sleep now?" He checked his timepiece. "Maybe I'll wait a bit longer then retire for the night. When the tides retreat, we know who's swimming naked, and when the fire alarm goes off in the middle of the night, we know who sleeps in the buff."

Chance finished his letter quickly, arranged it in an envelope, and signed the address. He'd remembered Gabby's suggestion on pickled walnuts and checked the farm's website.

A few minutes later, someone knocked on their door urgently. He opened it. Peter, the Lodge staff member, asked: "Is Felipe in?"

"Yes, where else can I go? I'm still waiting for my mother vessel to pick me up," Felipe responded and rose from his bed. "To what do I owe this pleasure? Anything the matter?"

Peter explained nervously, "Wilfred Perry is not in his room; neither is Amani Eden."

"Oh, don't sweat." Felipe smiled. "I've sent them to the library to do some desktop research on Edward VIII's craven abdication. I think it's a great case study for toxic leadership in times of crisis."

"But," Peter continued, "I've checked the library as well, and the drawing room, the sitting room, and the music room. They are not in any of those places either."

"Well." Felipe thought for a few seconds. "Perhaps they are in the washrooms? I liked tonight's offering of a chocolate mess, but too much chocolate could cause constipation, for it is low in fibre. Do you know that a Chinese philosopher said that the best three venues for thinking are on horseback, in bed, and when using the toilet? I think it's apropos given their damnable topic. Do you know that Mozart wrote a chunk of his pieces abed? Make a joyful noise unto the Lord and all that."

"If you see them, please tell me as soon as possible," Peter said. "And could you tell me what happened with the whiteboard?"

"Yes." Felipe leaned on the door jamb. "I was writing on it, it fell, and it cracked. I almost lost my tongue. I should be glad that it didn't smash my feet, or I wouldn't be able to think on my feet again for a while. Guess I need to be grateful for small mercies."

"I see. Though it does seem that some external force was applied to the panel," Peter said doubtfully.

"Now, I might have cracked it if I had a blackbelt in judo." Felipe smiled. "But I only have a blackbelt in Lean Six Sigma." He paused. "I checked the label, and it says that it's 'Made in England', so perhaps that's why."

Peter frowned upon this comment.

"I meant it in a good way," Felipe continued. "The UK is a top exporter of planes, suzerains, and automobiles as well as petrol and arms. Plastic products hardly make the top ten list. Oh, do you know that the UK is now the world's second-largest arms exporter? My sincerest congratulations on this milestone. I guess the no-holds-barred Saudis in Yemen need both Typhoon jets and JDAM kits. How do you put it in the local colours? Ah, kings have long arms."

Chance saw that Peter was upset.

Felipe gave tongue nonetheless. "And queens also. We must treat gender equality as an art form. I'm always solicitous about levelling the playing field and I'm a sister under the skin. The Nobel Peace Prize should really recognise the UK's queen-sized contributions in global peacekeeping, making, and building. But you'll have to wait till after the US gets it. Did you know, Peter, that George Washington wanted to become the first American King? Might be useful for a pub quiz. He won't be the first lying king, though. He wouldn't make it to the top ten list even. What can I say? That Britain's got talent? Oh, I didn't mean it as a compliment, merely a description. And don't you think that having someone who invented dynamite to host a Peace Prize is like having wolves sponsoring beauty contests for lambs? And the nomination processes trying to sieve out the most vegan wolf?"

Chance saw that Peter was truly ill-disposed towards Felipe now.

"Sorry for the vagaries of my mouth. I always find it difficult to sleep in a strange bed. Ah, Peter, here's a question I've been *dying* to ask you."

"Y...yes?"

"Did enslaved people build Buckingham Palace?"

"Ah...well...not–"

Felipe bombarded him, "And the materials they used, the lumber, the marble, the glass panels and the tea, sugar, tobacco consumed, were they all fairly traded and cruelty-free? The money that laid its foundations, was it as heavy as a pall and as pure as the driven snow? I've heard that 'mercantilism' is also known as 'commerce without conscience', 'destruction without remorse', and 'slaveowners without borders'. And do you know what's scarier than the Hagley Woods? MoD Abbey Wood."

"I would need to check my references."

"And what about Cumberland Lodge?"

"Well," Peter dodged again, "I'm afraid that I cannot answer these questions without referring to my sources."

"You're on. It's always important to get the facts and figures. I'm a numbers man myself and I'm anal about the specs. I won't ask you to stand and deliver. So long as you wish to prevaricate, Pete, you can't get away from the fact that British life and society is *in toto* built on and implicated in the slavery trade. Perhaps you can put that in your pipe and smoke it? Did you know that the British government's compensation to your slaveowners was the largest bailout in British history until the bailout of the banks in 2009? What can I say? That it's good to be property owners no matter at what time you live? It makes you wonder who'll make history next time." Felipe smiled. "In finance we say that cash is king and bosh is queen. But my favourite British rock band is indeed the Queen." He told Peter dismissively, "Don't worry about the whiteboard; my office will sort it out."

"Well," Peter replied impatiently. "We'll include the damaged item on the invoice, and please tell me when you find Wilfred and Amani."

"Sure." Felipe closed the door, moved back to his bed, and said to Chance, "I cannot make people swallow their tongues, but I might be capable of making their blood vessels burst to my heart's content. Ho. I think you can get to know a writer from their writings. If I ever write a book, I'll probably annoy people to death. Or they'll use it instead of toilet roll. Do you know that in Victorian times, toilet paper was called the 'unmentionable'? Remind me to do some market research on water-soluble paper. Well, I did see a magazine the other day called *The Toiletpaper*–"

A few short seconds later, someone rapped on their door again, this time more insistently.

Chance opened the door. It was Amani.

"Lao-shi!' she called out, "Mr Kazama told me to keep an eye on Wilfred and I saw him going into the woods with ropes in his hands! And he's crying!" Her agitated tone galvanized them into action.

"*Maravillosa*, the good only gets better!" Felipe sprang to the door swiftly like a clouded leopard. He checked his watch, "It's about time." He turned to her, "Thanks, Amani. Could you find Mrs Parker and talk to Peter about anything to buy us some time? The parky weather, tonight's dessert, and maybe even free-range chicken."

"Please check on Wilfred now!" she pleaded.

"Don't worry; we have every intention of doing so." Felipe grabbed his jacket. "Let's see whose head is stronger."

They hied down the stairs and hurried along the path into the woods. Shortly after, Chance saw something suspended in the caliginous night air and struggling under the thrilling moon.

It was Wilfred Perry in a hangman's noose.

He sprinted to the tree and held the boy's flailing legs to support him. The boy choked and retched and kicked him.

"Wilfred!" Chance cried. "Stop *kicking* me! I'm trying to help!"

"NO!" The boy cried back, winded, "No one can help me!" He twisted some more, and the rope snapped with a 'thock'. He fell on Chance, and the two of them tumbled down together at once, both screeching in pain.

"Pshaw, what a sorry sight." Felipe looked at them and lit a cigarette, "It's not worth the bother of killing yourself since you always kill yourself too late*. Wilfred Perry, death is no child's play. Death is not as easy as shooting fish in a barrel. In Japan, when adults try to leak gas to kill their families, the children often die, and the adults survive. What have you done now other than making a pig's ear of lopping off a branch and ruining a nice piece of rope? Today, I taught you that if you do a job, you should do it well. I can see that your tongue is hanging out. Do you want me to teach you how to tie a proper hangman's noose?" He walked beside them and picked up the snapped rope, "First, you need a sturdy rope that does not stretch. Hemp or manila should do. Then, you need some moral fibres."

Chance removed the boy from his body and held him up. He was now crying powerlessly with his head down. "Wilfred, tell us your troubles. We can help–"

Felipe stopped him. "Shush! You keep quiet and let me enjoy my *Saturday Night Live*."

He lolled against the tree. "Wilfred Perry, do you know from how high you have to jump to reach the *terminal* velocity? Do you know how many tons of sand can suffocate a person? I know someone who slashed her wrists with a shell. Some people can be creative, and some others are not that creative, right?" He kicked the boy's shin. "It seems that manners are in short supply these days. Wilfred Perry, hasn't anyone taught you that you should look at others when being spoken to?"

"Why are you so MEAN!" the boy raised his head and hollered.

"Thanks." Felipe smiled. "I'll take it as a compliment. I have average looks, average height, average tastes, but at least my pay is above average. Why don't you stop playing silly buggers? You haven't answered my question, Wilfred Perry. Do you want me to teach you how to tie a proper hangman's noose? I might consider it if you ask me nicely."

The boy cried more, "You don't even have sympathy for Mr Stevens!"

"Oh, I think it's a great grot. The bland leads the blind, and the ungentleman leads the inhuman—what a nice combo! This is a man eats man world, I tell you. Haven't you seen the news about the missing rozzer?"

Chance stepped in again. "Wilfred, we can help." He knew better than to tell the boy to snap out of it.

Wilfred kept crying and didn't say anything.

Felipe snubbed out his cigarette and then said, "Alright, Wilfred Perry, let me ask you this. Do you want to live?"

The boy murmured something.

"Can't hear you. Wilfred Perry, do you want to live?"

"Y...yes," the boy whimpered.

"Can't hear you," Felipe repeated. "Wilfred Perry, do you want to live!?"

"Yes!"

Felipe moved around as if searching for something. "Are pesky May bugs out so early? All I hear is buzzing." He barked once more, "Wilfred Perry, DO YOU WANT TO LIVE!?"

"YES!" the boy blenched. "I WANT TO LIVE!"

"Wilfred Perry, I'll only ask once more." Felipe grabbed the boy by his jumper collar, heaved him up, and shouted by his ear. "DO YOU WANT TO LIVE!?"

"YES! Mr Kazama, I want to...I want to live," the boy bawled. "Hel-help me!"

Felipe did not relinquish his hold. "And Wilfred Perry, what's the magic word!?"

"HELP ME PLEASSSSSE!"

"Very well." Felipe patted him on the shoulder. "Now that we've heard your SOS, tell us, Wilfred Perry, who put Will up the common lime?"

In between the boy's broken sentences, sobs, and the light breeze, they understood what had happened: once, he was browsing some adult material with his laptop's webcam on, and some people got hold of that video. They'd threatened that they'd leak it to everyone in his contact book. They asked him for a considerable ransom in Bitcoin, and when he told them that he couldn't deliver, they browbeat him and chivvied him to kill himself.

"You know what I think we should do, Wilfred Perry?" Felipe said. "We should commend you for being brave enough to speak up." He took off his jacket, handed it to the boy, and asked him to put it on and flip up the collar.

***

They got back to the Main Lodge and saw Peter waiting anxiously by the entrance.

"Blinkin' heck! Bugger me! What happened?" He eyed them. "I must say it's the group leader's responsibility to *ensure* that visitors stay within the grounds of Cumberland Lodge to ensure their safety!"

"Don't sweat, *compadre*," Felipe said. "Everything's just peachy and we are all alive and kicking. We were just out to take the air and gaze at the stars and hoping to find UFOs. But the cloud cover is a bit thick today, and I guess I better refer to my cloud atlas next time. That's a joke, by the way. But my favourite berry is indeed the cloudberry."

They entered the building, and Peter saw Chance doddering and Wilfred covered in dirt. "Cor blimey!"

Felipe continued as he handed Peter the snapped ropes. "Since we couldn't find the faults with the stars, we went off-piste and decided to have a go at grouse beating. You know, make hay when... Never mind.

Then I remembered that it's not yet the season for grouse and no hunting is allowed on Her Madje's demesne, and we are all honest and peaceful citizens. Oh, the boy's a citizen, and we are residents. Anyway, we had no intentions to encroach so we decided to practise *lucha libre*. You know, to enhance our cross-cultural competencies and nurture our global problem-solving mindset. They were shown the ropes. My favourite Kazuo Ishiguro book is *Nocturnes*. All good things come to those who wait, and all fun stuff come to those who stay up late." Felipe grinned. "I'll make sure these boys clean up and not sully your royal carpets and rumble what's under them. And might I suggest that you better check if your ropes are not made in England as well?"

"Now, what does that mean!?" Peter took umbrage at these remarks and almost rolled up his sleeves.

Felipe strutted by him. "No need to fret. It only means that I'm concerned about your procurement quality. Suppose it's not a rope of sand? White-collar crime is money for old rope. But hey, a cat may look at a king, and a rat may sit below a queen. Don't wait up for us."

"But—"

"Oh c'mon, don't be such a jobsworth. Your face tells me that you'd love a number two. Good nite, Peterman. You are released from duty tonight. Hope you have a lovely evening in the *arms* of Morpheus. Go and let it all hang out."

They accompanied the boy to his room to get his laptop, and then they brought him to their room. Wilfred showed them his communication with the blackmailers. Felipe first took screen shots of their conversation history, then told the boy to deactivate his social media accounts. Once that was completed, he asked Wilfred, "Are you certain that they have a video? Not a bluff? Ninety-nine per cent of the time when they say they have something on you, it's a bluff."

The boy shook his head unwillingly.

"Do you want to get the police involved? I'd advise you strongly to do so."

The boy explained that he came from a rigorous, exacting family of gentry, and he would never be pardoned if he caused a scandal.

"Don't have a cow. You could hardly call this a scandal. Let's say that a fictitious 'Prince Andrew' might be more notorious than Hannibal Lecter one day. He could well frighten the horses. And parents should stand by their children in times like this." Felipe looked at the screen. The blackmailers had asked for a ransom of a hundred Bitcoins, which was about forty-one thousand US dollars. "Tell ya what I'll do. I might as well pay it for you. I've told you that I don't trust Bitcoin. Well, well, guess what? My exes don't trust me either, and who doesn't have some nest eggs? I bet that even the Queen has some under the rose."

"But Mr Kazama, I...I don't have any money to pay you."

"Money is a trite idea, an activity. When you put money in a bank account, you are actually making a loan to the bank. And what's important is that money's only a number and numbers are only transitional objects. I bought a lot of the Bowie Bonds just for fun. Consider it an investment," Felipe said as he initiated the transaction. "Don't be flabbergasted if I ring your house bell thirty years from now."

"But...but Mr Kazama," Wilfred murmured.

Chance watched as tears welled up in the boy's eyes again.

"Wilfred Perry, are you trying to convince me that I'm making an unworthy investment?" Felipe kept his tone light and asked before hitting the 'Pay Now' button.

"N...no."

"I hope not, but it sounds awfully so."

The transaction went through.

"Mr Kazama," the boy cried again. He rubbed his face with his soiled hands, leaving streaks of mud on his face. "I'll remember you for the rest of my life!"

Felipe laughed, "Sonny, don't remember me. Just remember to tape your webcam next time you do business. Have you forgotten so quickly? What happens in this room stays in this room." He produced a small USB from his jacket pocket. "Go and smarten yourself up. I'm going to install some anti-malware wonders to fine-comb your computer."

"Thank you."

"Oh, and one more thing," Felipe added. "Now, how would you feel if people running around called you a 'tosser'? It feels bad, huh?"

"Yes." The boy hesitated. "I won't...I won't let my mouth puke shite again and I won't waste again." He gave Chance an abject apology, "So sorry for troubling you."

Felipe scolded the boy, "As I've said, Wilfred Perry, the British dish out apologies every day on trivial matters. Still, you should never apologise on behalf of some blithering jerks. Now go and posh up."

Felipe turned his attention to Chance. He was busy cleaning his snagged jeans. "Oops, I hope he didn't ruin your favourite pair of jeans. Once in a lifetime experience, wasn't it?" He winked at him. "*Amigo mío*, it's a myth that Bitcoin is untraceable and anonymous. I always do a belt and braces job."

Chance decided not to think about what he meant.

A few minutes later, Wilfred emerged from the washroom, this time more composed. "Mr Kazama and Mr Yang, thank you." He wrung his hands, and his ears flushed.

"What a night," Felipe commented. "I think an epic night like this requires a happy ending." He crossed his hands behind his head and said to Chance, "Why didn't you answer your question this afternoon?"

"Hmm..." Chance settled in the armchair and gestured to the boy to move his sleeping bag, and sat down on his bed.

"Well, I think we deserve some laughter in this room now." Felipe looked at him intently, "I've used up all my laughing stock and my quota for shouting this weekend. Don't worry; what happens in this room stays in this room."

Chance thought for a moment and offered his answer to the question 'What is the most embarrassing thing you've done?'.

He told the boy that a colleague of his girlfriend's had mistaken someone who went into a hotel with a 'chic Latina' as him and had tattled to her. She questioned him over dinner where he had been that afternoon. He'd shied away from her questions, and then she blocked his number.

"But where had you been?" Wilfred asked.

"Oh," he said, "I was at a colorectal clinic, and that's not your common or garden conversation opener at restaurants."

The boy gave him a face. "Well, my father has a similar ailment from sitting too long all day. He has very bad sciatica and sometimes it leaves his rear part numb. You can use...umm...syrup of figs. But are you back together?"

"Yes. And we make a dish of celeriac together sometimes."

They chatted a bit more about personal data safety, like using an email alias instead of the primary address and making regular checks on *haveibeenpwned.com* to see if your email has been compromised, or using a website called *Re:Scam*, which uses an email bot to automatically reply to scammers to waste their time.

Then Felipe told the boy, "Wilfred Perry, if you do a job, do it well. If you live a life, live it well. Have plenty of fibre in your diet and have plenty of moral fibres to rock on. Chicken can have pluck as well." He saw him to the door. "Go and get your beauty sleep. I always sleep better after a good cry."

After they went to bed, Chance had remembered something Felipe had said the previous day: 'If you're a good listener, you don't have to wait for people to open their mouths to know that they are sending out an SOS'.

***

Next morning.

They had a Continental breakfast with the group, not saying much, and gathered in the Hodgson Room. Wilfred looked as if he had heaved off a heavy burden, and Amani no longer tensed up.

Takashi had ducked out in the early morning.

A new whiteboard stood in a corner and stared at them like a sad clown. Felipe proclaimed, "The fickle British weather always makes me ratty with children. I'm in no mood to prescribe more snippy and snarky remarks or cast aspersions on the churlish chicken population today. I'm here to teach you what you cannot learn from books. I think I've accomplished that and I'm tired of speaking. Good manners will open doors that the best education cannot'. But if you have the manners of a hog, people will treat you as one. One day you'll all thank me for my guidance. What we'll do now is you'll write an essay. The best paper, judged by me, will win a DIY 'Chemistry of Monsters' kit sponsored by MEL Science. Whoever gets it, don't make anything that might explode in your house."

He took out the same pile of A4 papers that they'd used the day before and distributed them. "Here are the essay prompts. Art: What is the best way to fold a paper tiger? Public Policy: From a public health perspective, was the Virgin Mary a surrogate mother? Why or why not? Business: If culture eats strategy for breakfast, who eats what for lunch? Urban planning and management: If all humans are angels, what should we do with air traffic control? Literature: What would animal rights advocates think of Shakespeare's 'Why then the world's mine oyster, Which I with sword will open.' Ethics and Philosophy: Do you agree that adults are children with better morals and ethics?"

Chance decided that there was no need for him to stay any longer. He made his intention to leave clear to Felipe, went to pack, and asked the reception for a taxi.

Gabby was out in the driveway enjoying the sunlit lawn. He went out and chattered with her while he waited for his ride. She said remorsefully, "I had thought that Amani looked refreshed because the country air had done her good. Last night, she'd told me about the terrible things people at her school have been distributing, and she told me how relieved she was that someone had defended her. Mr Yang, I'm most grateful for your help. And I've wondered if Mr Kazama always speaks off the cuff. He has something...*sprezzatura* about the way he talks. Mr Yang. I..." Gabby faltered. "I...I have a friend..."

He only waited.

She half-turned to look at the Mews. "I have a friend and...she works as the housekeeper for an esteemed household in London. The lady of the house is a most caring employer, and she considers advancing social empowerment her cause. She's a governor for a local school and an active member of the Fabian Society. My friend is very honoured to be working for her. A few years back, her employer met an equally esteemed partner, and they filled their house with laughter. Then something changed."

She inhaled deeply. "Her employer discovered that her husband had been unfaithful, and she attempted to revert the situation. Someone told her that having a child in the house helps, so she adopted a girl... like Amani. Her uncle is a generous man, and he'd decided to hire the best tutors to help the girl. But someone had told her employer that no other man should enter her house. My friend had tried her best to carry out her employer's wishes. And once, my friend told me that she'd gone beyond her grief as she began to doubt the meaning of service when she'd helped her employer skin a pair of dead cats. Someone had told her employer that only by doing so would her husband return."

A pair of dead cats...

"Mrs Parker," he said, "are you certain...are you certain that your friend and her employer only used felines once?"

"Yes, Mr Yang, I'm quite certain." She looked at him questioningly. "They only needed a tom and a queen, and they procured a pair from a veterinarian...or so I heard."

Two were euthanized...

He pressed on. "Do you consider it possible that the employer of your friend might have procured more?"

"No," Gabby replied determinedly and smiled faintly. "You see, her employer has a faint heart and is squeamish when it comes to…matters like this. My friend told me that she wouldn't even touch the bag that had the poor animals." She hesitated. "And my friend told me how she wanted to offer her apology to those who were puzzled and troubled."

"Well, Mrs Parker." He thought for a moment. "Perhaps it's not for me to say, but as a fellow tutor, I feel that they would understand if they knew why."

"There's no need to worry anymore," Gabby offered. "Her employer's partner has returned."

He wanted to ask more, but then his taxi arrived.

He said goodbye to Gabby then got into the car. It was the same driver who had pulled a face on Friday.

Chance checked his travelling options. The trains from Egham to Paddington and Waterloo would take a considerable amount of time, or so he had deemed. He asked the driver if he had any other passengers booked and if he might be interested in driving him to Holland Park.

The driver agreed, and he sat back and mulled.

Back to the origin, he thought.

He didn't know how to account for the twenty-three cats that were either drowned or strangled. Gabby seemed to be telling the truth.

By whom? Amani?

If she couldn't keep a copy of *The Hunger Games* in secret in that house, it would be not easy to carry out acts like that. And there was no reason to bury them in the neighbour's backyard if Regent's Park provided a better choice.

Might it be Daniele Vidas? Everyone has secrets, he reminded himself
as the possibilities flitted through his mind.

During his earlier chat with Gabby, he had learnt that Wilfred's
father worked for the Financial Conduct Authority, and then he knew.
When the boy got home that afternoon and connected to the house
WiFi, whatever wiles Felipe had installed on his laptop would work
its wonders. Perhaps it was no coincidence that Nathan's father was a
prominent member of the UK's National Police Chiefs' Council.

Chance felt he had got himself out of a mess and landed in another
one straightaway.

He took out his phone and messaged Catherine as the car neared
Heathrow. She replied soon, saying that she'd just returned from her
Photoshop training centre on St John's Lane in Clerkenwell. He couldn't
be sure if she was happy to know that he'd be returning earlier than
scheduled.

The cab bumped on the poorly maintained roads, and his derrière
ached from his nocturnal episode.

And Eddy Robinson.

After last night, it seemed that sextortion was not so distant a
possibility as it once seemed.

The driver attempted small talk with him, encouraging him to
download their Gett app and grumbling how Uber drivers took business
yet failing to maintain the same safety standards; for example, his cab
had installed a camera, vehicle markings, and emergency warning
lights for customers' safety. Yet Uber cars were just cars without these
precautionary measures. He went on to talk about the local derby that

night.

Chance only listened with intermittent nods and 'I see's'.

As they approached Hammersmith, Felipe sent him a message: And the Best Poem goes to... (drum rolls*n).

He opened the attached photo and recognised Amani's handwriting. It had only a few lines:

Adults are all liars.

They said if we took up a gun, we would live.

They said if we hurt others, we would live.

They said if we were adopted, we would live.

Adults are all liars.

There is no learning curve for pain.

He had to pretend to look for something in his duffel bag to hide his tears.

Chapter 14

They arrived at Catherine's house. He paid the driver and tipped generously.

He then pressed on the doorbell and waited.

"Just a second!" he heard her calling.

"Sorry, I'm having a little...situation." She opened the door and disappeared like a gush of wind. He went in, changed into his slippers, put his bag down, and followed her into the kitchen.

There was molten sugar all over the range, the colander, the pan's handle, and even on Mr Darcy's whiskers and paws.

"Oh, my dear," he said. "Devil may cry."

"*Fie!* Mr Yang, I thought that candy apple was a simple dish, and now I know I'm mistaken. I shall never speak lowly of it again."

The pan was washed, the kitchen scoured, the cat cleaned, the dish remade, and they had a light lunch.

"How was your exam?" he asked.

"Passed it with flying colours. And Mr Yang," Catherine looked smug before popping a chunk of candied apple wedge into her mouth. "Why are you back so early?"

"Well. I wrote you a letter, and they told me that I needed to wait to post it and my patience was wearing thin, so I sent myself."

"I see," Catherine said, amused. "I thought that you were back early because you couldn't stand missing me."

"That's a major contributing factor as well."

The room was warm, so he took off his pullover. Mr Darcy jumped onto his lap instantly and rubbed his cheeks on his stomach non-stop.

"It seems that Mr Darcy missed you," Catherine commented.

He balanced the cat; it weighed like a small dictionary. "Is Mr Darcy the only one in this house who missed me?"

"No," she said with humour lacing her voice, "Esmeralda also missed you."

"Who?"

"Allow me to present you: Esmeralda." Catherine gestured to her verdant garden, and he saw a kumquat tree. "Hannah gave it to me. Better to nurture it than see it wither."

"Is she back?"

"No. She said she'd be back by early May." Catherine sighed. "They got it from the Columbia Road Flower Market."

"It does bring back some memories." He remembered to tell her about the filming location of *The King's Speech*.

After lunch, they decided to move their conversation elsewhere. They zhooshed the cushions and settled on the sofa, and Mr Darcy glued himself on Chance's lap.

Catherine found it mirthful. "Oh! Mr Darcy did miss you. He told me that you have grown upon him since you met last year."

"Did you miss me, little catling?"

"Yes. I've missed you terribly." Then Catherine realised something,

"You never call me 'Cathy'."

"Would you like me to?"

"I guess I don't mind. I prefer 'little catling' anyway when it's only us." Catherine retrieved something from her handbag. "Come live with me."

He took the newly cut keys. "Thank you, Catherine. Is there anything that I've missed?"

"Well." She sat back, and they snuggled together. "An told me about your...losses." She held his hand. "I've discovered that some of our pains are the same."

He thought for a while and told her what Amani wrote: that there is no learning curve for pain.

Catherine smiled bitterly, " And...I..."

"You have already told me with your eyes."

"I love you. I do. I see myself in you."

They talked for an hour or so. She'd told him why she didn't go to that vegetarian restaurant on the night when her parents passed away on their way back. She'd suffered severe menstrual cramps.

He told her what happened with Isabel and the true reason he had stopped drinking. The only thing he didn't tell her was that Isabel was the illegitimate daughter of Alexander Roxborough, Catherine's uncle. He'd given him his word, and he had no intention to renege on his promise. He had also kept quiet over a deceased solicitor with the surname of McCain.

Then he told Catherine how he acquired a phobia for white sheets.

"I went to visit my dad in his hospital room. The visiting hours were not over, but I felt dog-tired. He saw me and told me to go back home and have a good night's sleep. I thought, why not? I'll come back tomorrow anyway, and I'll spend more time with him. And the next morning, he was gone." He told the ceiling, "Catherine, I cannot stand that I was not there for them and that I...let them down."

"That's not true." She held him.

After a while, he collected himself. "I've learnt some things about you this weekend as well."

"Yes?"

"Like why you'd watch *Howards End* after *The Remains of the Day*."

He told her that Mrs Parker, the Edens' housekeeper, told him that she and her husband had met working at the Ritz in London. For a while, they had a period of relationship status uncertainty, and Gabby, the maiden, decided to quit her job and seek employment in Edinburgh. Before she left, she asked Mr Parker out for their last date at a cinema, and they had watched *The Remains of the Day*. After watching the film, they took a walk along the floodlit Victoria Embankment, and she asked him if perhaps one day he might sit on a bench on the North Bank and reminisce what-might-have-been, and Mr Parker decided that he didn't want that.

"Aww." Catherine was touched. "It's nice knowing there are happy endings in life," she said as she rubbed Mr Darcy on his flabby tummy.

Then he told her that Gabby had kindly taught him where to procure the ingredients for making top-line pickled walnuts. They decided to give it a try in July.

"And here's something that you might be glad to hear," Catherine said.

"What might that be?"

She kept him waiting.

"I know where you are the most ticklish as well, kitty cat." He picked up Mr Darcy and put him on the floor, but the cat jumped back onto his lap once again.

"Well. I might as well tell you, Mr Yang. Orla praised you."

"That's a first."

"And she wondered if there are traditional Chinese medicines that solve hair loss."

"I've heard that eating sesame might help."

She told him of Orla's engagement and how her colleague dithered over choosing her last name.

He considered and said, "Catherine, I don't wish for you to become Mrs Yang."

She froze.

He took her hands. "I'm more than fine if you are Mrs Roxborough."

She tilted her head. "Is this a proposal, Mr Yang? I think you can do better than that."

"Let's have a do-over." He moved Mr Darcy to the sofa arm and went out of the room. The cat followed him. A minute later, they each returned with a springy step.

"Catherine." He produced a velvety box from his pocket and looked at her, keenly. "I love you. Will you marry me?"

"Yes," she said. "Yes!"

It was simple and natural.

She had experienced a proposal once before. She had had the live quartet, the gold taper candle-lit dinner, the blooms, the kneeling, the flowery word of honour; but nothing was as reassuring as this.

He opened the ring box and presented an emerald-cut alexandrite ring with pavé diamonds, and put it on for her.

"Mr Yang," she questioned amusedly, "do you always go about carrying rings and tasers?"

He told her with his eyes and a kiss.

They settled back down, and Mr Darcy reclaimed his seat on his lap. Then Chance said, "Oh, I don't want any engagement, and I want the real deal now."

"You're as demanding as always." Catherine looked at him. "It's only fair if I speak about my conditions."

"Yes?"

"I've found that, given where we have progressed, I've decided to call you 'Tiger' as a pet name. It sounds very bad-ass."

"Ah." He acquiesced and then nodded. "Fair enough."

Catherine moved closer and snaked her hand around his derrière. She giggled. "Now I'm just patting my tiger on his butt."

He winced.

"You don't like it?"

"No...it's not a problem." He hesitated, "It is just that...I have a bruise on my hip needing attention."

"How so?"

He told Catherine what had happened.

Then they decided to move their conversation into the bedroom.

***

They got upstairs, and Mr Darcy followed them readily.

Chance took off his trousers, rearranged the bolsters, leaned back on the bed, and took the ice pack Catherine handed to him.

"Ohhh. It seems quite a bad bruise." She palpated his angry skin with damson spots and examined the hematoma. "Perhaps you should go to the GP? Or I can go and get a bottle of vodka now."

"I'm fine."

"Some cicabio salve to allay the pain, maybe? Or...I can kiss it better."

He smiled. "Will you stay with me for a while first? Your tiger needs you."

"An told me your sobriquet." Catherine dropped her rabbit ear slippers and they snuggled together.

"No one calls me that now. Except perhaps my aunt."

Mr Darcy jumped onto the bed and crept in between their warm bodies.

"Catherine." He dropped a few light kisses on her hand. "Do you know that today's your birthday in the Chinese lunar calendar? Whenever you think about your birthdays, I want you to remember only sweet memories."

She wallowed in her happiness and regarded her ring. "When did you get it?"

"Last time after you showed me your mother's alexandrite necklace, I asked Lynette, and she pointed me to a jeweller in Hatton Garden. Do you like it?"

"Yes. They pair up quite nicely. I like it very much." Catherine hesitated. "I love all your gifts, but...but I don't think that a...grand wedding would be necessary." Her thoughts drifted to her once planned wedding at Babington House.

"Just family and friends? That can be arranged."

They kissed ravenously but were soon interrupted by Mr Darcy. They tried again and the cat kept on third-wheeling.

Catherine mused, "I think I know why Mr Darcy is sparkly today."

"Because he has sensed your happiness?"

"Of course. That's a contributing factor. But..." Catherine paused. "When you cleaned him up just now, did you use the cat calming spray by his carrier?"

"I don't think so."

"He looks like he's under its effect. You know, Mr Darcy doesn't like catnip or valerian, but he fancies that spray very much."

"I see." He thought for a while, sat up, took off his jumper, threw it away from the bed, and the cat sailed after it.

"Catherine...would you mind if I make a quick call?" He explained, "I need to reach Felipe at the Lodge. It's something important."

"My tiger no longer needs me?" She pouted and made to leave.

He stopped her. "Go to my duffel bag by the umbrella stand. There's a letter for you in there. Why don't you read it while I make my call?"

"Okay! In fact, I've written you a message and I've put it in your mailbox."

Catherine left and Mr Darcy kneaded and purred on Chance's jumper noisily.

He took out his phone and called Peter at Reception, asking for Mrs Parker. He waited for a while, and she came along.

"Mrs Parker," he said. "Might I prevail on your kindness to ask some questions?"

"Of...of course, Mr Yang."

"What brand of red wine vinegar do you use when you make pickled walnuts?"

"Oh. I always use Lucini, but you can also mix half vinegar and half port. A cheap one would do. If you like to get merry, Mr Yang, you can also use half vinegar and half morello cherry gin."

"I see. Mrs Parker, I have to ask a few random questions, but they are of *vital* importance."

"Well, I'll answer to the best of my ability."

"Does your friend's employer have a nanny cam in her house?"

After a moment of hesitation she said, "Yes."

"Do you know when it was installed?"

Gabby told him.

"Do you happen to know when your friend and her employer procured the cats?"

Gabby told him again.

"And, Mrs Parker," he paused, "the bag that you took to Cumberland Lodge, the one in which you kept my jumper for me, the greige one–"

"Oh, that's not mine," Gabby explained. She wasn't planning on accompanying Amani to the Bootcamp, but because Felipe had insisted on it, she joined them. She didn't have time to go back and pack, so she'd borrowed a bag and put a few travelling amenities inside. The owner of the bag said that he wouldn't need it over the weekend.

Ambrose Eden.

Chapter 15

25th April, Monday afternoon.
Catherine's birthday.

Suave music played as Felipe and Chance adorned the dining room with streamers. Catherine helped Patsy decorate her funfetti cake using jimmies.

"Felipe, you're quite early today. I thought preferment would mean longer hours," Patsy commented casually.

"I pulled a sickie." Felipe passed a piece of ribbon to Chance. "I wouldn't miss this for the London traffic. I always treat my clients like friends and my friends like clients."

"Pat, I wanted to ask you, we have some beginners' courses at the flower academy and the staff can bring a student free of charge. Would you like to join?" Catherine asked. She wore a snazzy polka dot shirt dress that day.

"Absolutely. When is it?"

"Wednesday to Friday mornings."

"Then, I can't," Patsy said, a little let down, "I've got early shifts."

Catherine then told Patsy that Melody, her teacher at the flower shop, was delira and excira to hear her and Orla's news and she'd promised to design their bridal bouquets.

Felipe cut in, "I find that people who propose on birthdays just want to strategise and economise so they can buy one less gift and never forget the anniversary. But anyway, I'm happy for that poppet colleague of yours. You know, they say that the most important career choice you make is who you marry. My buddy here may not be supercalifragilisticexpialidociously dishy, but he has an alluring common touch. I know he'll be a paragon of making you happy. Considerateness is his wheelhouse." He carried on, "Patsy the Bennett, have you considered tying the knot with Cecil's pudgy fingers?"

"Ah. No. Well, I like where we are. It isn't on the cards for us now."

"It wouldn't matter anyway. You're already husbanding, and marriage is a serious undertaking." Felipe nudged Chance with his elbow. "I know someone in Italy who makes marvellous confetti! Now that I'm in London, I can invite myself to your wedding and finally get to meet your *madrastra*. Tell us, what did you say to win Cathy's heart? Did you say, 'Oh Catherine, there are supporting characters in your favourite stories named Catherine, but Catherine, you're the *protagonist* of my life! You're the light of my life! You're my *joie de vivre*!'"

"Nah!" the birthday girl burst out laughing. "That's so cheesy! Overly cheesy."

"Fine," Felipe said grouchily, "I'll save it for my own use then. Cathy, do you know any lassie who's named 'Catherine' and likes these fandoms that I can wolf whistle?"

"You know who you remind me of, Felipe?" Patsy recalled as she spread the cake icing. "You remind me of a patient who, when you asked him a question, would yak and clack on for a whole lot of ten minutes."

"Well. Emil Cioran says that we feel safer with a madman who talks than with one who cannot open his mouth. And let's not forget that idle hands are the devil's workshop; idle lips are his mouthpiece. And by that, I mean Mr Darcy, you better pull your weight. Why don't you hop on my shoulder and lend us your hands?"

Mr Darcy meowed on the sofa as Chance chuckled at this in-joke.

"See, this is exactly what I'm talking about," Patsy added. "You're always ladling out, always bending our ears, always larger than life, always feeling your oats, and always cutting a wide swath. And we can't refute you because what you say seems to make sense."

"Of course it makes sense. I have a knack for romancing the room, and I'm a Master Coach certified by the International Coach Federation. Patsy, you should be glad that I don't charge for this session for growing your mindset to a higher order. Well, one has to do some gratis work once in a while for the commensal common good. I've been told on many occasions that I'm smart as a whip. And you are already benefiting from my smarts, Patsy. I can feel it in the air, for I'm the life, the soul, and the lodestone of this party from soup to nuts."

Felipe steadied the chair that Chance stood on. "Cathy, do you know that a flock of starlings is called a 'constellation'? European starlings have exquisite tastes, and they eat grapes, currants, olives, and peaches. I think that's something you can use with your creative endeavours next time. Oh, and here's another fun fact. There's a *yokai* called a 'tenjoname'. It has an anthropoid body and a very long tongue. It likes to lick the ceiling of a house clean. I think that's something that Mr Stevens would be interested in recruiting. Do you know if they have any diversity, inclusion, and equity policy for the ménage at the hall?"

Catherine was in stitches. "Why do I feel that you're just pulling my chain?"

"Look it up, if you don't believe me." Felipe continued as he smoothed his Etro floral shirt, "I also know of another *yokai* called a 'kanbari nyudo'. It's a ghost that lurks outside washrooms on New Year's Eve. It peeks at the persons who are using the toilets. One interesting thing about this 'kanbari nyudo' is that it can blow a cuckoo out of its mouth. When people hear the cuckoo's calling, they must shout 'Shithouse Mouse!'. Otherwise, the creature will inflict constipation upon those who see it for the whole year. Oh, and in Italy, the populations scratch their cobbler's awls to keep evil spirits away."

"Felipe! Don't you have any other *finer* topics to discuss?" Patsy was not so pleased because she had just dredged a batch of chocolate chip oatmeal doughballs with sugar.

"By all means, Patsy. Would you consider oenology an appropriate topic? I know why you're so stroppy today. There isn't enough sunshine in London to cause wine faults. Or did you get stony broke at the Cheltenham Festival?" Felipe picked up a satin-bow-wrapped bottle of wine. "Cathy, you know that there's no Château d'Yquem 1992, so I got you '91, the year when you were conceived."

"Thank you, Felipe, that's very kind of you."

"*Prego*." Felipe flashed his signature smile.

After the room was festooned with the decorations, Felipe took up his glass of Horchata and had a gulp. "Oh, and my friend from a farm tells me that when you slaughter a male mammal, you must remove the head and the testes immediately, so the meat won't get tainted. Also, research has found that for humans, the brains and testes have the highest number of common proteins. And in Japan, when a bear eats people, people must hunt it down because it'll do it again once it tastes human flesh–"

"Felipe!" Patsy exclaimed again. "I don't think these grotty tommyrots are the suitable prandial topics that we should engage ourselves with on Catherine's birthday."

"These are the *very* topics we should engage ourselves with on Catherine's birthday and *especially* before the mastiffs arrive," Felipe said as he helped Chance to put away the ladder.

Patsy put down her pastry bag in disbelief. "Cecil is *not* a mastiff!"

"Of course, he's a mastiff and some more. And he's an old coot, a cantankerous spoilsport, and a prude and a bore. The corners of his droopy, dour mouth always almost fall to the back of his feet. He stuck horsehair in the ground and thought he'd grow a full-bottomed wig."

"Pish!" Patsy huffed. "Cecil's always sprightly and full of beans when we are together."

"He's full of Heinz baked beans. Do you know that they make it at Wigan? Who knows, might be handy for a pub quiz. Well, it takes all sorts to make a world."

"I think a *skiver* has no right to vilify someone industrious!"

"Hello potty. Let the one that's without sin cast the first stone. I've never dipped my pen in the company ink. And who's the delinquent one? Don't they teach ethical considerations at school anymore, Patsy? Or did you throw them to the four winds?"

"Cecil is *no longer* my patient."

Felipe smiled. "Maybe he's the one sprucing. He's a fat cat, a vanilla catch, and a chicken with the pip. Or maybe he has his *own* ethical considerations. I've heard that the word 'ethical' also means medication that's available only on doctors' prescriptions and not advertised to the general public."

Patsy put her hands on her hip and let rip. "Felipe Kazama! I've never seen any overbearing busybody as cocksure as you are in all my puff!"

Felipe inhaled profoundly and admonished, "Ñoña! I can have you fired in my company in a second for making such an abhorrent statement. How do you know if I hadn't had a penectomy?"

"Well…" Patsy stopped abruptly in confusion, and her tone softened. "Have you…did you?"

"Of course not. But when you *assume* you make an ass out of yourself. A sum of an ass. Next time, Patsy, you'll think twice before asking impertinent questions and *cocking* your snook. You'll remember to keep a civil tongue in your head and not in your cheek. It's called the Law of Effect."

Chance watched as Patsy sighed deeply and relented. "Catherine, do you mind sharing with us what your fiancé got for you?"

"Hmm," Catherine hesitated, "Chance got me a butler's desk." She then said, "Oh! My stockings are laddered. I better go and change them."

After she left the room, Felipe chided Patsy once more. "Bad Patsy! Bad! You've spoken the verboten word."

"Rot!" Patsy frowned, "I didn't say anything inappropriate or offensive just now, did I? Unlike *someone* who's lippy."

Chance explained briefly why Catherine might not be too fond of the word 'fiancé' on her birthday as he took out the millet rice cake with raisins he made earlier from the fridge. He had dressed the dish with the Great Park honey that he brought back. Mr Darcy jumped onto the dining table and neared the dish. He then excused himself to use the washroom before asking Felipe to mind the cat.

"Now, H Darcy." Felipe grabbed the cat by the scruff as if he was picking up a file folder. "You better behave and stop being a menace, or else I'll put you in your waistcoat."

The cat mewled insistently.

"Ha!" Patsy laughed incredulously. "If there's anything you should know about English literature, Felipe, is that the protagonist of *Pride and Prejudice* is called Fitzwilliam Darcy."

"Ha!" Felipe goaded, "It seems that you don't know American English literature at all. And it only proves that Cathy hasn't accepted you into our clique yet."

Catherine entered the room upon this remark, "Oi, don't say that!"

Patsy looked lost and hurt. "Am I being left out?"

"Oh, Pat." Catherine consoled her, "It's nothing top secret but not of general interest either. You've been talking at cross purposes." Then she told her about her fanfiction pursuits and her favourite ships.

"I like watching films. I like *The Tall Guy*, where Emma Thompson played a nurse. Hannibal Lecter... Wasn't there a poster that's banned?"

Catherine nodded eagerly, "Yeah, I have it in my collection. It's brilliant, actually."

Patsy picked up her pastry bag and shrugged, "I like horror films too. I love the Hammer horrors and the Claude Rains' phantom. I think it's the best adaptation bar none. And *The Human Centipede* is spine-tingling. A doctor at our hospital would use it to tell the interns how not

SHAWE RUCKUS

to operate."

Felipe sighed as he handed the cat to Catherine. "Patsy, you're making tonight intolerable. You'll never get to heaven if you ruin this evening."

Patsy ignored him. "Speaking of *The Remains of the Day*, I've had a patient who told me that when Kazuo Ishiguro wrote it, he'd heard...'Hey, That's No Way to Say Goodbye' by Leonard Cohen on the radio, so he decided to have Mr Stevens buttoned up to the bitter end."

Catherine was down in the mouth.

"Now, Patsy, my sensitive Euromonitor tells me that you've made Catherine sad," Felipe said. "Well, well. Cathy, as Wilde would say, everyone is worthy of love, except those who think they are. All good things come to those who wait, and all lush stuff to those who stay up late. All fun happens at night-time. That's my recent revelation."

"Hmm," Catherine reflected. "But life doesn't always have happy endings and sometimes it's a downer ending..." Her thoughts drifted to her parents and Hannah and Eddy Robinson again, and the last time she'd seen them.

"Let me cheer you up before laughing water is served." Felipe thought for a few seconds. "When I was still a member of the Great Unwashed, I liked to write diaries to practise my English. I recall an entry I once made. I was working as a chauffeur in Belgravia at that time. I wrote: Dear Deidre, ooops, made a slip of my pen. Dear diary, today's been another day when I've stared at the duplicate of Odilon Redon's *Vase of Flowers* in my room, and I've looped 'How Am I Supposed to Live Without You' all day."

Catherine sat down and smiled a bit. "Well–"

Felipe continued, "In the afternoon, I went to post a letter to an old friend. But then I didn't trust the efficiency of the Royal Mail and I decided to stop taking my blue pill, gathered my pluck, took the machine that always halted, and went to seek her. On my way, I saw an elegant couple thumbing a lift, and the turnspit in me made me stop. The couple was Doctor Swan and Mrs Swan. They had just returned from their residence in Vienna near the Belvedere. We've talked about many things, including fine wine, shoes and bags, grouse beating, Cligès the poem, and free-range garden varieties. The doctor asked me if I would be interested in joining their sequestered household in the Falkland Islands because England is no country for old men and the English weather is cold as any stone. Not mentioning that England is the most class-ridden country under the sun. I first declined his kind offer saying that I felt that I was neither fish, flesh, nor good red herring. And he said he knew how to treat a jaundiced eye. Mrs Swan seconded him, and she told me that she had met him at work at a hospital. The doctor also taught me a Latin phrase: 'omnia vincit amor'. He knew that in Japan, even monks could marry. He asked me what would I do if I received the austere accolade of the axe or the order of the boot? Would I encase and hide them along with the skeletons in my closet? Or would I clean them vigorously with more elbow grease? I considered my allotment after slaving away all those nights staring at the Orion and found that I had none. Then I remembered the time when they'd hacked off half of my chicken feed for breaking a bottle of wine already. How many times that I had witnessed an egg yesterday turn a feather-duster tomorrow. I decided to accept his invitation. I found my friend unscathed; we took wing for South America. We didn't even need a visa to go there. And as Bob Bitchin would say, the difference between an adventure and an ordeal is attitude. No one could cramp my style anymore. Well, Cathy, that's how I ended up as a seafarer once."

Catherine gave a small laugh and held Mr Darcy on her lap. "I don't know where you get all your ideas, Felipe."

"It's the universe that keeps on putting ideas in my mind," he said. "Do you know what I'll do one day, Cathy? I'll get a mansion and hire a housekeeper and a butler so you can match-make them."

The doorbell rang.

"Ah!" Felipe clapped his hands merrily. "The mastiffs have arrived!"

***

Much to Felipe's disappointment, it was not the 'mastiffs', it was An who had arrived.

"Happy Birthday, Catherine!" She came in and hugged her.

An settled on the sofa, and Mr Darcy sniffed her hand. Catherine noticed that her finger had healed.

"Are the mesh screens working?" she asked as she filled a glass of Horchata for An.

"Yes." An smiled. "My mother is so happy to know you are getting married! She invites you to go to China in the summer," she said as she petted the cat.

"What's your city like?"

"It's a small coastal city not far from Qingdao. It's a bit like Brighton but with a lot of wines."

"That sounds wonderful." Catherine handed her the sweet drink. She then offered the free beginners' course to An, but unfortunately, An had to spend more time on her dissertation.

"Ah, I forgot." An took out a gift that was wrapped like a large cupcake. "Many happy returns; I hope you like it."

It was a pair of pink lounge socks that had prints on the soles saying 'Wine is bottled poetry. If you can read this, bring me some wine'.

Felipe sat down on the sofa arm as Catherine opened her gift. He reached out his hand, "Hi. The name's Felipe Kazama. I've worked with your cousin, and I'm also Catherine's friend."

"Nice to meet you."

They shook hands.

Felipe continued loudly, "I'm a Peruvian national and Kazama is a Japanese word that means the time when wind pass—not passing wind, mind you."

"I see." An nodded in respect while Patsy grimaced.

Chance got back to the room, and they chatted for a while. Then Felipe stood up and retrieved some papers and a few small acrylic containers with various coloured sand from his Prada briefcase. He said, "Well, Catherine, we cannot get you a sandy beach, but at least we can get you some sand art." He asked Chance to help him to clear the table, and he took out some paper. He recognised it to be the pile of A4 paper they had used at the Lodge, but now it had cut-out patterns. Felipe spread the sheets one by one, fanned out the coloured sand, blew softly, and sifted the sand from the patterns.

"Behold!" Felipe straightened his posture, took away the papers, and then they saw a rainbow 'Happy Birthday' written in an ornate script font in the sand.

"Accha!" Catherine exclaimed. "It is wonderful!"

"Yeah! Give me five! Give me a Cambridge Five! Give me a 25 de Abril Bridge!"

They high-fived, and Catherine thanked him again.

"No worries. It's a no-brainer."

"Felipe!" Patsy sang out. "Don't get any sand on my cake!"

"Well, having kissed the Blarney Stone with the witchcraft in your lips and as inventive as you are, you can continue to build on sand, Patsy. Just make sure not to get your fingers sticky." Felipe looked at his watch. "Why don't we join the table and wait for the mastiffs as we wile away the sands of time? I'm Hank Marvin. Wouldn't some porkies and fibs be nice? Oh, I meant figs. Some kipers would do as well. Oh, I meant kippers."

"And what is a mastiff?" An asked.

Felipe grinned. "A mastiff is a synonym for a caitiff."

An didn't know what that meant, but she decided not to pursue it any further.

They sat around the table in an uplifting, *gezellig* mood. Chance and Catherine held Mr Darcy with An on one side and Felipe and Patsy on the other.

They had some small talk, and then An mentioned how thieves had been impersonating students on campus and stealing laptops. She was worried that she might encounter such an unfortunate incident and lose her research work.

"Hmm," Felipe said. "Let me tell you an episode. Once, I worked as a truck driver in Japan, and I loved this rice snack. But my salary was so meagre that I could only afford it once in a while. By the by, did you know that if you eat apple and cucumber together, it tastes like melon? I often tried it because fruits in Japan are costly, melons especially. One day, I finished a job, and I parked my truck in a parking lot. I decided to have a nap, and I left the windows open because it was very hot and I needed to save on gas. I had a bag of rice popcorn that I placed on the passenger side, and it was gone when I woke up. There was a children's playground nearby, so I asked them if any of them had taken it. Of course, no one admitted it. Then I went to the police and told them that I'd prepared some rice popcorn to poison the rats in my flat, but it had been stolen. They took it very seriously because once there was a case in Japan when some criminals put cyanide-laced Coca-Cola in public areas, and some high school students drank it and died. We found my snack in a snap."

"Oh, I see." An nodded cautiously.

Felipe continued, "What you need is a laptop lock or a security slot adapter."

"You mean like a lock on the...bag?" An asked tentatively.

Felipe compared and contrasted the differences between Nobel locks and Kensington locks in a lengthy monologue, and they remained silent.

Then Patsy remembered to ask about Catherine's toothache.

"It's okay now. I've developed a better hygiene routine," she said.

An said that one of her classmates had given up waiting for an NHS dentist appointment and decided to travel back to Thailand during their reading week because it would be quicker and cheaper. An also mentioned that her GP had hinted that she'd vote to leave because she'd considered that the NHS was insufficiently funded.

Patsy agreed. "I can say that many of my colleagues share the same sentiment. I see *The Remains of the Day* as a political satire. That the British, or at least a part of British society, always serve German and French interests willingly, but never our own. And what I felt was twisted about the film was how they made Mr Stevens' new employer American."

Felipe remarked, "Good, Patsy. At least you're not brainwashed with the righteousness of US dominance. But, Patsy, why do you have such a sanguine view on Brexit? As Upton Sinclair would say, it's difficult to get someone to understand something when their salary depends on them not understanding it. Brexit is only expedient to divide and diktat. In Ancient Rome, the government provided free bread and entertainment to keep the redundant happy. In Modern UK, the government offers free pablum and political ammunition to pander and pacify the doled substrata of society. Leave or remain; decline or decline further; Tories or Red Tories? That's the question in a cleft stick in the clear blue water with flotsam and jetsam. What the UK needs now is politics that make you feel good, not something you won't regret later. I've already seen a dangerous tendency in England where people scrape the barrel with their office supplies."

He removed a few sand grains from the table. "Patsy, you may be distancing yourself on regional integration, but there's no way to distance yourself away from the stinking continent physically. Perhaps rounds are being bought in Continental Europe this very second to celebrate the fact that they can finally get rid of the English hooligans. I think the UK's taxpayers should scratch your soft spot and question the funding for Buck House and BBC Wicked Service instead. Have you heard of the Pyramid of Capitalism? Who is selling England by the pound? Who are the actors on the chessboard? The top ones rule and fool you, the middle ones mangle and discard you, and the rest cook your goose and eat it for you. The Tories say they love the NHS, they'll spend more and Labour says they don't, so they'll spend even more. To borrow from an ex-Chancellor of the Exchequer of yours, you cannot fund the NHS on a just-in-time basis."

He shifted around. "Someone should tell you that there isn't a magic money tree. To my dismay, I can't say who because of the Chatham House rule. No names, no pack drill. But I can tell you that it's from the horse's mouth. The UK only repaid its debt accumulated during World War One last May. Not mentioning that, according to the British Standards Institution, the UK is among the top countries in the world for pharmaceutical theft. There'll be hell to pay–"

Then all of a sudden, Felipe called out, "Good grouse! Patsy the Bennett! Are you playing footsie with me? People will say that we are in love!"

"No," Patsy replied plainly, "I'm only trying to *step* on your toes."

"Stop ruining my brand-new monks and stop two-timing! I'm going to catch hell if my girlfriend finds out!"

She smiled cattily, "Oh, I didn't know that you're seeing someone, Felipe. Why didn't you bring her today and introduce her to our clique?"

Felipe cleared his throat. "Ahem. She's in another nation."

Chance and Catherine exchanged a worried, knowing look in anticipation.

"Huh. And where might *that* be?" Patsy asked as she flung out her napkin.

Felipe looked at her petulantly. "She's in the start-up nation, Israel. She's a ballsy Krav Maga instructor, and she went back for training."

"Oh," An asked. "Is Krav Maga a type of yoga?"

"Ah." Felipe smiled. "More like tango. I'm potty about her. She swept me off my feet."

Patsy hounded him, "No wonder you were talking about the *blue pills*, Felipe. Aren't you glad that they aren't *ethical*? I've learnt that smoking can cause harm in certain departments."

The opposite side of the table held the ring and looked back and forth between the two.

Felipe grinned and jeered. "Patsy, you should be concerned for your darling Cecil who's longer in the tooth. Aren't you *tired* of him being tired? I've heard that constant dripping wears away a stone. As busy as my body is, I'm perfectly capable of *inserting* the well-oiled machine to add value."

Catherine eyed the cake and feared that Patsy might slap it in his face.

Patsy only sighed. "Dear An, would you mind sitting with Mr Ho-hum from hell here? I can't be anywhere near someone without a soul."

"No...not really," An answered bashfully, and they exchanged seats.

Felipe carried on. "They say that to possess another language is to have another soul. I sold my soul to the devil, so what? I speak Quechua, Spanish, Japanese, English, and some good French. I've still got three more souls to sell." He grinned again. "Patsy, if pulchritude was earned, you'd be failing it."

"For God's sake, can't you belt up for a minute?" Patsy bit back.

"Well, Patsy, you should know that Mum's the word."

"Hell's bells! Go to Bath, sirrah! Go to Hell!" piped Patsy.

"I've been there, done that, got the T-shirt and back. The road to hell,

Patsy, is a roundtrip." Felipe smiled again. "And I think you should speak with a little more respect when you address someone with a handicap."

Patsy raised her brows in suspicion.

Felipe grinned. "I've got a golf handicap of 2.5."

Patsy was about to explode when Catherine intervened, "Felipe, please."

"She Adam-teased me first!" He said, "I'm only returning the favour."

Catherine insisted, "*Please.*"

"Fine. I won't mither again tonight. But I'm afraid it's going to be a meaningless assurance."

The doorbell rang again, and he went to get the door.

***

This time, it was Mick and Sam, Catherine's best friend and his spouse, who arrived.

Chance wondered if Cecil and Alexander Roxborough had simply decided to show up at the last minute to spend less time with Felipe.

Sam and Mick had gifted a set of bath bombs that they had hoped the newly affianced would enjoy. It was the first time that the couple had met An. After learning that she grew up in Inner Mongolia, Sam, a singing coach, engaged her in conversation about her childhood while playing with Mr Darcy. "It's quite dry and arid in summer. A little bit like the scenery in *My Mother's Castle*," An recalled. Sam liked a Mandopop singer called Wei Wei and they discussed a khoomei show or throat singing performance that An had attended.

Chance sensed that Felipe had got tired waiting for his opportunity to make fun of Catherine's godfather and uncle. He soon joined Catherine in tasting her birthday wine.

Chance heard him saying: "You know, Cathy. One-third of criminals are in jail in the US, one-third are on parole, and another one-third are not caught. I do believe that there are many on the lam. If you know, there's a ringleader sitting right in front of you, and you'd escape like a needletail instead of enjoying my congenial company. It's really about how to frame the question. I do think that if Richard Kiel played him, then you wouldn't be so interested as you are now. You have a movie, and a president was shot. Then you have this. It's understandable. Who wants to make a product that they can't market, and who wants to market a product that they can't sell? There was a TV series in Japan where the protagonist had a knife play. A student, aka copycat, killed his high school teacher with the same model of knife. You can never find a copy of that show in Japan now, and it's forever banned on air. If it makes you feel any better, think of it as a not very realistic sci-fi, for it defies gravity and physiology. I've never seen anyone who can raise both of their hands high above their head with a gunshot on their shoulder after a few hours. And chloroform is always quite messy. I've heard it takes minutes to knock people out lest they struggle. Movie crews are responsible for the box office, not for the scientific delivery of knowledge. Gee, they didn't even have a budget to cast bezzie Dee. Guess they had spent it all on the pigs."

He savoured his wine. "Or think of it as a Gucci promotion with its tomfoolery. Do you know why models smile in ads, but they don't in fashion shows? It's because they want you to buy their products, but they don't want you there at the show. People don't reckon time the same way,

I tell you. According to Chinese folklore, one day in the Hell of Tongue-ripping equals three thousand seven hundred and fifty human years. Oh! I've also heard of an urban legend that someone can open darbies with a fountain pen, and he always carries one on him. It's his skeleton key, no pun intended. He's a grandee among the criminals and he beats the rap all the time. Who doesn't have an extra sleight of hand? Let's not expect much from the fools, barbarians, and incompetents. If the FBI are so capable, they'd have found Paulette soon enough before she started to rot."

The doorbell rang for the third time that night, and the missing guests finally arrived.

They video-called Sophie, sang the song, shared the dishes, the cake, the sherbet, and some flying saucers with crisp fillings, gave their jubilant blessings, and successfully prevented Mr Darcy from jumping onto the cake.

The Murder Mystery Party was also a success. They played a script that Catherine had prepared herself, with the story revolving around an Agatha Christie style crime in a mansion in the late 1930s. All evidence pointed to the butler that Chance enacted. But in the end, Felipe the Constable managed to see through everything without offending everyone in the room and found that it was a visiting dignitary who had poisoned his political opponent and his cat.

Later, Mick, the ballroom dancer, offered one of his colleague's signature intensive waltz lessons to Chance to prepare him for the big day, but Catherine decided to take up the teaching post herself. She said it would be more fun that way. She then excused herself to talk with Cecil in the study.

They kept their conversation light and convivial on topics like Fred Astaire, events at the Sadler's Wells Theatre, the new production of *Frankenstein* at the Royal Opera House, the upcoming Chelsea Flower Show, and how Cecil would receive his honorary doctorate at the Oxford Encaenia in June. Yet, the theme soon drifted to Brexit again.

"I want the UK to remain," Mick said. "England and Poland are both my home. And we'll be strutting our stuff in Europe soon. Imagine all that hassle if we leave."

Alexander Roxborough, a sociology professor, told the table that he'd heard of a promotional red bus painted in spurious slogans saying that the UK sends the EU three hundred and fifty million pounds a week. "It's all fudging and steamrollering," he said. "People don't consider the rebates that the EU pays us. The ginger group does whatever to get what they want."

"Oh, but...but how much money *do we pay* the EU every week?" Patsy asked.

"Well, if you deduct the rebates, then the ballpark figure is around two hundred and fifty million."

"Wow." Patsy shook her head. "I don't think that it would make a difference. People might still think, why don't we spend that money elsewhere?"

"Like your world-beating N-H-S?" Felipe droned.

Patsy thumbed her nose at him.

She continued, "With the current budgets we've transformed from public health—helping people to stay well, to curative medicine—treating them when they are ill. There's a big difference in there, and if we can have more money with Brexit, then perhaps opting out it's not too bad a decision."

Felipe sipped his glass of van Nahmen juice with sparkling water filled to the brim. "I said I wouldn't let my mouth cause trouble again. But I'm afraid I did it because you'll feel better if I said so. Why do you have such a firm attitude, Patsy? Some things are the firmer, the better, but a naïve article of faith and bull-headed thinking cast in concrete are not one of them. Would you like some financial enlightenment or City manna to relieve you of your woolly thinking? Brexit will suit someone's book but perhaps never your own. I think Brexit is jolly good for some people because they can do more on less. Hmm. 'Do more on less' sounds like a whizzo Wagnerian leitmotif for the NHS. Do more on less staff, personnel, funding, and whatever. Limited efforts can only serve limited objectives when you tighten your belt. Dumbsizing. Here's my two cents: once the UK is out of EU governance, you can do more money laundering on less compliance and regulation. Money launderers in the UK can run their profits through the banking system with a ninety-nine point nine per cent success rate. It's no big secret that the London prime locations are already the surreptitious top choice to hide dirty money. Like Gaddafi's ex-house in Hampstead. Do you know what's even more spine-tingling than *The Human Centipede*, Patty? The human stampede. If Brexit happens, the UK will leave the Europol and no longer have unlimited and free access to the Europol Information System. You're sailing close to the wind. But, hey, to look on the bright side, perhaps you don't know, the European Space Agency is not a member institution of the EU, so Brits might still be able to enjoy life on Mars one day. But before that, don't you think it's better to keep your feet on the ground? Your high-flown Black Arrow Rockets failed two times out of four, and now you're trying to put it under yourselves? We shall see which way the wind is blowing, but I think you can't escape the Brussels Effect in the gathering storm and you'll only get stuck at the back of the queue *ad infinitum*."

"We can do what the EU does," Sam pondered. "We can fine the tech giants, and the money will come to us, right?"

"Yeah. It's feasible. The FANGs are a cash cow for the EU budget. Here's something superfine with the fines: when you levy a fine, they pay a lump sum. Dim sum. But here's the trick question, what's the size of the UK market and what's the size of the EU market?" Felipe snapped his fingers and captured An's attention. "Hermana, what's your city's population?"

An recalled, "It's a small city...seven and a half million at most."

"And what's London the zootropolis' population, anyone?"

"Probably about eight or nine million," Mick said.

"Vote to remain at the end of the day, people, if you don't want to go down the pan like a lead balloon. I'm not saying this to snub your bitsy Britain. I don't have an ancestral dislike against the long-ago British Empire as your iffy Mayor might surmise. FYI, neither of my parents was Kenyan and none of my ancestors was a sultan or a sou. I'm saying this as a Friend of Local London. Truth is always harsh to the ear, and idle lips are the devil's mouthpiece. People, please close your eyes and think of England. The fundament of survival for anyone is acrobatics and air-reading. Never stand in the wrong queue and never mistake air-raiding for air-reading."

Patsy sniped at him, "Huh! Felipe, who are *you* to take the Mic...who are you to take your turn and get on the soapbox and have your finger in the pie and lampooning and pooh-poohing? Brexit is *our* concern."

Felipe wagged a finger at her. "Now, now, now, now, Bratty Patsy, I pay more VAT and council tax in the UK than you earn in a year, and that entitles me to contribute some constructive opinion and engage in a courteous, enjoyable, and productive debate. Oh! The things I've done for England! Your NHS would never function without the generous support of UK taxpayers. Didn't you get your one per cent pay rise this month? I hope I've spent the pennies worthy and that you and your colleagues don't suffer from Baumol's cost disease. Enjoy the *jolly good* screw, please."

Sam laughed nervously, and Mick cut in as if on cue. "Hmm, perhaps you'd like to top up your juice?"

"Anyone want a nice brew? I'll go and put the kettle on," Sam suggested.

Felipe carried on, "Why are you Brits so scared of money talking as if you are talking about pimples on the Baked Bean's ass? Without money, the Atlantic Slave Trade would never have taken place and the British Empire would never have been possible. Florence Nightingale was the first female fellow of the Royal Statistical Society. And by now, you should know, Patsy, that number provides all distances and differences."

He commented, "Where would your aggravating tone and bombastic offensive get you? Your moral crusade and pursuit of so-called British national identity are only small and petty contempt at home. I understand your yearning for your lost golden age, I do, but 'Global Britain' sounds like nostalgia. Erstwhile glory hurts, doesn't it? As Edmund Burke said, nothing turns out to be so oppressive and unjust as a feeble government."

Felipe smiled. "Read some Pomeranz, people. Your long-ago Royal

Over-Seas League prospered because you exploited the ghost acres around the world. Now? I see the common, but I don't see the wealth. Heh! What a Tragedy of the Commons! Speaking as an *outsider*, you know what the problem of the rump of your day is? Other countries plan, do, check, and adjust, and the British Isles plan, delay, cancel, and apologise. Blame it on your *superbly* situated island mentality, maybe."

Alexander Roxborough seemed all het up with these sallies, and he made to leave soon. "Mr Kazama," he said, "I would rather spend this evening with Mendeley than listening to your mouth of a sailor."

"Zut! Shut my mouth!" Felipe feigned surprise. "Smart Alec, how did you know that I was indeed once a sailor? It's not available on my LinkedIn even. But I prefer the term 'seafarer'. You know, unlike you lordlings, I wasn't born with a silver spoon in my mouth. Little ol' me was born in a greasy spoon. And Alec, we've been waiting for you with bells on, and now you're leaving so soon? Feeling your age now? You just can't play along, can you? No wonder they say that leading academics are like herding cats. Even Patsy the Bennett here had poured scorn on you saying that you're a mastiff."

"Good Gawd! I *did* not!" Patsy clarified instantly.

"Duh! Of course you did. You said Cecil is not a mastiff hence implying Alexi is. Alexi, I hope I didn't take the wind out of your sails at the rate of knots. If I did, sorry not sorry. I don't mind diddly-squat if you leave now. Who's the snotty la-di-da putting on airs? Who's the incorrigible, freeloading *gentleman* who had singlehandedly facilitated the integration and disintegration of England and Continental Europe? Oh joy! Oh rapture! Wonders will never cease! We've finally managed to fix and bell the cat! How exalted for you to sublimate your passion into work now! You didn't plough your Greats, but did you not plough the school of life? I think you've failed fast like a *chikushou*' posho. And I think to be eligible to teach others, you need first think for yourself. What have you missed in your *own* education during the formative olden days?"

"Curse it! I shall not stand all this vituperation—"

Felipe interrupted curtly, "At least a dog knows when to bark, but you only seem capable of opening your mouth on the podium and in the bedroom." He looked at him indignantly. "Now, crusty old son, no need to give me that haughty look. Go home and have fun with your effing blue pencil and lonely eyelashes while you burn the midnight oil. Oh, remember to use some eyedrops, we must treat eye care as an art form. You can continue to curl up with Turnitin when the couples turn in. Tinkety tonk, old fruit."

Alexander Roxborough left in a fit of pique and he bailed without saying goodbye to Catherine.

The conversation then drifted to the symptoms of alcohol flush syndrome as Patsy explained that an enzyme called 'aldehyde dehydrogenase' caused it, and it was common in people of East Asian descent. An listened and nodded from time to time. When Catherine and her godfather returned, Patsy told her of a medical term called the 'Starling Equation'.

Then Felipe asked Chance to accompany him to the garden to see if any UFOs were out that night. They stood near the kumquat tree in the balmy night air under the dappled, light-polluted London night sky. Felipe said, "If Ambrose Eden enjoys the limelight that much, I can make sure that he dies a social death. He doesn't live up to his name.

Well, who knows, maybe he'll need a new identity to live on soon."

It's cheap to frame someone, Chance remembered Felipe saying. He decided to change the topic, "Are you really seeing Sidney?"

Sidney was the Krav Maga instructor that Felipe had mentioned.

"Of course. She's my *la chispa*. I'm thoroughly besotted and I love our fun runs in the parks. We have yet to poison the pigeons in the park, though. Oh, and I have good news." Felipe checked the leaf shape of the kumquat plant, "We've finally solved the orphan work on why the pizza arrived at Daniele Vidas' house."

"Why? What happened?"

"The Uber driver lied." Felipe paused. "He wasn't driving that day at all."

"Then who drove her?"

"You know what's in Barking and Dagenham?"

Someone called the pizzeria from a public phone in Dagenham, and the caller redeemed a free pizza coupon...

"Barking Sport House?"

"That and dispersed accommodation for asylum seekers," Felipe said as he watched the gnome decoration light flicker on nearby aquilegia grown in garden beds. "There's an asylum seeker from Albania. Daniele Vidas got in the car with her goodie bag from Starbucks and heard his stomach growling. He hadn't had a bite that day. She offered her food to him. She told him that her parents were migrant workers who struggled to bring bread to the table as well. When he got back, he found money in the bag. Then what did he do? He wanted to say 'thank you' and placed a pizza order for her address. He saw what happened on the news, but he couldn't stand out because he was working illegally. Anyway," Felipe smiled, "now he's being deported, so he doesn't give a hang anymore. Let's wish him all the berries."

Felipe went inside, and Chance mused over this inadvertent sad story paved with good intentions.

They got back into the room, and Catherine was saying goodbye to Mick and Sam. The two had offered to drive An back to her studio in Southwark, and they left together. Before they departed, Chance heard An asking for the spelling of 'mastiff'.

Shortly after, Cecil and Patsy were going as well.

"Has anyone seen my phone?" Patsy looked around the sofa and the dining table.

"*Guau*. So eager to get back and play doctor and nurse? And nope. It seems that it's neither here nor there." Felipe removed the sand as he said, "One thing for sure is that it's within the four seas that girth Britain. But here's what you can do, Patsy: leave no stone unturned and no stone unturned on. As for poor Feli, guess I'll go home and study J. M. W. Turner's wet in wet to enhance my cross-cultural competency."

Patsy bridled at his comment once more.

Chance accompanied Catherine and her godfather to the cloakroom. Felipe shimmied by Patsy and said in a low voice, "Psst, between you and me, Patsy the Bennett, no matter how you have Cecil in your pocket and twist him around your little pinkie, I know that you're only a tea leaf. I won't ask you to say it's a fair cop. I understand. I do. I was brassic lint once. Who doesn't have a bit on the side and who doesn't like a bag of sand? Now, if you want me to accept you into our circle, there's something that I'd like you to do."

Patsy shooed away the cat and found her phone under the cushions.

She stared at him with her eyes blazing like radars sweeping. "Are you trying to make sheep's eyes at me, Felipe? You seem to fancy yourself. You think you're a charmer, don't you?" She picked up a strand of cat hair on her chiffon blouse, blew it away, and snorted. "Between you and me, never waylay and mess with Patsy."

Felipe derided under his breath, "Yes, I've been called a charm offensive, a salacious spiv, a smarmy geezer, a wind-up merchant, a walking History Channel, a daffy freak of nature, a fart in a spacesuit, and a King Shit of Turd Mountain before. And no, Patsy, I don't want you to kick my Queen mum nor do I want to eat my humble pie. There are many ways of wrong-footing someone and inviting her for Her Majesty's pleasure at the Holiday Bay, but I'm not blowing the gaff for it brings nobody any good. And please don't mistake this as an invitation for an assignation. I'm only asking you to do a redounding good deed. There's a quarry I'm after, a piece of information that I need. I'd like you to get a line on it using your bush network in the zootropolis. I don't mind being called poetically shitty as long as I get the job done*."

He took out a burner phone from his briefcase. "Have a great evening with Cecil and his beans. Don't forget to put a bug in his ear in your own sweet way so he can update his codicil after drinking your wish-wash. You should know by now that I don't hold him in high regard. I hate the nobs, the toffs, and the parlour socialists. And they say that the enemy's enemy is a friend. If your plan works out, you'll be quids in and you can eat him out of house and home. Message you later."

Patsy took the phone and said nothing.

"Oh, and..." Felipe gave a beguiling smile, still holding on to the burner. "Love the cake-o."

And with that, she gave him a high five on the face.

Only Mr Darcy witnessed this exchange.

***

The guests left, the couple gave the tableware a lick and a promise, then they went upstairs and stretched on the bed with the cat in between them.

"Hum. What a night," Catherine reflected. "Unforgettable in every way."

"I hope you enjoyed tonight. Happy birthday, Catherine." He watched a smile tugging at her mouth corners.

"Thank you. I feel like a cat treading on air. I loved the presents, the wine, the sand art, and the cake. But you know what I liked the most?" she asked with amusement.

"Do tell," he encouraged.

"That when I said I was going to change my stockings, you came to look for me." She smiled. "It's very considerate, albeit unnecessary, for I've found someone I properly esteem and who holds me in the highest estimation."

"I dare say that's the most pleasant view that I saw today."

Catherine laughed a little. "Perhaps I can use it as an episode in my next story."

They were lost in their own thoughts for a while. Then he asked, "Do you perhaps want me to join your beginners' class?"

"Nope." She shook her head. "It's my first time teaching at the academy, and I don't want to get...distracted."

"You want me out of your sight again *so* soon?" he chaffed her.

"Well. I can give you some private tutoring in that respect. We can rise with the lark, go to New Covent Garden Market, and get the flowers of the flock."

Catherine turned to face him and sighed warily. "I don't know what's going on with Felipe and Patsy! I don't know what their bone of contention is and I don't like playing piggy in the middle. Poor Patsy! Felipe seems always running rings around her and setting her teeth on edge and An, they tied her up in knots!" She then inquired, "Do you know his girlfriend that he mentioned?"

"Yes." He told her about the Krav Maga Bootcamp that he had joined in April last year; that's where he and his business partner Dominic Turner met. Sidney was their instructor. "She was at the jazz bar's opening night as well," he recalled. "Sidney brought some friends for us to gain traction."

"I remember seeing her talking with Turner. I hope that nothing goes...awry with Cecil and Patsy." She mused, "But why would you want to join a Krav Maga Bootcamp?"

He told her that he wanted to brush up in case he needed to confront any 'stalkers'.

"I see." Catherine recalled the time they'd spent in her house as strangers and then said, "There is something else that I'd like to..."

"Yes?"

"Hmm..."

"Feel free to tell me, Catherine."

"You see... Hmm...here's the thing..." She trailed off again.

He had guessed the reason for her hesitation. "Cecil wants us to sign a prenup?"

Catherine let out a small laugh. "Why do you say so?"

"Well...I saw the buff envelope that he brought, and I connected the dots with your behind-the-scene talk." He considered, "Catherine, you can have everything that I have, and I want nothing from you. I only want you."

"Aww," Catherine purred, "and Mr Darcy?"

"I only want you and Mr Darcy."

"And Esmeralda?"

"Well. I only want you, Mr Darcy, and your garden fauna and our future."

"Good to know and no," she told him, "Cecil showed me my father's will again. I didn't know that there was a codicil regarding the house. Anyway, he said he'd sort everything out for *us*."

He wondered briefly if he should draw up a will.

She drawled delightedly, "And do you know what I want to do now?"

"Hmm?"

"I want to try my new bath bombs."

"That can be arranged."

She splayed her fingers and caressed his face. "I want us to try it together." She smiled serenely. "I was told today that all fun happens at night-time. Let me put on some mood music and we can get our jollies."

He kissed the palm of her hand and got up to draw the bath. Catherine turned on the stereo, and Eddie Higgins played. Something kept on nagging at his mind.

What was amiss?

The dead, sous-vide cats were accounted for, so was the puzzling pizza delivery...

Then a lingering doubt crossed his mind.

Only the missing voice recorder...

Perhaps he should ask Gabby about her friend again. Only this time, he needed to consider his approach more carefully.

He turned on the taps, and the water flow soon inundated the jazz tune.

CHAPTER 16

As things turned out, he didn't have to contact Gabby at all.

On Wednesday morning, shortly after the routine fire alarm sounded in his flat, Gabby called him.

"Mr Yang, have you...have you seen Amani? Did she contact you?" Gabby asked worriedly.

"No," he stood up, "not since Cumberland Lodge. Is there anything wrong?"

"Well. She...she skipped school this morning and...we can't figure out where she is now."

Gabby explained what had happened: Georgiana had upbraided Amani for her close relationship with Nathan again over their get-together revision arrangements over the weekend.

He felt it was a potted version of what happened, but he didn't ask for more. "Well, Mrs Parker, if I see her, I'll ask Amani to go back."

The call ended. He contemplated the places where Amani might go, and realised he knew very little about her. He called Nigel, and asked him if Nathan might know where she was. The answer was no. Then he decided to try his luck at the London Graphic Centre.

He grabbed his wallet and keys, tucked the taser into his waistband,

and by the time he came out of the lift, his cell rang again. It was Felipe.

He let the call through.

"Holá!" Felipe said, "I thought that you might want to know that I'm at the flower academy now, with your student."

Chance made his way to Catherine's workplace as Felipe carried on. "I had a sleepover at Sidney's, and then I saw Amani loitering by the road. Do you know what the probability of running into an old friend in London is? I guess I better try my luck with EuroMillions."

Chance had no reason to believe what Felipe offered. He even wondered if Felipe had not kept a GPS tracker on Amani somehow.

He got to the flower academy and entered the basement. Catherine and her colleague Orla were teaching a beginners' taster lesson on floral arrangements that day. It seemed that the class was having a break, for neither Catherine nor her colleague were in sight. There were vases of sweet peas and hydrangea flowers on various work stations.

He saw Felipe clad in a black Hard Rock Cafe T-shirt and jeans swanning by the duplicate of *Venus Verticordia* on the wall and around the work stations with one red rose in his hand. Felipe also wore a black Phiten necklace. Amani sat on a chair and made minor changes to a vase of flowers that now looked like a viny monster.

Amani saw him and waved slightly.

"How do you like my interpretation of Biollante?" Felipe asked Chance casually. "In case you don't know, Biollante is a cloned version of Godzilla with modifications from the genes of a rose. O Rose, thou art sick." Felipe didn't wait for his reply. "Amani, have you got any plans for the Early May Bank Holiday? Why don't we invite Nathan and his pal Wilfred Perry and we can go to the zoo together? Or we can picnic and discuss Leibniz and Calculus under Shakespeare's Tree in Primrose Hill?"

"Umm..." Amani said, "I don't...I don't know."

Chance quickly typed a message to Gabby asking her not to worry anymore.

"Primrose Hill is a wonderful place, isn't it? H.G. Wells made it an aliens' base. Here's a fun fact for you, Amani. Have you seen *Paddington*? They filmed it there. Do you know that Paddington is a Peruvian national? Well, 'national' might not be the right word, but Paddington is definitely a Peruvian native and he's from Darkest Peru. Dani Rodrik is an economist at Harvard and he always asks his students: Would you rather be rich in a poor country or poor in a rich country. I guess Paddington knows that it's way better to be an émigré in a rich country taking into consideration absolute and relative poverty. I wonder if the Browns voted for Labour though." Felipe continued, "Anyway, pity that Paddington didn't apply for a visa before coming to the UK or else he'd know how racist the people here can be. Of all the British embassy people I know, they always think that my life goal is to run away from South America and escape the jungle. Oh, here's something that I didn't dare to say during our Bootcamp: Trump's a dog."

Finally, Amani laughed.

"I meant it. William Hogarth had a pug dog called Trump; he made a sculpture of it. It's on display at the V&A. Maybe we should go and have a look. Let's hope there won't be any dog's dinner or dog's breakfast for us. And that we won't need to take any biscuit. There's a poem called 'April is a dog's dream', and May is certainly a dawg's American Dream." Felipe shrugged. "Or we can go to the British Museum and check on the Parthenon Sculptures before they return to their rightful place in Greece.

People had stored them in the Aldwych Underground during World War Two. Gee, you'd wonder why Prince P still hasn't done a redounding good deed for his homeland. I hope he's not becoming too slitty-eyed having stayed in that bleak house for too long. Amani, remember that we must treat eye care as an art form. Prince Philip once said that if he were to die and reincarnate, he'd like to return as a deadly virus and contribute to solving overpopulation. I do hope that he had not thought of it as a modest proposal when he let it slip from his lips to God's ears. Amani, do you know what *wuyazui* or a crow's mouth is?"

Amani nodded slightly, saying that it meant a 'jinx' in Mandarin.

"Merchants of gloom can be quite brutal. Hmm. If I were to die and reincarnate, I'd like to return as a magpie so that I can make droppings on my enemies' heads, and they can't do anything about it. What would you like to become, Amani?"

"Well. Maybe a...an umbrella acacia tree that's far from people."

Felipe went to the bin, found a sheet of discarded A4 paper, and made an origami of Godzilla. "A tree? Good choice. Do you know that magpies belong to the crow family? But I oversee my mouth now. People always have to mind what they say, really. Public speaking is an art form. The British always say 'with the greatest respect', and then they say something terrible. Every day is a school day. I have learnt, Amani, that it's unwise to put the cat among the chickens. Tsk. I was given to understand last week that Mercury's been blacklisted from all properties of the Crown Estate indefinitely. What can I say? I guess that they can't accommodate diversity when exchanging views and inspiring minds. Am I bovvered? I guess I'll squander elsewhere then. I have learnt my lesson to keep schtum in the silentium. Whereof one cannot speak, thereof one must be silent. Ludwig Wittgenstein said it. He went to the same school as Hitler did."

Felipe said as he nipped off the stem of the rose, "Do you know that in the British Museum, there's a sculpture called the *Tree of Life*? It's not a real tree, of course. The sculpture is made from the decommissioned firearms collected in Mozambique." He inserted the rose into the mouth of the Godzilla origami, and Chance instantly felt sorry for the flowers.

It looked like a miniature Triffid.

"Hoo. I think we better slip before the artists find out and vent the roof. Guess that I have no feel for beauty." Felipe grabbed his jacket. "I didn't have anything to eat this morning. How'd you say if we go for a bite now?" He carried his art with one hand.

Amani nodded.

Chance followed the two out, and he caught a glimpse of Catherine with a cup of coffee walking down the road. They walked to the Five Guys on the end of Long Acre. There were not many diners there. Felipe asked what Amani liked and ordered for them.

"Do you know that the first Five Guys was opened in Arlington, Virginia?" Felipe peeled his burger wrapper as he spoke. "Catherine was overjoyed with this trivia when I told her. I do miss the Bluegrass Country Radio. Amani, do you know that Five Guys claims that there are more than two hundred and fifty thousand ways to customise their burgers? It's really about permutation and combinations. Life is all maths. According to Kleiber's law, we can only have Godzilla on the big screen because no creature can support a large mass with a volume of its size. And that's why Earth's largest animal, namely, the whales, have to rely on buoyancy to help themselves."

Amani ate quietly, and Chance had a milkshake.

Afterwards, Felipe ordered an Uber car and said to him as they neared Gloucester Avenue, "I thought I might ask Georgiana if she's interested in a martini lunch. You know, to enhance my cross-cultural competencies. Gee, last time, I wore sneakers to Sushi Samba. They didn't let me in because they have a dress code. They don't live up to their name. I bet that, Amani, if I show up as a *sambista*, they'll scream and run away."

They arrived at the Edens' house, and Chance saw Gabby waiting by the roadside.

"Oh! Amani!" she called out as the passenger door opened. "Where have you been? We were so very worried!"

Amani didn't say anything.

"AMANI!" Georgiana Eden dashed out; she was off her face again. "When will you ever stop me from worrying!? How *on earth* did you have the gall to play truant? I knew that those books wouldn't do you any good–"

"Well, well," Felipe interrupted, "Georgiana, perhaps you should encourage children to read more. As Richard Steele would say, reading is to the mind what exercise is to the body. And what's so wrong with some social snacking?"

"Tush! She has exams coming up! It would not do for her to give up a future simply because of some brazen material!"

"Whooo, lovely kitten heels you've got there. Love the leopard prints and you definitely bring out the best of them than a certain dismay. And look." Felipe tried to divert the tensions. "I've got you here my latest creation, which I have named as 'Dogzilla'. You can put it in your garden to keep evil spirits away." He showed them the flower. "Perhaps next time I can get you a *Puya chilensis* to brighten your parlour? No need to worry about Customs; I know a professional pickup crew in importing and exporting. How would you like a martini lunch with me? Do you know any Taco Bells around here?"

They moved into the house, then Amani said determinedly, "I'm not taking the exams."

Gabby took a deep breath, "But, Amani, surely you don't want all your efforts to go in vain?"

Amani shook her head, "I don't want to be a bargaining chip for anyone anymore."

"AMANI! YOU MUST TAKE YOUR EXAMS WHETHER YOU LIKE IT OR NOT! I, AS YOUR MOTHER, DEMAND YOU TO TAKE THEM!"

Chance sensed that these words triggered something grave within Amani. She ran into the kitchen and returned with a knife in her hand.

"And you know what happens when you piss them off? The goat attacks, charges, and bunts you, whereas the lambs take to their heels."

He had remembered what Felipe said word for word.

Gabby shrieked and nearly fainted. Felipe held her and helped her to sit on the sofa. He then settled the Dogzilla on her lap.

"You are not my mother!" Amani shouted. "You never have been, and you never will be! You're just a stranger! You keep me here like an animal in a zoo—some exotic animal imported from Africa as part of your menagerie. You force me to have good diet regimes. You corral me in the house in the name of protecting me from outside influences! You show me off like a trophy prize once or twice in a year!" She then turned the knife to herself. "I've seen far more people die, so what would it change if I see one more? I've decided that if I die, at least I will die by my own hands."

She seemed calm, which was a dangerous signal. And she was hemmed in by the sofas.

"AMANI! YOU ARE OUT OF YOUR MIND!" Georgiana shouted back.

"Amani," Chance said, "please **drop** what you are holding." He had the taser ready, but did not want to use it on his student.

"Blast! What in *blazes* is this argy-bargy all about? I'm trying to have a conference call upstairs!" Ambrose Eden ventured downstairs and saw the scene. "What–"

Chance heard a series of zapping sounds as Ambrose Eden called out and fell. Amani had dropped the knife at this sudden turn of events as Ambrose Eden whined and cried.

"*Ooops.* Sorry," Felipe said, holding the taser. "I just wanted to try it. I thought...I thought it was bogus. But don't worry, I'm a First Aid at Work provider, and I can get him up and running in no time."

He handed the taser to Chance. "Take care of the ladies while I CPR the gentleman here. Hup, two, three!" He man-hauled the half-conscious Ambrose Eden into the dining room and closed the door.

Chance picked up the knife, looked around, and dropped it into a large floor vase.

THUMP! His heart sank at the same time.

A few minutes passed. Gabby seemed to be recovering while Amani stared unseeing at her hands, shaking.

"Will he die?" Georgiana cried suddenly. "Will he die?"

"No, no," he assured her. "Mrs Eden, what has happened today...
Perhaps you and Mr Eden should seek some professional help from
social workers. It's apparent that Amani is not happy in your house and I
dare say that, according to my observations, you have not been fulfilling
your obligations–"

"What do you know!" Georgiana said to him, coldly.

"What do *you* know?" Amani said. "And what you did? Did you
or did you not take Daniele's voice recorder!? I heard you two arguing
about some cats only days before she died! You said that she was a bad
influence, then she died! If I stay here, I might die one da–"

"Now, now, now." The dining room door opened, and Felipe dragged
Ambrose Eden out. "There's no need for such pessimism. I've sensed that,
Amani, you have a *sakabashira* in the house that's badly infected with
termites."

Ambrose Eden's nose was bleeding, and the blood fell freely onto
the floor drop by drop. Chance didn't remember seeing any part of him
bleeding a while ago. He hoped Felipe had punched some of his lights
out.

"Now," Felipe threw Ambrose Eden on to the single sofa as if he was
handling a cat, "I believe that Mr Eden has put a foot wrong."

"I...I..." Ambrose Eden wiped his nose with his uncuffed white shirt
sleeve. "Georgie, I..."

By the time he finished, Georgiana Eden had summoned her
solicitor to begin the divorce paperwork at once.

***

Later.

Chance helped Gabby to make some tea as Ambrose Eden packed and left.

According to Georgiana Eden, she had long discarded the voice recorder into Regent's Canal. The device had some snippets from a few book chapters. It seemed that Daniele Vidas was doing some volunteering work for the visually impaired, and she also collected urban and natural sounds.

Amani wanted to have a walk, so Chance and Felipe went with her.

"Where do you want to go?" Felipe asked her.

"I...I don't know."

They made their way slowly to Regent's Park. The girl remained silent all the way, and then she said with glassy eyes, "It's probably best that I stay away from everyone.... I'm...violent. I'm alone and I don't fit in."

Felipe considered, "Now, kid, there's no need to make life more difficult than it is. Let's not make the most innocent become the most guilty*–"

"But I've...I've burned down houses! I've hurt people! And I've made people scream! I hear them scream in my dreams! Where does it leave me? I'm in a fugue state all the time.... I'm out of place all the time...."

"Where does it leave you?" Felipe continued, "It leaves you right here and right now. Things they could not enjoy, you enjoy it for them. They cannot study anymore, so you do it, double, triple, paying tenfold the efforts. You eat their shares, live their dreams, and never let them go. There is no saint without a past, and some sinners are always entitled to a future. Even Pope Francis was in the Hitler Youth as a boy. Sometimes, great sinners make great saints. Put your best foot forward, Amani. Go places, have fun, eat lots of meat and fibre. Life is like maths. You don't understand why things happen, and you just get used to them. And stop acting the goat. I once fired a gun in Japan. Most weapons hurt, but education is a weapon that can change the world for the better. You don't have to learn the wrong lessons. Never say die, Amani. You don't deserve an easy way out. Stop thinking about the lives that you could have saved. Save yourself first. And you know what I think you should do? I think you should go and read history at Oxford and join the Rhodes Must Fall campaign. Look ahead, kid." He gestured.

They looked ahead. People were laughing, smiling, and relaxing in the park. Some flew kites, some read, some blew bubbles, and some threw frisbees with chasing dogs.

"Look ahead and tell me," Felipe said, "if history is not healed bit by bit by these moments?"

Amani looked down with a bleat.

They just stood there and Chance looked skyward. A jet had left a fresh trail.

***

He got back to his flat shortly before three, found his way to the study, and locked the door.

Catherine was still teaching at the flower academy, that he was certain, but he could not take any chances this time.

His phone buzzed; Turner had called several times. He put off calling him back.

He plonked himself down on his swivel chair and took out a small SD card from his coin case. It was from the nanny cam in the Edens' dining room. They had walked Amani home before Felipe had gone back to his office for a brown bag seminar. Chance told Georgiana that Felipe had requested him to recover the item and she believed him. She asked him again to keep what happened in her house in there.

He woke his laptop, inserted the card, and checked its contents.

There were some files. He click-opened one and fast-forwarded until Felipe and Ambrose Eden came into the frame.

Felipe dumped his cargo on the nearest chair as Ambrose Eden cursed and swore, losing his moccasins on the way.

"Now, Hurry Hooray Henry, there's no need to go ballistic and splodey. There's really no need to put your foot in your mouth. Hasn't your mother taught you how to deal with difficult guests?" Felipe looked around. "Oh! I see that you've got a Philippe Starck lemon squeezer? What a marvellous design! It looks like an alien *pulpo*, doesn't it? I've heard that he'd positioned it to be a conversation starter."

Felipe took the metal object and smashed it into Ambrose Eden's face. The thing dented; blood gushed out.

"Ow!" Ambrose Eden whimpered like a hurt hyena and gurgled as if he had dry ice in his mouth.

"Now, we can talk." Felipe dragged a chair out and sat down. He wiped the juice squeezer with the hem of his T-shirt like a killer would clean his knife. "Do you like to read comics, Mr Eden? My recent favourite is *Hellboy*. There's a Nazi villain in it called Karl Ruprecht Kroenen. I've heard that they based the character on an actual Nazi. When he was captured post-war, they shaved off his nose and ears, and sliced off his eyelids and lips."

Felipe took off his necklace, and Chance saw a fountain pen on the chain.

"I won't play Mr Nice Guy. I have something called an X-Acto Z model here. I usually use it for kirigami and whittling, but-but-but-*but* I don't mind engaging it for alternative purposes." Felipe grinned. "Tell me, Mr Eden, do you know that the X-Acto brand started selling scalpels? The founders soon gave up because there's a pain point in user experience. It's too messy when *sterilising*. Pun intended. Would you like a face by Picasso? No, I think a Szyszlo might be better."

Ambrose Eden held his nose and scoffed snappishly, "You're only bluffing."

"You think you're brainy, don't you? Let me help you to ring your *zako* bell'." Felipe grabbed him and nutted him. Ambrose Eden squealed like a stuck pig and Felipe sat back smiling. "Do you think that you're a tough nut to crack? I regret to inform you, Mr Eden, that your shoes are not on any other foot now. You're no one to high hat me. How about if I snap your head off and see if you'll live like Mike, the headless chicken? Is there a cleaver in your toy chest that I can borrow? Now, I've heard that you like a bit of rough and that you wished to throw your hat in the ring? I can think of a more visual image. If you like cats that much, I can put a feral fellow in your pants. Why don't my furry friend and I help you throw your pen in your Willis' ring? I'm sure you wouldn't mind another 'doctoring'."

Felipe gave a perplexed sigh. "Mr Eden, I once did a balloon debate experiment in Cappadocia. Up or out. Someone pushed off his two mates, thinking he'd live. The only thing that survived was a Pelican case out on a limb." He shrugged and then looked at his nails nonchalantly. "What can I say? I guess that politicians, philosophers, and economists should shoulder more responsibility for the scientific delivery of knowledge."

"You stark raving mad blighter! You'll be dead the second I tell Georgie's uncle!" Ambrose Eden snuffled. "He'll give you what for! He won't–"

"Aren't you an expert on dontopedalogy? Well, well, they say that inanity can only be cured when an idiot dies. Would it make you feel any better knowing that the *gentleman* himself has delegated me to iron out the unpleasant? Should I tear you from limb to limb? Or would you prefer your Lotus totalled by a lager truck? Should I use a Purdey and shoot you down like a grouse? Perhaps you would choose to end up in a ditch near Primrose Hill like Godfrey?"

Felipe thought for a few seconds. "How about if I *defenestrate* you by grabbing your stacking swivel and make you go out of the window without leaving a trace? I'll spare you the nuts and bolts and the ins and outs. Do you know how many Britons are reported missing every year in England and Wales alone? Two hundred and forty-two thousand and three hundred and seventeen last time I checked. And do you know how many *mispers* leave remains behind? I can rub you out in no time. Now, let's play a game called Truth or Dare."

He stood and hauled Ambrose Eden up by his scruff. "You can choose to cop a plea by telling the truths to your beloved wife, or if you dare me and look for Barney Rubble, you'll have no time to cry. You better pin your ears back and mark my words. I can assure you that there's method in my madness and I always make *good* my promises.

It's no skin off *my* nose if you don't listen. If you don't wish to become some remains one day six feet under, I advise you to choose sensibly. And please refrain from the art of circumlocution. Chop, chop, *catmeat*."

Chance watched as the two left the room, then he gaped as a long breath caught in his throat.

On the screen, Felipe turned and gestured 'rock on' to the camera.

Chapter 17

C atherine left the flower academy at seven-thirty pm, reflecting on her first day of teaching and her batch of students. Everyone did well, perhaps except for the more abstract, gothic representation that Felipe had left halfway.

She got back to Kean Street. Hannah Robinson had messaged her that she'd be back in a week.

Catherine passed the automated glass doors. The Robinsons' mailbox was almost overflowing. She picked up a few letters that had dropped onto the floor and squeezed them back to their proper place.

A minute later, she unlocked the flat door with her keys as a bird squawked somewhere in the open-air atrium.

No light was on inside the room. Catherine had thought that he was not back yet.

"Catherine," he said roughly in the dark.

She barely made out that he was sitting in front of the butler's desk with his back to her. The balcony door was ajar.

"Oh. I thought you weren't in." She moved closer like a curious yet cautious cat. "It's very dim in here. Do you want me to click on the lights?" Catherine watched as the BT Tower glistered afar.

"I didn't save it," he said.

"Y...yes?"

"The bird. I didn't save it."

Catherine remembered him telling her that he had once fallen out of a tree as a boy because he wanted to return a birdling to its nest, but wasps attacked him.

"But you did save a child just days ago. I think that's a feat in itself, Mr Yang," she offered genuinely.

She waited for a reply, but none came. Soon the silence was unbearable.

"Tell me what you're thinking," she asked softly.

He gave a heavy sigh. "I'm thinking about *The Remains of the Day*. The...the film ending."

"Yes?" She pushed for more.

"An had a good childhood friend. They were neighbours and lived opposite each other. The boy's uncle raised racing pigeons. Sometimes we would go to his dovecote. He always told us that if we saw a frightened or injured bird, we should never attempt to scoop it up and throw it in the air hoping that it would fly, because the birds might go into shock, and they'll just crash onto the ground and die."

"Well..." Catherine pondered, "movie crews are only responsible for the box office and aesthetics, not so much the scientific delivery of knowledge."

More silence.

"Oh, and Amani came to the shop today. Felipe had invited her to join our taster session. They slipped away halfway, though. I hope I haven't done a lousy job in teaching."

After a moment, he said despondently. "I don't like tutoring."

There was a steely edge to his profession.

"Hmm. You can always consider a career in other fields." Catherine sat down on the sofa and tried to keep her tone light. "I think that Felipe will be more than glad to write you a recommendation letter."

The pre-set rice cooker started to whir.

"If children are suffering, and people approach it the wrong way, it would be like hogtying them and throwing them out of the window." Having said this, he rose from his seat and turned on the accent lighting.

Catherine saw bags of deflated Pipers crisps on the kitchen counter.

She felt that he had so much more to tell, but in the end, he only smiled feebly. "How would you like some fried rice for dinner?"

***

A week later.

When the copper railings outside Oxford Circus Station are hot to touch, you know that summer has come to London, Catherine thought as she rode in the lift to the ninth floor.

She had remembered this line when Daniele wrote it to her.

Catherine's first floristry course was more or less a success. She had received some feedback from her students that warmed her heart. She wanted to write to Daniele again; perhaps they could discuss the design of a particular centrepiece for a dinner.

She pondered the whereabouts of her pen pal as she moved through the open-air atrium. Catherine hoped she was enjoying what life had to offer. She wondered if Daniele was still in London.

Soft, puffy clouds floated in the tender-coloured sky, and Hannah Robinson's plants seemed to have regained their vibrance.

Hannah had returned.

She seemed better. She had told them that she took much solace in supporting Donald Trump's presidential campaign back home.

A pigeon flitted across the blue, and Catherine recalled her lover's dense declaration from a week ago.

"If children are suffering, and people approach it the wrong way, it would be like hogtying them and throwing them out of the window."

And X and Y...

Perhaps they would talk about it later.

Catherine pigeonholed her questions and glanced at the Robinsons' briefly. The corner of her eye caught a shadow through the mullions of the picture window by Hannah's kitchen.

Wait...is that? She doubted her eyes.

Lordy!

In a blink of a second, the shadow vanished, and she stood there, dumbstruck.

Her thoughts had drifted to the tales of the world's most haunted theatre, the Theatre Royal on Drury Lane, that Orla had told her about earlier.

The Man in Grey...

And the lady who passed away in the bedroom upstairs...

She swallowed nervously and suddenly felt like an insect under a microscope, being observed by some unknown force.

Stop being such a fraidy cat, will you!

The early May warmth did nothing to take the chill off Catherine, and she hurriedly took out her keys and unlocked the door.

"Catherine, Catherine, Catherine! You're right!" He met her with open arms and gave her a bear hug. "He's a different person! It wasn't Eddy at all! The man in the video is his twin brother!"

"Waouh." She let out a breath that she'd been holding, "Well. I...I saw him, I think, just now." She laughed bitterly. "And...and I thought that Eddy's wraith had come back."

A few minutes later, they settled on the sofa with two cups of honey grapefruit tea as he recounted what happened. "I told you that I'd contacted the uploader of the videos but to no avail. Last week, Turner called and said that he'd received some private messages on the site, and that's how we found him. Eddy only got to know of his existence last year and they would meet up every few weeks." He sighed. "The day when Eddy had a stroke, he met him at the hotel where he...he did a shoot–"

Someone rapped on the door rapidly. Catherine got up and opened it.

"Oh! Catherine!" Hannah Robinson cried out agitatedly. "I should have never given away all of Eddy's stuff! I was a *darn* fool! I should have believed him! I will regret it forever now!" She wiped her tears with a posy-dappled bandana.

"Mrs Robinson," Chance walked up by the door, "please don't concern yourself about it. Hmm. I took some liberty the other day when Catherine told me that you'd donated Eddy's things to the Oxfam store. Well–" He hesitated as Catherine gave him sidelong glances. "There was very little we could do with the clothing items, but...but we've managed to get hold of his CDs and records." He took out a business card for the jazz bar. "Here's the address, and my friend would be very happy to return them to you."

"Oh! You're a star!" Hannah Robinson took the card and hugged them both. "The white rabbits worked! Are...are they open now? I'll go now. And I must call Sarnai. There are dust bunnies all over the place!"

A few minutes later, the open-air atrium quieted again, and spring had finally returned.

***

They got back to Holland Park after lunch.

Catherine hummed a song jauntily as she relaxed on the lounge chair, reading fanfiction on his tablet and wearing the pair of pink socks An had gifted.

By then, he knew that it was 'A Thousand Years' by Christina Perri.

"Why did you do it?" She tilted her head and asked.

"Hmm?" He started to trim Mr Darcy's toe tufts as the cat was leaving trails of dirt after using the litter box.

"Why did you help Eddy and Hannah?"

He considered for a moment. "I don't really know. I felt it was the right thing to do and, in a way, I'm doing myself a favour... Turner knew the shop manager, Tim, and he notified us as soon as the records were up on the shelf. No harm done."

"Hmm." Catherine put down the tablet and mused. "Smart cookie you are, Mr Yang."

"Not a sweet one?"

"That as well," she smirked.

"Not cloying like Pop-Tarts or...gungy like Twinkies?" He mirrored how she had asked him once.

"By no means, Mr Yang; you are sweet as flying saucers to me."

"Why do you still do it?" He cleaned the trimmings and smoothed Mr Darcy's whiskers.

"Yes?"

He sighed slightly. "Catherine, why do you still call me 'Mr Yang'?"

"Well. Old habits...live long." She sighed in response. "I wonder how Eddy felt when he first knew of his twin brother's existence. Strangers of bonding."

Catherine picked up her reading while he thought about Eddy and his brother.

A minute later, Catherine smirked, "Ohhh! I've just read a one-shot called 'A Little Friendly Banter' and it's brill." She put down the tablet and joined him on the sofa. "I'm thinking of writing a corresponding piece called 'Pastime with Good Company'. Maybe I'll even do a crossover with *Entrapment*. What do you think?"

"I think it sounds lovely."

"Would you like to be my BETA before Daniele gets back to me?"

"Gladly."

He held the cat as they enjoyed each other's company.

"What TV do you like to watch?" she asked.

"I liked *Golden Balls* and *The Crystal Maze* and programmes where you go into a supermarket, they give you a budget, and you pick a basket to get close to that number. It's a good exercise for mental arithmetic."

Catherine smiled. "Well, now we know whom to entrust our weekly grocery shopping with from now on, and Mr Darcy will see to it that you have a shopping list."

He laughed. "I'd be delighted."

They huddled together, and Mr Darcy purred contentedly as Catherine scratched his favourite spots behind his ears.

"My pen pal once wrote to me that when the copper railings outside Oxford Circus Station are hot to touch, you know that summer has come to London. It's going to be the first summer that we spend together... Do you have any favourite ships?"

"Of course, I do," he said airily. "I ship *us*. You are my leading lady, Catherine."

"Hmm." She smiled ruefully. "I can think of some scenarios already." She mused, "We can go to the Chelsea Flower Show with Hannah."

"And we'll make pickled walnuts," he added.

"And we can go riding in Hyde Park and I'll teach you to waltz." A smile bloomed on her face.

"And we can go and picnic on the River Dee."

"And we'll go to China in the summer. I've asked Melody for leave. We can celebrate your birthday there and we can go gallivanting halfway around the globe. I'll look into the visa application tomorrow. It's not so bad a pastime it seems when I'm in good company."

"And I'll make you something sweet tonight, then we can watch something of your choice."

"We can watch *Lark Rise to Candleford*. You remind me of Miss Lane somehow." Catherine moved closer and said fondly. "My dear tiger, we certainly do have an inspiriting agenda ahead of us, but I can think of one or two items to add value now." She kissed him deeply, and they decided to move their conversation into the bedroom again.

Sometime later, she told him, "I've been thinking about what you said the other day."

"Yes?"

"Those at the FBI. They scooped up a broken starling and threw her into the air, forcing her to fly. They demanded fidelity, bravery, and integrity of her, but they showed her damn all. They slammed the door to the aviary in her face and wondered why she wasn't in the room.... Some birds are never meant to be caged and manhandled."

Mr Darcy crept on their bed and rubbed his cheeks on their entwined fingers.

"I think I'll have a kip now." She hugged him and the cat and then fluttered her eyelashes. "And when I wake up, Mr Yang, would you indulge me with a bath and a rub down?"

"Of course." He stroked her hair tenderly. "Some cats are *always* entitled to be pampered and cherished."

She laughed as she shut her eyes. "We'll count on you then."

He propped himself on one elbow and watched Catherine, and Mr Darcy catnapped in tandem.

Everything seemed fine. Gabby had messaged him. Her employer had begun to enthusiastically support the Fawcett Society and in two weeks, Amani would have her first Core Maths paper.

He did not doubt that she would do well.

A police siren sounded somewhere distantly.

He sensed that perhaps Eddy's long-lost brother had been economical with the truth. He thought about the possibilities of what might have happened in that small hotel lobby in the hinterland of his mind.

His heart began to wilt as he thought more about Eddy Robinson, Daniele Vidas, and the two Brits that were still missing.

Felipe is right. It's all chaos out there.

But now, here, and this time belonged to them.

EPILOGUE

December 2015.

"Atishoo!"

She waited on the pavement in the bone-chilling cold and overheard someone complaining: 'She's such a beast! I've never given a thought that *quid pro quo* sexual harassment would bloody happen to me!'

She listened as the man walked away in anger with his phone in his hand and let out a sigh. She was certain that life was rearing its ugly head again and again for many others.

A mother and her young child walked by, discussing which equestrian brand to buy for their Christmas shopping.

She recalled a conversation that she had had with her pen pal, Cat, on dressage and different English riding bits and saddles.

She wished her well as she warmed her numb fingers with the hot coffee.

Once, she had told Cat of her plight, and she asked her if she fooled herself with all the malarkey of the Eloquence Stone at Blarney. It was an awakening call of a sort, and what a roller coaster of fate her life had been.

Perhaps she would send her a message tonight to ask her whereabouts and if she might be interested in signing up for the London Zoo's Gir Lion Lodge experience.

Her Uber arrived, and she got in.

"Brrr! Brass monkeys, isn't it?" She held her coffee cup carefully on top of her right knee.

The driver looked at her through the rear-view mirror and spoke with a heavy lisp, "Sorry, I speaks zie 'ittle Inglish."

"Don't worry. My parents didn't speak English. It's cold, isn't it?" She settled and put on her seatbelt. "Not the best time to go to the zoo and see the lions."

They drove in silence as she sipped her coffee. Shortly after, the driver's stomach growled.

"Sorry," the man said with a smile. "I no eaten today."

"Oh." she squeezed her take-out bag from Starbucks. "I... Would you like some cookies for a snack later? I know what it's like to feel the pinch. My parents were migrant workers, and they pared down all the time."

"I no know. I ran away blood...feeud here."

She searched her pockets, found what she was after, and put the paper bag onto the passenger's seat. "You can eat it later."

"No." The man said decisively. "No han-dout."

"It's a hand up. Have it to fend off the cold, please." She unbuckled her seatbelt as they neared her house. "I'm paying it forward."

She got out of the car, paid on her phone, and looked at her neighbours' house. The light upstairs was on.

Perhaps she would talk to Georgiana Eden about the cats again sometime later.

But for now, she thought, maybe she could make some juice with chicory.

Maybe.

Notes and Terms

Sadness is a Bonfire

Chapter 2

jubilación – Spanish for retirement.

leche de tigre – Spanish for a marinade for curing fish in Peruvian ceviche.

Wabi-sabi – Japanese for the acceptance of the transience of life.

ichigo ichie – Japanese for a once-in-a-lifetime encounter.

ichigo ame – Japanese for candy-coated strawberry.

Chapter 3

unten menkyo – Japanese for a driver's licence;

hokenshou – Japanese for an insurance card.

Chapter 4

nekojita – Japanese for a cat's tongue, literally meaning unable to eat hot food and beverages.

Chapter 5

sheng – Mandarin for a Chinese wind instrument with vertical pipes.

Tsumaranai mono desu ga – Japanese for a customary expression used when people give presents.

ikebana – Japanese for the art of flower arranging.

Epilogue

'The Law is not the only reality in a lawyer's life. Pettifoggers have rent to pay, status to achieve, and heights to scale.' – Felipe adopts a quote from *The Evidence of Things Not Seen* by James Baldwin.

toshikoshi soba – Japanese for a traditional noodles dish eaten on New Year's Eve.

The Learning Curve of Pain

Chapter 2

UST – Fanfiction term for 'Unresolved Sexual Tension'.

nagajuban – Japanese term for a robe that people wear under their kimonos.

Chapter 8

'There is a 'hell' in 'Hello'. There is even a hazard in 'Thank you'.' – Felipe refers to the Japanese term 'Thank you Hazard' describing situations when drivers flash their hazard light to thank each other.

'I also read of murders, wars, bankruptcies, jackpot winnings, and Shakespeare.' – Felipe adopts a line from *The Miser* by Mona Van Duyn.

'It's hell to be seeing it when you're very little and very angry, and no mother's lips to kiss you anymore.' – Felipe adopts a quote from Ouida.

'A longitudinal study of 323 child soldiers in Sierra Leone finds that," Felipe said, "forty-seven per cent experienced anxiety and depression; twenty-eight per cent had PTSD, and eleven per cent attempted suicide.' – Felipe cites from the following research.

Betancourt, TS, Brennan, RT, Rubin-Smith, J, Fitzmaurice, GM & Gilman, SE 2010, 'Sierra Leone's Former Child Soldiers: A Longitudinal Study of Risk, Protective Factors, and Mental Health', *Journal of the American Academy of Child & Adolescent Psychiatry*, vol. 49, no. 6, pp. 606–615, viewed 28 February 2019, <https://www.ncbi.nlm.nih.gov/pmc/articles/PMC3157024/>.

Betancourt, TS, Thomson, DL, Brennan, RT, Antonaccio, CM, Gilman, SE & VanderWeele, TJ 2019, 'Stigma and Acceptance of Sierra Leone's Child Soldiers: A Prospective Longitudinal Study of Adult Mental Health and Social Functioning', *Journal of the American Academy of Child & Adolescent Psychiatry*, vol. 0, no. 0, viewed 18 March 2020, <https://jaacap.org/article/S0890-8567(19)30392-2/fulltext>.

ohisashiburidesu – Japanese for a formal way of saying 'long time no see'.
shibazuke – Japanese for a type of pickle.
Ja na – Japanese for 'see you!'.

Chapter 10

zozobra – Spanish for anxiety and stress.

'People with no vices are going to have some purty annoying virtues.' – Felipe quotes from Elizabeth Taylor.

'We are but one of the multitude, in no respect better than any other in it.' – Felipe quotes from *The Theory of Moral Sentiments* by Adam Smith.

Chapter 12

MARCH – Acronym for five elite universities in Japan.
omae wa hajishirazuda – Japanese for 'You are shameless!'.

Chapter 13

'Do you know that a Chinese philosopher said that the best three venues for thinking are on horseback, in bed, and when using the toilet?' – Felipe refers to Ouyang Xiu (1007–1072), a Chinese essayist from the Song Dynasty.

'It's not worth the bother of killing yourself since you always kill yourself too late.' – Felipe quotes from Emil Cioran.

'Good manners will open doors that the best education cannot.' – Felipe quotes from Clarence Thomas.

Chapter 15

Ñoña – Spanish term for shit (vulgar).

chikushou – Japanese for a beasty person.

'I don't mind being called poetically shitty as long as I get the job done.' – Felipe adopts a line from *Deathwish* by Vivek Narayanan.

Chapter 16
'Let's not make the most innocent become the most guilty–' – Felipe adopts a quote from *High-Rise* by J. G. Ballard.

zako – Japanese for a small fish, literally meaning a nobody.

Willis' ring – Also known as 'Circle of Willis', an anastomosis that supplies blood in the brain.

Acknowledgement

My thanks to M·F for the opportunity for a short stay at Cumberland Lodge.

Also By Shawe Ruckus

A Chinese Remedy
Mercenaries in Suits Book 1

You may have heard how rich Asians spend, but do you know how they kill?

On April Fool's Day 2015, married pharmacist Tilly Wurman gets a surprise text message; one that definitely isn't a joke. Her ex-girlfriend Joyce Peng has been forced out of her Holborn flat by an underground fire and needs somewhere to stay the night. It soon becomes clear that something isn't right with Joyce. So, when Joyce's dead body is discovered a few days later, it looks like an open and shut case of suicide. But is everything really what it seems?

In another part of London, just returned from a year-long trip to India, Catherine Roxborough also gets a surprise when a man appears at her kitchen window and smashes the glass. Recently separated from her fiancé, Catherine lives alone and is terrified that a stalker is lurking in the shadows.

These two very different mysteries bring two very different men to London. Reticent Chance Yang and flamboyant Felipe Kazama, consultants for Mercury Investments and Securities, are tasked with investigating Joyce's supposed suicide and keeping Catherine safe. This isn't an ordinary day's work for Chance and Felipe, especially when personal feelings start to emerge. And the deeper their investigations go, the harder it gets to uncover the truth...

From London to Shanghai, this thrilling and surprising mystery will take you on a journey that keeps you guessing until the very end...

Available in mainstream e-book and audio book stores.